Carol McCleary was born in
Kong, Japan and the Philippir
now lives on Cape Cod in ar
the ghost of former occupant
at www.carolmccleary.com.

Praise for Carol McCleary:

'Packed with historical detail and humour' *Elle*

'Meet Nelly Bly, investigative reporter, self-assured, gutsy and funny, in her first outing. *The Alchemy of Murder* is a brilliant debut full of historical detail and peril which will entertain you right till the last page. Can't wait to read more of her adventures' David Headley

'Carol McCleary does for the City of Light what Ann Perry has done for Victorian London and what *The Alienist* did for 19th century New York. A gripping, atmospheric, electrifying masterwork!' Barbara Wood

'Meet Nellie Bly, America's first female investigative reporter. She's feisty, funny, opinionated, persistent, and as tough as any male she meets. She has to be, because in *The Alchemy of Murder*, she's swept through a tale of peril and pursuit that is sure to keep you turning pages long after you should have been asleep. You'll find yourself on the mean streets of nineteenth century New York, in Victorian London and in Paris as the Eiffel Tower rises and deadly things – men and microbes – stalk the streets. It is a dazzling entertainment, so well constructed – and it has Oscar Wilde too!' William Martin

*Also by Carol McCleary*

The Alchemy of Murder

CAROL MCCLEARY

# The Illusion of Murder

HODDER &
STOUGHTON

First published in Great Britain in 2010 by Hodder & Stoughton
An Hachette UK company

First published in paperback in 2010

I

Copyright © Carol McCleary 2010

The right of Carol McCleary to be identified as the Author of
the Work has been asserted by her in accordance with the
Copyright, Designs and Patents Act 1988.

All rights reserved. No part of this publication may be
reproduced, stored in a retrieval system, or transmitted, in any
form or by any means without the prior written permission of
the publisher, nor be otherwise circulated in any form of binding
or cover other than that in which it is published and without a
similar condition being imposed on the subsequent purchaser.

All characters in this publication are fictitious and any resemblance
to real persons, living or dead, is purely coincidental.

A CIP catalogue record for this title is available
from the British Library

ISBN 978 0 340 99845 8 (A)
ISBN 978 0 340 97844 3 (B)

Typeset in Plantin Light by Palimpsest Book Production Limited,
Grangemouth, Stirlingshire

Printed and bound by
CPI Mackays, Chatham ME5 8TD

Hodder & Stoughton policy is to use papers that are natural,
renewable and recyclable products and made from wood grown
in sustainable forests. The logging and manufacturing processes
are expected to conform to the environmental regulations of the
country of origin.

Hodder & Stoughton Ltd
338 Euston Road
London NW1 3BH

www.hodder.co.uk

To Hildegard.
Who doesn't know the beauty, kindness,
intelligence and wisdom she possesses.
But that is what makes her so
extraordinarily special.

# Preface

*I discovered that Egypt is a land of both mystery and magic, an exotic place where trees talk and men turn staffs into snakes, so it should not have come as such a surprise to me that death would also be mysterious in this ancient, haunted land of pyramids, mummies, and the eternal Nile . . .*

Journal of Nellie Bly, 1889

These words were recorded by Nellie Bly, the world's first female investigative reporter, during the race around the world she made in 1889 to beat the record of Jules Verne's fictional hero Phileas Fogg in the novel, *Around the World in 80 Days.*

That journey of nearly 22,000 miles by steamship, carriage, and iron horse brought her not just into contact with exciting and exotic cultures during Victorian times, but into the intrigues of great nations at a time when ancient magic and a mysterious prophecy of the Sphinx threatened to stain the Nile red with the blood of foreigners.

While Nellie's adventurous journey was related for the public in her book, *Around the World in 72 Days,* those of you who have read Nellie's previous accounts of her investigations are aware that she also maintained a secret journal of what actually happened during her investigations, beginning with the murder and mad science she encountered when she spent ten days in a madhouse in order to get a 'man's' job as a reporter.

Many readers are already familiar with the fact that the discovery of Nellie's secret journals – found in the rubble when the old building that housed her employer, the *New York World*, was razed – has been the subject of both litigation and accusations that Nellie's actual accounts were liberally altered to include murder and intrigue.

This accusation is firmly rebutted.

While it was necessary to make modest editorial corrections to the journal, the reader may once again rest assured that they may compare our truth and veracity to that attributed to that lioness of literature, Lillian Hellman, by none other than author Mary McCarthy.

THE EDITORS

Nellie Bly
*Setting out on her race around the world
with a small valise*

# Prologue

I discovered that Egypt is a land of both mystery and magic, an exotic place where trees talk and men turn staffs into snakes, so it should not have come as such a surprise that death would also be mysterious in this ancient, haunted land of pyramids, mummies, and the eternal Nile.

That I could meet a bizarre end in this strange land has not occurred to me until now as I stand, frozen, staring down at the long black snake I've stepped on.

I don't dare lift my foot; I can't even breathe; I just stand stiffly in place, the toe of my shoe pressing down on the serpent as it thrashes and tries to coil.

Darkness is closing in as a burning torch on the dirt a few feet from me fades. When the bundle of sticks burns out, there'll be just me and the snake – in the dark.

*In the dark where?* This is a burial chamber, for sure. A sarcophagus is off to my right and I can make out on the wall a scene from the *Egyptian Book of the Dead* – an aged painting of a boat that has the head of a lion, a tail and clawed feet at the stern; aboard are wailing women, some with hands

1

outstretched, others covering their faces – mourners for the dead.

The stone coffin, pillars and faded hieroglyphics are the only remnants of what was perhaps the magnificent tomb of some long dead pharaoh. Once filled with unimaginable treasures, it now contains nothing but dust and cobwebs; thieves have taken everything but the ghosts.

Shouting for help will do no good. No one knows I'm here except the person who imprisoned me; someone I've yet to put a name or face to, but who has murder in their heart, and who knows I'm trying to flush them out.

The snake's tail whips against the side of my leg and I nearly jump out of my skin.

I have no idea what kind of snake it is, but this country is famous for its asps – deadly horned vipers and cobras. Cleopatra tested their venom on condemned prisoners to find out which killed the fastest and most painlessly before she had one bite her.

How I came to be imprisoned in an ancient tomb with one foot on a snake and the other on my own grave has me wondering how I've managed to offend the gods of this ancient land so quickly. A mystifying artefact of Egyptian black magic is the source of my troubles and I have been forewarned – possession of it has already caused blood to soak into the primordial dust of the Nile valley.

It is not the first time I've stepped into a snake pit, so to speak, but it's never happened literally before; at times like this I wonder if there is something about me that attracts the strange and the dangerous.

My name is Nellie Bly and I'm a reporter for Mr Joseph Pulitzer's *New York World*. With too much boldness for my own good, I bullied and bluffed my way into having the newspaper send me on a race around the world in which I had to beat the 'record' set by Phileas Fogg in Jules Verne's novel, *Around the World in 80 Days*.

That it was the thirteenth day of my journey when I made landfall in Egypt should have told me that this was not an auspicious time to visit a place where priests once made people eternal with dark magic, and the land blistered under ten plagues hurtled at it by the almighty Jehovah.

The snake twists and thrashes violently, and I press harder – at least I think I do. My body is blue-cold, I can't feel my toes, and my knee is shaking wildly as if it has a life of its own.

*Did something move at the sarcophagus?*

I'm sure I saw something move.

*Dear God, let it be a trick of the light.*

The fading torchlight is casting eerie shadows. There can't be anything in the stone coffin, not something alive, unless it's true that Egyptian priests could embalm in a way that preserved life indefinitely.

More snakes?

The thought of being in the dark with snakes, scorpions, spiders and God knows whatever else lurks in ancient tombs causes the shaking in my knee to work its way up to my hip and my whole body trembles. I want to cry but I can't spare the strength and instead press down harder on the snake.

The torch flickers and hisses as if it's burning through the last of the pitch. I have to get to it and somehow keep it going until I can find my way out of this nightmare. There has to be a door somewhere.

My knees and my courage are giving way and I keep imagining I'm letting up the pressure on the struggling serpent. I know I can't keep this awkward stance any longer. I have to do something now before the darkness completely embraces me.

The creature underfoot thrashes violently, whipping its whole body. It starts to slip out from under my shoe and I scream as I push down on it again, my heart pounding so hard that I'm breathless and sway dizzily, almost losing my footing.

Shutting my eyes tightly, I ask God for help. I don't think He will listen; unfortunately I'm one of those people who never talks to Him unless I'm up to my neck in alligators, but I try anyway, though I don't think that the Good Lord would approve of my present association with the dark side of Egyptian magic.

I can't be left blind in the darkness with a deadly snake. I need to get both feet on the snake and jump up and down until I'm sure it can't harm me, then get to the torch before it dies.

I start to bring up my other foot up as I look down.

*It's gone.*

The snake has slipped out from under my foot.

Mortified, I can't move, can't breathe. It could strike at any second.

*Mother of God, how did I get myself into this mess?* Ancient curses, magic amulets, esoteric mysteries from the *Egyptian Book of the Dead*, murder and fanaticism; it's all madly peculiar for a young woman from Cochran's Mills, Pennsylvania, population exactly 504.

As the darkness closes in on me and my breathing takes on the hoarse rasp of a death rattle, I ask myself what I could have done differently when I decided to flush out a killer in a land blessed by the sun and damned by ancient curses.

# PART ONE

## DAY 13

*I shall now speak at greater length of Egypt, as it contains more wonders than any other land, and is preeminent above all countries in the world for works that can hardly be described.*

Herodotus (450 BC)

# I

Thirteen days after I leave New York, the *Victoria*, the ship that will see me all the way to Ceylon in the Indian Ocean, anchors in the bay at Port Saïd, the gateway to the Suez Canal. The bay is too shallow for large ships to reach the docks and they must lie out and be fed coal for the boiler by coolies on barges.

My effort to beat the eighty-days-around-the-world record of Jules Verne's Phileas Fogg has progressed nicely. By carriage, train and ship – the *Victoria* being the third ship to convey me – I have put over 5,000 miles under my feet.

Particularly gratifying is that my membership in the female gender has not in the least delayed or otherwise hindered my travels. Mr Pulitzer had planned to send a newspaper*man* on the assignment because he believed the race too dangerous and strenuous for a mere woman.* But more about that later.

* Pulitzer's concern was well founded. The world in 1889 was infinitely more dangerous than it is today, not to mention the lack of modern conveniences – no aeroplanes, automobiles, credit cards, ATMs, not even mobile phones! It was a time when 'high-tech travel' was on trains called iron horses, and steamships had auxiliary sails to use when the boiler failed. The Editors.

7

When I hear the anchor chain clanging I dress to go out on deck and get my first sight of the ancient land by dawn's early light.

As I step out of my cabin, a man down the corridor is closing the door of his room behind him. He gives me a studied look as if to judge whether I have come out because of him, then turns away without a 'good morning' and hurries to the companionway that leads to the outside deck.

He's dressed rather peculiar for a passenger, his attire looks more like the work clothes of a sailor, and he's carrying a small sea bag not unlike those I've seen sailors tote. Most unusual about his clothing is that the pants are a little too long, the shirt a bit too roomy, looking to me as though they are borrowed or bought on short notice.

He is an intense-looking gentleman, perhaps close to thirty years old, to whom I've offered a 'good day' a couple of times in the passageway since I boarded at Brindisi two days ago, but have had hardly a nod in return. He takes his meals in his cabin and appears very preoccupied with his own private affairs, so much so that he forgets common courtesies; a man on a mission, the boys back in the newsroom would say. Caught up with his own importance, I'd say.

If he asked, I would tell him that he'd have more success keeping his own affairs from public scrutiny if he acted less like a nervous squirrel hiding nuts.

Out on deck, the last lingering moments of night along with a fine mist hanging in the air make my first impression of Egypt not the golden land of the eternal sun, but the gloomy outline of a dark city, with a line of buildings along the shore appearing as a great serpentine beast with humps that has lain down along the water's edge.

No gaslights glow in windows or on street lamps, nor is there the tell-tale bounce of carriage lamps that one expects in a city. By crossing the Mediterranean, I have left behind the world of the modern conveniences of steam-powered engines and Mr Edison's newfangled electric lights, and stepped into a land that has changed little over the centuries.

A chant coming from a tall, slender tower silhouetted against the breaking dawn reminds me that I have arrived in the Islamic world. It is a call to prayer made by a muezzin from a balcony near the top of a minaret that rises next to the domed roof of a mosque. Neither spoken nor sung, the summons to face Mecca and pray is strange to my ear, a mournful wail like a plea to Allah for mercy and bounty in a harsh, dangerous world.

I spot the peculiar passenger from my corridor and realize why he's dressed in work clothes – he's standing on a small wooden platform being lowered to a rowing boat below. He must be in a hurry not to have waited for the accommodation ladder, a gangplank that will be placed on the side of the ship later to assist passengers in boarding shore boats. Is urgent business, perhaps even a family emergency speeding his exit from the ship?

A movement at the railing on the deck above catches my eye. Someone, a man I think, but I'm not sure because the individual is wrapped in a hooded overcoat, is at the rail, watching the passenger being rowed ashore.

My neighbour at least is entertainment on an otherwise dark and gloomy morn.

When the call to prayer ends, a violent gust of wind blows from shore, buffeting the ship and creating an eerie murmuring in the rigging.

'The poisoned wind, the A-rabs call it,' a crewman says as he passes by. He pauses and catches my eye. 'They say it comes out of the desert to blow us foreigners back to where we came from, and there's plenty in Port Saïd who believe it. Don't go ashore without a good man's protection, miss.'

A passenger slipping ashore under cover of darkness, a watcher in the night, a wind full of menace?

I return to my cabin to get ready for an excursion ashore, wondering what other curious things await me in the uncanny land of the Nile.

# 2

The night before we anchored, Herr Von Reich, a gentleman from Vienna, invited me to join him on an excursion to the city's native bazaar on our first day in Port Saïd. There, he assures me, I will find the mysterious and unimaginable, along with everything under the sun to buy, from rings to rugs and 'Even a camel if the captain will let you bring it aboard.'

Accompanying us will be Lord and Lady Warton, a British couple who have business ties with Von Reich, an engineer and inventor who once worked in Egypt.

There are sounds of discord when I go to meet my companions at the accommodation ladder. Arab boatmen below are shoving and shouting at each other in a mad haste to be the rowing boat closest to the platform that passengers step off at the bottom of the stairway.

Von Reich grins down at the chaos. 'We need only one boat and there are six warring to serve us. Lord Warton and I will clear the way with our canes. You ladies should keep your umbrellas handy.'

Both men carry Penang lawyers, thick walking sticks with bulbous, leaded heads.

As I follow the two men down the nearly vertical narrow stairway on the side of the ship, Lady Warton, coming behind me, says, 'You'll find that a sharp blow from a cudgel is the language these natives best understand.'

I glance back, nearly losing my footing, and gasp instead of making a retort. Having been formally introduced to the woman only last night, and in light of their generous acceptance of my presence, it would be ill-mannered of me to point out that a stick beats more ugliness into a person than it ever beats out.

The steep stairway sways and scrapes against the side of the ship and I hold on tight, wishing I wasn't wearing the long dress that far increases the risk that I will take a neck-breaking tumble. For sure, it was an inconsiderate man who made up the rule that only men can wear pants.

At the bottom platform I bite my lip as the canes swing right and left to drive back all but one boat. Lady Warton lashes out at a grabbing hand with her umbrella, but I have no intention of using mine in such a rude manner against fellow human beings. It's obvious that rowing passengers ashore is the only way these boatmen have of earning their bread, and it's a small loaf at that.

Forced to leave high school due to a heart condition, then living hand to mouth as a factory girl until the age of eighteen my sympathies lie with the poor wretches.*

Von Reich and Lord Warton board a boat to assist us ladies and I step aside so Lady Warton can go on first. Swells lift the platform and I step back, reaching for the support of the railing, when a boatman on the other side grabs my arm and

---

* Nellie lied about her age to maintain her 'girl reporter' image. She was actually twenty-one when she left the factory for a reporter's job. She was twenty-five years old in 1889. Leaving school because of a 'heart condition' was also a fib. She left school to work because her widowed mother could not afford to keep her in high school. The Editors.

I am literally dragged into his rocking boat. It happens so quickly I only get out a 'Well!' after I'm seated.

Von Reich shouts, 'We'll see you on shore, Nellie,' and I give a brave little laugh and hold onto the sides of the boat for dear life, finding myself a prisoner of four Arab rowers who are naked except for loincloths.

*This is an adventure*, I tell myself, a mantra I repeat when it appears I am going to hell in a handbasket and have no control over the situation.

I smile at the man who dragged me aboard. 'Get me to shore dry and I shall be very grateful.'

He unleashes a long statement in Arabic and I just smile and nod. I have no clue as to what he is saying, but I am sure he understands and is agreeable to my needs. I wish I could tell him how sorry I am that my companions found it necessary to administer the cane so freely and lavishly, and that I marvel at their stubborn persistence even while cringing under the blows.

I am reflecting upon the unkind attitude I heard expressed aboard the *Victoria* by Europeans and Americans about people of less fortunate nations, when I realize the rowers have stopped rowing and we are rising and rocking in swells a hundred feet from shore.

The man I spoke to gives me a nasty smirk, holds out his hand and says in perfect English, 'More money or you swim.'

I stare at him – gape at him – thoughts and emotions convulsing in my head like the shifting patterns of a kaleidoscope. Manhandled, kidnapped, and now I'm threatened and blackmailed by people I sympathize with.

Rising in the unsteady boat, I raise my umbrella and tell the ungrateful devil, 'Get me to shore!'

# 3

Safely ensconced in an open carriage with my companions as the sun's oppressive heat beats down on us, we make our way down a narrow, unpaved Port Saïd roadway alive with people and animals, the swirl of dust, and noise from every quarter – a street symphony punctuated by the braying of donkeys, the shouts of street vendors and the glee of children.

Two- and three-storey buildings with large enclosed balconies projecting far enough to shade the crowded passages below shoulder both sides of the street. Made of wood tarnished by time, the balcony windows are latticed with lovely Eastern motifs.

My companions busy themselves talking about the strategic importance of the Suez Canal, and while the uncommon sights, sounds and smells make Lady Warton's nose wrinkle, I smile in wonder as a cloud of pigeons on a terrace above take wing as a black-veiled woman walks among them like a magician releasing an entire flock.

We pass a train of camels carrying firewood, kicking up dust on an old man sitting cross-legged on the curb, years of hardship etched on his face, loaves of flatbread for sale lined up on newspapers beside him. A fat merchant wearing a red Turkish fez and straddling a small donkey clutches a metal box tightly to his chest as a fierce Saracen with a wicked-looking curved sword clears the way in front of him.

The streets are alive and the people have a strange flavour to me: servants – *slaves*, Von Reich says, despite the pretence of slavery being illegal – get up from sleeping on the ground outside their employers' houses and go inside to work; men and women are clothed from head to foot in long, loose-fitting cloak-like garments. Girls without veils and women with their faces hidden go to a nearby well to draw water and carry it back in clay pots balanced on their heads; a little boy leads a cow with a rope from house to house, milking the cow into jars brought out by householders. The milk boy carries a stuffed toy calf to fool the cow into giving milk.

'Would a cow really believe a stuffed toy is her child?' I ask Von Reich, our expert on everything Egyptian.

'Perhaps not in America, but in Egypt, who knows? In this strange land, where it is said that the Sphinx rises on moonless nights and runs across the desert like a jackal, and mummies dead thousands of years rise from their tombs, the unexplainable is not always unimaginable.'

We rumble past a line of men balancing bulging goatskin bags on wood poles across their shoulders.

'Public water carriers,' Von Reich says.

Their bodies are skeletal, as if the hot desert sun had melted away all their flesh except for a layer of skin as rough as papyrus. Though they're not in shackles, they remind me of a chain gang. 'How do they survive such hard work in this brutal heat?'

'Necessity.'

My companions for the day appear to be strange bed-fellows not only to me, but to each other. The Viennese inventor is relaxed and amiable, displaying plenty of bonhomie, while the British peer and his wife appear aloof, standoffish to the point of snobbishness, but I suppose they have a common ground in business. Von Reich has told me he is traveling with the Wartons to Hong Kong and on to Washington, D. C. on a business matter concerning an explosive he has patented.

The Austrian introduced himself to me while I was walking on deck the first morning at sea after we left Italy.

A dapper gentleman with well-cut clothes, Von Reich is broad-built with a closely shaved head and a gold monocle which looked custom-manufactured to fit comfortably and securely in his right eye. His flamboyant moustache with its long curved ends resembling the handlebars of a bicycle defies gravity with the help of a generous application of wax. His whole appearance is very much in vogue with men of wealth and position – and those who imitate such models of success. It always amazes me what great lengths men go to in order to portray a certain look – and they say women are vain.

After Von Reich made several overtures on board towards me in his blunt, central European manner – approaches that my mother would have deemed cheeky – I amused myself by asking him if *Frau* Von Reich would be joining him en route.

After assuring me rather stiffly, 'Frau Von Reich is faithfully awaiting my return,' he broke out laughing and told me that the only *frau* in his family is his mother.

He certainly is a handsome figure of a man, but an onboard flirtation is not in the stars for me. As I tell myself each morinng, I have rivers to cross, mountains to climb, castle walls to storm, dragons to fight . . . and in this case, pulling a man along would slow me down.

After I refused an invitation of a walk on the deck and

some liquid refreshment afterwards, his ardour cooled significantly.

However, when he told me he was going with friends to the bazaar, I boldly hinted that I would be delighted to join him. It was cheeky of me, indeed, but I am cabling my experiences back to New York and it will provide local colour.

Kids swarm across the street, causing our carriage to stop. A cyclist wearing an Arabian robe with a closely drawn hood quickly swerves to avoid them. His front wheel catches in a pothole and both man and bicycle go down hard.

'I hope he's okay,' I blurt out.

'What does it matter if one of these lazy natives is bruised?' Lady Warton asks.

*Charming woman.* Her husband refers to her as Eleanor, but she is Lady Warton to me. Eleanor is much too sweet for the woman's sour personality.

As the cyclist gets up, his hood slips down to show the side of his brown face, but oddly enough a flash of pale white skin above the boot on his right leg is also exposed. Rather than the sandals that the Egyptians prefer for their hot climate, the cyclist's footwear appears to be the same type of brown boots I've seen on British soldiers.

Brown face, white legs, army boots. How odd is that?

I start to share the observation with my companions when a racket erupts that sounds like the hounds of hell have broken out of their cage.

'Good gracious!' Lady Warton snaps. 'What is that horrid noise?'

'Hopefully it's not trouble with the Mahdi,' Von Reich says.

'What's the Mahdi?' I ask.

'A fanatical group who have unleashed a jihad, a holy war,

to drive the British and other Europeans from Egypt and kill Egyptians who consort with them. The name actually refers to a Muslim messiah, a Christ-like figure who will return to Earth during the End Days to rid the world of evil.'

I recall reading about the movement. 'Are they the fanatics who defeated a British army several years ago?'

'Actually, it was a British general leading an Egyptian army that was overwhelmed by vastly superior forces. Cutting off the head of Chinese Gordon, the general, and mounting it on a pike fired the movement. If the self-proclaimed Mahdi had not died of typhus, he may well have continued down the Nile, driving Europeans and the Egyptians who tolerate them into the sea.'

'Is there any danger to tourists?'

'There have been incidents of violence against foreigners, but we will be safe.' He pats his chest near his heart. 'Lord Warton and I are armed.'

Wonderful. After battling rowing boat pirates who threatened to cast me into the sea, I have been dropped into a hornet's nest of murderous terrorists.

'The Egypt government's rather ineffective, isn't it?' I ask. 'Under British control?'

'Yes, the government went broke and couldn't pay its debts, but the real interest of other nations isn't Egypt herself, but the Suez Canal. The country that controls it can put an economic stranglehold over other countries.'

'Britannica rules the seas,' Lord Warton says, 'and that little ditch scratched into the sand is a strategic route to India and the Far East.'

A mounted company of Egyptian cavalrymen with British officers trots by, heading in the direction of the noise.

'What do you think is going on?' I ask Von Reich.

'Noise can mean a celebration or trouble. This sounds like trouble.'

'Our troops can handle any situation,' Lord Warton says.

I didn't point out to him that the troops were Egyptian; only the officers were British.

The clamour grows louder and our carriage-driver pulls off the road as a large crowd of men come up the street repeating the same shouted phrase. The Arabic words mean nothing to me, but its violent tone is similar to one I once heard from a mob that had gathered after strike-breakers left union men dead, and it frightens me.

A squad of foot soldiers led by a British sergeant double-times smartly into place near us and our male companions leave us to speak to the noncommissioned officer as the crowd gets closer.

Perhaps a hundred men are in the crowd, no women, though a number of children are prancing along. Most of the men are wearing the djellabah, a loose-fitting hooded robe that is the universal male attire here unless one is working in the water or at the beach.

It doesn't strike me as an organized demonstration, at least not in the sense of people in a parade, but more of a crowd that was sparked into action spontaneously.

Egyptian horse soldiers with British officers, perhaps the ones we saw earlier, are in single file on both sides of the advancing crowd, acting rather like cowboys herding cattle.

*Time to return to the ship*, I think. However, too inhibited to show a yellow streak, I keep this thought to myself as our gentlemen return with the British sergeant.

'Sergeant O'Malley says we will be safe this close to his troops,' Lord Warton tells us.

The sergeant touches the rim of his pith helmet with his fingertip in greeting. 'Don't worry, ladies, we won't let the rabble get out of hand.'

'What are they shouting about?' I ask.

'The Father of Terror,' Von Reich replies.

'The Father of Terror?'

'That's correct, madam,' the sergeant says. 'That's what they call the Sphinx. Seems a tree told them that the Sphinx was going to get up from where it's squatting at Giza next to the pyramids to drive us demon foreigners from Egypt.'

It occurs to me that the cyclist I saw might be a British spy on the lookout for troublemakers.

Sergeant O'Malley busies himself lining up his men to assist in crowd control while our driver gets our carriage off to the side of the road.

'Trees talking!' scoffs Lady Warton, sounding personally offended, as if they were talking behind her back. 'What will these ignorant people imagine next?'

She appears wedded to hats with netted veils and wears them even on the ship. I assume she has facial blemishes she doesn't want to share with the world, or that she wishes to protect her skin from the sun.

Something about my expression causes the woman to direct her ire at me. 'Young woman, I suppose *you* believe in talking trees.'

I smile sweetly. 'Well, I was thinking that not far from here God spoke to Moses from a burning bush and commanded him to lead his people from Egypt.'

Von Reich doesn't say a word, but it is easy to see that his jaws are clamped tight to keep a laugh from erupting.

# 4

Our carriage is pulling up to the arched stone entrance to the bazaar when a man on a bicycle passes us.

'Isn't that the same man who took the spill?' I ask.

Von Reich shakes his head. 'I really can't say.'

'He had the same boots,' I mutter, more to myself.

'Shall we enter the den of thieves, ladies?' Von Reich asks as we step down from the carriage.

He had described the marketplace as a caravanserai, a place where camel caravans stop to drop and take on loads. I expected a sprawling dirt field with camels, tents and a bit of dung underfoot.

Instead, passing through the gate we go back in time, not to the ancient Land of the Pharaohs, but to medieval Baghdad of the *Arabian Nights*, to Ali Baba who spoke the magic words, '*Open, sesame*' to steal the treasure of the Forty Thieves, and to the mysterious Arab quarters called kasbahs.

The bazaar is dark and labyrinthine, exotic and puzzling, all at the same time; a heady blend of people, merchandise and animals that looks as if it has been laid out by an artist for his canvas.

The passageways, scarcely wide enough for two people walking abreast, are covered with canopies of Nile reeds, turning the walkways dim and shadowy even in the daytime.

The muted light and hooded robes and turbans add to the aura of fathomless mystery belonging to this culture that has lived along the Nile for thousands of years.

Rather than a world of organized shops, the bazzar is a menagerie of tiny cubbyholes crammed with merchandise pouring out like horns of plenty, some occupying spaces so small they are no more than cupboards.

People press up against the walls to keep from being trampled as donkeys and camels laden with goods force their way through the walkways, yet no one seems to be bothered. The chaos is organized.

The atmosphere is spellbinding as a contortionist prances along with us, twisting his limbs into impossible positions while a tumbler makes great leaps in the air, jumping, bouncing and rolling like a rubber ball. As with the camels, people simply move out of their path.

I catch the pungent scent of spiced Turkish tobacco from an open-air café where men wearing djellabahs drink muddy Turkish coffee and mint tea from tiny glass cups and share hookahs.

Copper pots and carpets are for sale, as are clothes ready to buy, cloth ready to be sewn, and cloth still being woven on looms – cotton, lamb's wool and goat hair. A man takes a live chicken from its cage and with one quick blow, chops off its head – blood splatters onto his robe and mixes with the blood of chickens now roasting over hot coals. 'Genuine' papyrus paintings of pharaohs in chariots and dancing girls with their bosoms bare can be purchased for the cost of a pack of gum back home. Goods are everywhere – flutes, drums, bells, cymbals, jewellery, spices . . . There are no bare spaces, even the passageways themselves are full, and some are so narrow we are almost shoulder to shoulder with the merchandise.

The exotic Eastern marketplace is everything I imagined and nothing I expected. I'm sure if I looked close enough, I would find frankincense and myrrh, and perhaps behind the public facades of shacks lining the alleys, I could buy treasures looted from the tombs of pharaohs.

'I find the stench of a marketplace insufferable, but his lordship enjoys contact with the natives,' says Lady Warton, fanning herself with a very pretty pink silk fan that has a design of small flowers on it. 'He served in Morocco for a year with the Foreign Office, advising the local officials on growing grains.'

'He's a farmer?'

'Of course not! He has farmlands on his estate. Naturally the farming is overseen by his manager, not by his lordship.'

'Of course,' I murmur, keeping myself from wondering aloud why the Foreign Office didn't send the farm manager to Morocco instead.

Tattered beggars with bodies so dirty that their skin is hardly discernable from their fouled rags approach us with outstretched hands and heartrending pleas: '*Baksheesh, baksheesh . . .*'

Lady Warton glares at them and swings her umbrella to shoo them away. 'Go away, go away.'

I give them coins, remembering my mother's admonition whenever she saw a person with a deformity: 'But for the grace of God go any of us.'

'Feeding lice only causes them to multiply,' she says.

'Sorry.'

Finding myself ill at ease with her insufferable attitude of superiority, I button my lips as any well-mannered guest should. The boys in the newsroom have an expression for her ladyship's type, one that I willingly embrace: *rich bitch*.

Lady Warton was obviously born with a silver spoon in her

month – one filled with vinegar. She and her pompous husband no doubt believe that their position in the world is due to nothing less than the divine rights of kings, rather than an accident of birth.

The strange sights and smells that surround me bring to mind a book I've read: the adventures of Allan Quatermain, the hero of Rider Haggard's tale *King Solomon's Mines*.

'Isn't this place exotic?' I offer.

'Exotic? My dear, you are surrounded by half-naked, unwashed natives who eat and drink things that poison the stomachs of civilized people. The Côte d'Azur is exotic. This is a wasteland.'

'I find it captivating. Egypt is a place to come in search of adventure. If I had been born in a different time and place, perhaps I could have been an adventurer searching for lost treasures.'

Lady Warton stares at me as if I have something dribbling down my chin.

'Are you feeling ill, your ladyship?' I ask.

'Frankly, my dear, I am deeply disturbed and puzzled by the concept of a young woman tramping around wild animals and savage natives in search of treasure. That is certainly not a proper ambition for any *woman*.' She surveys me with a look of contempt that sweeps from head to toe. 'One has to wonder how a young woman who possesses ideas that are the proper attributes only of men was raised.'

I turn away and bite my lip. I've learned to rein in my temper because being a reporter carries with it the necessary evil of having to deal with all kinds of people, but I draw the line at remarks about my upbringing. If she says another word about my mother, I will knock her onto her noble behind.

My reaction to her is aggravated by my resentment of

people who have licked the cream off the top all of their lives. Not having to earn their bread, they don't understand that there is more to life for women than just being the helpmates and sexual playthings of men.

I soon wonder if we aren't going in circles, for the alleys appear to be a confusing and intricate network of passages that all seem to repeat themselves.

'Does your husband know where he's going?' I ask Lady Warton. 'I feel lost in this maze.'

'His precious sister in England specifically requested that he get her a trinket from a particular dealer she heard about, so we must humour him.'

We enter the jewellery section, where tiny merchant shacks offer jewellery boxes and ornaments of every kind, from copper bracelets to gold chains, anklets and nose-rings of leaden-looking silver and brassy gold.

Lord Warton says, 'We're getting close, I'm sure of it.'

His wife leaves me to join him and Von Reich drops back to walk with me. He takes my arm as we stroll along, watching beggars and the purveyors of 'ancient' artefacts competing to relieve people of their money.

'How do they talk?' I ask him.

'Who?'

'Trees. Do they speak to people passing by, that sort of thing?'

'Only with the written word. You see all around you the elaborate artful swirls and waves of the Arabic language, none of it decipherable to us of the West. Those flowing lines are sometimes repeated in nature, on tree leaves, carved in the sand by the wind—'

'So the pattern on a leaf is interpreted as words, and fanatics start shouting that it's a message from God.'

'Exactly.'

I confess, 'I'm afraid I'm not doing too well with Lady Warton. I don't want to be a bad guest, but anything I say seems to offend her.'

'You're at a disadvantage, trying to hold a conversation with a woman who has never used her brain. As you pointed out with the Bible story, that trees talk here should not come as a surprise. Egypt is part of the Holy Land, a place of mystery, where an angry God sent plagues of pestilence to punish a stubborn pharaoh, where staffs turn to snakes, and the sea itself parted for God's favourite.' He squeezes my arm. 'But you must appreciate that it is also a place of dark magic, of pharaohs with eternal lives, mummies that rise from their graves—'

'And a sphinx that gallops across the desert – and eats foreigners.'

'*Ja!* In this country there are few precise boundaries between what is, and what might be.'

'I confess that I'm not a person who embraces the supernatural. Perhaps because so much of my life has been spent keeping a roof over my head and putting food on the table, I leave the uncanny to those who have the time and energy. But ever since I walked out on deck this morning and saw Egypt through mist and darkness, I've felt *something*.' I shake my head. 'I can't explain it, and certainly won't share it with my editor in a cable for fear he'll believe I have brain fever, but I've had a sense of not being alone.'

We come to a clearing where a crowd is gathering around a man standing on a small mound, holding a staff.

'You have to see this,' says Von Reich, and steers me towards the man. He is wearing a long black robe and a white turban that rises to a peak with a dark green band—

'Good Lord!' I exclaim. 'That's a snake, not a hat band.'

A cobra fanning its neck and showing its fangs is wrapped around the turban.

'That evil creature is looking at me,' I tell Von Reich. There is no doubt about it, the thing is staring right at me.

'Nasty devil, isn't he?' he laughs. 'It's easy to see why the pharaohs used the cobra as a symbol of their power over life and death. The Egyptian cobra they call the asp is one of the most venomous snakes in the world.'

'What happens if it gets off the turban?' I ask.

'Someone dies. But it's sewn on so it stays wrapped around the turban and can't move its head enough to bite.'

It doesn't look sewn on to me. 'The man's a snake charmer?'

'More than that, he's a *psylli*, a magician who handles snakes,' replies Von Reich. 'They're not just marketplace entertainers. *Psyllis* are descendants of an ancient tribe of desert people who work wonders with snakes, especially the *Naja haje*, the deadly Egyptian cobras. They're exposed to snake bites while still young and claim they have an immunity. They're said to be servants of Wadjet, the Green One, the Egyptian goddess with a snake's head.

'Stories about them go back thousands of years. There are *psyllis* is the Bible, – like the pharaoh's magician-priests who dueled with Moses and his brother Aaron.'

'The ones who turned staffs into snakes?'

'Yes, their favourite trick, and it is a clever bit of conjuring. Today they earn more money drawing out snakes from people's houses than from entertaining people. It's not uncommon for snakes to get indoors and once inside they can be impossible to find – until a cobra reaches out from under your bed and bites you.'

I shudder at that thought.

'*Psyllis* go into people's homes and sing a tune that seduces the snakes into leaving their hiding places.'

The magician speaks to the crowd and Von Reich interprets the gist of what is being said.

'He's going to show us his power over snakes and then he will forever immunize people from snake bites – for a price, but not a bad investment considering how many people die of bites in the country.'

I'm wondering how many people die from the 'cure' when Von Reich grabs my arm.

'Watch this!'

The man raises his staff into the air and points it in our direction – then tosses it right at us. The wooden rod hits the ground and instantly turns into a wiggling snake that coils and rises up, fanning its head.

Gasps erupt, including mine, and we move back. Von Reich keeps his own cane in front of the serpent to attract its attention as we edge backwards.

Once the snake has been captured and placed in a sack by one of the magician's attendants, the four of us regroup and walk away.

'Please, tell me how it's done,' I say to Von Reich as the Wartons stop to examine a rack of jewellery. He told me aboard ship that he's an amateur magician and showed me several clever card tricks.

'Obviously, the man calls upon the snake goddess to empower him.'

A man with a big flamboyant moustache has to have an ego to match, so I play on his conceit to draw out the answer. 'I'm sorry, I just thought you might know, being a magician yourself.'

He pretends to look around to see if anyone is within hearing range.

A man coming towards us is selling scarabs and I keep an eye on him as we walk. It occurs to me that these beetles, once powerful amulets used to ward off evil spirits and slay enemies, are now employed largely to fleece tourists. Still, I've decided that I would like to pin one on my dress as a memento of Egypt.

'The *Naja haje* cobra has a unique characteristic,' Von Reich is saying. 'A spot on the back of the snake's head, when pressed, causes the snake to extend to its full length and become rigid. It snaps out of its paralysis when it's tossed by the magician and hits the ground.'

I raise my hand to signal the scarab seller to come over, but he turns to a man who is suddenly by his side. The man's wearing a djellabah, but a distinguishing feature of his clothing draws my attention: British army boots.

It's the cyclist I saw earlier.

From the expression on the scarab seller's face, I sense tension between the two of them. The seller turns to move away and the hooded man grabs a scarab and abruptly spins around and starts to walk toward us.

The scarab seller yells in Arabic and the cyclist breaks into a run, but he goes only a few paces before an Egyptian steps in front of him, his back to me, and I see the flash of a blade.

It all happens so quickly, I see it, but my mind won't accept it – the Egyptian has stuck a dagger into the cyclist's belly.

Murder is being committed before my eyes.

The dagger man shouts, '*Allah Akbar! Allah Akbar! Allah Akbar!*'

God is great!

# 5

The two men face each other, so close that the cyclist grips the wrist of his assassin as if they are about to dance, his face a mask of surprise, his mouth open, almost as if the assault has left him with an unfinished question: *Why?*

The assassin pulls the bloodied dagger out of his victim's stomach.

Staring down, the wounded man puts both hands over the spreading patch of blood on his abdomen.

The assassin strikes a second time, shoving the blade into the man's abdomen again. The cyclist's legs fold and he drops to his knees, then onto the dirt, as his attacker holds the bloody dagger high in the air, repeating, *'Allah Akbar! Allah Akbar!'*

He turns towards us, dagger in hand, his robe spattered with the victim's blood.

*'Shoot him!'* Lady Warton shouts to her husband.

Lord Warton seems paralyzed, frozen in place, his jowls quivering as he stares at the murderer.

My feet won't let me move. Like Lord Warton, I just stand and gawk at the man coming at us with a bloodied blade.

Von Reich pulls out a double-barrelled derringer and fires. The bullet knocks the man back, his own face mimicking the surprise that his victim showed only moments before as he falls backwards onto the dirt.

Quick strides bring Von Reich hovering over the man. The assassin looks up and says something in Arabic as Von Reich takes careful, deliberate aim and fires, the bullet catching the man in the centre of his foreshead, snapping his head back against the ground, his legs twitching, and then he is perfectly still.

The second shot brings me out of my trance and I rush to the cyclist who has got back up on his knees. He clutches at me, grabbing at my clothes. Seeing him close up, I realize he's my neighbouring passenger from the *Victoria* who made such an unorthodox departure from the ship.

I try to hold him up but he slips back to the ground. Kneeling beside him, I cradle his head. 'Get a doctor, he's still alive!'

He grabs me, pulling me closer.

'It's all right, we're getting a doctor.'

He's trying to tell me something, so I let him pull me to him until my face is inches from his lips. He whispers something I don't catch. 'What?' I ask.

'*Amelia . . . Amelia . . .*'

That is all he says before he slumps in my arms and I feel the life slipping away from him. He spoke with a British accent.

Lord Warton grabs my arm and pulls me up and away from the man.

'We must get a doctor!' I yell.

'There's nothing you can do.'

'No!' I struggle to get back to the man, hoping he might still be alive but knowing he isn't.

Lord Warton is holding me tightly as he pulls me away, while Von Reich and others crowd around the body. He finally releases me when Von Reich takes my arm.

'He's dead,' says Von Reich.

31

I jerk my arm away. 'Leave me alone!' He's right, there's nothing I can do, but I need time to gather my wits and let it sink in.

'What did he say to you?'

'Amelia.'

'What?'

'His wife's name, Amelia, that's all he said. We must get him a doctor, maybe there's something . . .'

Von Reich shakes his head as he reloads his pistol. 'A doctor can't help him now.'

'You poor dear,' says Lady Warton, leading me away with another firm hold on my arm. 'His lordship and Von Reich will take care of everything. You've been through enough.'

Lord Warton looks up from kneeling beside the cyclist and yells to her, 'Go back to the boat. Von Reich will see that you get there safely.'

'But we can't just leave.' I plant my feet firmly on the ground. 'The police—'

'You're not in America!' Lady Warton snaps. 'This is *not* a civilized country. If we are to sail with the *Victoria*, we must hurry to the carriage before we get involved in a deadly dispute between two natives.'

'Natives? The man's a British passenger on our ship.'

'Why do you say he's British?' Von Reich asks.

'I saw his face . . . heard his voice . . .'

They steer me back towards the bazaar entrance as we talk.

'I saw and heard the same as you did,' says Lady Warton. 'His face was brown, he's obviously a native.'

'No, I'm sure he's British.'

'That's not possible,' disagrees Von Reich. 'He appeared Egyptian to me.'

'You had a momentary glance at a hooded man,' Lady Warton insists.

'I saw his face.'

'He's brown.'

'Not his legs.'

'His legs? What about his legs?' she demands.

'His robe got pulled up when he fell of his bicycle. I saw white skin.'

Lady Warton gives Von Reich an exasperated look. He shakes his head and says, 'Nellie, I saw only brown skin.'

'I know what I saw. He spoke English.'

'Many Egyptians speak the Queen's English. We run the country,' Lady Warton declares.

Holding back tears, I raise my chin and stand my ground. 'The man is a passenger on our ship. I will not abandon him, even in death.'

'I'll take another look at the man,' Von Reich concedes. 'Keep going, we can't have the carriage leave without us when word spreads of trouble.'

He hurries back in the direction we came. Still gripping my arm firmly, her ladyship deftly marches me out of the maze and straight to the carriage as easily as if she'd left breadcrumbs to guide us.

We're at the carriage when Von Reich comes back, breathing hard. 'I've examined the man thoroughly.'

'Arab?' Lady Warton asks.

'All over.'

'I have to see for myself.' I start back to the entrance of the bazaar.

'Get involved and you'll be detained for questioning,' says Von Reich.

That stops me in my tracks. 'Detained for questioning' would mean not finishing the race. I hesitate, shifting from one foot to the other, not knowing which way to turn.

Lady Warton turns to board the carriage. 'I don't know about you, young woman, but I have no intention of staying for months in this godforsaken hell while the slow wheels of bureaucracy grind down.'

The mere thought of it chills me even in the hot, dry desert air.

I hate her words, they're hard and cruel, but I know she's right. 'I suppose there's nothing that can be done for the poor man.' It sounds like an excuse, even to me, but it's also the truth. 'What about Lord Warton? Shouldn't we wait for him?'

His wife shakes her head. 'He'll be fine. His lordship has had plenty of practice at dealing with natives.'

Von Reich helps me board the carriage. My knees are shaky and I am still fighting back tears. 'She's right, *Fraulein*. You cannot imagine what the police of these backward countries are like. Things can get very ugly.'

Things already start to look ugly as we begin to move off. A crowd has gathered and the driver looks worried. 'We must hurry. Word spreads.'

'What do you mean?' I ask.

'A Mahdi follower was martyred by an infidel. The Father of Terror is rising to drive the infidels from our land. That is what people are saying. We must hurry,' he repeats.

We haven't travelled a hundred feet before a mob pours out of the marketplace from different arteries, chanting, '*Allah Akbar! Allah Akbar!*'

We duck and cover our heads with our hands as stones start flying at us.

# 6

The carriage takes us out of the reach of Stone Age weapons but anger and fanaticism travel faster than the wind. All along our path men on the street shout angry words and shake their fists at us.

I can't stop thinking about the man we left behind at the marketplace. A man who died in my arms and spoke his last words to me. He wanted me to do something for Amelia, whom I assume is his wife. How do I find her? What do I tell her? That her husband's life-blood was spilled on the dirt of a Port Saïd marketplace? That if he's a foreigner, the local people would celebrate the death as a sign from God?

*If he's a foreigner.* The doubts of my companions have me wondering if the man really was the secretive passenger I saw disembark before dawn. I saw white skin on the cyclist, but it's possible that it wasn't the same man. I wouldn't recognize my own brothers if they were covered head to toe in Egyptian robes.

'You must stop agonizing over what occurred,' Lady Warton says, reading my thoughts. 'Life is cheap in these backwards countries. They express themselves with violence because they have no books or newspapers. Unless you can breathe life into the dead, there is nothing you could have done.'

'Except make sure his wife Amelia is notified of his death.'

35

'Did he tell you his wife's name was Amelia?' asks Lady Warton.

'No, I just assumed—'

She gives me a dark look that says I will never learn. 'You must have heard an Arabic word that sounded like the name.'

I keep my peace rather than cause a confrontation. I'm certain he was speaking his wife's name in his last moment. I don't have a clue how, but I shall see that the man's wife is properly notified. At the moment, though, I need to get my feet solidly back under me and keep focused on the demands of the race I have undertaken.

I could not have imagined the tragic events in the market-place when I took up my challenge and sailed from New York thirteen days ago. When Mr Pulitzer informed me that a man would be sent because a race around the world was too great a task for a woman, I told him to go ahead and start his man – and I'd set out for another newspaper and beat him.

When the powerful publisher finally yielded, he gave me only three days' notice to prepare for the trip. But there were other reasons for my trip to Egypt besides Jules Verne's remark that a woman was not capable of making the trip in the eighty days his fictional hero had managed. The seed for such an adventure was sown two years earlier, when no New York newspaper would hire me as a reporter because I was a woman.

To prove that I was as capable as a man, I set out on my own to expose the shocking conditions at a woman's insane asylum by getting myself committed as a patient. It required me to convince a boarding house landlady, policemen, three psychiatrists and a judge that I was a lunatic. The final diagnosis stated that I was a hopeless case, quite incurable, requiring commitment to the notorious women's asylum on New York's Blackwell's Island.

I spent ten days in the madhouse and wrote an exposé for Mr Pulitzer's newspaper that revealed the brutal conditions mentally ill women were subjected to at the asylum.\* That venture not only got me a job as an investigative reporter on Mr Pulitzer's *New York World*, but ultimately took me to Paris, its magnificent World's Fair, and a confrontation with preternatural evil.

When I returned to New York, Mr Verne's taunt that women were too fragile and required too much baggage for such a trip stayed with me. Such a notion is pure poppycock, brewed up by men who underestimate the power and determination of women just because society forbids them from wearing pants. 'Nellie's Folly' is what the other papers will call it if I fail. Worse, the effect that failure will have upon the ambitions of women to succeed in a man's world will be severely damaged.

This is why I accepted the challenge and why I must succeed.

I was certain I could do it. The available transportation – steamships, trains and carriages – are all about the same as those used by Phileas Fogg sixteen years ago, but two great advances have reduced travel time: the Suez Canal, which means it is no longer necessary for ships to sail all the way around Africa's Cape of Good Hope, and the completion of the transcontinental rail line from San Francisco to New York.

---

\* Nellie also wrote a book in 1887 called *Ten Days in a Mad House*. Her experiences in the madhouse ultimately led her to Paris and the events told in *The Alchemy of Murder*. The Editors.

Knowing that I would have to sometimes scurry to make connections, I brought only one small handbag, a valise about sixteen inches long and seven inches wide. I never realized the capacity of an ordinary hand-satchel until dire necessity compelled me to exercise all my ingenuity to pack one with the following: two travelling caps, three veils, a pair of slippers, toilet articles, ink-stand, pens, pencils and copy-paper, pins, needles and thread, a dressing-gown, a light jacket, a silk bodice, a small flask and drinking cup, several complete changes of underwear, a liberal supply of handkerchiefs and fresh ruchings and, most bulky and uncompromising of all, a jar of cold cream to keep my face from chapping in the varied climates I should encounter.*

The travel dress I put on the day I boarded the ship in New York is the same one I am wearing today and will wear for the entire trip of nearly three months. I also have an ulster to keep me warm.

The evening before I started out I went to the office to say goodbye and to obtain £200 in English gold and Bank of England notes. The gold I carry in my pocket, with a few pieces hidden in the heel of my left shoe. The Bank of England notes are in a chamois-skin bag tied around my neck. Besides this, I have some American gold and paper money to use at different ports, as a test to see if American money is known outside the forty-two states and territories.

Even though it was quite possible to buy tickets in New York for the entire trip, because I might be compelled to change my route at almost any point, no intinerary was made

* Veils were in fashion and also commonly used to hold ladies' hats in place. Ruchings were lace trim on collars and sleeves that could be taken off and washed. The Editors.

and the only transportation I arranged on leaving New York was my ticket to London.*

A fellow reporter suggested that a revolver would be a good companion piece for my travels, but I had such a strong belief in the world greeting me as I greeted it that I refused to arm myself. I knew if my conduct was proper I should always find men of any nationality ready to protect me.

Now, though, the life's blood of two men soaking the dirt of the marketplace made the suggestion that I carry a revolver seem like sage advice.

Raucous noise jolts me out of my thoughts and I tense up as a group of people turn onto the street. Women at the head of the procession are shrieking and wailing.

'The Mahdi?'

'A funeral procession,' answers Von Reich. 'The barefoot women at the front howling the loudest and tearing their clothes are professional mourners.'

'What nonsense is that?' Lady Warton demands. 'Why in God's name would they hire people to make those awful noises and rip their clothes?'

'It's how they honour the dead; the more grief, the more the dead person will be missed. The black-robed women wait outside the house like a flock of crows until they're told the deceased has passed and then they begin their expressions of grief, all the way to the cemetery and until the last shovel of dirt is thrown.'

* Not buying tickets for the entire trip was a good decision since Nellie missed the mail boat at London and instead crossed the English Channel to Boulogne, then travelled across France and down the boot of Italy to Brindisi by rail and carriage, where she boarded the steamship *Victoria* for Port Saïd. The Editors.

I close my eyes tight and turn my head to avoid looking at the group as they pass, but it does no good – the wails for the dead penetrate my bones, chilling my marrow.

Who will cry for the dead men in the marketplace?

We reach the beach where several boats are available to take us out to the ship.

'You ladies stay here and I'll find our boatman,' Von Reich says.

He returns with a disgusted expression on his face. 'It's arranged, but the boatman would not permit us even to board until I paid him. His price is double what he charged to bring us to land. These people are robbers.'

'And murderers,' Lady Warton snaps.

# 7

The moment our feet are on the deck Lady Warton excuses herself, proclaiming she has a 'horrid headache' and heads straight for her cabin and her headache powders.

Perhaps it is only my strained state of mind, but as she flees I'm left with the singular impression that in her estimation, it is somehow I who am responsible for her distress rather than the fact that we have witnessed two violent deaths in the marketplace.

Instead of going directly to my cabin, I walk on deck, pacing swiftly from stern to bow, a habit I have of wearing off nervous energy and mulling over the day's events before I retire.

This time I need to walk off ragged nerves. My body aches because I've been so tense. I watched two men die today. How will their deaths affect me? Touching the side of my neck, I can still feel the dying man's breath as he whispered his last word to me – *Amelia.*

I know I've left the violence at the marketplace and the rage on the streets where a mob thirsted for blood – my blood – yet I sense I've carried some of the malevolence back to the ship with me, just as I brought the dust of Port Saïd on my shoes.

They were still coaling the ship from a barge when we boarded, dust-covered men with sacks of coal rushing up the steep gangplank between the barges and the ship. The men are not working quietly. Judging from the noise, every one of them is yelling something different, according to their own fancy and humour.

The frantic bustle is soothing in an odd sort of way, and just for the moment the aching memory of the horror in the marketplace fades.

I don't know the identity of the cyclist who died in the marketplace, but regardless of who he was, in the morning I'll ask Lord Warton what happened after we left and if anyone is planning to locate the dead man's wife. If not, I shall attempt to. The man's resemblance to my fellow passenger and his British accent still bewilder me, but I have to put aside my doubts and move on.

Returning to my cabin, I find the steward's luggage cart parked outside the cabin belonging to the man I thought was the cyclist. The door is slightly open.

Passenger names appear on all the cabin doors, and this one bears the inscription 'John Cleveland'.

I hesitate briefly, my good sense telling me to move on and mind my own business, but my curiosity prods me to peek in. I nudge the door open a bit more. Raymond, a ship's steward who also serves as my attendant, is placing clothes on the bed. Behind him are two steamer trunks.

I push the door further open.

'Madam? Can I help you?'

'Is Mr Cleveland in the vicinity?'

'No, he went ashore, madam.'

I glance at the clothing on the bed and the trunks. 'Is Mr Cleveland leaving us?'

'Yes, he's staying in Port Saïd. I've been instructed to send his luggage ashore.'

'Really? Who told you he was staying?'

The steward avoids my eye. 'Those are my instructions, madam.'

'I'm just wondering if the instructions are correct. I saw Mr Cleveland a short time ago and he never mentioned that he was leaving.'

'The instructions came from Lord Warton.'

'I see.' But I don't – not at all. Lord Warton tells me that the dead man isn't my neighbour on the ship and then gives instructions for the man's possessions to be left behind. That makes it all as clear as mud. Except for one thing. 'Lord Warton isn't on board the ship.'

'Her ladyship delivered the instruction for him.'

'I see.' More muddy waters, though it is readily apparent that Lady Warton received instructions to which I was not privy and neglected to share them with me.

'I'm only obeying instructions, madam.'

He's getting defensive – he probably thinks I suspect him of stealing. 'Of course. Do go on with his lordship's instruction.'

As he turns back to his task, I add, 'Raymond, I have a dreadful headache. Would you please go to the infirmary and fetch me some powder?'

'But madam, I brought you some headache powders yesterday—'

'Yes, I know, but I need some more. Here—' I pull a three-pence coin out of my pocket and slip it into his hand. 'I'll watch Mr Cleveland's possessions until you get back.'

Resisting the impulse to push him out of the door, as soon as he is gone I start searching – for what, I don't know. I haven't a clue as to what to look for, but I obey my instincts, which are screaming that something is not right.

Why the devil makes me do these things has always been a mystery to me. As a fellow reporter once told me after I narrowly escaped a brothel owner's wrath, some day I will end up sticking my nose in the wrong place and get it chopped off.

Quickly checking the dresser drawers, I find them already emptied. Leafing through the items on the bed reveals an ordinary collection of shirts, collars, cuffs, shirt fronts, bow-ties and other accessories. Taking care not to ruffle the clothes too much, I press down on the piles to feel if anything is hidden beneath . . . and find nothing.

The two steamer trunks are unlocked and empty.

In a box on the floor are books and a case of fine kitchen and dinner knives branded with the name of a cutlery manufacturer in Liverpool. Inscribed on the cutlery case is the passenger's name: John J. Cleveland.

My gallows humour dispatches a most inappropriate thought into my head: a cutlery salesman was stabbed to death by a knife.

I look through the books: there is one on hunting rifles, a thin volume called the *Handbook on Egypt* and a hefty tome entitled *Compendium of Laws of the County of Yorkshire*.

A small piece of paper marks a page in the law book. Written on it in pencil are a series of numbers that have no apparent order, at least not to me. It makes no more sense than if I had sat down and written numbers at random, but the numbers must have meant something to Mr Cleveland.

Shamelessly rummaging through the man's possessions, I find no indication that he has a family – no pictures of a wife or children, no letters.

*So if Mr Cleveland was the cyclist, who is Amelia?*

Even if she is a lover rather than his wife, might he not

have a picture of her? Some keepsake such as a lace hand-kerchief with her favourite scent, or a farewell note?

I hear footsteps in the corridor and almost drop the book. *I'm going to be caught.* I shove the paper back between the pages, the books back into the box, and race for the door, opening it and snagging the heel of my shoe on the threshold as I stumble out.

Getting my balance, I stare at a man who has opened the door to a cabin on the other side of the corridor. The foot-steps I heard were his. He stares back.

'I—I—' No alibi comes to my normally liquid tongue and I give him a smile instead.

'Good evening,' he says.

I choke on a reply as I hear two voices coming from the stair-well that leads into the corridor. *Lord Warton and the steward.*

I leap forward and rush at the man, causing him to step backwards into his cabin and nearly fall over a piece of luggage. I step in and slam the door behind me.

For a moment, we just stare at each other, his mouth agape.

'You'll catch flies,' pops out of my own mouth.

He starts to say something and I can see that words fail him.

He is older than me, perhaps in his late thirties. My first impression is that he needs a shave, a haircut and a bath. Soap, hot water and a good scrubbing by the ship's laundry would also make his clothes presentable. His appearance suggests he has come aboard directly from an expedition of some sort, rather than an hotel.

A tall, handsome man with sapphire blue eyes and a muscular build, he appears perplexed, perhaps even slightly amused that a mere slip of a woman has forced her way into his room.

'What I meant was, your mouth was open. You'll catch flies that way if you aren't careful.'

'Who told you that?'

'My mother, when I was a little girl.'

My mouth is flapping nonsense but my ears are pricked in anticipation of the sudden banging on his stateroom door that I expect at any moment, along with a demand that I come out and face the music.

He nods in a knowing manner. 'I can see that your mother, dear woman that she no doubt is, probably spared the rod too much with her daughter. May I ask why you have stormed into my room?'

'I—I—'

'Yes, I've heard that much.'

His voice tells me he is British, something I had already assumed from his appearance and clothes.

'I'm trying to avoid a masher.'

'A masher? On the ship? Come, we'll inform the captain – after I thrash the man.'

I hold out a hand to keep him from getting around me to the door. 'No, we can't.'

'Why can't we?'

'I—I—'

'Perhaps the truth might come out easier?'

I sigh deeply and lean back against the door. I don't know why lies are getting stuck in my throat. A compulsion to tell the truth has rarely crimped my speech before now.

'I did something I shouldn't have done. A man was murdered—'

'*You murdered a man?*'

'No, of course not, a man was killed at the marketplace. Two men, in fact.'

'Yes, I heard something about that. A dispute between locals.'

'No, the first man attacked was British. I'm sure it was Mr Cleveland, the cutlery salesman across the hall.'

He starts to say something, opening his mouth wide enough again for flies, then closing it.

'You think I'm mad.'

'Not at all,' he says, calmly. 'I think that something I ate or drank came from the Land of the Lotus Eaters and has caused me to imagine that a young woman has barged into my room, telling me a wild story about the death of a cutlery salesman in a marketplace.'

'Lord Warton says the dead man is Egyptian, but I say it was Mr Cleveland.'

'And what does Mr Cleveland say?'

'You haven't been listening to me. Mr Cleveland is dead.'

'Miss—?'

'Bly, Nellie Bly. I'm an American. Mr—?'

'Selous, Frederick Selous.' He gives me a gentlemanly nod–bow. 'I am British and it is obvious that you are an American. No proper British woman would barge into a strange man's room at night. However, the fact that you are American, madam, does not make Mr Cleveland dead.'

'The fact that you are British, sir, does not make Mr Cleveland alive.'

'Quite true, Miss Bly. But the fact that I spoke to Mr Cleveland only a few minutes ago does mean he was not murdered earlier in the marketplace.'

*Oh, Lord* . . . a big hole has opened under my feet and I am falling into it.

# 8

I'm sure I left Mr Selous's stateroom on two feet, but when I'm in the corridor and his door slams behind me, I feel I've crawled out on broken glass.

'Nellie, girl, you did it this time,' I moan out loud.

*Mr Cleveland alive?* I can't believe I have been so bull-headed, stubborn and stupid.

The corridor is empty – praise the Lord for that – and I walk slowly, in a mental fog, towards my cabin at the far end. How will I face Von Reich and the Wartons tomorrow? More importantly, how do I get myself into these things?

'*Madam!*' a voice behind me snaps.

I spin round. The steward has come out of Mr Cleveland's room and I brace myself for the accusations that I am certain will start flying. Full of guilt, I'm ready to confess my sins.

'You forgot your headache powders.'

I breathe a sigh of relief. 'Thank you, Raymond.'

My head really is ready to explode.

After taking the headache powders, I throw myself onto the bed, cover my head with a pillow and groan into it. What a fool I have made of myself! It'll be all over the ship by morning.

My short time in Port Saïd has been nothing but dreadful.

Witnessing a murder and what amounted to an execution in a medieval bazaar, then being chased by a mob of murderous fanatics, all confirms Mr Pulitzer's opinion about the dangers of international travel.

Somewhere along the line I have made a complete fool out of myself with important people who have been kind to me and who I will be seeing every day for the next several weeks.

This last realization prompts me to pour another glass of water and add more headache powder.

I can only conclude in my defence that the dark side of Egyptian magic has reached out from a secret tomb buried in the desert sands and turned the day into a nightmare.

What grates the most is that Lord Warton will likely attribute my insistence that the dead Egyptian in the marketplace was John Cleveland to a combination of too much sun and the weakness of a 'female disposition'. And I have provided all the necessary ammunition. A hysterical female, for certain, is what I have managed to make myself.

I should never have challenged Lord Warton's assessment of the identify of the dead man. He is a lord, after all, even though I'm not quite sure what that means – is he an earl or baron? Whatever his title, it's something very prestigious because everyone from the captain to the other passengers fawns over him. Compared to a nobleman, what do I know?

A thousand regrets swirl within me as I take off my dress to shake the dust out of it. As I'm giving it a good jerk, some-thing drops out and hits the carpet.

A scarab, the magic amulet of the pharaohs.

'Where did you come from?' I ask as I examine it.

The stone beetle is a couple of inches long and an inch wide, larger and heavier than the ones I've seen used for jewellery. Red with black eyes and a black spot on its back, the beetle has six brown legs and two short autennae.

The only way it could have got into my pocket was if the dying man put it there as I held him. Why would he slip a symbol of Egyptian magic into my pocket? It was his last act, besides uttering the name Amelia.

What is so important about this scarab that a man was murdered over it – and passed it to me in his dying moments?

Nothing about its appearance makes it appealing. It lacks the gems or fine workmanship that would give it value beyond that of a marketplace trinket. The flat bottom has two snakes on each side, their heads meeting at the top, but no other symbols or hieroglyphics. The scarab's back is smooth with no distinctive horizontal or vertical lines. It does have an unusual feature – it's meant to be opened. A crack along the side suggests that it's made of two pieces wedged together.

A piece goes flying as I pry it open with a nail file and bangs against the wall, breaking into fragments. In a cavity between the two sides is a key, similar to the one my father used to use to remove the big metal cover from a piece of machinery at the mill he operated in Cochran's Mills when I was a child. When he bought a new machine, he gave the key to me because I loved the odd shape of it. I still have it, safely tucked away in my jewellery box at home.

The mill was started by my father and named for him, Elizabeth Cochran being my true name. Those who have followed my career know that when I was hired as a reporter I was forced to take the pen name of Nellie Bly to hide my identity, since news reporting is considered immodest employment for a woman.

The key in my hand also looks like it belongs in a factory,

around machinery. Nothing about it strikes me as Egyptian. It's definitely the product of an industrialized country.

Events have taken on an even stranger line. That was no dispute between locals in the marketplace, but something smacking of intrigue. But why was the key slipped into my pocket?

The cyclist who exposed white skin, the man whose dying words were spoken with a British accent, a man with a face I'm sure I passed in the corridor – it had to be Mr Cleveland. Lord Warton taking charge of his luggage, sending it ashore, it cannot be a coincidence.

A British man named John Cleveland died in the marketplace in a dispute over a key hidden in a cheap scarab. I'd stake my life on it.

Staring at the key, I wonder if I have done exactly that.

I push the thought aside. I'm on a British ship. No one can harm me. I hope.

Still, I have no idea why he gave me the key. Or why the key was important to him. What would it mean to Amelia? Was it a link to assets he wanted his family to receive?

Those are not the only unanswered questions: what was Mr Cleveland doing in Port Saïd disguised as an Egyptian? Why was the key concealed in the scarab? Why was Lord Warton hiding the fact that the dead man was British?

Finally, and of greatest significance, how could Frederick Selous believe he'd spoken to Mr Cleveland if the man had died in my arms?

Is there an intrigue that involves the British and the religious radicals trying to drive them from Egypt? But Warton doesn't strike me as a spy. Not that I have met any, but I do have a reasonable notion that spies are clever and devious.

Warton is stuffy and arrogant, rudely so, and my impression is that his intelligence comes more from education than from any innate wit or cunning.

And his insufferable wife – that mean-spirited woman doesn't fit my romanticized notion of how a spy's wife would act.

It seems to me that Lord Warton is much more likely to have stumbled accidentally into a murderous situation at the bazaar than to be involved in any intrigue. But if so, why hide the fact that the murdered man was British?

Protecting the precarious British situation in Egypt would be the obvious motive. Having served in the diplomatic corps, Lord Warton would be sensitive to the fact that Egypt is a tinderbox ready to explode. His first instinct might have been to hide the fact that Mr Cleveland was British. It might serve as fuel for the radicals in their campaign to win converts.

I slip my dress back on because none of this makes any sense if Mr Cleveland is still alive. And there's a man down the corridor who says he is.

Frederick Selous answers the door only after I have knocked several times. The door is jerked open to reveal that he is a bit dishevelled and not in good temper. I suspect he had already dozed off.

'I need to talk to you.'

'Miss Bly, it is—'

I make a frontal assault again, stepping in as he makes hasty steps backwards. Being caught standing at a man's door at this late hour would be scandalous.

He stares at me as if I have entered with a snake in my hand. 'You are completely demented.'

'I am a newspaper reporter for the *New York World*. I smell a story.'

'For your information, I am also a newspaper reporter.'

It is my turn to gape. 'No!'

'Yes.'

'What paper? The London—'

'The Cape Town *Lion*.'

'The what?'

'A newspaper in South Africa.'

'Never heard of it.'

'Miss Bly, that statement exposes your ignorance of history, geography and sociology. Africa was populated with humans when dinosaurs still roamed New York.'

It is obvious that this is not a man I will win many arguments with.

'Mr Selous, I need to ask you a very simple question. What did Mr Cleveland look like?'

He takes a deep breath. It is easy to see that he is struggling with the temptation to remove me physically from his room. But I am confident that a British gentleman would no more manhandle a woman than an American would.

Hopefully.

'The man,' he says slowly, deliberately, 'was perhaps in his thirties. Medium build. Average height. Hair . . . brown, I believe. Eyes . . . I'm not sure, my inclination is to say brown.'

'Medium build, brown hair, brown eyes – that description would fit most of the men in the Western Hemisphere.'

He gives me a tight grin. Like a dog ready to bite. 'I am certain that is neither Mr Cleveland's fault nor mine. Now, madam, would you mind leaving my room so I can get back to bed?'

'Where were you when you spoke to him?'

'I was standing beside my luggage on the beach, waiting for a boat to take me to the ship. He told me his name was Cleveland and asked me to tell the captain he would be staying ashore in Port Saïd. A business matter, he said.'

'Ah . . .'

I can see he is restraining himself. 'What does 'ah' mean? You make it sound as if you have had a revelation from the gods on Olympus.'

'You had luggage with you, you were obviously boarding the ship for the first time. The man knew you wouldn't recognize him, while passengers who had come across with him from Italy would.'

'I was the only person on the beach.'

'Very convenient.'

'What does *that* mean?'

'Don't you see? You don't know that was John Cleveland, he was just a man who walked up to you and—'

'*Miss Bly*. I am not in the habit of being approached by *dead men* named John Cleveland and asked to carry a message. Now I suggest you take your hysterics out of my cabin before I am forced to have you removed by ship's officers.'

I can see that a harmonious relationship with the man who has identified himself as a fellow reporter is impossible.

I open the door to leave, but pause after stepping out to put a parting shot over his bow.

'I don't know how reporting is done in South Africa, but from your attitude I must assume your efforts are restricted to news of weddings, funerals and dog bites.'

After delivering that fine retort, I slam the stateroom door hard enough to wake the dead.

Whipping round, I'm doomed to meet the steward coming out of Mr Cleveland's stateroom again.

Seeing me leave a man's cabin at night, the rogue gives me a knowing grin.

I respond with a searing glare that wipes it off his face.

Frederick Selous in the heart of Africa

# 9

I return to my cabin but pace like a trapped animal, more questions buzzing around my head. Wouldn't Cleveland have come back to the ship to apprise the captain of his decision rather than leave matters to a stranger on the beach? And why leave orders for his luggage to be sent ashore with Lord Warton?

One conclusion I reach is that the key must be put in a safe place until I can figure out what to do with it. The best place I can think of is the secret compartment in my shoes.

The dear shoemaker who made my shoes for the trip suggested that I let him make the heels hollow, so I'd be able to put some gold coins in them. 'That way if your purse is stolen, you shall still have some money.'

The pieces of the scarab are evidence I can't hide, so I do the next best thing: toss them out of my porthole.

With that resolved, I should be able to sleep, but it isn't possible. Thoughts are knocking at my brain with the insistent rhythm of a woodpecker. Instead I throw on my ulster and begin my usual stern-to-bow pacing on the deck in the hopes of giving my overloaded mind some relief.

Raymond the steward is lowering luggage down the side of the ship in a net as I come out on deck. I'm sure the trunks are the ones I saw in Mr Cleveland's stateroom.

A shadow falls over me as a man comes up to the railing and stands beside me.

'I couldn't sleep, either,' says Mr Selous.

He appears a bit hesitant at having approached me. Perhaps he didn't realize it was me until it was too late to politely flee. Or is he implying that I'm the cause of his sleeplessness?

'Mr Cleveland's luggage going ashore.' I nod down at the meshed bundle being lowered.

'Quite,' he says, using that uniquely British response.

'I suppose Mr Cleveland is anxiously waiting on the beach for the boat to bring his luggage to shore,' I say facetiously, staring at the beach that is too far away and too dark to see anything on. 'Can you see him?'

Mr Selous makes a guttural sound that conveys he is sorry he attempted to be polite and now is *quite* finished with my intrigues. As he turns to leave, a shout comes from below.

A steamer trunk has slipped out from the meshed bundle, striking the side of the boat waiting for it. The trunk snaps open as it hits the boat and falls into the water, opening for a second before a boatman grabs it.

'It's empty,' I whisper.

'What?' Selous turns back and peers over the side. 'It's too dark to see—'

'I saw when it hit. It's empty.'

From his expression I think he's trying to give me the benefit of the doubt but is uncertain as to whether I deserve it. He starts to say something, then appears to shrug it off and pushes away from the railing.

'Good night, Miss Bly. We should both get some sleep and rise early, for tomorrow we pass through the greatest man-made waterway in the world.'

I stay at the railing for a moment, staring down at where the luggage is being unloaded onto the boat. The trunk was definitely empty; yet more questions are buzzing around my head.

When I turn to leave I make eye contact with Raymond.

I give him a frown that lets him know I am no fool, that I know there are shenanigans afoot, and get back an unexpected dark look.

*Learn not to signal your punches*, I tell myself, on my way down the dim stairwells and corridors that lead to my cabin.

A dark figure appears ahead of me at the far end of a corridor before disappearing into a stateroom – the mysterious woman in black who I've glimpsed on deck before during my walks. I've taken a fancy to the notion that she is none other than Sarah Winchester, heir to the Winchester Repeating Arms Company fortune.

Mrs Winchester fell into a deep depression after the untimely deaths of first her daughter and then her husband, and came to believe that she was haunted by the ghosts of the thousands of people killed by the famous Winchester rifles that helped win the Civil War and massacred most of the nation's Indians.

That she has only worn black since the death of her loved ones is one of the more mundane rumours about her strange behaviour; another is that she is using her vast fortune to build a house with an endless number of rooms because a spiritualist advised her that as long as she kept adding rooms to the house, the ghosts of the Winchester dead would not attack her.*

I first saw the woman come up the gangplank after I boarded at Brindisi. It wasn't her widow's black garments and net veil that were memorable, but the coffin being carried by porters behind her.

Both woman and coffin disappeared into a first-class state room and neither have been seen since – except for the fleeting glimpses of her that I've had at night.

The name she boarded under was 'Sarah Jones', and the widow Winchester is known to travel incognito in her own Pullman car with the shades down, and to use a false name when staying in hotels.

Her first name, widow's clothes and reclusive habit all indicate that she is indeed the Winchester woman, but it's the coffin that clinches it for me. While I've never actually heard of Mrs Winchester bringing a coffin along during her travels, such an oddity would fit the public image of the woman – and provide me with new evidence of her eccentricities for a story.

Is it the body of her young daughter in the coffin? Or her husband?

The thought of sleeping with the dead in a stateroom gives me gooseflesh . . . a goose walking over my grave, as my mother would say.

I make sure my door is securely locked before I put on my

---

* Mrs Winchester kept the house under continuous construction for the last 38 years of her life, from 1884 to 1922. Once seven storeys high, it was damaged in the great earthquake of 1906 and is now only four storeys, containing 100 rooms, forty-seven fireplaces and 10,000 panes of glass. The Editors.

nightgown. I'm about to undress when there is a knock on my door.

Certain it is Lord Warton coming to accuse me of searching Cleveland's room, I open the door and find Von Reich instead.

'I thought I should check on you and make sure you're well.'

I lean against the doorframe and rub my forehead. 'My head has split in two and I've lost one of the halves.'

'After what you've been through, it's amazing you have any head left. Tomorrow the Wartons and I are taking another day excursion—'

I shake my head no and even that hurts. 'I am going to stay aboard and rest.'

'I'm sorry to hear that. We are going to feast with a sheikh in the desert that will be like nothing you have ever imagined, then we are visiting the ruins of ancient Tanis, the city that once was the capital of Egypt. But since you—'

'I'm coming!'

He grins. 'We leave before the dawn. To avoid the sun. And trouble.' He starts to leave, then turns back to me. 'It's rather like the biblical Revelations, isn't it?'

'The feast?'

'No, no, the story of the Mahdi. The Muslim holy book says he'll return to Earth amidst a time of war and destruction, much like the Bible says the Four Horsemen of the Apocalpse will create.'

He looks at me for a long moment. 'I told you that you must expect the unexpected in Egypt. It's an ancient land, one still haunted by thousands of years of intrigues, wars, and hexes.'

'What's the surprise for tomorrow?' I ask.

He raises his eyebrows. 'A miracle, dear lady, you shall stand witness to a true miracle.'

Von Reich leaves and I carry his words to bed with me.

Holy war, apocalyptic horsemen of war and death, the intrigues of modern nations and ruins of an ancient one, all mysterious and exotic and not at all what I expected when I made the impulsive decision to race around the world.

Now I'm to witness a miracle.

I could use one at the moment. So could Mr Cleveland.

I feel guilty for having silently ridiculed him for acting so secretively. He obviously had his reasons, though whatever intrigue he was involved in, he didn't play it well – at least not well enough to keep from getting himself killed.

Von Reich's invitation sounds to me as innocent as a pickpocket with his hand in my purse. With the Mahdi on the warpath, I have to wonder if the miracle won't be that we get back to the ship with our heads still on our shoulders.

I would have foregone tomorrow's excursion, but it's just too convenient that we all ended up in the marketplace as murder was committed. I have to find out if it was a coincidence, or something else.

Exhausted from the day, I sit down to take off my shoes. Right after removing the first one, I stop. In the corner of my eye a movement catches my attention and I look up.

*Something* – a shadow, a figure – is at my porthole.

Gripping my shoe, I slowly get up to see what, if anything, is there. Just inches away from my porthole a man's face abruptly appears. Someone might as well have thrown a spider in my face. I drop my shoe and the face, draped by a grey, striped hood, disappears as quickly as it materialized.

Without any thought I run for my door, throwing off the

other shoe, and barrel out of the doorway, racing down the corridor to the companionway and out to the deck.

Breathless, my heart in my mouth, I make myself slow down so as not to draw attention to myself and cautiously walk down the deck toward my porthole.

Several male passengers are ambling about, enjoying their evening cigars and brandy, none in Egyptian hoods. I look in every direction, trying to figure out where the hooded man went.

My feet are wet from the deck's evening washing and even though it is not cold, I shiver. Lifting my chin and shoulders up, I'm determined to strengthen my resolve. I know there was a face at my porthole with the same hood as Mr Cleveland's when he was killed in the marketplace. Whoever is trying to frighten me can go to hell.

I march back down the deck to the companionway, meeting Frederick Selous returning to his cabin.

Staring down at my bare feet and lack of a night coat, he asks, 'Is something wrong, Miss Bly?'

'Does it look like something is wrong to you, Mr Selous?'

I leave him with that until I am past him. He pauses at his cabin door and appears to wish he could say something.

'Don't worry, Mr Selous, I don't frighten easily. In fact, when I get scared, I get mad.'

I strut into my cabin six feet tall and filled with strength.

Once the door is shut behind me I collapse against it and try to get my breathing back into a normal rhythm. Then I lock it and push the cabin chair under the handle.

*What the devil?* What madness is this? Someone's idea of a bad joke?

No, not a joke, but something much more cruel – an attempt

to frighten me, perhaps even send me running to the captain screaming that the ghost of John Cleveland has paid me a visit. If someone wanted to discredit me, that would certainly be grist for their mill.

I didn't get a good look at who was in the porthole, all I saw was a dark face half hidden by the hood of a cloak, but I have no doubt that it was meant to frighten me into believing it was Mr Cleveland.

I draw the curtain over the porthole before slipping into bed, still angry and tense from the invasion of my privacy. The face in the window has had a powerful effect – it has brought home the fact that the murderous rage that spilled blood in the marketplace has followed me back to the ship.

The small cabin suddenly makes me feel confined, with an eerie sense of being cornered. I'm no longer certain I'm safe aboard this ship. I feel exposed – even trapped – rather than safe and cosy, because I don't know who I can trust and there's no place to run and hide.

The key in the scarab cost John Cleveland his life. Now it is a magnet bringing danger and intrigue to me on a ship I should feel safe aboard.

And I lied to Frederick Selous.

I do get scared.

New York World *November 14, 1889*
*the day Nellie left on her trip*

*Nellie racing around the world*

*Travel clothes and veils of Victorian women*

# PART TWO

## DAY 14

*Port Saïd*
The Miracle

*Lighthouse and entrance to Suez Canal as Nellie saw it*

# IO

Riding in a carriage through Port Saïd, in an early dawn darkened by angry clouds, I no longer see the land of the eternal Nile as an enchanted place. Instead, I feel as if I have been transported back to the malevolent Egypt of the Old Testament, where mighty pharaohs who called themselves living gods ruled with the whip, and the God of the Israelites turned the Nile red with His wrath. Only this time, the blood that stains the waters might be my own.

I try to shake off my feelings of gloom, and anxiety about whether an angry mob might drag me from the carriage, but the murder of John Cleveland and the deadly rage of the Mahdi has cast a long shadow in my mind, feeding doubts, confusion and fears that I can't share with my companions or anyone else on board.

I regret accepting Von Reich's invitation but struggle to grin and bear it – with clenched teeth – as I sit in a carriage fit for a king en route to a feast given by a Bedouin sheikh near the ruins of a great city of antiquity.

Von Reich is pleased with our transportation. 'The sheikh sent his own carriage for us. It would not have embarrassed a pharaoh.'

The gilt carriage has ornate carvings of snakes curling up around the poles, the black tongues of the reptiles hissing towards the sky as if they are challenging the gods; fish in vibrant shades of green, yellow and turquoise that appear ready to leap off the poles mingle with the snakes; and sitting on top of each pole are white doves of peace, each holding a bright lime-green leaf in its beak.

A silk canopy made of the most soothing sea-blue turquoise protects us from the sun. Plump aquamarine, azure and violet pillows with gold tassels are laid out on the seats.

Two fierce-looking Bedouins on camels armed with rifles and swords ride as our escort. So much for the white doves of peace.

From their conversation earlier on the beach road as we waited for our conveyance, it's obvious my companions are pretending nothing happened yesterday in the marketplace. Rather than the shocking events and the possibility that we will be attacked by another mob, they chat about the lack of good service and food aboard the ship, the poverty of Egypt, the unusual scenery . . . anything except that the blood of men was spilled on the dirt of the marketplace before our eyes.

The pretence leaves me tense and unsettled, full of questions and a sense of distrust, especially of Lord Warton. I have no doubt he's the instigator of the game. He throws me solemn looks intended to communicate to the others that I am a hysterical female who has been so traumatized by yesterday's deaths that raising the subject would cause an imbalance in my delicate feminine constitution.

I've handled crooked politicians, convicted murderers, burly street toughs and tough editors who would make mincemeat out of this pompous British lord. I have worked undercover as a mad woman in an asylum, walked mean streets posing as a prostitute to investigate how their male customers treated them, taken employment as a maid to expose the abuse of servants, even danced in a chorus line and received shooting lessons from Annie Oakley . . . all without upsetting my 'delicate constitution'.

I feel like asking the haughty gentleman exactly what his achievements are, besides trying to show Moroccans how to grow wheat, a task I'm sure his employees would be far more qualified to perform. Or reminding him that yesterday he froze in fear and confusion as a man with a dagger came at us.

Our carriage is rumbling over Port Saïd potholes when Lord Warton suddenly catches me by surprise by mentioning yesterday's incident after all.

'What did the man in the marketplace give you yesterday?'

'Excuse me?'

'Someone told the police he passed something to you.'

'What is he supposed to have passed me?'

'That is the question, young lady – what did he give you?'

'If someone believes they saw me being passed something, let them ask me directly. I don't intend to answer an anonymous accusation.'

Lady Warton pats her husband's arm as his cheeks colour from what he no doubt considers my impertinence. 'Let us talk about more pleasant things, dear.'

I avoided an outright denial just in case someone actually did see the man slip the scarab into my pocket. I'd like nothing better than to take the key out of my heel and have a spirited discussion about it, but my instinct is that if I give it to Lord Warton, it would find its way to the bottomless pit of British bureaucracy.

Learning the truth about Mr Cleveland's death and carrying

his last word to his loved one are responsibilities I have accepted
. . . and Lord Warton made a mistake when he set out to make
me look ridiculous.

What other malice he holds in my regard is still to be determined. At the very least, he has appointed himself manager
of whatever involvement his country has in the marketplace
incident, a role with which I sympathize since I would take it
on myself if I thought Mr Cleveland was American. But two
issues niggle at me. The truth needs to be exposed to ensure
that no skullduggery took place and, most importantly, a man
was murdered before my eyes – a man who selected me as
the instrument of his last wish, to carry an object to his beloved.

Despite my feelings, however, I am an invited guest and it
would be rude of me to say anything, especially since the
Wartons have a business relationship with Von Reich, who is
doing his best to make me feel welcome. But I will not let the
matter rest.

Von Reich points to the two-hundred-foot-tall, brick-walled
lighthouse near where the canal meets the Mediterranean.

'The Statue of Liberty, that colossal statue the French put
up in New York three years ago, was originally meant to be
placed here to commemorate the Suez Canal. The original
design was that of a fellah, an Egyptian peasant, with beams
of light emitting from a headband and a torch he held.'

'How did it end up in New York?' I ask.

'Money. The Khedive of Egypt ran out of it and the *Light
of Asia* peasant turned into the goddess Liberty and became
*Liberty Enlightening the World* in New York harbour.'

I make a mental note of this story to include it in a cable
back to my editor. Everyone knows that the statue was a gift
from the people of France, and that Monsieur Eiffel built the

frame in the same fashion as he did his much-criticized tower in Paris, but the fact that the concept made its way from Egypt will be of interest.

As we leave the city, Lady Warton turns the conversation to me. The woman seems slightly bemused – or amused, I'm not sure which – both by my job, and by my current undertaking

'My dear,' begins Lady Warton, 'you must tell me so I can advise the ladies I play bridge with . . . why would any young woman work in a man's profession and race around the world to beat a man's record?'

I smile politely. 'It's a challenge, and I believe I am as capable as any man.' Personally I would like to ask her if she ever goes outside without asking her husband about the weather.

Lord Warton's face again contorts with displeasure as if my very existence sours his stomach. 'We can all hope that women will stay in their place and not attempt to imitate men.'

'Now, now, dear.' His wife pats his arm again. 'We must not pick on our guest. She's still young, but someday she will learn what really matters in life.'

I return a very forced polite smile and resist the urge to be catty. What keeps me from lashing out, besides politeness, is that I know these pompous snobs have had so much given to them – and have accomplished little themselves. Unlike Lady Bluenose, I have had to work for my daily bread, and it has never struck me as God's will that I should labour as hard as a man for less money or opportunity.

Coming to the top of a ridge, the desert unfolds before us as a purple-grey carpet in the dull light. The road is a stony dirt track hard enough to support the carriage wheels. Far beyond, like a desert mirage, is a vast expanse of water.

'Lake Manzala,' says Von Reich. 'The eastern delta of the Nile. Tanis and our rendezvous with the sheikh are on the other side, at a tributary of the Nile.'

'It looks as big as a sea,' I say.

'It's quite large. The Suez Canal actually runs through the eastern edge of it.'

A caravan of camels moves across the sands, their long, slender necks swaying in unison with their rocking gait. I brighten a little, reminding myself I am away from murderous mobs and faces in my porthole.

Von Reich purchases dates from a cameleer whose animals are laden with them. It's my first taste of the oval-shaped fruit and I find them sweet and sticky.

A shadow passes over the dunes as a falcon glides gracefully above us, his blue-grey feathers glistening in the sunlight. He slants his body to the left and dives. Just before he appears certain to crash into the ground, his claws come out and grab something from the ground. When he soars back up into the sky a rodent is struggling in his grip. I'm in awe that the raptor could spot such a small thing in this vast ocean of sand, yet at the same time I feel pity for the little critter.

I notice that the two Bedouins riding as our escort to the rear also saw the falcon and smiled when it captured its prey.

'My brothers and I against my cousins . . . my brothers, cousins and I against the world,' Von Reich is saying.

His comment catches me by surprise. 'Excuse me?'

'The Bedouins have a view of the world that is narrowly restricted to their own families, which is the meaning of the phrase. It's the code they live by and they mention it often.

It's said that a Bedouin owns only three things – his clothes, his animals and his women.'

'What do the women own?' My question pops out before I can control my tongue.

'A lifetime of misery.'

Lady Warton gives our escorts a frown. 'Bathing water is definitely not on their list of possessions. They smell worse than their camels.'

We board a small steam launch that puffs and chugs across the lake. I would prefer a sailing boat, but Von Reich says the steam launch is faster and we don't have the time to spare.

With my practical travelling cap attached securely to my head, I try to keep from laughing as Lady Warton struggles to keep her dainty canary-feather hat attached to her head as winds skipping across the water pummel us. I'm envious of the lightweight pith helmets the men wear, smartly secured with a chin strap. Made of a cork-like material, they provide shade and contain holes for heat to escape. With these and their white linen suits, the two men look very much like colonials coming to do their duty as masters. Lady Warton also wears white, an unfortunate colour for all of them since the damp wood seats leave brown patches in an unmentionable place

Our boat passes a long narrow craft loaded with bales of cotton; the men aboard chant as they row with long oars, a rhythmic song of labour carried across to us on the breeze.

It is easy to imagine Cleopatra and her court attendants instead of cotton bales, and a slave master cracking a whip over the heads of the rowers.

'What are you smiling about?' asks Von Reich.

I just shrug my shoulders because I can't explain. The gentleman from the city of Mozart and Strauss, the Viennese Waltz and the glittering court of the Habsburg emperors, would not understand how marvellous this land is to a young woman who once thought she would spend her entire life underpaid and worked to the bone in a factory in a small American industrial town.

# 11

The ruins of Tanis appear as our steam launch brings us to a dock in the late afternoon. I am far more interested in seeing the ancient city than sitting down to dine with a sheikh. The thought of coming nearly six thousand miles without catching a glimpse of the remnants of Egypt's golden civilization is quite alarming.

A servant is waiting to escort us to the sheikh's tent. 'It is a short walk,' he informs us.

'Tanis was built a thousand years before the birth of Christ,' says Von Reich resuming his usual role of pedantic showman, 'around the time God sent the plagues and parted the sea for Moses. The great civilizations of Greece and China had yet to arise when the monuments that you're about to see were built – monuments that have excited and puzzled people for three thousand years.'

He must have noticed my eyes light up at the thought, because he leans closer to me and speaks in a confidential tone so as not to be heard by the others. 'Do you know what I like most about you, Nellie? How little things excite you so much and make you smile so brightly.'

Little things?

'You've missed your calling, Von Reich,' Lord Warton calls out. 'You should have been a tour guide. Tell us about Tanis.'

'Tanis was the capital of Egypt several thousand years ago. The city was an important port until it was finally abandoned because the lake's waters began to rise Its most important complexes are the Temple of Amun, the king of gods, who is usually represented as man with a ram's head, and that of Horus, a god of the sky and war.

'The city has been ravaged by time and tomb robbers, and much of the area has gone back to desert, but be aware – the spirits of gods and kings still walk among the vestiges of its magnificent past.'

Scattered about us, as though we were in the stone garden of a giant, are granite statues and monuments, some colossal in size, many lying prone.

I'm already writing in my head the story that I will send with my cable back to New York.

'Some very fine artefacts were found here by an English Egyptologist who spent several years working on the site,' adds Von Reich. 'There are probably many more, but excavation is time-consuming and expensive, so it comes in bursts.'*

'He must be devastated,' I say.

'Who's devastated?' asks Lady Warton.

'Him.' I gesture at a fallen statue of what appears to be a pharaoh. Standing upright it would be several times my height.

'He has had to just lie there and watch over the ages as thieves carry away the treasures of his city.'

She gives me a look that expresses at the same time both doubts about my sanity and contempt for my thinking process.

* In 1935, a French archaeologist unsealed a Tanis tomb and discovered treasures that rivalled those of King Tut. On a lighter note, Tanis is the city where the Ark of the Covenant was found in the first Indiana Jones movie. The Editors.

I suppose in her world of tea parties and formal balls, stone kings don't have feelings. But as I stand here, humbled in his presence, and look at his finely chiselled features – large eyes, a bold, almost Roman nose, a full mouth, all worn by time – I still sense his power and majesty and can't help but believe he's watching us.

As I am admiring the beauty and timeless workmanship of all these fallen edifices, I hear Lady Warton announce, 'It appears to me that this place needs masonry work and a good coat of paint.'

I'm choking back a retort that I know I would regret when I hear Von Reich shout, 'Come here!'

As Von Reich lectures the others on something he has found, I quietly slip away. I much prefer to walk among the ruins. Maybe I'll stumble on some artefact other explorers have overlooked.

Behind the crumbled ruins of the pillars, I find a stately granite sphinx. Close by is a statue of another pharaoh and more stone structures.

Something I've read comes to mind. 'The longer man lives upon the earth, the more the ground grows ancient beneath his feet.'

Standing on ground where history has been made, I picture men toiling in the scorching heat as whips rain down on their naked backs because they are not working fast enough. Perhaps thousands of people died to build Tanis and centuries later many of the monuments are still here – more a testimony to the common people who built them than to the pharaohs.

The huge statue of the long-dead pharaoh intimidates me. The way his penetrating eyes bear down puts the fear of the unknown in me, and I'm not one drawn to the occult. Without a doubt, they made him this size so people would tremble before him.

His most menacing feature is the king cobra placed on the front of his crown, its neck fanned into that distinctive hood, indicating that it is ready to strike a deadly blow whenever it desires.

'What do you think about your tombs being looted and your monuments broken and scattered like stone weeds?' I ask the pharaoh.

'*I am eternal.*'

I nearly jump out of my shoes.

A man wearing a long black robe that cloaks him from the top of his head down to his sandals is standing in the shadow of the colossal monarch. A narrow gap in the hood exposes little of his features.

'That is how he would answer your question.'

I glance back to make sure my companions are still within shouting distance.

'He is eternal, like the Nile.' The man steps forward and I can see he is elderly, with wrinkled features and wisdom's white beard. 'He and the river will still be here when those who sacked his tombs and cities are dust scattered by the wind.'

'Do you work here?' I ask.

'I am the caretaker of all this.' He waves at the ruins around us. 'A city of vanished glories, containing only what the thieves of history have left behind.'

He appears educated; not a fellah farmer or labourer.

'Are you an Egyptologist?' I ask.

He gives me an appraising look. 'Nothing so grand. When the Englishman Flinders Petrie was working on this site, I had the privilege of overseeing the workers. What little knowledge I have comes not from books, but from working with others, mostly foreigners.' He studies me for a moment. 'You are not British.'

'I'm American.'

'An American . . .' He seems taken aback by my nationality and ruminates for a moment before finally adding, 'Egypt sees many foreigners; British, French, German, Italian, but few Americans. You are the first I have met.'

'Who is this gentleman?' I gesture at the giant statue of the pharaoh.

'Ramses the Great. Unearthed by the men who worked with the English archaeologist.'

'Ah, Ramses. The pharaoh who caused Egypt to suffer ten plagues when he refused to let Moses and the Jews leave.'

I didn't add that about everything I knew about Egyptian pharaohs was either learned in Sunday school or came from Von Reich. I nod at the sphinx. 'What a magnificent creature.'

The sphinx is six feet high and about twice as long; its body is taut, its claws extended, giving the impression of being ready to leap. I walk around it as I speak to the man. 'I think I saw his brother in the Louvre museum in Paris.'

'Yes, one of the sphinxes from Tanis is held prisoner in the French museum.'

'Held prisoner'? That's an interesting way to put it, but I suppose if another country were to remove the Liberty Bell from Philadelphia I would view the act in much the same manner.

'He must also cringe at how the city has crumbled,' I say. 'I've heard the winds that sweep off the desert can be brutal.'

'It's the sea breezes that have blown invading armies to Egypt's shores that have ravaged the remnants of our past. The great powers of Europe have plundered the treasures of Egypt since Roman times,' his hoarse whisper tells me. 'There are more obelisks, sphinxes and treasures of the pharaohs in London, Paris and Rome than in Cairo or Alexandria. Some of them are there because of the greed of my own people. Even our kings filled their coffers with monies they obtained selling our treasures to foreigners.'

He gestures at the great stone edifices around us. 'Left alone, these ancient monuments would have defied even the scorching desert winds that can flay the flesh from a camel, but the hands of man are too ruthlessly covetous to leave the treasures untouched.'

I change the subject to something less thorny. 'Have you heard of the Riddle of the Sphinx? Which creature goes on four legs in the morning, on two during the day, and in the evening upon three?'

The caretaker smiles and nods. 'I know the puzzle from Flinders Petrie. People crawl on all fours as babies, later they walk on two legs, and finally in old age they need a cane and that gives them a third leg.' He narrows his eyes. 'But you must not think that the power of the sphinx is a tale for children. To us who know her well, the Great Sphinx at Giza is the Mother of Terror.'

'Yes, I heard that shouted in Port Saïd. People believe that the sphinx will drive foreigners from Egypt.'

'It is said that the Nile will turn red from blood once again, just as it did when Allah punished the pharaoh. Only this time it will be the blood of foreigners that colours the river.'

I turn away from the chilling prophecy as I hear my name

shouted. My companions are coming up the hill and I wave at them.

'Over here,' I yell, when I realize the statues and stone wall are blocking their view of us.

As they reach me, I say, 'This gentleman—'

He's gone. I hurry around the sphinx and the pharaoh.

'What in heaven's name are you doing?' Lord Warton demands.

'He was here a moment ago.'

'Who was here?' asks Von Reich.

I throw up my hands in frustration. 'We were talking about the Great Sphinx killing foreigners—'

'The sphinx was talking to you?' exclaims Lady Warton.

'No, of course not. I was talking to a man about it. He's disappeared.'

Lady Warton offers me her parasol. 'You'd better keep your head shaded, my dear. The heat is making you delirious.'

# 12

I've been in circus tents smaller than the sheikh's pavilion.

The sprawling tent is held up by a forest of poles, with the sides rolled up to let air circulate. Off to the right is an oasis, with trees and date palms surrounding a pond.

A sea of sand, then in the middle of nowhere, a small lake surrounded by grass and trees . . . one of God's miracles, my mother would say.

'Is the sheikh the head of a Bedouin tribe?' I ask.

This provokes a chuckle from Von Reich and a snort from Lord Warton.

'He's actually a prince and a pasha,' replies Von Reich, 'because he's the brother of Tewfik Pasha, the Egyptian king they call a Khedive. He has palaces in Cairo and Alexandria, but he puts up a tent in the desert once a year to impress people with his Bedouin roots.'

'There is no Bedouin blood in the line,' Lord Warton says with contempt. 'The ruling family dates back to a Turkish officer of Albanian descent who won a bloody power struggle after Napoleon's army left. They have as much Bedouin ancestry as my bird dog.'

Drinking at the oasis are Arabian stallions, horses of the desert noted for their intelligence, speed and grace, and the wonderfully awkward and charmingly ugly camels: the animal world's version of Beauty and the Beast.

'Arabian horses and camels are considered among the finest gifts of Allah,' Von Reich tells us, as though reading my thoughts. 'The horse for its beauty and the camel for its strong back.'

Over our heads as we enter the pavilion are hanging baskets of flowering plants, hundreds of them, adding a sweet scent along with moisture that is a relief from the parched desert air. The entire interior is carpeted with thick Persian and Turkish rugs. Golden candelabras as tall as a person are everywhere.

'What in God's name is this?' Lady Warton asks, staring at the round, knee-high tables surrounded by saddles and cushions that are scattered throughout the tent.

'When a Bedouin comes to dinner, he sits on a rug and brings in his camel's saddle to rest against,' Lord Warton replies. 'We used them in Morocco, too, though not at the dinners you attended.'

'We're expected to sit on the floor to eat? How uncivilized,' she grumbles.

I stare around, fascinated by the sheer opulence of it all. I can't even imagine what this 'Bedouin' tent must have cost. Or how many fellahs broke their backs in the cotton fields that produce the country's cash crop to provide it.

The marble-white porcelain plates lining the tables are exquisite. In the centre of each one is a dark blue image of a warrior pharaoh in a golden chariot drawn by one horse. His arm is raised high, ready to hurl a spear at a charging tiger.

'Bone china,' says Von Reich, noticing the direction of my

gaze. 'It's made with ash from calcified ox bone. That's what gives it that brilliant but brittle look.'

'Where are the utensils?' I ask.

'You eat with your fingers and *only with your right hand*.' Von Reich says. 'The left is for personal use and considered unclean.'

'Obviously they don't have civilized facilities for relieving oneself,' Lady Warton sniffs.

'Dinner is served with gold and silver utensils in his palace, but using one's fingers is for his desert warrior image.' Von Reich leans closer to us and adds in a low voice, 'Oh, and when you sit, don't point your feet directly towards someone else. The Egyptians consider it bad luck.'

'Thank you. Anything else I should know?' I ask.

'Let the men do the talking.' He grins and gives me a wink. 'Women are considered decoration.'

With that said the two 'gentlemen' leave us to mingle, abandoning me to her ladyship, whose scowl appears painted permanently on her face.

'I need to quench my thirst,' she announces, heading for a bare-chested man dressed only in big, billowing yellow pantaloons and a red turban. He's holding a large silver platter filled with glasses of pomegranate juice.

Von Reich told us earlier that the foreign men attending the banquet will be mostly European businessmen and some military officers. The few other European women present are no doubt the wives of these men, since a single woman would not have been invited – nor indeed would any Islamic women.

The women remind me of those I have encountered at the high-society tea parties I used to cover for the *Pittsburg Dispatch* – overdressed and overpowered. Like Lady Warton, they are wearing flowery silk or lace dresses fastened in the back with tiny buttons smaller than the tip of my pinkie, which require assistance from maids.

Making no claims to be a great beauty, I dress for comfort, preferring clothing that is simple, with little lace, frills, or those prickly petticoats intended to make dresses full, or as one dressmaker told me, 'lady like'.

Von Reich and Lord Warton have changed from their travelling clothes. A few of the European men are in black or dark grey morning dress, the daytime version of white tie with its cutaway coats, striped pants, and silk top hats, but most wear the same type of white linen suit worn by Von Reich and the British peer.

The military officers are all dressed largely the same, from pith helmets to boots with highly starched uniforms inbetween.

While a few of the Egyptians and Turks present wear Western suits and fez hats, the only men who appear comfortable in the warmth of the afternoon are the ones in traditional Arab desert clothing, which permits air to circulate – flowing white tunics with sleeveless cloaks of blue, green and yellow, made of cotton, linen or silk, that fall to just below their shins, while loose tassel belts of braided gold silk adorn their waists. Even their rope sandals look cooler than most footwear.

A weapon is one item all the males agree upon – the British with their Webley revolvers and the French with their officer's version of the Chamelot-Delvigne. The Arabs have hanging from their belts scimitars or daggers decorated with all sorts of precious gems; weapons that lack the range of a pistol, but are no doubt just as effective if one has been raised cutting their teeth on such blades.

I would not have been surprised to find women carrying derringers in their satchels, especially the French women, who tend to be worldlier than most others of their sex since their country is at the crossroads of everything international.

It's rather amusing to watch the British and French men sipping the rich, Turkish coffee out of dainty little demitasse cups – they look so out of place, their pinkies sticking straight up in the air. I'm sure they'd rather be drinking brandy, but the Egyptians are teetotallers – at least in public.

A low rumble begins that gradually intensifies into a loud, deep boom, as a large gong is struck and bronze trumpets blare, announcing the arrival of a group of men on camels.

It's obvious that the man at the front is our host – he's riding the only pure white camel. His Bedouin robes are silk, not cotton or linen, and are trimmed with precious stones – glittering rubies, sapphires and diamonds. But the real confirmation comes when a servant goes down on all fours beside the sheikh's kneeling camel so the sheikh can step on him as he dismounts the animal. I wince as he steps onto this human footstool – the sheikh is not a small man; he must be close to two hundred pounds.

He walks on a red carpet that has been rolled out from a table heavily guarded by Saracens with long swords, and pistols tucked in their waistbands.

'I'm afraid you ladies must fend for yourselves for a while,' Von Reich announces. 'His lordship and I have been invited to join the sheikh at his table.' There's a little pride and male superiority in his tone.

As they head for his table I notice with astonishment who is taking a seat next to the sheikh – Frederick Selous.

Before I have recovered from that surprise, another man

emerges from a dark area behind the sheikh and joins them at the table – the marketplace magician, the one Von Reich called a *psylli*.

I start to tell Lady Warton that I shall run screaming from the tent if John Cleveland materializes, but she has slipped away, presumably to get another drink. When she returns, I ask if Von Reich and her husband are friends of the sheikh.

'Von Reich met him in Cairo. My husband has never met the man, but they have a common interest – horseracing. My husband breeds racehorses, and the sheikh requested he join him to discuss their animals.'

'I love horses – I used to have one of my own. I used to compete at county fairs in the States. I even won a few ribbons.'

'How nice.' She makes it sound as if I won a consolation prize at a penny arcade.

Keeping a polite smile fixed to my face, I groan inwardly, telling myself that I have to stop trying to hold a civil conversation with this disdainful woman and simply make non-committal responses to whatever she says.

The sheikh sits down at his table and claps his hands . . . we are now allowed to sit.

The soulful wailing of a woodwind instrument fills the tent as barefooted, veiled women enter. They're dressed in lush purple silk garb that clings to their bodies, emphasizing their graceful contours. Yellow scarves, fringed with coins, are tied around their hips.

Every feature of these women is exquisite – they all have long, silky black hair, golden skin, ample breasts and curvaceous hips, all perfectly proportioned. Swaying to the hypnotic music, they extend their arms outwards, beckoning us to join them. The top part of their costume slips ever so slightly off their shoulders as their hips sway in a circular, hypnotic motion to the rhythm of the music.

Tiny cymbals held between their fingers make a light tinging noise, as they perform incredible feats of flexibility with their belly muscles. As they gradually bend backwards until their tresses sweep the carpet, shouts from the men grow deafening. I too find myself captivated by the way the women's hips sway with such charged precision, back and forth. The yelling stops and I start breathing again. What an erotic performance.

'Raqs Sharqi,' whispers Lady Warton, 'the dance of the Orient. It claims to be the oldest dance in the world.'

'Amazing,' is all I can say.

The gong shatters the silence and brings us out of our trance as the women leave as gracefully as they came.

Male servants enter the pavilion carrying silver platters laden with vegetables, wooden bowls filled with couscous, and crystal bowls overflowing with shredded coconut, honey, dates, figs, olives, grapes and pomegranates.

It's all so lavish, but it's also wasteful because it's impossible for us to eat all this food. I'm sure that in Port Saïd there are families who would survive a month on just a few platters of the food served here.

Two men carry in a dish bearing a whole lamb and place it in front of the sheikh. He plucks the eyes out of the lamb and pops them in his mouth.

I force myself not to react. He *really* looks like he's enjoying them. But as my grandmother always said, 'To each his own, said the old lady when she kissed the cow.' I'm just glad I'm not eating them.

The Sheikh proceeds to cut off a leg, then takes a stuffing

of dates and figs from inside the belly with his right hand. When he's done, the lamb is passed to another table where a man cuts out the tongue.

I'm quickly losing my appetite, but my real focus is not on the food. I'm keeping a surreptitious eye on the men at our host's table.

I can't tell what they are talking about, but I wouldn't be surprised if it is about me, the key and John Cleveland. And maybe the *psylli* is telling them he could put a cobra in my bed.

'Have you eaten something that disagrees with you?' asks Lady Warton. 'You have the oddest look on your face.'

'No, I'm fine. I was just thinking about what a small world it is.'

She raises her eyebrows. 'In what way?'

'Oh, all these people from so many places, all assembled here. Look – even the snake magician from the marketplace is here.' Unable to resist the temptation, I add, 'I wouldn't be surprised if Mr Cleveland paid us a visit.'

She gives me a shy smile. 'Let's hope he does, so you will be able to dismiss those silly notions about him being dead.'

The dishes are cleared away and once again the gong booms. Dozens of men in djellabahs appear outside the tent.

The men lie down on the sand, arranging themselves in a row like sardines in a can each one pressed so close to the next there is not the slightest space between them. It looks as if they're forming a floor. A man casually walks down the line of bodies.

Lord Warton and Von Reich join us after the sheikh leaves his table, leaving Mr Selous and the magician huddled together in what appears to be a deep conversation.

'Why is that man walking over them?' I ask Von Reich.

'To make sure that the human plank will hold.'

'Hold what?'

'They're preparing for a ceremony called *doseh*, which means treading.'

'Treading?' I ask.

'Yes, but it's best not to tell you what's going to happen. After it's over, if you like, I'll explain why it's done.'

Trumpets ringout and the sheikh appears astride a white Arabian stallion led by two grooms. Its thick mane flows down its side, its tail high in the air.

The sheikh makes a clicking noise with his tongue and the grooms let go of the stallion.

The horse advances with long, exaggerated steps, stepping up onto the human plank. With the sheikh aboard, it must weigh close to fourteen hundred pounds.

*And it's walking on the men!*

# 13

'The treading,' Von Reich tells us, enjoying his customary role as scholar, 'is a ritual done in memory of a miracle performed by a Muslim saint. The saint rode his horse into Cairo over earthenware jars without breaking them. It's believed that the sheikh who re-enacts this ceremony cannot hurt the prostrate men, just as the saint didn't break the jars. If any of the men die, it's due to their sins.'

'That's horrible.' I see it as an act of arrogant oppression by the mighty against the helpless. I gaped at the brutal spectacle, unable to move an inch, as the horse's powerful hooves came down like sledgehammers on one man then the next. 'Why doesn't the sheikh just use jars, as the saint did?'

'And take the risk of cutting the hooves of his prize stallion? His horses are much more valuable,' Lord Warton replies.

Everyone – except me – has a good chuckle over the sheikh prizing his horses over his subjects, egging the peer on. 'All Arabs, from princes to desert nomads, love, admire and cherish their horses—'

'Sometimes more than their wives,' Lady Warton interjects.

'Well, my dear,' Lord Warton grins at the other men, 'wouldn't you agree that if one has several wives, as many of these Arabs do,' – he pronounces it A-rabs – 'sometimes they'll find sweeter dispositions in the stables than in the main house?'

The men enjoy another chuckle.

'The Prophet Mohamed said every man shall love his horse,' Von Reich adds. 'Bedouins will go without food before they let their horses starve.'

'But what about the men who have to endure the sheikh's horse?' I ask in vain, knowing these people have no compassion for the underdog.

'The peasants consider it a privilege to be trod upon,' replies Lord Warton.

'Really? I wonder how any of us would feel if we had to lie on the ground back home and let royalty walk their horses across our backs.'

Von Reich gives me a small grin, but I get stony silence from the others. When they start comparing Arabian horses to quarter horses, I wander off, heading for the back of the tent in the direction I saw Mr Selous and the *psylli* exit.

They seem to me strange bedfellows: the magician who was performing where a man was killed, and the Briton who talked to the dead man. The two are huddled together, walking slowly, talking too quietly for me to hear. It is very discourteous of them, not allowing me to eavesdrop.

They disappear into the ruins and rather than running to find them and making a perfect fool of myself by getting caught, I veer off to look at the monuments by the light of the flaming torches set up to permit guests to enjoy the antiquities.

It's a bit eerie seeing these ancient stones under the ghostly glow of the full moon and the flickering torchlight, but a few other people are wandering about, too.

I round a pillar and find myself abruptly face to the face with the magician. He is not blocking my way, but not moving either, just staring at me with the blackest eyes I've ever seen. I glance quickly about, but his British companion is not in sight.

Forcing a smile and a 'Good evening', I start to walk around him when I spot a scarab hanging from a gold chain around his neck. Not a brother to the one that was slipped into my pocket, the magician's amulet is a blood-ruby, almost heart-shaped and encrusted with precious stones.

*Worth a fortune*, I think, as I raise my eyes to meet his. Not at all what one would expect a marketplace magician to be wearing. Neither are his clothes, which are not the simple cotton he wore yesterday, but black silk trimmed with pearls.

'Do you know the magic of the Heart Scarab?' he asks in heavily accented English.

'No, but I would certainly like to hear it.'

'A bearer of the Heart Scarab is assured of rebirth after death.'

'I see . . . and how is that?'

'When people die, the gods weigh their hearts. Hearts that are full of sin are heavy, and are eaten by the destroyer of hearts. But if the dead person's heart is replaced with a scarab before it is weighed, the sins are not discovered and the person is reborn.'

'Is that how Mr Cleveland managed to get from the market-place to the beach where he spoke to Mr Selous? And stare at me through a porthole? His heart was replaced with a scarab?'

He gives me a look that would fell a two-ton Tanis sphinx.

'You are on sacred ground where gods still walk. Their wrath falls upon those who mock them.'

His staff comes out from beneath his robe and I flinch, but

the rod taps the ground with a thud as he sweeps by me, leaving me cold despite the hot night.

I shake off my unease and keep an eye out behind me for snakes as I head deeper into the site. What a creepy character.

That he wasn't surprised when I mentioned a dead man talking to Frederick Selous didn't astonish me; he probably got an earful of that subject at the sheikh's dinner table. But he could at least have raised a curious eyebrow about a port-hole peeping Tom.

More regrets about having come on this excursion begin to stack up in my head but I shake those off, too, determined not to let an Egyptian bogeyman keep me from my chance to soak up some more of the land of pharaohs. I'm happy to visit the ruins without Von Reich's pedantic chatter and Lady Warton's caustic view of everything, including me.

Night is falling, the sky taking on an ashen glow as an early full moon rises behind a blanket of dark clouds. Tanis is a ghost city, its greatest monuments shattered, the souls of its ancient dead scattered by the desert wind, but the faint moon-light takes just enough edge off the darkness for a little imagination to bring its past glories alive. It's not hard for me to imagine a pharaoh on a golden chariot, his soldiers using their spears to push back a crowd staring with awe at the living god.

My feet bear me far enough from the tent for the music and party sounds to fade, taking me past the Great Temple of Amun and beyond to where a short fence has been put up at an excavation site near the Temple of Horus.

A large cavity has been opened and fenced off with stalks of river reeds, but the desert sand that coats everything makes it appear as though the whole project was abandoned years ago. The opening reveals a crudely excavated stone stairway, steep and broken with missing steps patched by wood supports. The broken stairwell disappears into a pool of darkness that the moonlight doesn't penetrate.

The crudeness of the opening makes me wonder if it wasn't made by thieves rather than professional archaeologists, and what priceless treasures the tomb held before raiders vandalized it.

A smaller fence is about thirty paces away, next to the end of a tall wall where a torch is mounted. I wander over to see what it's guarding and find another cavity, a hole about six feet wide. Like the fence at the stairwell, this one is also flimsy, not meant to hold a person back but just to mark the opening.

I edge closer, bracing myself with my left hand against the granite wall, careful not to put any weight against the fencing which appears ready to blow away with a strong wind. The flickering light from the torch at the end of the wall is at my back and casts little light into the hole but there's enough moonlight for me to see a mound of rubble ten or twelve feet down. From the debris and irregular shape of the hole, I assume that I'm standing on the roof of a tomb or whatever the chamber below is, and that the opening was created by accident, perhaps from a cave-in when the area was excavated by workers inside the cavern who entered through the stairway

The chamber is lost in a dark void but it doesn't take much for my mind's eye to envision markings on the walls – perhaps the tale of a war won by a pharaoh, a royal marriage or a king getting sage advice from a god.

I'm leaning over the opening, trying to see more, when the torchlight behind me is cast into shadow and I hear the crunch of a footstep.

'Is someone—?'

A black blur comes at me and impacts with the side of my head, the blow slamming me against the wall. My legs collapse and I fall to my knees, head spinning, putting my hands out in front to keep from going down on my face. Something drops next to me – a rock – and I see a swirl of cloth. My senses are half knocked out of me, but I realize I've been hit by a rock wrapped in material. The cloth goes over my head and around my throat, a knee pushes into the small of my back and the cloth is jerked back to strangle me. I pull on it and try to twist out of it, my head spinning from the blow, but blind panic giving me some strength. Suddenly the pressure is released from my throat and I manage one gasp of air before something slams against my head again and I see stars.

I feel hands all over my body, exploring, searching, pressing and grabbing, the strength of them telling me they are a man's hands. As the fingers squeeze my breast I get a flash of my drunken lout of a stepfather and I rise up, pushing back against the man pawing me, banging my head against his chin.

He relaxes his grip on me again and his hands go behind my shoulders and give me a shove, forcing me forwards against the reed fence. I scream as the fence parts like feathers against my weight and my body plunges into the abyss.

As I hit the bottom, the wind rushes out of my lungs and I see a flash of light in my head before my mind goes dark.

# 14

I lie sprawled out, not moving and with a strange sense that I'm still tumbling down a bottomless pit. As I reach out to break my fall I realize that my hands are already on solid ground, as is my whole body. I've landed on a layer of sand covering the rubble pile created by the cave-in. The fine grains feel soft and cool when I scrabble at it with my fingers and push back with my feet in a weak attempt to move. I feel more sand with hard objects beneath.

Struggling to get up, I raise dust and such, clogging my windpipe, polluting my lungs, and I start to choke, unable to keep the cloud of particles that's floating in the air from getting in my nose and mouth and eyes. I clamp my teeth together to try and filter the air between them, making it a little easier to breathe in the stifling atmosphere.

Looking up at the opening lit by moonlight, I sway dizzily, and I have to steady myself to stay upright in order to keep from falling over. The opening is much too far away to reach, even standing on the debris.

A torch that must have fallen with me is lying on the ground. It gives out little light, leaving the area around me mostly lost in dark shadows. I have to keep it going.

Taking a step, I feel something move under my foot. I look down and freeze in place.

*I've trodden on a snake.*

It slips out from under my foot and I frantically step back down on it, pressing hard just behind its neck.

It thrashes, whipping its body back to hit the side of my leg. I feel it escaping again and I follow it with my foot, pressing still harder, trying to keep the toe of my shoe close to the head so it can't bite me.

I don't know what to do. I can't move, can't reach the torch, can't even bend down to grab a rock. Fright chills my blood. I feel faint, and the foot holding down the snake is beginning to turn numb.


'She just wandered away from the table,' Lady Warton tells her husband Von Reich and Fouad, the sheikh's majordomo.

Frederick Selous joins the group in time to hear her statement. 'In which direction did Miss Bly go?' he asks.

Lady Warton waves vaguely towards the back of the pavillion. 'I don't know, I wasn't paying attention.'

'Has anyone checked to see if she's returned to the launch?' asks Selous.

All the guests but the group from the *Victoria* have left the pavilion, most of them to return to their steam launches.

'Yes,' the majordomo says, 'I sent a servant to check. She has not been there. No one remembers seeing her anywhere in the grounds. I'm told she spoke earlier to the site's caretaker. I have sent a man to his house to discover whether she told him anything that would provide a clue as to her whereabouts.'

Lord Warton snorts. 'Frankly, it wouldn't hurt my feelings if the young woman was left behind when the ship sailed.'

'She's on a race—' Von Reich starts.

'The race be damned. She's been nothing but a nuisance, starting rumours about what happened in the marketplace.'

Frederick Selous gives Lord Warton a restrained smile. 'I think our first concern should be her safety.'

'Of course,' replies Lady Warton, 'that goes without saying – though I share your sentiments about her,' she tells her husband. 'It's just like the foolish young woman to wander off when our boat is ready to take us back to Port Saïd.'

'What efforts are being made to find Miss Bly?' Selous asks the majordomo.

'I've sent servants to scour the area. The problem besides the darkness is that there are so many perils. Thieves have dug numerous holes in search of treasure, sometimes reaching the burial chambers.'

'Are the openings marked?' Selous asks.

'Only a few are fenced because one cannot keep up with the work of those who lust for the treasures of the pharaohs. There have been hundreds of pits dug over time. Thieves will often cover the openings to their holes so they're not obvious.'

'The thieves work at night?' asks Von Reich.

'Yes.'

'So Miss Bly could have run into these tomb raiders?'

'Anything is possible,' replies the majordomo. 'She could simply have wandered away from camp and lost her way back. And there are more dangerous creatures at night than those who walk on two feet. There are packs of lions and jackals—'

'Human jackals, too, I imagine,' says Selous. 'How much Mahdi activity is there in the area?'

'The fanatics are found everywhere in Egypt where there is sand,' the majordomo declares.

Selous nods at a large group of guards who don't appear

to be assigned to any task other than standing around talking and smoking.

'You say servants have been sent out to look for the young woman. Can you have those guards join the search?'

The majordomo smiles with false sympathy. 'I regret that His Highness has more servants to spare than guards.'

*It's gone.*

Dear God, the snake has slipped out from under my foot.

I don't budge an inch, but I'm shaking so badly I'm sure the snake will interpret it as movement.

Looking in front, to the back, all around, I don't see it. It's slipped away into the darkness. It could be coiled and ready to strike the moment I move, but I can't just stand here forever. The light is fading, the shadows are thicker. I have to get to the torch and use it to find a door, or I'll be entombed with the snake and whatever else is lurking about.

I'm sure I saw something move at the sarcophagus a moment ago. I don't want to even think about what could be in the stone coffin – or anywhere else in this chamber, with its morbid images from the *Egyptian Book of the Dead* on its walls and pillars.

Letting out a sob, I go for the torch, sure that I'll feel the snake's fangs biting into me before I reach it. I grab it off the ground and wave it to keep the flame going. It's just a bunch of sticks tied together and dipped in pitch. The light it casts is hardly more than a kitchen match, but it's all I have.

Most of the chamber is lost to me in shadows and darkness, with a slight edge taken off a pitch black area in the direction of the stairwell I saw from the outside.

It makes sense that the chamber I'm standing in is accessed

by the stairway and that what I see across from me is a small doorway. I don't rush towards it because I can't see well enough to know if there's a big pit between me and the door – not to mention that whoever pushed me in might just be waiting there to finish me off. And finish his search, too. The man wasn't feeling my body out of lust – he was searching for the key, I'm sure of it.

I don't see or hear anything that tells me someone is up there at the opening. I have no idea where my companions are – or the caretaker, for that matter – and I don't know if one of them might even have given me the shove, but I have to try and let someone know I'm in harm's way.

'Help! Help!' I yell up. '*I'm down here! I need help!*'

No one is coming, I know that, but I yell out of desperation anyway. The thought that I may never make it out scares me, but I can't let it control me. *Take a step*, I tell myself, *one step at a time, just keep moving, never give up, never stop fighting back.*

There must be a way out, perhaps through the door that I think leads to the stairway. I don't know what or who is on the other side of it, but if it's someone who is coming down to finish what he started, I am already trapped, so I must drive myself forwards and meet my enemy head on, rather than have him jump on my back.

Moving towards the door takes me out of the light coming from the opening above and I step slowly, cautiously, praying the snake has returned to its hole.

My foot hits something that feels like wood. Squatting down to get a closer look I make out the shape of a ladder covered by sand, or at least it seems to be a ladder of branches tied together by twine. It's not at all what an archeologist would use – the rickety-looking thing doesn't feel very sturdy and was most likely made by locals who come down and hunt for artefacts.

I don't dare use it to climb up to the opening because whoever shoved me in might still be up there, so I keep moving in the darkness towards what I believe is the door and stairway. Until I hear the tumble of rocks breaking loose.

Backing away, I nearly fall when my foot hits the ladder again. Grabbing one end, I pull it up, completely out of the sand. It's surprisingly heavy and awkward but my adrenaline is pumping. I start raising it, trying to keep my footing as I push up, one rung at a time, getting it higher and higher until I lift it into position in the opening above. It is just tall enough to reach the hole.

Starting up the crude steps, rocks and dirt rain down on me as the ladder breaks loose some of the debris at the top. It is very rickety, I can't imagine it held the weight of a man; it seems more for children. A rung breaks as I take a step and I hold tightly onto the two vertical posts to take some of the weight from under my feet.

Another step and it feels like the whole thing is just about to disintegrate and collapse in a heap. Slowly, I place my feet towards each side, hoping that there will be more support where the rungs are tied to the vertical posts.

Another two steps and as I reach up for the lip of the opening, I feel the ladder shifting under me. I freeze in place, holding even more tightly onto both vertical posts to keep them stable, but the ladder starts to twist, one post moving away. I can't keep it straight and I hear the twine holding the rung under my foot snap as I reach for the rung above. I barely get a handhold when the steps under my foot come loose and I start to fall. I let go, landing on my feet, then pitching forward.

Sheer panic gets me back on my feet as the sound of someone coming down the passageway becomes obvious.

I look around for a weapon. But what can I use? A piece of the ladder? The dry rotted wood would hardly batter a fly. Bending down to grab a rock, I see what looks like a black whip. The whip moves and I nearly jump out of my skin.

*A snake.*

It starts to move away from me as a door opens and light flows into the room as a man enters. I see only a black figure.

Screaming, I grab the tail end of the snake and throw it at the man approaching me. It hits him on the chest and falls to the ground. He quickly picks up the snake and steps towards me, moving into the light that's shining from above.

Gripping the writhing snake behind the head, he holds it up. 'Good snake. Eats rats.'

The caretaker smiles at me.

'I heard your cries for help.'

# 15

*Why me?* Why am I lucky enough to nearly get killed, then end up subjected to the tender mercies of a dreadful woman who probably gives out pieces of coal to mudlarks at Christmas time.

Out of the chamber and reunited with my companions, Lady Warton helped brush me off, but with such unspoken disapproval that her true feelings about the incident were abundantly clear.

No one else said a word, but the verdict expressed on each of their faces was the same: I clumsily 'fell in'. I had leaned too close and the fence gave way; I fell, hit my head and imagined being attacked by a strange man. The other scenario, offered by Von Reich to assuage my anger, was that I had run into a tomb robber who wanted my purse and jewellery. I was too embarrassed to mention that my assailant's hands violated my body searching for the key.

I pretended to accept Von Reich's assessment only because I couldn't counter it with my belief that I was attacked for the key – not without revealing I have it. I came close to revealing what I believed was the attacker's motive when I told him that the man wasn't a local but one of the guests who followed me after I left the tent.

'Why would a guest do that?'

'Because they— they— I don't know,' I stammered, tripping over my tongue as I swerved verbally to avoid mentioning the key.

'Who would do such a thing?'

'Anyone!' I snapped and walked off in a huff to kill the conversation.

'Who' could have been anyone in the pavilion, from the sheikh to his guests, who knew I had gotten the scarab in the marketplace. That included my companions, Frederick Selous, the snake-loving magician, and, I had to admit, just about anyone else in the tent who had a secret interest in the marketplace intrigue.

I know I was attacked and nearly killed for the key, but even I can find holes in my story because I can't reveal all the facts. There is nothing I can say, nothing I can do, to repair my reputation. All but the man who attacked me are convinced that I have a weak female constitution that drives me to hysterics.

I'm so angry I need to blow off steam. I feel like screaming, but that would really seal their opinion of me. If they knew that in New York I once actually convinced a host of doctors that I was hopelessly insane . . .

We're approaching the dock to board the steam launch for the trip back across the delta when an eerie sound floats to us on the night air . . . not one from an animal, but a deep, steady rhythmical chant that pierces my soul like sharp daggers.

'What's that horrible noise?' Lady Warton asks Von Reich.

'*Ababdehs*,' Von Reich tells us, 'nomads who wander through the desert, always on the move. They have been around forever, long enough to have witnessed the rise and decline of ancient Egypt. Every night the men sing and dance by their fires, chanting praises to Allah. If memory serves me correctly, they dance in a great circle, moving incessantly from left to right, to the faithful moon of Shawal. They believe the chant presages success for the sword of the Prophet.'

'What about the sword of the Prophet?' Lord Warton asks.

'They're chanting about how much infidel blood will be on it.'

'Look – there they are.' Lady Warton points off to our right.

In the distance a group of people are chanting and swaying under the light of the full moon. Dressed in flowing garments of white, they appear ghostly as they lift their arms to the sky.

'Are they pointing something at the moon?' she asks Van Reich.

'Yes, curved palm-stalks, just part of their ritual.'

It makes no difference that their uncanny howls and ghost dancing send chills down my back and up my legs. It doesn't matter if they are putting a curse on me. I don't care if the Sphinx gets up from where it's crouching and swims down the Nile.

All that matters to me at this moment is that someone tried to kill me. A morbid sense of dread follows me back to the ship, because I know I have not left danger back at Tanis.

# 16

*I am a messenger of the Father of Terror.*

Ahmed Kamil bows his head to Allah one more time before slipping into the still dark water of Port Saïd Bay.

His time has come. Tonight he becomes a warrior for Allah.

*I am a messenger of the Father of Terror*, he repeats the phrase to himself as a mantra while he slowly swims, cloaked by the dark of night and careful not to draw attention by splashing. His instructions are to board the steamship *Victoria* unnoticed and before the ship leaves the port.

His objective is the bow of the ship, which he has been told is the best place to avoid detection because the area is crowded with anchor hoisting and other machinery and equipment. He has been warned to stay away from all other areas even late at night, since many passengers sleep on deck instead of in their cabins because of the oppressive heat.

*I am a messenger of the Father of Terror*, Ahmed sings silently to himself.

While rumours race like wildfire that the Sphinx will rise against the foreigners who occupy the land, it is not the powers of ancient Egypt that Ahmed has sworn homage to, but one that has flowed down the Nile River valley from the Sudan and ignited the minds and hearts of the people: *jihad*, the Struggle.

Ahmed joined the battle to make the land pure for the return of the Mahdi because those who toil in the Struggle are to be among the Chosen. To join the Struggle one must be a warrior for Allah, a *mujahid*, with a willingness to be a martyr for the cause.

Ahmed is a poor fisherman, and in death he will find freedom from a harsh life of relentless desperation just getting enough food each day to stay alive. He has no wife or children because he cannot feed them, but his parents and the people of his village will honour his name when they are told of his deed.

Giving his life will be an opportunity to honour the will of Allah and receive the rewards given to martyrs.

Ahmed knows he will not return from the task assigned to him. He will take a life and give his in sacrifice and receive his reward on the Day of the Resurrection – paradise for an eternity.

When he was told a woman must die, he was at first shaken, even frightened. Like all the men of his village, he was raised to protect women. But if her death is the will of Allah, so be it.

Reaching the thick bow anchor chain, Ahmed mounts it, using his hands and feet to pull himself up until he is able to belly over the bow railing.

On deck he crouches down, looking around to make sure he's alone before he loosens the rope strapping down the canvas cover of a lifeboat and quickly slips underneath.

Peeking out from beneath the cover, he remembers standing on the river bank as a boy and watching crocodiles hiding in the murky water, just their eyes and snout visible as they waited patiently for a victim.

Now, he will be that patient crocodile.

'The woman will come to you,' his leader told him.

Nestled inside the lifeboat, his mind swirls with what he was told after he was named the chosen one:

*My mission for Allah is to deliver a message in blood.*

*I will be blessed and enjoy the fruits of paradise for an eternity.*

*I am a messenger of the Father of Terror.*

*Allah Akbar!*

*Tanis Sphinx*

# PART THREE

## DAY 15

*Suez Canal*

# 17

Getting a look at the Suez Canal dragged me early onto the deck when I would have preferred to stay in bed and bury myself under the blankets. Having no desire to be stared at or hear gossip about a young woman who imagines dark plots and cries 'Murder!', I am at the rail when most of the ship is still asleep.

The famed canal is an enormous ditch with high sand banks that the ship moves through so slowly, no breeze is created over the deck. Even this early, the thick heat presses down, making it feel as if I'm standing on a hot plate.

The oppressive air puts me in a brown study. Normally, seeing one of the greatest man-made monuments in the world would have put me into a high state of excitement, but my body is still sore and my anger still raw at nearly being killed.

'It's really quite amazing, isn't it?' Frederick Selous edges next to me at the rail. This time he has obviously approached me when he could have avoided it.

As he has such a gentlemanly air about him, I tell myself not to badger him further about what occurred between him and the ghost of Mr Cleveland. It would be flogging a dead horse.

'Yes, it is, though it's really just a big ditch.'

'Quite, but it's a ditch one hundred and twenty miles long,

which connects two great bodies of water. There were doomsayers who predicted it would cause the Mediterranean to pour into the Red Sea with such force that the entire planet would be thrown off kilter.'

He is freshly shaven and has had a haircut.

'Bath, too,' he says, amused by my rude inspection of his toiletry. 'I roused the ship's barber early out of fear passengers who saw me would think I was a pirate who'd boarded the ship.' He leans beside me on the railing. 'I was away from civilization for a week, taking a look at Mount Sinai. 'Fraid what little water we had couldn't be wasted on washing.'

'Did you find the Ten Commandments?'

'Actually, my friends were convinced Noah's Ark was there, but we didn't find that either. See that caravan?' He points to my left at a camel caravan travelling parallel to the canal. 'They call camels ships of the desert, but that is no doubt what the caravaners are saying right now about this ship.'

'Why would they call it that?'

'Because our ship is lower than the sand banks of the canal. From a distance you can't see the water, so it looks as though the ship is actually moving on sand. So you see – it truly is a ship of the desert.'

'That must be a marvellous sight.'

His eyes drift out to the desert and I feel like he's looking past me to places no one else sees.

He is a striking figure of a man: tall, broad-chested, with well-carved features that are both aristocratic and sensuous. I find few men able to convey both personal warmth and a strong masculinity, and Frederick Selous manages both.

While he impresses me as strong and assertive, I also detect a reserved, perhaps even intellectual side to his nature, not at all like most newspapermen I've met, and certainly a far cry from the boys in the newsroom back home who like to roll up their sleeves, put up their dukes and wade into a story – when they aren't hawking tobacco juice into a spittoon.

However, all his admirable qualities dim in comparison to the fact that I can't trust him. His discussion on the beach with a dead man can be excused because anyone who had not met John Cleveland would have taken the man's identity at his word. But Selous's presence at the sheikh's table, his suspiciously intense conversation with the *psylli* and his cosiness with Lord Warton means not only can I not rely on him to be an ally, but also I sense he is deeper into the quagmire than he lets on.

Not one to remain in silence for long, I pipe up: 'It must be the greatest man-made construction project in history.'

'I suppose that's true, since we can't really count the Great Wall of China because it was built in segments over the centuries.'

'You've seen the canal before?'

'Many times.'

'On news assignments?'

He smiles. 'I'm not actually a reporter – at least not a professional one and certainly not the calibre of one who is racing around the world on a story. I decided to take a sea journey and a Cape Town newspaper kindly asked me to send back observations of my trip. I'm a big-game hunter.'

'Is that a profession? Or a sport?'

'In my case, a profession.'

I have never met a big-game hunter, though I have read stories of men who explore trackless jungles on the Dark Continent in search of wild beasts and adventure.*

'You should read *King Solomon's Mines*. You'd probably enjoy it. It's about a safari hunter, like you.'

Mr Selous gives me a quirky smile, as if I've made a joke and don't know it.

'Yes . . . I should. Egypt's quite a fascinating country, don't you agree?' he asks. 'So much colourful history.'

'I've seen little of it, but what I have seen has made a lasting impression upon me.' This is an understatement.

He looks away, then back to me with sympathetic eyes. 'What happened in the marketplace was a terrible thing for any woman to witness.'

'For anybody to witness.'

'Quite so. Having the poor devil speak his dying words to you must have given you an even more significant connection to the tragedy.'

I nod. 'Ah . . .'

'There is that 'ah' again. What revelation have you received from the gods this time?'

'Lord Warton told you the man spoke to me. Or was it the magician who told you?'

Briefly, he appears at a loss for words. 'You certainly don't beat around the bush, do you? It was his lordship who told me you held the man in his last moments. As for the magician,

---

* Frederick Selous was more famous to the Victorians than Nellie was. The most notable explorer of Africa and big-game hunter in an era in which such men were admired as the epitome of manhood, Selous was the inspiration for Rider Haggard's hero in *King Solomon's Mines*. The Editors.

I was talking to him about the snakes that have tried to put me in an early grave more than once.'

'Did Lord Warton attribute my belief that the murdered man was British to female hysterics?'

'Lord Warton was concerned for your female constitution under such trying circumstances, as any gentleman would be.'

'Mr Selous, let me assure you that my female constitution is just fine. It is my sense of justice that is being trampled.'

He raises his arms. 'I surrender!'

'I don't take prisoners.'

'Yes, I can see that. I've faced charging rhinos that are less aggressive than you.'

I suppress my ire and turn back to the canal, in need of changing the subject before I make a fool out of myself – or worse, put him so on his guard that he never slips up and exposes his true part in the intrigue.

Changing the subject, I say, 'I left New York so suddenly, I didn't get a chance to research the places I'd be going to see. Is it true that the lives of 100,000 labourers were sacrificed in the building of the canal? A ship's officer told me that.'

'I'm sure the authorities were not counting the bodies, but I have heard that same estimate and from stories about how the canal was dug, I have no reason to doubt the figure.'

I pat my face with my handkerchief. 'This heat is quite oppressive. We could use a good sea breeze.'

'Yes, but we won't feel one until the ship can gather speed. Ships have to travel slowly, at no more than five knots, or they create wakes that erode the sandy walls.' He hesitates, as if he's choosing his words carefully. 'That incident in the marketplace, what convinces you that it was John Cleveland? Were you acquainted with Mr Cleveland?'

'We were never formally introduced, but we passed each other in the corridor several times during the voyage from Brindisi to Port Saïd. As he lay dying in my arms, I'm certain it was Mr Cleveland's face I was looking at.'

'But you never spoke to Mr Cleveland on the ship? Or heard his voice?'

'True on both counts. But we can assume that he had a British accent.'

I don't mention that I know he was British because I searched his room.

'Yes, that is a reasonable assumption. But as you know, British accents are like American ones – they vary according to where one is brought up. And there are many places in the world where the local peoples—'

'Yes, I am fully aware of the fact you Britons have scattered your accent around the world. But what about the white legs?'

That gives him pause. 'White legs?'

I describe the fall the 'Egyptian' took on the road.

'And you are certain that the man on the bicycle is the same person you saw in the marketplace?'

'Yes.'

'Frankly, I'm forced to question your powers of observation. If a hundred of these followers of Mohamed appeared before us right now, I would venture that we would remember their robes and hoods but few personal features. Why am I to believe that your powers of observation are any better than these of the rest of mankind?'

That does it. '*Mr Selous* – I see no evidence that entitles you to judge me. You were not there. *I was.*'

He holds up his hands in surrender again. 'You're correct,

you were there. My concern is that you have been put through so much trauma in a short time. First the violence in the marketplace, then that accident at—'

'Accident? You mean the attempt to kill me?'

'Miss Bly—'

'If you'll excuse me, I have important matters to attend to. I'll leave you with your errands for Lord Warton.'

I stalk off, my stomach and jaw tight. What insufferable insolence, but I'm irked at myself for being ruled by my emotions. Angry tantrums not only keep me from learning anything, but confirm Warton's opinion of me. It's hard, though, to maintain a reporter's unattached, professional assessment of the situation when I'm the damned victim.

# 18

Barely able to keep from boiling over, I move down the deck to another spot as far away as I can get from Frederick Selous and everyone else. But something tells me I am not rid of him. He didn't appear to be a man who would step aside from a problem – even one acting like an angry bee. But at the moment I'm tired of duelling and wish I could have an ally rather than an opponent.

What have I gotten myself into? Why I'm staying in this mess as a target is another good question. An easy way out would be to hand over the key to the ship's captain and publicly declare that the man who whispered his last word to me was an Egyptian. But if I turn tail and run, I would do the same the next time I am confronted by a threat of violence. Shakespeare said something about meeting danger head on so it doesn't get the advantage, and that's what my instincts tell me I must do. It's not as though I can jump overboard and swim to the next port.

A moment later Mr Selous is beside me again at the railing.

I don't give him the benefit of even a glance. 'I'm going to ignore you in the hope you will go away. Rail leaning has become a bad habit on your part, at least when it's next to me.'

'Did I mention I considered a career in law before I took up hunting?'

'That doesn't surprise me. Your manner is that of a bullying lawyer.'

'Yes, I deserve that. But may I ask you what I believe would be a lawyerlike question?'

'Why? To discredit my observations?'

'I can assure you that is not my intent.'

'But is that Lord Warton's intent?'

He chews on that for a moment. 'As an American, you may not be fully aware of all the ramifications of the presence of my country in Egypt. I have spent my entire adult life in Africa and I am acutely sensitive to the situations we face in our colonial empire – and the fact that the Mahdi movement along the Nile is the most violent opposition we face at the moment.'

'If you're trying to tell me that Lord Warton has the best interests of his country in mind, that has occurred to me. But he hasn't come to me as a gentleman and expressed that sentiment. Instead, he treats me as though I am a foolish woman with a wild imagination. And he acts as if he has some official authority concerning the matter in the market-place, rather than just being a witness, as I am. Who exactly is he, anyway?'

Mr Selous leans closer and speaks in a confidential tone. 'I became acquainted with him yesterday for the first time, but I do know he has served in the Foreign Office. Briefly and without distinction. Rumour has it that the only thing that entitled him to a position was his title and his old school chums.'

'In other words,' I whisper back, 'his lordship is probably not a spymaster.'

He clears his throat and hides a grin behind his hand. 'I'm

not aware of all his activities, but that is not a role I would pen for him if I were writing a story about the marketplace killings. More likely a chance bystander, but as a staunch British gentleman, ready to defend Queen and country if he sees a threat.'

He gives me an appraising look. 'I suspect that Lord Warton's reaction to your appraisal of the situation may well be coloured, since he believes you're a reporter noted for, shall we say, sensationalism?'

I give him the smile that Mr Pulitzer once described as the grin of a barracuda.

'I believe I am noted for my objective reporting, sir, and that it is the wrongs of those I investigate that are sensational, not my accounts of them.' I tap his lapel with my forefinger. 'I am not a threat to Queen or country. I just want the truth. If someone would reveal it to me, you may rely upon my discretion and the fact that I would act in a manner with which neither you, Lord Warton nor your Foreign Office would find fault. You can report that to him.'

'You're right, you deserve the truth. The Good Book says that the truth will set us free. And I apologize for approaching you as an inquisitor, even if it was with the best of intentions. I trust that you are a person of great moral responsibility and would not do something that could result in furthering the already terrible toll of death and disorder the Egyptians are suffering. Now please, tell me exactly what you observed in the marketplace.'

I laugh and shake my head, and get a frown in return.

'I'm not laughing at you,' I say, 'it's just that you are the same as me, always peeking under the rose to see what is hidden.'

He grins and offers his arm for a stroll. 'I confess that sometimes I also get pricked by thorns when I stick my nose under the rose to snoop. Would you care to accompany me on a quest to find a cool drink – some lemonade, perhaps? And share with me the details of what you observed?'

We sit on deckchairs shaded by an awning and sip our lemonade as I relate what occurred from the time I first observed the victim on his bicycle and later at the market-place.

I omit my search of Mr Cleveland's room and my discovery of the scarab and key.

'So you believe that he spoke his wife's name,' says Mr Selous.

'That was my impression. I'm certain he said Amelia, not an Arabic word. Whether Amelia is his wife is yet to be seen, but that she's a woman in his life is entirely probable.'

'Did you find anything of interest when you searched his cabin?'

I keep from giving a start. Fortunately, it's too hot to make any quick movements, giving me a chance to mull over the question. He saw me leave the room, but he doesn't actually know I searched it. I have to tell him something, throw him a bone so he doesn't think I'm being evasive.

'Not really. He was a cutlery salesman from Liverpool.'

'With a wife named Amelia?'

'I found nothing about a wife. But I only made a quick search.' I yawn and stretch. 'I suppose Lord Warton told you that I tricked the steward into leaving me alone in the room.'

He gives me a grin. 'Actually he didn't but I assumed as

much since you escaped from his room and into mine when you heard them coming. You also recognized the luggage being taken off the ship last night.'

Damn . . . He bluffed me into a confession.

'Empty cases,' I point out. He doesn't respond but I don't let the subject drop. 'You didn't see the trunk open?' He said he didn't last night, but I wonder what his response will be now that we are on friendlier terms.

'No, I must confess, I didn't, but I don't doubt that's what you thought you saw.'

'*Thought* I saw?'

He holds up his hands to block my attack. 'Sorry, I didn't mean to put it that way. It's just that it was dark and it happened so quickly. And I really can't imagine why anyone would conduct a charade about the luggage.'

Neither can I.

'You really saw nothing of interest in your search?'

'Not as such. I found his lack of personal correspondence unusual, but he may have only recently begun his journey away from home. He had a book about Egypt and one on the laws of Yorkshire.'

'Not that unusual.'

'I suppose not. There was a series of numbers on a piece of paper in the law book.' I give Mr Selous a mischievous grin. 'Perhaps he's also studying the law.'

He shrugs. 'Perhaps. The incident at Tanis, is there any possibility that you were overcome by the desert heat—'

'And fainted because of my frail constitution? Or perhaps from a lack of oxygen when I was strangling myself.'

'Yes, I see we should avoid Tanis. May I ask you this: If a man's life depended upon your testimony, could you with complete confidence state before God and a jury that it was John Cleveland who was murdered in the marketplace?'

I let out a big sigh and lean back, fanning myself. *The white of his leg. The British accent. Amelia. The key I can't tell Selous about. John Cleveland's sudden decision to stay in Port Saïd. The empty steamer trunk.*

It all adds up to a scheme to keep the dead man's identity a secret.

'I admit there was nothing distinguishing about the man's face that leads me to conclude it was him. However, my impression is that it was.'

'You didn't answer my question. It calls for merely a simple yes or no.'

I fan my face more furiously. 'Is this the way you badger your wife? A demand for simple yes and no answers?'

'I don't have a wife.'

'I can well understand why!'

'Madam—'

'Sir – I suggest you direct any further *lawyerlike* questions to Lord Warton, or anyone else but me. Good day!'

'Miss Bly!' he yells as I hurry away.

I swing around – reluctantly.

'We'll stop at Ismailia shortly to pick up passengers. There will be time for a brief visit ashore to see the Khedive's palace. Will you join me?'

I make a small bow. 'I shall be honoured to do so, kind sir.'

It is a relief to go below and get away from the sweltering heat of both the air and the cross-examination, but I have discovered three things of importance:

I need more proof that the dead man is Mr Cleveland.

Frederick Selous wants me to accompany him on a trip to shore.

And he is not married.

Von Reich steps out of the smoking lounge as I come by.

'Nellie, how are you feeling?'

'Hot and sore.' I could add that I am more angry about the damage to my reputation than the bruises to my body.

'I see that I have competition for your favours,' he says. 'That Englishman who wanders in jungles.' He gives me a knowing look. 'A friend of Lord Warton's.'

'Hmmm.' I suspect there is more to come. 'You're also a friend of Warton.'

'A business acquaintance. He needs money and can open doors for me.' He glances around. 'I happened to see Warton and the jungle man huddling together at a very early hour. Watch out for them.'

*What was that all about?* I wonder as I head back to my cabin. Certainly not jealousy on Von Reich's part. He distributes his attentions towards women aboard rather indiscriminately. So why did he give me a warning?

I like the man from Vienna – find him amusing, though not the Romeo he obviously aspires to be. He might have confided in me as a friend, or more likely out of sympathy for the terrible situations he has inadvertently put me in.

Now what am I to think about Mr Frederick Selous and his interest in me after I find out that he plotted with Lord Warton before approaching me on the deck? He didn't approach me as a single woman he could casually pass time with aboard. For sure, he has joined with Warton to make sure that Nellie Bly, reporter, keeps silent about the murder in the marketplace.

Finding Mr Selous both interesting and attractive despite his machinations, I shall be disappointed if his only interest in me is to sabotage my reputation.

I'm tempted to ask the steward what was done with the contents of the empty trunk I saw, but decide to leave well enough alone. But I'll be on my guard, especially with the gentleman who has invited me for a shore excursion.

# 19

Mr Selous and I board a small boat to go ashore after we anchor at Ismailia. The boatmen who swarm the ship to carry passengers are gathered at the bottom of the ship's ladder, but they suddenly become quiet and well mannered after Mr Selous shouts down at them.

I don't know what he said – something in Arabic, I imagine – but I'm certain that his size and powerful voice are intimidating. No doubt the long-barrelled six-shooter in the holster strapped to his hip also influences their decision to act in a civilized manner.

'Planning to bag some big game?' I ask.

'Just a precaution. The pilot boat carried news that there have been more disturbances in the country, though none reported in Ismailia.'

He starts to say something else but stops, and I don't let it lie.

'You were about to confess that you brought the pistol because I might be a Jonah. I certainly hope I'm not a magnet for trouble.'

'What I *was* about to say is that I hope our little excursion ashore doesn't bring any more hell into your life.'

'So do I.'

Lord Warton stares down from the railing as our little boat

pushes off and nods to Frederick. Catching my eye, he gives me a nod too, and I throw back a small smile that doesn't reach my eyes. If he looked into them, he'd know exactly what I think of him.

As usual, his manner appears haughty and condescending. And it isn't the fact that he's standing on a much higher vessel that leaves me with the impression he believes he's looking down on someone beneath him.

Ismailia Bay is hot, calm and flat. I feel as if I am on a wooden plate floating across a pot of hot water. Frederick – he insists I omit 'Mr' and 'sir' when addressing him – has sensibly provided a very large umbrella to protect me from the sun.

His own protection is a wide-brimmed safari hat that is rounder and appears softer than a cowboy hat. It reminds me a little of the hats worn by the Argentine gauchos. He's dressed very casually in a lightweight tan shirt and pants, and well-worn, knee-high brown boots.

'To protect against snakes,' he says, when I glance at the boots, 'in the jungle. But I don't expect to be bitten in Ismailia.'

Beggars, tumblers and sellers of trinkets compete for our attention and coins on the beach. A magician shows us a clever sleight of hand trick with a disappearing bead in a handkerchief, and I reward him with a coin.

'Are you aware that a number of magicians from around the Mediterranean region boarded the ship at Port Saïd?' Frederick asks.

'No. Why are they aboard?'

'A magic conference in New York, I'm told. One of those preternaturally wealthy American robber barons with an interest in the spiritual world has invited the finest magicians on Earth to demonstrate their powers. A rather large monetary prize awaits the conjurer whose trick can't be guessed by a committee of judges.'

'Perhaps one of them can show us how Mr Cleveland can manage to be both dead and alive at the same time.'

He stops and searches my face with his eyes. 'What must I do to convince you that I am not lying to you about having spoken to John Cleveland?'

'I believe you are as mistaken about having spoken to the man himself as much as you believe I am mistaken about him dying in my arms.' Brushing a bit of lint off his coat, I look into his eyes with all sincerity. 'The matter can be resolved by having one of those magicians who've come aboard conjure him up.'

'Mind what you wish for. Stranger things have happened.'

Frederick hires a carriage that takes us into the town. Ismailia is quieter and smaller than Port Saïd; the ship stops here only because the government mail contract requires it. The streets are unpaved and even more rutted than those of the Mediterranean port, but at least there are no mobs shouting for the blood of foreigners.

I spot an English-language newspaper office, the Ismailia Post, housed with the cable office – a not uncommon arrangement, since out-of-town news comes by wire.

'I try to pay my respects at news offices as often as I can,' I tell Frederick, certain that as a thoughtful gentleman, he will urge me to make a brief stop.

He glances in the direction of the establishment. 'Yes, quite.' Suddenly he points at a store selling musical instruments. 'Those drums are made from fired clay with sheep's guts stretched over one end. They make a rather good sound.'

I turn cold, then angry. 'Stop the carriage.'

I startle both Frederick and the driver, who reins in the horse and looks back at me.

'You can have this back.' I shove the umbrella at Frederick and step down from the coach, slamming the door behind me.

Frederick stares gravely at me. 'What are you doing?'

'I saw your look. You're trying to divert me from the cable office. You invited me along to make sure I don't send my editor the story about the marketplace.'

'Regardless of what you think, you must understand that you risk arrest if you send an inflammatory cablegram.'

'I don't intend to send one. But when I do, you will not be able to stop me.'

I wave down another carriage and tell the driver to take me back to the beach.

I am so mad, I'm ready to howl at the moon.

The scheme to keep me on a leash and my lips sealed smacks of Warton in his role as the self-appointed, self-righteous arbiter of my conduct.

I didn't plan to send a cablegram. I considered it, but rejected the notion because I'm a foreigner in what amounts to a war zone and I know I could be arrested if I dash off something about spies and government cover-ups. Besides, I would be going off ill-prepared because I don't have all the facts. If the story was proved to be wrong, my reputation as a credible journalist would forever be tainted.

The newspaper world in New York is a battlefield, where a publisher's heart beats with the same rhythm as the paper's circulation figures. Mr Pulitzer would drop me like yesterday's news if I made a mistake that allowed his competitors to heehaw.

The same is true of the race I've undertaken. Sitting in jail in Egypt, or even being detained for questioning for a few hours while my boat sails would cost me the race. And my career, my very life blood. The *World* has made my trip a lead story, boasting that its reporter will succeed. If I don't beat the eighty-day mark, I will not only curl up and die from shame, but Mr Pulitzer will make sure I am a pariah in news reporting.

By the time I reach the beach and hire a boat to take me out to the ship, my anger has evaporated and the heat and dark thoughts have filled me with weariness and a sense of anxiety.

I feel so alone, so exposed – halfway around the world from friends and family and not a soul I can turn to. Lord, what I would give to have the man who has trekked through pathless jungles and faced charging beasts as a friend and ally. Instead, with every word and thought, my relationship with him becomes a deeper morass.

As I'm being rowed out to the ship I realize that the source of my anxiety is a question.

When is the other shoe going to drop?

# 20

*Once upon a midnight dreary, while I pondered weak and weary* . . . sings in my head as I take my late-night constitutional from bow to stern. Perhaps the poem slipped into my thoughts because it was a night in the 'bleak December' that Poe's raven knocked on the door of the lover distraught over the death of the lovely Lenore.

December has come to me, too, and this first day of it is indeed a bleak one – the dark and angry clouds that hung over me have followed me aboard and put me in a melancholy gloom. The thick atmosphere from the heat coming off the Arabian Desert presses down on me, despite the paltry breeze provided by the forward motion of the ship.

It's an overcast night, and the pale ghost of a full moon doing nothing to relieve the darkness brings to mind my mother's belief that ghosts are spirits who have stayed behind because they have unfinished business, and need help to cross over to the hereafter.

John Cleveland, of course, is the ghost haunting my mind's attic and I haven't been much help in getting his spirit to rest in peace. I don't want him to end up like Poe's character, his soul trapped beneath the raven's shadow, to be lifted 'nevermore!'

*Stop it!* Groaning, I hit the side of my head with my palm

to knock some sense into it. I don't know why my mind is always conjuring up these strange thoughts. I'm too superstitious, too willing to accept that there is phenomena beyond my five senses. I've even been wondering whether breaking the scarab and throwing it overboard brought an ancient Egyptian curse into my life.

I don't have to worry about threats from the spirit world – I have plenty to deal with in this one. I just have to keep myself grounded and remind myself that the man who instigated Mr Cleveland's death puts on his pants one leg at time, just like everyone else. The face in the porthole was a real person trying to frighten me, and ghouls are created on stage with mirrors.

When I reach the bow, I look quickly behind me to make sure no one is watching, because I don't want to get caught and really give the captain a reason to throw me overboard. Slipping under the rope, I ignore the 'No Entry' sign.

The bow is the least visited area of the ship, roped off to keep passengers from strolling through because it's where the equipment for hauling up the anchor and raising the sails is stored. There's also a danger of being swept overboard as the ship ploughs through the seas.

I enjoy my late-night visits to the bow because it benefits from both port and starboard breezes when the ship is underway, and unless the anchor is being raised or lowered, it's the quietest place on board. When we're in rough seas, I sometimes sneak onto the bow to feel as if I'm riding a giant sea creature as the ship drives deep into the waves and then rears back up, blowing back salt-water spray.

I know I'm not the only one violating the captain's order. The woman in black, also a nocturnal deck walker, uses the area, too. Knowing she desires privacy, I'm careful to avoid the bow when I see her there. I'm glad I don't see her tonight, for I really need this time to be alone.

Away from the deck lights, it's midnight-black as I carefully step over chains and steel cables and weave around the big winches and lifeboats. I reach the forward end of the ship, my little haven of peace and quiet, and I suddenly realize how tired I am as I lean on the railing and let the warm wind ruffle my hair and clothes. Heat tends to drain my energy, and it's relentless in this hot, dry climate that is also afire with political passions.

I hear something behind me, and as I turn a man slips out from under the canvas cover of a lifeboat – an Egyptian, clad only in a loincloth.

*With a large knife.*

Letting out a yell, I make a dash amidships but my foot trips on a cable stretched between machinery and I fall, hitting the deck squarely, face down. The Egyptian's feet find the same cable and he goes down to my left with a startled cry.

I get myself up in a panic and he rises as I do, the knife still in his hand.

I scream and turn to run again but my feet slip out from under me as I spin around and fall sideways, hitting my head against the metal housing of some machinery. The man with the dagger is suddenly upon me, knocking me against the housing again, sending me back to the deck.

There is a whirl of motion, grunts and heavy footfalls erupt around me and I realize someone else has joined the battle.

I raise my hands to protect my face and curl up in a foetal position as feet stamp around me. The fight is suddenly no longer happening above me and I hear a startled yelp and look up to see two dark forms at the rail, one of them going over. From the shape of the dark figures, it looks as though it was my almost-naked attacker that went overboard.

It's too dark to make out anything about the other person except that it must be a man, then he's gone, too, down the deck, leaving me there with my head spinning.

Someone hovers over me again and I let out a startled cry.

'Are you all right?' the woman asks in English.

The accent is not British, but continental – French, I think.

A whiff of perfume emanated from a female figure wearing a veil. For a second I think it's Lady Warton, but the face beneath the veil is close enough for me to realize it isn't.

'I—I—' I'm not certain what my condition is. I am still on my back and my head is swimming.

'What's going on here?' a shout comes from a few feet away.

I recognize the voice as that of the first officer.

Without a word, the woman leaves.

As I am assisted to my feet, I can smell the woman's lingering perfume. I'm certain that was the woman in black who also walks the decks at night.

Her features have stirred in me a sense of haunting familiarity, one that I can't put a finger on. For certain, I was wrong about her being the eccentric Mrs Winchester, who is much older and dowdier than the woman I've just seen.

Another certainty is that whoever tried to kill me at Tanis came back to finish the job.

Questions bounce around like rubber balls in my sore head.

Who was my rescuer? Obviously, a man who did not want to stay around to receive my thanks because he wanted to keep his identity a secret. The woman in black did likewise.

Someone has tried to murder me again. Stowing away and lying in wait would have required some planning. Have I gotten the entire Mahdi movement into a murderous rage against me because of the key in the scarab?

# 21

'Miss Bly, because of your insistence to my first officer that you witnessed a man go overboard, we have done a roll-call of all the crew and passengers and everyone is accounted for. Everyone.'

The captain's jaw is tight and he is not in good humour.

I have been taken to the ship's infirmary to be examined by the doctor. When the captain came in, I quickly learned that an attack on a passenger aboard the ship was a scandal he was keen to avoid.

'I told your officer I was attacked by an Egyptian wearing a loincloth.'

'We have no Egyptians aboard – not even stowaways. And, young woman, the last time I looked, none of the passengers was wearing loincloths.'

'Which means that whoever attacked me went overboard.'

The ship's doctor, who has been pottering in his medicine cabinet to find a salve for my scrapes, says, 'We have had incidents in the past where thieves have come up the anchor chain while we were—'

'We were underway, doctor,' the captain snaps. 'There are no thieves aboard the *Victoria*.'

'Of course not, captain,' the doctor says.

'What about the witnesses?' I ask. 'The man who came to my aid, the woman who—'

'No one lays claim to having seen the alleged incident.'

'Alleged? Are you implying that I made up the attack?'

'I am merely giving a commonsense interpretation to what you have reported. You sneaked into an area that is off limits because of hazards, tripped and banged your head. That much of your story is evident. Your report that a man came at you with a knife and that someone intervened is still under investigation. Your exact statement to my officer is that you blacked out after striking your head and that all you saw around you was a blur of dark figures. Is that an accurate rendition of what you have previously stated?'

'I did bang my head, but—'

'Doctor, exactly what injuries did this young woman sustain during her *trespass* in the restricted bow area?'

'A few bruises and scrapes, a blow to the head—'

'A blow to the head. The fact that she became disoriented and even blacked out briefly shows it was a pretty severe blow, does it not?'

'Oh yes, yes, perhaps even a concussion.'

I could see that I had lost the doctor to the demands of keeping his job. 'The head injury occurred because I was attacked.'

'My dear,' says the ship's doctor as he applies ointment to a scrape on my arm, 'you took such a nasty fall, I'm afraid your memory is not solid. I won't be surprised if you have occasional blackouts for the next few days. You're a very lucky young woman.'

'Will she suffer any permanent impairment?' the captain asks.

'No, though there could be some short-term effects. How severe, I can't say, but I believe with plenty of rest, she should be back to normal in a few days. In the meantime, though, she might still have hallucinations.'

'*Hallucinations!*'

The two men jump at my exclamation. If Mr Selous, the great hunter, had heard my retort, he would have likened it to the howl of a wounded jungle cat.

I lock eyes with the captain. 'It was a personal attack on me. An attempted murder.'

The captain turns shades of red and purple and appears to be suffering from apoplexy. I hope he doesn't drop dead, if for no other reason than that it might delay our passage.

He regains his composure and turns to the doctor with a meaningful look. 'You do recall we have been warned that this young woman suffers from an overabundance of imagination and paranoia. I suspect that this entire episode is a case of female hysteria generated by a blow to the head. There was no attacker, no gallant rescuer; it was all conjured by the imagination of an impressionable young woman who has read too many penny dreadfuls. Don't you agree, doctor?'

'Most definitely. Yes, most definitely.'

The captain stiffly spins about face as if he were in a military parade, jerks open the infirmary door and steps out, slamming it closed behind him.

But just before it closes, a mirror on the wall reflects the image of two men standing in the corridor outside the infirmary.

Lord Warton and Frederick Selous.

I slip off the examination table to confront the two slanderers but the doctor grabs my arm.

'Miss Bly, you're aboard a ship. Under the laws of the

seas, the captain has exceptional authority over you, powers that can be exercised with little restraint.' He gives me a fatherly smile. 'If you cause trouble, he'll put you ashore at the next port and you will have to complete your race by swimming.'

# 22

My anger turns from hot to cold fury as I head for the state-room of the woman in black who hovered over me at the bow. Hot anger is for bursts of temper. When I get an icy chill, my intent is to wreak vengeance and havoc. 'Pink,' my mother has said, using my family's pet name for me, 'you are the meanest when you are silently angry.'

*Hysterical female indeed.* Those pompous, ignorant bastards. And I make no apology for my language.

I can understand the captain's eagerness to protect the reputation of his ship, but I draw the line when it is done at the expense of both the truth and my good name.

I'll stop short of a confrontation with the captain because the ship's doctor is right – I could be put off the ship and forfeit the race. But I can't let an attempt on my life go unanswered or have my credibility trampled. Spotting Selous with Warton outside tells me what side he has picked again. War has been declared, the lines drawn; no quarter is to be given.

I'll need allies in the battles to come, and the woman who came to my aid on the bow seems the most likely – and indeed only – candidate at the moment, since the man who threw my attacker overboard will not come forward.

Although I'm hesitant to call on the woman because she

goes to extreme lengths to protect her privacy, I need to know what she saw on the bow.

Did she see the struggle? If she did, I could rebut the 'hysterical female' accusation the captain has stained my reputation with.

Puzzlement over the features I saw under the veil is sitting in the back corner of my brain and teasing me. There's something about her that strikes a chord, yet I can't put my finger on it.

I decide a frontal assault is necessary.

Pausing at the woman's door, I take a deep breath, and tell myself to relax. Barging in as I did with Selous could alienate her.

Tapping lightly on the door, I wait for a response. None comes.

Tapping a little harder, I wait.

Harder, even – a good, strong pound because the woman is probably asleep.

'Perfectly obvious,' I mutter to the door. The woman is not going to open it.

Has she been forewarned by the captain that I might pay her a visit? Or is she so intent upon maintaining her privacy that she will not open the door even if the ship is sinking?

I am tempted to yell that the ship *is* sinking, but I stop myself. Causing a panic aboard would only confirm the captain's opinion of my mental state and get me deposited ashore with my luggage at the next port.

'All right.' The door is not going to be opened to my knock. That much I understand.

Resisting the desire to give it a good kick, I turn to leave, but driven by one of those impulses I'm helpless to stop, I turn back to the door and try the handle.

The knob turns and I push open the door.

Across the room, a woman in a long black negligee is lounging on a velvet quilt on the closed hood of a coffin. Beside the casket is a tall golden candelabra, with little globules of wax sliding down the candles like teardrops.

Lazy smoke curls up from a cigarette held in an ivory holder as she looks up from a magazine and glares at me.

'*How dare you?*'

'I—I—'

She slips off the coffin lid and comes at me, no doubt to slam the door in my face.

I stare at her in paralyzed astonishment. It's not possible. It's unbelievable. It can't be.

'My God – you're—you're—'

She lets out a shriek and grabs me, almost jerking me off my feet as she pulls me into the room and slams the door behind us.

# 23

'I am sorely tempted to leave her behind at Suez city,' says the captain.

The ship's doctor, the first officer, Lord Warton and Frederick Selous are assembled in the sitting room of his quarters for brandy, cigars and a discussion about the young newspaperwoman who has become a nuisance aboard.

'More's the pity, but I don't dare,' he continues. 'Her employer, a man named Pulitzer, would lynch me with printer's ink in his newspapers if I caused her to lose this ridiculous race she's conducting.'

'Yet she needs to be reined in,' says Lord Warton.

'She's very centred on this incident in Port Saïd,' adds the doctor. 'Not that she shouldn't be. It must have been a terrible trauma to Lady Warton also and yourself, of course.'

'Quite so. Her ladyship was upset by the incident, but she has not turned it into a *cause célèbre* to embarrass our country.'

'Ships sailing in this region do occasionally suffer thieves and stowaways,' the first officer says. 'It sounds as though she may have had the bad luck to run into one that came aboard when we were anchored.'

'You didn't actually see anyone attacking her, did you?' asks Lord Warton.

'No, but I got there after the man who supposedly came

to her aid had fled. It's strange no one has come forward to take credit for that apparent act of heroism.'

'It certainly wasn't me,' Lord Warton replies. 'I would have thrown *her* overboard.'

The first officer nods at Frederick Selous. 'And it wasn't you, Mr Selous – you were playing cards with the captain and me. So who—'

'It doesn't matter if someone assisted her,' Lord Warton says. 'We're dealing with a woman who has not only imagination, but both an appetite and an outlet for sensationalism. Pulitzer's newspaper in New York thrives on providing vulgar thrills to its readership.' He takes a long drag from his cigar and blows the smoke in the air. 'It's our duty to ensure that she does not upset the delicate political balance in Egypt by having her take unrelated incidents and create a bloody mess for us.'

'Hear, hear!' the captain offers with his raised glass, and the others follow suit.

Lord Warton takes another drag and stares up at the ceiling as he slowly exhales.

Selous, quietly observing the man, concludes that the peer loves the limelight.

'It goes without saying,' his lordship continues, 'that my friends in the Colonial Office would hold the steamship company and its employees responsible if this young woman is permitted to damage our position in regard to the canal.'

The threat is unnecessary, Selous reflects; the ship's officers are not only patriots, but they are not stupid when it comes to protecting their employment. If the shipping line were barred from use of the canal, it would be forced out of business.

As the discussion rumbles on, Selous savours his brandy, swirling it, sniffing it, to avoid participating in the conversation. Something outside the room – at the bow of the ship precisely – requires his attention, and he wants the session to be over with as quickly as possible.

Listening to Warton speak of his brief service in Morocco as if he had been at the right hand of the Foreign Secretary himself, Selous has a hard time keeping himself from smirking.

Having spent the last two decades mingling with Colonial and Foreign Office personnel, he has heard a bit about Warton, and knows infinitely more about Warton's type – a man who got his job because of who he knew rather than what he knew.

Selous, the third generation of immigrant French Huguenots who fled persecution in France, has a different view of the world from the peer's. For one, his name – Frederick Courtenay Selous – is not 'British' sounding, a fact that got him into more than one fight at school with types like Warton, who could trace their roots back to the Saxons.

The first lord in the Warton line was a wool merchant, who bought his title by providing the king with an eighty-gun ship of the line.

No other Warton has worked for a living since.

Although the situation with Nellie Bly has made them allies, Selous knows that Warton considers him his social inferior, despite his admiration for Selous's adventurous spirit, his personal accomplishments, and the fact that his family has a long history of success in business and science.

Selous has heard that Lord Warton is not one to jump into anything new or radical. With financial problems due to bad management of his estates and his bad luck at cards, he went into government service not for Queen and country, but because he needed the employment – and the contacts it gave him.

He has now left public service after a short, undistinguished career, and has a reputation of being accessible to businessmen who want to do business with the government. Some, like Von Reich, are foreigners.

'Egypt is a tinderbox ready to catch light,' Lord Warton is saying. 'When it does, thousands will die, our own people among them – not to mention that a loss of the Suez Canal would have political and economic ramifications around the world.'

He locks eyes with the captain. 'I recommend that any cables Miss Bly gives to the purser to send at our ports of call be reviewed by me, to ensure there are no politically explosive false allegations.'

The captain looks to the others and back to Warton. 'Rather unusual, don't you think, spying on a passenger's cables – and censoring them?'

'Based upon my connection with the government, you can consider the request an official one.'

Selous stifles a yawn. The man's a complete ass.

'Most business passengers prefer to send their own cables when they reach port,' the captain says.

'Well, then, something will have to be done about that, won't it?'

'That tactic has already met with resounding defeat,' Selous says.

# 24

After the captain's meeting ends, Selous wanders on deck, smoking a cigar, and makes his way towards the front of the ship. He waits in the darkness at the bow area, making sure no one is in sight, and then slips under the rope barrier to the area where Nellie was attacked.

With little light coming from the moon and a thousand nooks and crannies for a small object to hide, finding anything on the deck is not going to be easy. But being a great hunter, Selous has an eye for fine detail – a broken limb in a forest of trees, a single crushed leaf among thousands: the smallest detail can reveal his prey.

He knows the ship's officers have inspected the area, but their examination would have amounted to walking to the bow and, short of tripping over a body, finding nothing of interest because they didn't know how to look.

Evidence of a struggle on deck is obvious to him: smudges made by the bare feet of one man, the scuff marks made by the shoes of another as the two struggled, their feet trying to gain purchase on the damp deck as they shoved at each other in a fight to the death.

Using the soles of his shoes, Selous wipes out the marks.

Reconstructing the fight from the evidence, he finds what he came to look for; slid into an opening at the base of a piece of machinery is the crude, wooden-handled dagger the assassin wielded.

Taking a quick look around to make sure he is not being observed, Selous tosses the weapon overboard, hearing a faint plop as it hits the water and begins its journey to the bottom of the sea.

Making his way back to his cabin, he thinks about the newspaperwoman who has thrown a kink into the best-laid plans of men – and nations.

She has botched things up on many levels. It's easy to see that she will keep getting in the way – if she manages to stay alive.

# 25

'They're trying to murder me, not you. They thought you were me, that's why you were attacked.'

The statement from the woman barely penetrates my brain because I'm still in shock after realizing her identity.

I can't keep from staring impolitely at her.

That she has just announced she was the intended victim of the deck attack is unimportant. All that seems completely irrelevant at the moment as my mind tries to deal with the incredible sight in front of me.

Had Cleopatra herself boarded the *Victoria*, I would not have been more surprised.

'Sarah Bernhardt,' I whisper.

'Yes, yes, I've already told you, in the flesh.'

'The Divine Sarah.'

Sarah Bernhardt is not a person – at least not in the sense that I am one, that the President of the United States and the occupants of the next stateroom are persons.

The Divine Sarah is a living goddess.

The most glamorous actress in the world, the most revered tragedian, most beloved, most sensuous, the most *everything*, whose fame, brushes with scandal and love affairs provide juicy titbits for gossip columns and afternoon teas all over the world.

The woman every woman desires to be – *the woman every man wants to love*.

From reading the gossip columns I know that she was born in Paris, her mother was Jewish, her father probably Dutch, but no one knows for sure because his sole contribution appears to have been slipping into her mother's bed for just long enough to contribute his seed.

When she struggled to earn a living as an actress, she became a courtesan, her beauty and charm making her a favourite of nobles and royalty – her love affair at nineteen with Belgium's Prince de Ligne produced her only child.

Now here she is, pacing in front of me: the living legend whose lovers are rumoured to include even the Prince of Wales. She must be over forty, but she looks a decade younger.

She sits back down on top of her coffin and blows cigarette smoke at me. 'Young woman, we must get beyond your amazement that I am on board.'

'I thought you were that Winchester woman.'

'Who?'

'It's too complicated to explain. What are you doing on board, incognito? Hiding in your cabin?'

Sarah slides off the coffin again and paces with the nervous energy of a caged animal, using her foot-long ivory cigarette holder as a music conductor's baton to highlight her words.

'I cannot reveal my mission. It is a matter of importance that is unequalled in human affairs.'

I have no idea what she is talking about, but it sounds important. Exciting, in fact. 'Unequalled in human affairs' brings to mind images of the march of armies across darkling plains; war ministries called into secret sessions; dispatches carried through the night by spies on galloping horses.

She is the greatest actress in the world and I naturally assume that she is playing a role, but it doesn't alter the fact that there was a murder in the marketplace, and an attempt at Tanis and now aboard the *Victoria*.

It cannot be a coincidence.

The world's greatest actress, the consort of kings and millionaires, the toast of three continents, is telling me that she is involved in the same intrigues that have entangled me – but she won't tell me her role, even though she has cast me as her understudy for the attack on the bow of the ship.

Just as important, she is offering me no clue as to what game is being played that could mean war between nations.

As I watch her pacing, something occurs to me: had I not been such a dunderhead, I would have realized Sarah Jones's real identity days ago.

Everyone knows the Divine Sarah sleeps in a coffin because it helps her understand roles involving suffering and tragedy.

*'Life has taught me that if one is to be somebody,
it can only be after death.'*

Sarah Bernhardt

# 26

Trying to get Sarah to sit still and discuss the situation is about as easy as stopping the ship by dragging my foot in the water. It is not so much that she is flighty, as bursting with energy. I suspect that she needs a release after being cooped up in a cabin for days.

When she finally sits quietly back down on her coffin, and has me sit in a chair, she looks me over.

'I've heard about you,' she says. 'My steward says you're an eccentric, rich American heiress, travelling about with a hairbrush and a bank book, with nothing to do, so you do strange things to get attention.'

At first I'm furious, then I break into a giggle. 'I am guilty of having a hairbrush.'

'Who are you exactly?'

'Exactly, I am a newspaperwoman. I have written a number of exposés that have brought about social reform or exposed corruption.'

As she asks pointed questions about my career, I give her details explaining how I got started as a reporter when, angered by a *Pittsburgh Dispatch* article that essentially said a woman's only worth was as a helpmate to a man, I wrote a Letter to the Editor and signed it 'Lonely Orphan Girl' out of fear I would lose my job.

That letter got me a job as a reporter, but after a few searing articles about how the common worker was being mistreated, a group of businessmen paid a visit to my editor and I found myself covering weddings and funerals . . .

Even after I made a daring trip to Mexico at my own expense to show I could handle a foreign correspondent's job, I was still assigned a 'proper job for a female reporter' – the society page.★

'I left my job in Pittsburgh and went to New York, certain my success would open doors for me. Instead, I found that there was no room for a woman reporter even in America's largest city. After banging on doors for months, and down to a trolley fare – which I had borrowed after my last cent was stolen – I barged into the office of Joseph Pulitzer and informed him that I could write a story that would turn the city on its head.'

I tell Sarah the story of Blackwell's Island.

Sarah laughs. 'You should be on the stage.'

'I find I can only act in real life. I have been on a stage just long enough to find out that I cannot fake it.'

'Tell me why you have come knocking – pounding – at my door.'

'Are you aware that a man was murdered in the market-place in Port Saïd?'

She shrugs. 'My steward said there was some native dispute.'

'I don't think so.'

★ Nellie went to Mexico during a violent era of revolution and banditry and left after receiving a message that she would be risking her life if she wrote any more exposés about conditions in the country. After she became famous, she wrote about her experiences in a book entitled *Six Months in Mexico*. The Editors.

I relate the events from seeing the murdered man fall off his bicycle, to him whispering Amelia's name, to my fall into the Tanis tomb and the attack that brought her to my side. I omit my search of Mr Cleveland's cabin.

After I finish my tale, she says, 'Frankly, my dear, I don't think your little marketplace matter is connected to the matter I am dealing with.'

*Little marketplace matter?*

'Sarah, I need to know more about the situation you are in. If you'd share with me—'

She brushes away my need to know with a wave of her cigarette holder. 'I have been sworn to secrecy.' She gives me a dark look. 'Speaking to a newspaperwoman would hardly satisfy that oath. No word of it will escape my lips even if I am stretched on an inquisitioner's rack. However, I *am* frankly bored to death locked in this sardine can. Helping you with your little mystery would give me some relief. Tell me what you know about this man Cleveland.'

Admitting to my burglary, I tell her how I managed to get rid of the steward so I could make a search of Cleveland's room.

'That was naughty of you,' she says with a big smile.

Sarah's estimation of me has gone up.

She asks what I observed in Cleveland's luggage and lets out a shout when I come to the books and writings.

'That list of numbers you saw is a secret code. That's what one of the books was for, probably that law book that struck you as odd for a cutlery salesman to lug about. I once had a lover who was a spy. An Italian count. He used ordinary books to construct his codes.'

'How is it done?'

'It's so simple a child could do it, but impossible to decipher unless you have the right book. The spymaster gives his spy a book that is not in general use in the foreign country where the spy is being sent—'

'That Yorkshire law volume would be perfect,' I add.

'Exactly. To compose a message, they find the correct words in the book—'

'The numbers are the page, line and position of the word.'

'Nellie, you are quick, aren't you? Since both the spy and his supervisor have the same book, it's easy for them to decode messages. My lover sent his messages in invisible ink, especially the ones to me.'

'Why did he use invisible ink?'

'He was married.'

'Oh.' I am amazed that she is openly admitting to having had a married lover.

'Don't sound so prudish, my dear. Certainly you have had a love affair with a married— ah, yes, I see from your blush that you have. To read the messages, I ran a hot iron over the paper or held it over a radiator.' She sighs. 'He was a wonderful lover, warm to a woman's needs, and generous. They caught him spying and hanged him. Your spy, that cutlery salesman, he may have used invisible ink, too.'

'The paper I saw had writing on it.'

'Of course – a sheet of paper without writing on it would raise suspicion. The invisible words are written between the lines.'

I snap my fingers. 'Lemon juice! My brothers used it to make invisible writing when were children. Milk, too. What did your lover use?'

'Nothing so ordinary.'

She leans forwards and whispers in my ear. I blush from head to toe and quickly change the subject.★

'I suspect you're right about the books,' I say. 'It made little sense for a cutlery salesman from Liverpool to have a book on the laws of Yorkshire, though I could understand why he might have one about Egypt. And you might be right about the invisible ink. The numbers I saw may have been a draft he prepared, to be turned into an invisible message between the lines of an otherwise innocent-appearing correspondence.'

'It's too bad you don't have the paper with the numbers on it and the book. Is the luggage still in Cleveland's suite?'

'No.' I tell her about seeing the empty trunk hit the water.

'Did *all* the luggage appear empty?'

'Now that you ask me, yes, I believe so.' I shake my head to stir up the memory. 'The way the boatman handled them so easily, taking them out of the lowered netting and tossing them back to his mates. They may well have been empty.'

'So, the contents may still be aboard with your British lord sitting on them – who may not even know their importance.'

'I'm sure Lord Warton and the others must realize Mr Cleveland was a spy. Or at least suspect it.'

'That doesn't mean they know how the spy game is played. Or are aware that invisible ink could be part of what the chief of the Paris police calls their *modus operandi*.'

I have to wonder if the Parisian police chief is her lover, too.

Sarah lets out a great sigh. 'Well, my dear, it is very late,

★ Nellie is too inhibited to reveal the substance used by Sarah's lover, but a clue can be found in the story of Sir George Smith-Cumming, who entered British intelligence in Victorian times and was the model for intelligence chief 'M' in the James Bond stories. Smith-Cumming had his men use semen for invisible ink. The Editors.

and now that I have listened to your tale, there is only one thing for you to do.'

'Which is?'

'Go on with your own affairs, your race to beat the record around the world, and leave matters of spies and revolutions in the hands of the politicians. No matter what you do, you'll receive no thanks for your efforts and may actually jeopardize your goal, because all politicians are devils.'

It is good advice, and much more palatable coming from a woman of the world who wants me to succeed than from Mr Selous whose advice is based upon my gender.

I look her in the eye. 'Sarah, do you want to share with me your—'

'No!' She gets up and sweeps dramatically to the porthole and opens it, staring into the dark night. 'It is a secret I cannot share. If the secret is revealed, armies will march, empires will tremble.'

I am awestruck. 'Are *you* a spy? Entrusted with a national secret?'

'Me? A spy? Of course not.'

'Then . . . then who's trying to murder you?'

'My lover's family, of course.'

# 27

My head is pulsating when I leave the great actress to return to my own cabin. So many things have happened so quickly since I arrived in Egypt. Now I find Sarah Bernhardt, the most famous actress in the world, is on the *Victoria* – and she has become my friend and confidante. I wish I could wire Mr Pulitzer and tell him about it. But she has sworn me to secrecy about her presence.

The ship is underway, moving down the canal towards Suez Bay and I step out on deck to get some air, joining the other passengers seeking even the trifling breeze that the forward movement of the ship brings over the deck, before I am banished below so the men can have the deck to themselves.

Crewmen are hanging lights at the front of the ship and a group of us watch as they put the lights over the side.

I lean against the rail and eavesdrop as a man tells his companion that the lights are electric, powered by the ship's steam engine, and that before the introduction of electric head-lights, ships were compelled to tie up in the canal overnight because of the great danger of running into the sand banks.

Being near the bow reminds me of my close call with the grim reaper. I didn't make an issue of it, but I'm not convinced that Sarah was the intended victim any more than I believe I leaned too heavily against the frail railing at Tanis, or mistook

'Amelia' for an Arabic word. I was searched at Tanis for the key, and I'm sure a Mahdi dagger man came aboard to kill for it, just as another did in the marketplace.

The key and the death of Mr Cleveland are directly related to the political unrest in Egypt, I'm sure of it. What I can't comprehend and the great actress won't help me with is how these matters are related to her problems with her lover's family.

Having worked out nothing that sounds like a solution, I return to my cabin, certain that once more I will not be able to sleep.

As I step into the tiny cubbyhole that serves as my bathroom I smell face cream.

My cream is in an airtight jar which I have not touched since this morning. Opening it, I can see that the contents have been stirred around.

Bending down, I take a sniff of the drain opening in the sink bowl and smell a hint of cream.

Someone has opened the jar and tampered with the contents. In the process, a blob of cream fell into the sink and was washed down to cover the intruder's tracks. They were obviously looking for the key.

I look around seeking other clues that someone has invaded my room. I find none, but I have no other explanation for the condition of my cream jar other than that someone made a thorough search of my cabin. Certainly my male steward has not been playing with my beauty products.

My sense of having been violated once again fills me with indignation, but a more practical thought sneaks in: Sarah's speculation that the contents of Mr Cleveland's luggage might still be aboard.

From Sarah's description of the process, I'm certain that Mr Cleveland did write a coded message, though I don't know if what I saw was the finished message or one in progress. Or if he had another message hidden on the papers in invisible ink.

Knowing what Mr Cleveland wrote in the coded message might flush out my enemy.

How can I go about finding it without jeopardizing the race . . . or my life?

However, more urgent at the moment than secret messages is the matter of not being murdered in my bed by an intruder who returns to search my person.

I wedge the chair back under the door handle and crawl into bed, clutching my pair of scissors.

# PART FOUR

## DAY 19

*Parting the Red Sea*

# 28

Leaving the Suez Canal behind, the ship takes us the length of the Red Sea and to the Gulf of Aden at the western part of the Arabian Sea. Hopefully, I have left behind in Egypt the curse of the pharaohs that has brought so much hell into my life.

Just before we come to the British port known as the Aden Settlement, we pass a row of high brown mountains.

'They are known as the Twelve Apostles,' Von Reich informs me when we meet during an early morning deck stroll. 'In Aden there is a tradition that the town dates back to Genesis and that Cain and Abel are both buried there.'

Even though I read the same thing in the ship's Bulletin, I permit him to expound in his didactic manner.

Watching his expression, I wonder if I can find any clue to his change in attitude towards me since I have become a pariah to his British friends and the ship's captain. He reveals nothing, not even the concern he expressed earlier, but I suspect his recent lack of interest in me has been fed by the overtures I see him making to other women on board.

We sail into sight of the British colony at Aden and it looks like a large, bare mountain of wonderful height, but even with the aid of a spyglass I'm unable to tell whether it is inhabited.

I continue my morning constitutional as Von Reich stops to watch a soccer ball being booted back and forth on deck by a group of young men.

After the ship stops to drop anchor in the bay, the breeze dies and I escape inside. I have a mission to undertake.

I give the assistant purser a big smile and a cheery 'Good morning' and hope the devil has well oiled my lies.

It's obvious that Lord Warton has taken custody of Mr Cleveland's possessions, but where are they now? While Warton could have some small items in his own cabin – the books, for instance – he must have arranged for storage of the larger pieces, since the only storage area in the cabins is for steamer trunks slipped under the bunks. I'm hoping that the pompous peer is as unfamiliar with spy codes as I suspect he is with the process of growing wheat in Morocco.

'I'm planning to purchase a large item in Aden and will need somewhere to store it. Is there a place on board to store something too large for my cabin?'

'What type of item?' asks the assistant purser.

'A Persian rug.'

'I suspect Aden isn't the best place to find Persian rugs – Egyptian ports generally have a better selection. If you do make a purchase, however, you can store it in the passenger luggage compartment.'

'Where is that?'

'On the utility deck below the last passenger deck.'

'I'd like to take a look at the facility, to make sure it's secure.'

'Oh, it's certainly secure.' He nods back at a key on a

large ring hanging on the wall behind the counter. 'That's the key.'

'May I borrow it to look over the area?'

'No, ma'am, we can't let passengers go down there, they might get hurt in the working area of the ship. Also, you know, some passengers have been known to rummage through the stored luggage of others. Not that you would do that, of course.'

'Of course not.'

'When you bring your purchase back, just give it to your steward. He will get the key and stow it for you.'

*In a pig's eye he will.*

Trust the steward? Poppycock! He has already been bought by Lord Warton. Offering him money would only whet his appetite to get more from others.

But how will I get my hands on the key if I can't enlist the steward's help?

Speaking of the devil, as I return to my cabin I find the steward at my door with a written message.

'A chit from Mr Selous. The gentleman requests a response.'

The note is an invitation to join him in an hour to take a tour of Aden.

It is signed, '*Your Devoted Admirer*'.

The steward holds out a pencil. 'Does madam wish to reply?'

'Yes.' And 'Yes' is what I write on the chit.

Interesting. An invitation from a man who I left suddenly – and on no uncertain terms – after he tried to keep me from the Ismailia cable office. My suspicious nature doesn't fail to register that the ship's bulletin says there is a cable office in Aden.

Frederick Selous isn't a stupid man or a crude one. He would hardly try the same trick twice, at least not after I had flung it back in his face.

The excursion will offer me the opportunity to see what I can discover from him, and to find out if he is trying to get information for Lord Warton. Besides, while I find my attitude morally weak, I admit that I find Frederick Selous very attractive.

When I am not angry at him.

As I come onto the deck I find the heat very strong and am glad I have selected my silk bodice rather than my heavy wool waist. With my hat and umbrella, I feel ready to risk the sun. It feels even hotter than in the canal area, perhaps because we have travelled 1,500 miles closer to the equator since we left Port Saïd.

I hesitate as I see the Wartons approaching Frederick Selous at the accommodation ladder. I'm behind them and they haven't noticed me yet.

'Going ashore, too?' Lord Warton asks Frederick.

Frederick looks past them at me and says, 'Yes, I have offered to show Nellie a bit of Aden. I've been here several times.'

Both Wartons turn to look at me. Lady Warton gives me an insincere smile from behind her mesh veil. 'Would you two mind if we shared a carriage? That way we can all benefit from Frederick's wealth of knowledge.'

'Of course not,' we both mumble, and I flash her a smile that I hope doesn't reveal too plainly that I'd rather take a pair of Egyptian cobras as companions than her sour personality and arrogant ass of a husband.

Frederick's look says 'I didn't plan this', and I smile forgivingly because I don't think he did. It's the luck of the draw, the boys in the newsroom would say, and we have drawn the black queen and the knave for this hand.

As we await our turn to descend the temporary gangplank strapped to the side of the ship his lordship looks as though he expects some kind of gesture from me.

Perhaps he thinks a peasant like me should kneel and kiss his signet ring.

Near the pier where we land are shops, a hotel, post office and cable office. The actual town of Aden is five miles distant.

Lord Warton tells us that Aden was first occupied by his country to halt piracy, some of it from Somalia. 'It is now an important station for ships to take on coal and water for their steam engines.'

Unable to resist a display of childish behaviour, I stare pointedly at the cable office as we pass across the street from it.

Frederick pulls me away towards a row of street vendors selling everything from ivory trinkets to salted fish. I already know why he has drawn me away from the others – to chasten me for this antic.

'You are an impertinent young woman.' He says it with a smile, in a tone that hints at if not approval, then at least respect.

'And you, sir, are a scoundrel. Your last invitation was a bald-faced scheme to keep me from a cable office.'

'Guilty as charged. But since you had the opportunity to send a cable, and did not, it is clear that you have no intention of stirring up trouble for my country. I apologize for my rudeness.'

'I accept your apology. And since this is a free country, you won't attempt to stop me from going over to that cable office and sending one off, will you?'

'Of course not. It's a free country, as you say, and I would exercise my freedom to inform the local authorities that you are an agent provocateur stirring up a revolt against the Crown. And you can spend the balance of your eighty days pacing around a prison cell.'

'Mr Selous—'

'Frederick.'

'Mr Selous, the more I am around you, the more I discover what it is about you that I like.'

'Which is?'

'Nothing. Absolutely nothing. You have no redeeming social graces whatsoever.'

He takes my arm and steers me towards a bookstall.

'Actually, knowing your feelings towards me, I was hesitant to invite you. I worried that you would return my invitation with a well-deserved slap to my face.'

'I'm taking a rain check on the slap.'

'Of course, there is one comment you made that cut me to the bone.' He narrows his eyes.

'Ah . . .' I know exactly what he is referring to – my accusation that he is Lord Warton's lackey. 'Well, was it the truth?'

He purses his lips for a moment. 'Yes, I was urged on by his lordship, but I also felt it was the right thing to do at the time.'

'Then I owe you no apology.'

He takes my arm in a gentlemanly fashion. 'Do you know what I like about you, Nellie?'

'I'm afraid to ask.'

'Everything. Your smile, your wit, your courage, the way you throw punches to protect yourself. But if you will forgive a man who has spent his adult life battling the worst that Mother Nature and the animal world can throw at one, you have a fault.'

'A fault? No!'

'Nellie, you only know how to throw punches. You have to learn how to duck once in a while – even run, when the odds against you are too great.'

'Mr Selous—'

'Please call me Frederick.' He shakes his index finger in my face. 'If you argue with me, I will be forced to tell Lady Warton that you are in great need of her maternal ministrations and wish to spend the rest of the voyage at her side.'

'Ouch! I would rather swim with the sharks in the bay.' I immediately regret my unladylike comment but he merely nods and mutters, 'Amen to that.'

I buy a backscratcher, a stick with a carved hand on the end, not for a keepsake from Aden but because it occurs to me that I could have a use for it later, something that whoever carved it never dreamed of.

He suddenly reaches for a book. 'What's this?'

The title is *Handbook on Aden*.

'Interesting,' he says. He gives the vendor a coin and we walk away, ignoring the man's jabber in Arabic, no doubt an insistence that the book was a family heirloom worth many times more. He tucks the book into an inside pocket.

'A guidebook?' I ask.

'In a way.'

'A spy manual?'

This is a shot in the dark, based on the book I saw in Mr Cleveland's effects.

He stops and gives me a grave look. 'As I said, you don't know when to duck. You're right, it is a book prepared by the intelligence branch at the War Office. There is a handbook for every country and colony detailing the political, economic and military state of the country.'

'Does it contain secret information? For spies?' I ask.

'Not the stuff of troop movements and war plans, if that's what you mean, but the information in the books is considered confidential, to be read only by high-ranking Colonial and Foreign Office officials. And spies, I suppose, to gain familiarity with a country.' He locks eyes with me. 'I am not a spy, if that's what you're wondering, but I do have friends in the Colonial and Foreign Offices and they have made references to the books.'

Leafing through the book, he says, 'I doubt there is anything in here that would blow the lid off Aden, but nonetheless it belongs in the hands of our administrators, not the locals.'

'How do you think it got into a pile of odds and ends?'

He raises his eyebrows and shrugs. 'Theft by a servant? A wife disposing of household items when packing for a return to Britain not realizing it's confidential? Quite the thing that would ruin a man's career if discovered.' He smiles. 'Or even cause the loss of the kingdom. Do you know what Richard III said after his horse fell in battle? My kingdom for a horse?' He recites:

*Because of the nail, the shoe was lost*
*Because of the shoe, the horse was lost*
*Because of the horse, the rider was lost*
*Because of the rider, the battle was lost*
*Because of the battle, the kingdom was lost*
*All because of a horseshoe nail!*

'All because a housewife discarded an old book,' I add.

'Quite. So you saw a *Handbook on Egypt* when you searched Cleveland's room, making you believe he was a British agent.'

His casual remark catches me off guard and I take a moment to respond.

'Actually, the fact that he sneaked off the ship in the wee hours, ran around Port Saïd with his face stained brown and tangled with Mahdi killers made it rather obvious that he was on a secret assignment.'

'What else did you discover in his room that you haven't told me about?'

I raise my eyebrows. 'I'm sure you know better than I do the contents of his cabin. I had only the briefest moment to look through his things and saw nothing of consequence.' A lie, but necessary.

'I never saw his personal effects.'

'Ah . . .'

'There's that mysterious exclamation again.'

'So Lord Warton has not shared his booty with you?'

Frederick gives me a twisted grin. 'No, he hasn't. The *Handbook on Egypt* was a guess on my part. His lordship acts as if the survival of the British Empire itself has been placed upon his shoulders. Frankly, he strikes me as a rather small man who has stumbled into a rather big mess and sees himself as the general leading a charge to rout the enemy.'

Lady Warton approaches, raising a curious eyebrow as she sees Frederick and me strolling arm in arm; no doubt this is her way of showing she's aware of a romantic interest between the two of us, but she reminds me more of a grinning shark than a matchmaker.

Lady Warton and I stroll along the edge of a cliff which provides a view of our ship in the bay below. When we are out of the men's hearing, she pauses and eyes some native women coming down the road.

'He married one, you know,' she says.

'Who?'

'Selous. He married an African native woman and had a child by her.'

'Really?' It's all I can think of to say. I'm not sure why she is sharing this personal information with me.

'He's not really British, you know.'

'He isn't? He sounds like it.'

'He was born in England, but his great grandfather was a French Protestant, a Huguenot who fled persecution in Catholic France.'

By my calculation that makes Frederick at least third or fourth generation British, depending on how one counts. He might be British going back centuries on the side of one parent.

Lady Warton gives me a sympathetic look, but my impression is that of a vulture eyeing a piece of meat.

'You poor dear, you must still be suffering from that terrible incident at the marketplace.'

'Oh, no, I've forgotten the whole thing. It's all behind me now; I'm feeling just fine. Should we join the gentlemen?'

I don't give her a chance to answer because I need to get away from the cliff's edge. I am too tempted to shove her over it.

A great ball of anxiety rises in my stomach, threatening to shoot up into my throat.

Frederick lied to me about being married.

What else is he lying about?

# EN ROUTE FROM ADEN TO COLOMBO

Tonight we have a lantern slide* exhibition that is very enjoyable. The loyalty of the British to their Queen on all occasions, and at all times, has won my admiration, and it is once again apparent during the show.

Though born and bred a staunch American, with the belief that a man is what he makes of himself, not what he is born; still I cannot help admiring the undying respect the British have for their royal family.

During the lantern slide exhibition, the Queen's picture is thrown on the white sheet which evokes a warmer applause than anything else that evening.

We never have had an evening's amusement that does not end with everybody rising to their feet and singing 'God Save the Queen.'

I cannot help but think how devoted that woman, for she is only a woman after all, should be to the interests of such faithful subjects.

With that thought came to me a shameful feeling that here

* A lantern slide show was an early form of slide projection. The slides were glass plates upon which pictures were painted. The slide could tell a story or show exhibits of art, history, and so on. Over time, a technique was developed to use transparent photos and the modern slide projector came into being. The Editors.

I am, a free born American girl, the native of the grandest country on earth, forced to be silent because I cannot in all honesty speak proudly of the rulers of my land, unless I went back to those two kings of manhood, George Washington and Abraham Lincoln.

Nellie Bly, *Around the World in 72 Days*

*Steamship* Victoria *with sails furled*
*Italy to Ceylon run*

# 29

Magic is on the programme tonight.

Magicians will take to the stage to perform their acts, and I will attempt some magic myself, in a more private location. I just hope the wizardry I have planned doesn't come back to bite me.

I have deliberately planned my scheme for tonight because the next port is Colombo, Ceylon, where I will change ships for the Far East leg of my journey. Since I will be disembarking the ship anyway, the captain won't be able to go through with his threat to strand me at a port. However, my plan is so audacious, I have to wonder if he might take punitive action while I'm still aboard. Of course, the captain's wrath will only come into play if I am caught . . .

The risk is worth it because I'm running out of time to search Cleveland's possessions and I'm unsure what Lord Warton will do with them once he has to change ships. The British mission at Colombo is much larger than the one at Aden; he will have to take the items off the ship, so Colombo seems an obvious place to dispose of them to officialdom, unless he decides to hold onto them for some reason.

After the lights are turned down in the entertainment room and up on the stage, a pair of magicians come out and introduce themselves: Carolina Magnet, a woman billed as the Strongest Woman on Earth, and her assistant, who we already know is her husband.

Her husband is the master of ceremonies for her act, informing us that she will prove her strength to us with 'tests in which she pits herself against the strongest men aboard the ship'.

This is quite a claim, since she doesn't appear to be a particularly large or muscular specimen of womanhood.

'Any volunteers, gentlemen?' the man asks. 'We need three men true and strong from the audience for Carolina Magnet to test her strength against.'

Three large men, two fellow passengers and the ship's second officer, are coaxed onto the stage.

Carolina Magnet grasps a cue stick, holding it up at about neck level as the master of ceremonies instructs the ship's officer to also take hold of the stick. 'Carolina Magnet,' he bellows, 'has the ability to use the mysterious power called 'magnetism' to create a force that makes it impossible to move her.'

The man steps to the side so the audience can get a full view of the woman and the ship's officer facing off, each grasping the cue stick.

It is obvious to me that without a 'trick' up the woman's sleeve, the officer will easily push her back. But, of course, watching her succeed is the fun of it.

'If this manly officer is able to push the Strongest Woman on Earth back a step, he will have accomplished a feat that no man has succeeded at before.'

'The man will best her,' a well-boozed male shouts from the audience.

The tug of war begins and the officer can't move her, no

matter how hard he tries. It's as if the woman's feet are nailed to the floor. I lean forward, trying to get a look at her shoes, wondering if they bear some sticky material that keeps her from sliding back, but even if her shoes were nailed to the floor, the man would be able to push her upper body back, and he can't do it.

There's a round of applause, then the other two men attempt to push her back and fail also.

I'm highly intrigued and as usual my curiosity is chomping at the bit for an answer. To ensure that I get one, I've placed myself at the same table as Von Reich and sworn on a stack of Bibles beforehand that I will never reveal the secret of any conjuring he explains. I know his loyalty towards the world of magic evaporates whenever his ego is excited by a woman's plea.

'How does she do it?' I whisper. 'Please, I'll die if I don't know.'

He grins smugly as he leans close to murmur, 'If she pushed towards the men and they pushed back at her, she would be easily defeated. Instead, she holds the stick high and as the men push towards her, she pushes *up* on the stick. It takes very little effort on her part to hold back the much greater strength of the men because she has deflected their force up, instead of against her.'

'It's that easy?'

'We can try it later and you'll see. If you push up, I won't be able to push you backwards.'

'Now the incredible Carolina Magnet will demonstrate her ability to use the mysterious power of magnetism again, this time by lifting more than twice her weight,' her husband informs us.

A large dumbbell atop a wheeled cart is rolled out onto

the platform. The dumbbell, an iron bar with a large iron ball on each end, indeed looks hefty – each ball is the size of a very big, round melon. It's obvious from the squeaking of the wooden stage how heavy the weight is.

Once again three men are invited up onto the stage. None of them are able to lift the dumbbell off the cart.

With a roll of drums from the ship's band, the woman who claims to be able to manipulate the powers of magnetism, a secret which confounds the greatest scientists in the world, steps up to the dumbbell and lifts it, to the amazement and applause of all except Von Reich.

'Child's play,' he snorts. 'The dumbbell is very light, but the cart holding it is very heavy. There's a hidden latch that keeps the dumbbell stuck to the cart. When the men pulled up on the dumbbell, they were actually attempting to also lift the cart, which weighs several hundred pounds. When it's her turn, she releases the latch and easily lifts the fake dumbbell off the cart.'

In some ways, it's better not to know the secret of how it's done. But from my point of view, the most interesting conjuring is about to be performed – my own.

I slip out of the entertainment lounge when the next magician, billed as a master of Chinese rings, comes on stage. I will find out later from Von Reich how the magician manages to loop what appear to be solid rings in and out of each other.

The ship is rocking a bit from a tropical blow and people are leaving with me, some already queasy, making my own exit seem natural.

The interior corridor of the main deck is deserted as I hurry down it. Passengers are either watching the entertainment, or in their cabins, while the service crew has retired to get some sleep before their early morning chores.

The assistant purser is on duty behind his counter, looking bored and sleepy.

'How is the show going?' he asks.

'It's amazing. A small woman bested three large men at shows of strength.'

'How does she do it?'

I lean across the counter and whisper, 'Mirrors, it's all done with mirrors.'

'It's astonishing what they can do, making it look so real.'

'Incredible, isn't it? Now, I want to make sure the rug I purchased in Aden made it into the passenger storage compartment.'

He removes a clipboard hanging next to the key to the storage area from the wall behind him. He sets it on the counter and I put my hand on it.

'One more thing. You keep a record of cablegrams passed to passengers, do you not?'

'Yes, ma'am. We have a board in the back room on which we post all cablegrams sent over to the ship from cable offices, along with the time and date they are delivered to passengers.'

'I believe a cable addressed to me has fallen through the cracks at some point since I boarded at Brindisi. Could you please check?'

'That will take a moment, ma'am.'

*That's the idea.* 'Thank you. I'll check on my rug while you look at the cablegrams.'

The moment he disappears into the back room, I unhook the backscratcher that I have hidden beneath my dress and belly up on the counter in a very unladylike pose.

Extending it as I lean across the counter, I hook the passenger luggage compartment keyring and pull it back towards me, slip it into my pocket, then quickly flip through the luggage manifest, turning immediately to Port Saïd.

Lord Warton checked in three boxes the evening Mr Cleveland was killed. I was with him and his wife for almost the entire time they were in the city and I never saw them make a purchase.

The log shows the boxes are stored at B5-3.

The assistant purser returns, shaking his head. 'Everything has been delivered to you, Miss Bly.'

'Thank you, that's a relief.'

'Did you find your rug?'

'No, but I just remembered it might still be in my room. I'll give it to my steward in the morning.'

A passenger is approaching the desk and I move quickly away, leaving the purser a bit perplexed. I've already decided how I will get the key back to him after I search the luggage compartment. I'll come up to the desk, suddenly stoop down, then rise up, holding the keyring, and announce that I found it on the floor.

I'd be in awe of my own cleverness except that my stomach is tied in knots because I'm scared half to death by the realization of what I have just done – I've stolen a key to enter a restricted area, and I'm about to search boxes belonging to a peer of the British realm.

Completely batty, that's what I am – no doubt about it. My ten days in a madhouse must have turned me into a real lunatic. Why in God's name would I put myself in harm's way like this again?

Perhaps the real question, though, is why I have these moments of remorse only after I have done something completely insane.

# 30

My nerves are still on fire as I quickly descend the stairs to the utility deck.

Opening the door to the luggage hold, I fumble around with my hand until I find a switch on the wall. I turn it, and a single naked light bulb hanging in the middle of the storage area comes on.

Thank God they have installed a newfangled electric light; although the bulb is dim, at least it takes the edge off the darkness. Too bad it doesn't take the edge off my jangled nerves.

Slipping inside, I leave the door open just a hair and place the key in the inside lock, rather than take the risk of losing it.

'This is not going to be easy,' I mutter, staring at the rows of passenger baggage.

There are storage areas on both sides of the aisle, three tiers in height, with luggage and boxes stuffed four or five high in the compartments of each tier. Each compartment is screened by floor-to-ceiling netting that keeps the items on the shelves in heavy seas. When I find the correct section, I will have to release the netting in order to gain access to the items piled on the shelves.

Getting close enough and squinting, I quickly learn the

numbering system. The two lines of storage areas split by the centre aisle are A and B respectively, with B being the one on my right. It begins with the storage compartment labelled B1-1.

Passing down the narrow, claustrophobic passageway, with the ship's motion causing the luggage to strain back and forth against the netting like a great beast's innards as it breathes, makes me feel like Jonah inside the whale.

Finally reaching the section I'm looking for, I groan. B5-3 means the items are located on the third tier, access to which is gained by a narrow ladder that a monkey would find challenging, never mind a woman in a full dress with heeled shoes.

Similar to a tall stack-ladder in a library, the ladder rolls sideways along the floor to where you want to ascend. However, book ladders don't move all by themselves like this one does, sliding back and forth as the ship ploughs though seas whipped up by the blow.

*I'll probably break my neck.* They'll find my crumpled body when they empty the hold at the next port. But there's no turning back; it's too late. I have no place to go but up, literally. I've crossed the Rubicon and I don't even have Caesar's army to back me.

Somehow I manage to reach the third level, unhooking the netting as I go up, but I'm only halfway home. Cases and boxes are stacked two deep and three or four high in the space. The only saving grace is that the items are not piled completely to the top, permitting me to move some of them as I hang onto the sliding ladder, worrying that the whole shebang will come flying off the shelves with the violent roll of the ship.

If I hadn't boasted to myself about my cleverness in plotting this ransacking of the ship's luggage hold, I would abandon the project. Only stubborn pride and a lack of good sense keep me going.

With very dim lighting it's hard to see the numbers on the individual items, but there are only five boxes and three of them should be the ones that Lord Warton has stored.

Now I am in a dilemma. I can't get them down to the floor to search them, then bring them back up, because they are too awkward and heavy. They will have to be searched on the tier, and that will only be possible if I can get both hands free instead of one clutching a ladder rung while grabbing out with the other to keep the ladder from sliding.

As I shove and restack everything, I manage to move the cases apart to create a hole big enough for me to squeeze into. I find myself standing upright on the third tier, hot and sweaty and a little nauseated from the ship's motion as I hang onto the top box of a stack I want to go through.

*Never, never, never again will I be so stupid.*

Each box has twine tied tightly around it and I don't have a knife. I am angry enough to rip it off with my teeth.

However, since my teeth aren't strong enough, I use an object that for centuries women all over the world have found as handy as the tools of men: a hairpin.

With sheer stubborn determination I manage to untie the string, open the box and find Mr Cleveland's books.

Removing the piece of paper with numbers written on it and the Yorkshire book of laws, I take turns holding each of them in the direction of the light to see the printing.

The first set of numbers lead me to the word 'extreme'; the second sends a quiver down my spine: 'danger'.

Hanging on tight as the ship rolls, I quickly check the written number scheme for the next word and find 'for'.

My knees tremble with so much excitement, I'm ready to collapse.

As I'm reading the fourth set of numbers, I hear voices and the door opens. Terrified, I freeze in place.

'Here it is! In the door. You must have left the key here the last time you brought down some luggage.'

It's the purser, shouting at his assistant.

'But, sir, I would swear—'

The ship rolls and I let out a startled yelp.

'Who's there?' the purser snaps.

The two men are sent staggering against the compartment to their left as the ship rolls again. The stack of boxes I'm using for support moves, and I throw myself deeper into the compartment to keep from being flung off the tier by the motion of the ship.

The ship pauses for a moment at the end of its roll, then starts to roll again in the opposite direction.

Frantically I grab at luggage as everything around me begins sliding off the shelves – no longer restrained because I have removed the netting.

Unable to keep my balance and with nothing left to hold on to, I follow the avalanche down, screaming bloody murder.

# 31

'With thirty years' naval experience, from stoking the boiler to raising the sails and commanding the entire ship, I can tell you that despite any old sailors' tales, a woman is not bad luck at sea.'

The captain is leaning back in his chair, staring up at the ceiling as if he is expecting a missive from heaven.

Sitting perfectly still, I stare straight ahead, my hands in my lap . . . waiting for lightning to strike.

He leans forward and shifts a little to meet my eye, but I turn away.

'No madam, despite my officers' suggestion that perhaps there *is* something to this superstition, I reject their contention. You are not bad luck – you are a regular Medusa, worse than the plagues God threw at the Egyptians.'

The purser and first officer are standing behind me, shaking with smothered laughter.

I just cringe. I know my face is flaming red and I am so angry that I have to struggle to keep my composure – not angry at the captain or the ship's officers, but at myself. I have made a complete fool out of myself. *Again.*

'Well, what do you think, gentlemen? What shall we do with this young woman who has flagrantly disobeyed the rules of the ship?'

'Keelhaul her, captain,' the first officer replies.

The captain leans forward in a pretence of gravity. 'Do you know what keelhauling is, young woman? We run a line from one side of the ship to the other and tie the end of it around the miscreant. Then we throw him into the sea and pull him back aboard – only we pull from the opposite side, so he is dragged under the keel, and his flesh is rubbed off by the barnacles that attach there.'

If they don't end this charade soon, I will scream. I know there will be no punitive action against me except the one I dread most . . . humiliation.

What a pretty picture I must have made, flying off the tier and onto a mountain of baggage.

I'm mortified at making such a fool of myself. I will never go back out on deck where people can see me, I will never return to the dining room, I will have to take my meals in my room. Or drown myself.

What bothers me most of all is the dishonour I have brought to the death of Mr Cleveland.

'Keelhauling is too harsh for a woman's delicate skin, captain,' the purser says. 'I say we put her in irons and throw her—'

I leap out of my chair, push past the two officers and flee, their laughter flying at me faster than I can move.

Frederick is in the corridor outside the office and I rush by him, breaking into a run.

'Nellie! Wait!'

I shake my head without turning back and hurry to the stairway to my deck. Thank God it is late and there is no one in the corridor. I will throw myself overboard if anyone sees me running like a dog with my tail between my legs.

Not bothering to knock, I fly into Sarah's dark stateroom, pouring light in from the corridor behind me.

Her coffin lid is open and she sits upright, startled. Her face is covered with cold cream, her hands are in gloves, her hair soaked in some other cream and bundled under a cap.

'What are you doing?'

'They've beaten me!' I wail.

'Who?'

'Warton, Frederick, the British Empire!'

'Well . . . that certainly narrows it down.'

I cry for the damage I have done to the memory of John Cleveland. And Nellie Bly.

'Nellie—'

'No, not Nellie – my real name is Elizabeth Cochran. Nellie Bly is the name of a reporter. I'm nothing, just a factory girl who thought she knew everything.'

# 32

Lord Warton stalks back and forth, glaring at the pile of baggage that fills the end of the passenger luggage compartment aisle.

He whips round and demands from the captain, 'Well, where are they?'

The captain and the first officer look to the assistant purser, who squirms under their stares.

'The books were here,' he says. 'They fell out of a box Miss Bly had opened before she took her tumble. When everything came off the shelves, the box dumped its contents. I saw them right there.' He points to an empty spot on the floor. 'Three books, scattered about along with some papers.'

'If they were here,' Lord Warton yells, 'where are they now? I demand you search the room of that troublemaking reporter.'

'She was with us when the books went missing,' the captain answers. 'Someone took them when my officer went to find crewmen to clean up the mess.'

'Who? Who took them?'

The captain gives Lord Warton a tight grin that says he has had about enough of the man's demands. 'Sir, obviously I don't know, but I suggest that in order to find out who, we start with *why*. What's the importance of these books?'

'You told me the woman said there were writings in a secret code,' Lord Warton says, directing his statement at the assistant purser.

'That's what Miss Bly claimed when we extricated her from the mess she created,' the man responds.

'What secret was she talking about?' the captain asks Lord Warton.

'It is a matter of national security to which you do not have privity.'

The captain looks to his officers. 'Well, gentlemen, then I suggest none of us lose any more sleep about a matter to which *we* don't have privity.'

'*You!*'

I let go of the handle to my cabin door as if it is a hot poker, and spin around in surprise.

Lord Warton is the source of the exclamation.

'You are in deep trouble, young woman, more than you can imagine.'

'I beg your pardon.'

'Name your co-conspirator, the one who took Cleveland's books, or I shall have you arrested.'

'I don't know what you're talking about.'

'You know exactly what I am talking about. You told the assistant purser that those books contained a code. I demand you turn them over to me so they can be given to the proper authorities at Colombo.'

I'm speechless, not because of his demand but because it means he was unaware of the secret writing. I'm also not going to be bullied.

'I don't have the books, and I didn't even know they were

missing. But now that you've explained the matter, I can see your problem.'

'*Your* problem, you mean.'

'No, sir, I'm not the one who appointed myself custodian of Mr Cleveland's possessions. I'll leave it to you to explain to the authorities how you stored them in a *public* place and now cannot find them.'

I slip into my room, throw across the latch and lean back against the door, breathless.

I can't believe Warton didn't know the numbers were a code. So why did he have the contents of Cleveland's luggage repacked into boxes and go through the charade of having the cases sent ashore?

In a strange way, I am greatly relieved, even elated to hear that someone has stolen the books. It validates my suspicion that they contain a secret.

I don't think the captain and his chums will be laughing so hard now that they know I was on a serious quest. But I also find it strange that the captain was amused rather than angry.

Completely exhausted, my knees are wobbly as I shuffle to my bunk. I talked with Sarah for over an hour and she set me right about myself by telling me what she went through early in her own quest to establish a career.

When she was still a teenager and had ambitions to be an actress, her mother pushed her into being a courtesan, providing 'favours' to wealthy men in order to get acting roles.

She acquired them, but they came with contempt from other stage players who were less fortunate. 'And less talented,' Sarah said. Ultimately, her God-given talent won the day and the origins of her success were overshadowed by the universal proclamation of her talent.

'But along with success comes challenge,' she told me. 'You will never stop having to prove yourself.'

Her story is a good reminder to me. I have always believed that the only course to be taken when I'm knocked to the ground is to get back up and fight. Perhaps Frederick is right; I don't know how to duck, I only know how to throw punches, but some of those punches land, as one did tonight.

I had assumed that my adversary aboard was the British lord, who I now discover was entirely ignorant of Mr Cleveland's secret.

The same person who searched my room for the key has taken the books, and it is someone who is aware enough of my movements to allow them to slip in and steal them in the wake of the chaos I have left behind.

A person hidden in the shadows, one diabolical step ahead of me, all the way.

Someone I know and trust?

PART FIVE

DAY 22

*Colombo, Ceylon*

# 33

We steam into the bay at Colombo, Ceylon on a bright day.

The large island is close to the southern tip of India, with the Indian Ocean stretching landless for thousands of miles to Australia and the Antarctic in the south.

I have to stay in the city for several days before I board the ship that will take me on to the Far East. After registering at a hotel, my plan is to find the cable office and send a story back to my editor in New York. The cablegram won't contain anything about the incident in Port Saïd or my trials and tribulations, as all that will be written when I have the full story. However, a second cable I send will contain a query to the paper's London correspondent for information about a cutlery salesman named John Cleveland.

Standing by with other passengers, I wait patiently for the ship to drop anchor. Once again, the bay is too shallow for our ship to reach the dock and we must be ferried ashore. A number of steam launches are already coming out to meet us.

With its abundance of green trees, the island appears restful and pleasing to my eyes after the spell of sweltering heat we passed through on the Arabian Sea coming from Aden. The shoreline is dotted with low buildings fronted by arcades which look, in the glare of the sun, like marble palaces.

Forming the background to the town is a high mountain called Adam's Peak. A man standing beside me explains there is a tradition in Ceylon that Adam and Eve were banished to the island paradise after they were cast out of Eden, and are buried here.

'The beautiful blue sapphires found on the island are tears of Adam and Eve that crystallized as they wept after being banished from the garden.'

It is a charming anecdote, and I make a note, as I did of the link of Cain and Abel to Aden.

The beach, shouldered by a forest of tropical trees, looks as if it starts in a point out in the sea, curving around until it forms into a blunt point near the harbour, the line of which is carried out to sea by a magnificent breakwater surmounted by a lighthouse.

The land curves back again to a point where a signal station stands, and beyond that a wide road runs along the water's edge until it is lost at the base of a high green eminence that stands well out over the sea, crowned with a castle-like building glistening in the sunlight.

When I looked in on Sarah earlier to see if she wanted to accompany me to shore, her door was half open and she was pacing furiously, cold cream on her face, a cablegram in hand, while her steward was packing a steamer trunk.

The pilot boat had delivered cables to the ship before the ship entered the bay.

She waved the cablegram at me angrily. 'They will not force me to run for cover with their stupid threat!'

'What threat?'

She immediately drew back, tucking the message into a pocket of her dressing-gown. 'It's nothing, a small problem with a role I am to play.' She turned around and glared at the steward. 'Much more important is what I shall do with this cretin. He has damaged my best hat with his sloppy packing.'

'I dropped by to see if you wanted to go to the hotel together.'

'I'll meet you at the hotel. If I am able to get off this ship with my possessions and my mind intact.'

I wondered about the cablegram as I went back out onto the deck and got in line to go ashore. A threat from her lover's family? What sort of threat would one send by cablegram?

Besides the cable and the damage to her hat, it seems Sarah has another good reason for having a black day. Because we have to stay ashore, she must leave the sanctuary of her state-room for a hotel – not a significant problem for most travellers, but no doubt fraught with complications for a woman who travels with a coffin.

I consider myself a seasoned traveller, but I would be hard pressed to arrive at a hotel with a coffin – in Colombo or anywhere else in the world – yet Sarah appears more daunted by the condition of her favourite hat than the reaction that can be anticipated from hotel staff. Then again, there is a great deal of drama in the mere notion of arriving at a hotel with a coffin, and as the greatest actress in the world, she is a master of melodrama.

My only regret at leaving the *Victoria* is that the steamship *Oriental*, which will take me to China, is not yet prepared to sail because it awaits the arrival of a ship from Australia. Getting away from the bad service, poor food and the looks I get from the officers and crew will be a relief.

Colombo is a setting-off point for ports in India, Australia and New Zealand, as well as for the Far East. Thank God, most *Victoria* passengers will not be accompanying me on to China.

However, I will not leave behind my reputation as an agent provocateur when I transfer ships: from prior conversations, I already know that the Wartons, Herr Von Reich, Frederick Selous and several others will also be on the *Oriental,* and then on the same ship as I will take to cross the Pacific to San Francisco.

Each day of delay in Colombo will weigh heavy on me, but at least it will be spent in what I am told is one of the most beautiful places on Earth.

I am mulling over Sarah's reaction to her cablegram and wishing the slow-moving steam launches would move faster as the line to get ashore is a long one, when Frederick is suddenly beside me.

'If you're game for a little adventure, I can get you to the hotel while most of the passengers are still waiting to go ashore.'

He catches me by surprise. He no doubt believes that my deliberate avoidance of him is due to the fiasco over my search of the luggage hold, but he does not know it actually dates back to Aden, when Lady Warton told me that he was married.

I am still contemplating my reply when he takes my arm and pulls me along.

'You'll have plenty of time to tell me what a cad I am on our way to shore. Your other option is to let everyone get ahead of you and claim the best rooms at the hotel before you get there.'

'You treated me callously by not rising to my defence,' I tell him, as he leads me by the arm to a gangplank the crew is utilizing to unload luggage.

'I kept you out of the brig.'

'I'm certain there is no brig on board this ship.'

'True, but the captain had planned to lock you in your cabin.'

'What!' I try to stop but he pulls my arm to keep me moving. 'He wouldn't have dared.'

'He would have been perfectly within his rights after the books went missing.'

He gives my arm another tug as I try to pause and defend myself. 'The captain thought the whole matter was a joke.'

'Only after I spoke to him and pointed out that it would be wiser to laugh about it than to have it appear a serious matter in his report to his home office.'

'So you told him I was a clown?'

'Would you rather I told him you were a felon?'

'I'd rather you go to hell.'

He gives me a sharp look. 'Is that any way for a lady to talk?'

'If I wasn't a lady, I'd tell you what I really think of you, *Mr Selous*.'

'Frankly, *Miss Bly*, you should be thanking me. My biggest fear was not what the captain would do, but what would be said to the authorities after we docked. I'm sure you realize you could be arrested.'

'Nonsense.' But I suspect he's right.

'Don't worry,' he says, 'I've spoken to both the captain and Warton. Neither wants to have a chat with the authorities that will expose them as having been bested by a woman reporter, and having lost valuable materials.'

I find myself once again vacillating between having warm feelings for this man – and deep distrust. I don't know what to expect from him. He lies to me, then protects me. Slams

209

me down, then lifts me up. Makes me grit my teeth one moment, then makes me want to nestle close to him the next.

We pause and I stare down at the cluster of odd-looking boats below.

'We are going ashore – *in one of those*?'

'We will if we don't drown.'

The boats are awkwardly shaped, rudely constructed things, with a sitting area probably five feet in length and two feet in width across the widest part, narrowing down to the keel, until it is not wide enough to allow one's feet to rest side by side in the bottom. There are two seats in the middle, facing one another, which are shaded by a bit of coffee sack that must be removed to make room for passengers to embark.

At each end of the peculiar boat a native sits with a paddle – a straight pole with a board the shape and size of a cheese-box head tied to the end of it.

Too narrow to sit upright in the water without support, the little vessels are balanced by a log the length of the boat that is fastened by two curved poles that extend out three feet from the boat.

At the bottom of the gangplank, I step into one of these boats as gracefully as an elephant climbing into a bathtub, certain that I will end up swimming to shore.

When we are settled in, the oarsmen paddle rapidly. We cut through the water at an amazing pace, passing the steam launches that chug along.

'What do they call these things?' I ask Frederick.

'The locals call them catamarans, though tourists call them outriggers. Native fishermen take them out to sea. I'm told that they are so secure against capsizing, no sinking has ever been reported.'

On the dock he guides me past the line of carriages awaiting passengers still to be deposited from the slow-moving steam launches.

'Carriages are slow on these crowded streets,' he says.

He takes me to a line of two-wheeled carts with a top that can be raised to protect against rain. They resemble sulkies, the light, one-horse carriages designed to carry a single person, only the horsepower for these carts is human – short, slightly built men.

With a little rough English and sign language, the first driver in line insists he can carry both of us. I'm not disagreeable about the notion of being pressed up against a handsome man with startling blue eyes, but I don't want the poor labourer injured.

'Are you sure he can pull us both?'

'The wiry build of Sinhalese men is deceptive. They're all muscle.'

As in all hot countries, the men wear very little clothing and these are no different – they wear hardly more than a sash across the groin, though their hats are broad affairs that remind me of big mushrooms.

The lovely castle-like structure I saw from the ship is the Grand Oriental Hotel. Seeing it close up does not lessen its elegance.

After we step out of the ricksha, Frederick asks, 'Will you join me for a cool drink after we register at the hotel?'

I hesitate, but reply, 'Yes.'

'Followed by lunch?'

'If I am still speaking to you. I don't think I like you very much.'

'I don't blame you. I don't like myself much, either.'

I wave away his attempt at humour with my hand. 'Why didn't you tell me you were married?'

'Ah, yes, I see. A little gossip from her ladyship?'

'The source is not important. The fact that you are a barefaced liar is.'

'You asked if I was married, I told you truthfully that I am not. Had you asked whether I have ever been married, I would have told you the truth, that yes, I have been. My wife passed away. She was African and was taken by one of those fevers that seem to come suddenly from nowhere and leave a path of death. I have a son at school from that union.'

'I'm sorry. For your loss and for my rudeness.'

Two things are heavy on my mind as I make my way to the hotel desk. Will Frederick change his mind and put the police on my trail if he finds out about the Cleveland cablegram I plan to send? And that thought is coupled with a sudden insight into the disappearance of Cleveland's books and code.

Frederick proved to me that he knew the importance of the handbook when he showed concern about the one he found in Aden. But Cleveland went far beyond just possessing a handbook – yet Frederick showed little concern when he talked about the missing books.

*He must have stolen them himself.*

Now he has gone out of his way to keep me from the hands of the police.

Why? Is he trying to help me? Or does he have something worse up his sleeve?

# 34

I register at the hotel before Frederick and wander for a while, looking at my surroundings as I wait for him.

The Grand Oriental is a fine, large establishment, with tiled arcades, corridors airy and comfortable, furnished with easy chairs and small marble-topped tables which stand close enough to the broad armrests for one to sip the cooling lime squashes or the exquisite native tea, or enjoy the delicious fruit while resting in an attitude of ease and laziness.

In this lovely promenade the men smoke, consume gallons of whisky and soda and peruse the newspapers, while the women read their novels or bargain with the pretty little copper-coloured women who come to sell dainty hand-made lace or with the clever, high-turbaned merchants who snap open little velvet boxes and expose, to the admiring gaze of the charmed tourists, the most bewildering gems.

My wide eyes see deeply dark emeralds, fire-lit diamonds, exquisite pearls, rubies like pure drops of blood and the lucky cat's-eye with its moving line, all set in such beautiful shapes that even the men, who begin by telling the vendors, 'I have been sold these before by some of your kind,' would end by laying down their cigars and papers and examining the glittering ornaments that tempt all alike.

'I could take up permanent residence here,' I tell Frederick when he joins me in the lobby.

I immediately sink down into a large lounge chair, feeling wonderfully lazy, and sip a lime squash while Frederick enjoys a cold beer and a fine cigar.

He is both intriguing and attractive, when I'm not annoyed at him. I have met men like him before, men of the West who live by the gun – shooting buffalo and bears, of course, not lions and elephants. Generally they are hardened, solitary souls, rough hewn in all aspects, who prefer the companionship of prairie dogs over humans.

Frederick, though, is a cultured gentleman. When I am with him my suspicions melt and I feel warm and comfortable, free, even – feelings I don't often get with men.

Frederick nods towards a high-turbanned merchant who is displaying a wide selection of gems to guests seated nearby. 'You'll find that most of the jewellery bought and sold in Colombo is sold in the corridor right here, in the Grand Oriental. It's much more pleasant than visiting the shops.'

'I heard on the *Victoria* that the gems in Colombo are good value.'

'Quite so. No woman who lands at Colombo ever leaves until she has added several rings to her jewellery box, and the rings sold here are so well known that the moment a traveller sees one, in no matter what part of the globe, he will say to the wearer, 'Been to Colombo, eh?' Let's get him over to show his wares.'

'Sounds like fun, but I haven't the money, nor can I add anything to my valise – there's no space.'

'Then you can add it to your finger or wear it around your neck so your case remains unburdened.' He holds up his hand to quell my objection. 'I know I have been a bore and a cad towards you. I want to make it up to you.'

I catch my breath. This handsome man is going to buy me a gem. I would love a blue sapphire to match his dazzling eyes.

He turns to call over the gem merchant when a woman so beautiful that she puts to shame the sparkling rubies and sapphires of Ceylon glides towards us.

Frederick pauses mid-motion and gawks as if the Queen of Sheba has entered the hotel.

'Oh, there you are, Nellie dear.' Sarah flutters her handkerchief at me. She is not wearing her netted veil, but has it in her hand. 'I was worried that we'd find ourselves at different hotels.'

'*Good heavens!*'

The exclamation comes from Frederick. It is a shout, but one that is barely audible – more of a shouted whisper, hoarse and full of awe and amazement.

I hear his quiet exclamation loud and clear, and I know exactly what his next words will be.

'Sarah Bernhardt!'

A man of the world, cultured and educated, he has no doubt seen her on the stage in London and Paris. His tone suggests he has just caught sight of a goddess.

The gem merchant gives me a look and I shake my head, sending him away.

As with all men who gaze upon the Divine Sarah, Frederick's mind has gone, he is no longer capable of rational thought or action.

I hunch my shoulders and shrivel up, tucking in my chin, clutching my arms to my body and curling my fists, feeling small and gawky, an ugly duckling in the presence of a graceful swan.

# 35

We part for our rooms to unpack and bathe with Sarah and myself invited to join Frederick in two hours for tiffin, which he tells us is the name for lunch on the Indian subcontinent.

The invitation forces upon me the awkward choice of sharing his attention with one of the most desirable women in the world . . . or sulking in my room.

I graciously accept rather than succumb to my lower instincts and appear petty and jealous.

After a cool, refreshing bath, I dress hastily and leave my room. I have an errand to run and need to complete it before I meet them for lunch.

I decide a ricksha will get me to my destination faster than my feet.

There is a definite scent as we move along the street, and it doesn't derive from the city. Besides the fact that they dress in nothing but a sash around their private parts, these ricksha drivers seem to cover themselves in oil or grease. When the day is hot and they run and sweat, one wishes they would wear more clothing and less oil! The grease has an odour that is entirely its own.

I feel rather ashamed, going around the town in a cart drawn by a man, but after I have travelled a short way, it occurs to me that this is the way the man earns an income to feed his family.

The roads I've seen are perfect. I can't decide, to my own satisfaction, whether the smoothness of the road is due to the blessed absence of beer wagons, or to the absence of the New York street commissioners.

My destination is the local newspaper office at which I find two clever young Scots who run both of the city's newspapers. They are quite excited by the story of my trip and ask many questions.

Enquiring about news coming out of Egypt, I'm told that there have been reports of murderous attacks by Mahdi fighters, but no mention of one in a Port Saïd marketplace, and I do not pursue the subject further.

When it is time for me to leave, I put into action my plan of deceit.

Knowing that the newspapermen are in constant touch with the local cable office, I pass them the draft of my cables and money to cover the transmissions to my editor in New York and to the London correspondent of the *World*. 'Could I ask you to send these for me?' I request sweetly. 'I am tied up this afternoon . . .'

They kindly take charge of the dispatches, promising to cable them as soon as possible.

The New York message contains a brief summary of events since I left Port Saïd and omits any reference to the attempts on my life or the incident in the marketplace; the London cable asks the correspondent for information about cutlery salesman John Cleveland.

I request that the reply be sent to Hong Kong, since that will provide time for a thorough check.

Now I don't have to worry about being followed to the cable office or being treated like an agent provocateur.

As I make my way back for tiffin, I leave the ricksha a few blocks from the hotel so I might enjoy the exotic sights on the streets, especially the snake charmers. They are almost naked fellows, sometimes with ragged jackets on and sometimes turbans on their heads, but more often their heads are bare. They execute a number of tricks in a very skilful manner.

The most wonderful of these tricks, to me, is that of growing a tree. They show a seed, then place the seed on the ground and cover it with a handful of earth. They cover this little mound with a handkerchief, which they first pass around to be examined, that we might be positive there is nothing hidden in it.

Over this they chant, and after a time the handkerchief is taken off and up through the ground has appeared a green sprout.

Those of us gathered around look at it incredulously, while the performer says, 'Tree no good; tree too small,' and, covering it up again, he renews his chanting. Once more he lifts the handkerchief and we see the shoot is larger, but still it does not please the trickster, for he repeats, 'Tree no good; tree too small,' and covers it up again.

This is repeated until he has a tree several feet high. Then he pulls it up, showing us the roots.

Then the trickster asks if we want to 'See the snake dance?'

I say that I would, but that I will pay to see the snake dance and for nothing else.

All of us take a few steps back as the man lifts the lid off a basket and a cobra crawls slowly out, curling itself up on the ground.

Like its Egyptian cousin, this is one of the deadliest creatures on Earth, yet the snake charmer moves casually about it, as if he's dealing with a harmless garden snake.

The 'charmer' begins to play on a little fife. The serpent rises up steadily, its neck fanning as it darts angrily at the flute, rising higher at every motion until it seems to stand on the tip of its tail.

The snake suddenly darts for the man, but in a flash he deftly catches it by the head and with such a strong grip that I see blood gush from the snake's month.

He works for some time, still firmly holding the snake by the head before he can get it into the basket, the reptile meanwhile furiously lashing at the ground with its tail.

When at last the snake is covered from sight, I draw a long breath and the charmer says to me sadly, 'Cobra no dance, cobra too young, cobra too fresh!'

Quite right; the cobra is too fresh!

I tip the charmer generously for the sake of his family. I suspect snake charming is not an occupation with a bright future.

'Aren't you going to ask me how the trick is done?'

Von Reich gives me a grin. I didn't see him approaching.

'This one is obvious, isn't it? The snake sways to the music—'

He is already shaking his head. 'It cares nothing for the music. It's the motion of the flute that the snake is following. Cobras are used because they seem to become transfixed by the motion and are relatively slow-moving when they strike, at least compared to other snakes. That one was too young; it needs to be trained up.'

'Are you staying at the Grand Oriental?' I ask as we walk in the direction of the hotel.

'No, unfortunately a lesser establishment. By the time I arrived, all the rooms at the Oriental were taken. I did not have the benefit of a seasoned traveller in these parts racing me to shore.'

I let the remark pass without retort, but praise the Lord as I imagine this means the Wartons are probably not at my hotel either.

The Viennese gentleman strokes his long golden moustache and looks at me out of the corner of his eye as we walk.

'I am hurt, *Fraulein*, that you find the company of that English hunter more pleasant than mine.'

'Not at all. I have accepted Mr Selous's overtures a few times because you have been busy romancing every available woman on board. Not to mention some who are supposed to be *unavailable*.'

He gives a small chuckle. 'I am merely trying to provide a little companionship to lonely women.'

'Some of these lonely women I see you flirting with have husbands.'

'I'm doing their husbands a favour, too. They can enjoy their cigars and brandy and I can enjoy their wives.'

He gets a big laugh out of his own wit and I join him.

'Well, at least you are honest about your roguish intentions.' I decide to do a little digging.

'Did Lord Warton tell you that he made some rather nasty allegations against my character?'

'Little mention is made of you around his lordship, since he tends to go into a fit of apoplexy whenever your name is spoken.'

He roars with laughter again.

'You understand, of course,' I say, 'that I am entirely innocent of any wrongdoing.'

'Of course you're *not* innocent, at least to him. He believes you are a meddlesome newspaper reporter who is determined to stick her nose into the controversy over who will keep control of that ditch that connects the Mediterranean to the Red Sea.'

'And what do you believe?'

'I believe you have a very pretty nose. And that it is going to get cut off if you keep putting it in places where you shouldn't.'

Arriving back at the hotel, I find Sarah and Frederick waiting at the dining room door. They are engrossed in conversation like old friends.

Putting on my bravest smile, I let Frederick guide us into the dining room, determined not to reveal my feelings of jealousy and inadequacy, emotions I hate and would not reveal in public even if I was suffering the infamous Chinese torture of a thousand cuts.

'I've stayed here before,' Frederick says. 'The food is very good.'

'Then you should order for us,' Sarah replies. 'We will be helpless, otherwise.'

*Oh my God* – she really knows how to warm the cockles of a man's heart. Her veil is back on. Too bad she wasn't wearing it earlier. In fact, it would have been even nicer if, like Von Reich, she had missed out on getting a room at the hotel.

*Petty, petty, petty, Nellie . . .*

Carol McCleary

The dining hall is pleasant in its coolness and matches the other parts of the hotel with its picturesque stateliness. The small tables are daintily set and decorated daily with the native flowers of Colombo, which are rich in colour, exquisite in form, but void of perfume. I find this particularly agreeable – I don't know why, but many perfumes give me a headache. I believe it's a quirk I acquired from my mother, who never wore perfume for the same reason.

Above our heads are long strips of cloth, fastened to bamboo poles that are suspended within a short distance of the tables. Frederick tells us they are called punkas. They are kept in motion by rope pulleys, worked by men and boys, and send a lazy, cooling air through the building, contributing much to the guests' comfort.

As Sarah asks Frederick a question about the beautiful breakwater we saw from the ship, I look around, soaking in the atmosphere and the scent of exotic foods. Suddenly my reverie is interrupted by an exclamation, and the clap of Sarah's hands.

'I'd be delighted,' she cries.

'After dinner, at about nine, would be the right time to head out,' Frederick says to me.

'Sorry – I was thinking about something.'

'There's a magic show tonight I'm sure you would both enjoy. And Sarah wants to see the famous breakwater. We can stop there on the way to the show.'

'Why don't you two—' I begin, my feeling of being ugly and unwanted taking over.

'You must come,' Frederick insists. 'It's a once in a lifetime opportunity to see a performance of the world's greatest magic trick.'

'Please, Nellie, it'll be such fun,' Sarah implores.

'All right.'

The only thing stronger than my jealousy is my curiosity – and the dread of being left out of anything. My mother says she never deprived me of anything as a child, but perhaps my fear of being excluded comes from being one of the youngest in a family of thirteen children.

While climbing the steps to return to my room, a thought pops into my head, filling in a blank that I wasn't even aware was there.

Sarah wore her veil to lunch.

She always wears her veil in public.

But not when she met Frederick and me in the lounge area, she had it in her hand.

Why would someone who is so easily recognized have taken off her veil?

Finally, a question to which I have a ready answer: She wanted to be recognized by Frederick.

*But why would she want him to recognize her?*

# 36

*Sarah's cablegram.*

The answer to Sarah not wearing a veil when we first met at the hotel came to me when I tried to nap before dinner.

She had revealed herself to Frederick because of the cablegram.

*A stupid threat*, she had said. A physical one? One that would make her seek out the friendship of a well-known hunter for protection?

Threats of bodily harm are not sent by cable – the message had to be more subtle than that – but from her anger, there is no doubt that the contents were meant to intimidate her. Certainly they infuriated her and drove her to make contact with Frederick. So . . . Frederick has a connection to Cleveland . . . now Sarah has a connection to Frederick. Does that mean Sarah has a connection to Cleveland?

Sarah's friendship isn't a safe harbour for me. She's part of the intrigue that began in the marketplace and that still touches me, reaching out from Port Saïd like the tentacles of Jules Verne's giant squid.

I never have been comfortable with the notion of there being two separate intrigues aboard, but trying to connect the love affair of a famous French actress, a fanatical religious uprising in Egypt and the machinations of powerful countries

224

over control of the vital Suez Canal, is threatening to give my small brain a big headache.

Since attempting to get any kind of rest is futile, I pull myself off the bed. Maybe a leisurely bath will relax me for the evening that I'm about to spend with a beautiful actress who obviously has an interest in the same man as I do.

After viewing myself in the mirror, I decide that the only way I could get Frederick to notice me when Sarah is present would be to throw myself in front of an oncoming train. And then it would only be the sound of the train's horn that would direct his attention to my mangled body . . .

Frederick and Sarah are waiting for me at the carriage stand in front of the hotel when I come out.

I keep a dispassionate face but I find the way they stand near each other and talk interesting for its sheer subtlety. Rather than standing face to face as one would when conversing with an acquaintance, they face slightly away from each other, almost as if they don't want anyone to know they are talking. A casual observer might not even realize they knew each other. Or that they had been talking.

Why the charade? What are they up to?

We board a carriage and set out. From the number of people on the streets, it seems that everybody at the hotel and the city at large has come out for a drive, the women and many of the men going bare-headed as a cool evening breeze sweeps in.

When we are out of sight of other Europeans, Sarah takes off her netted hat to get the full benefit of the light breeze. She looks rather young for a woman who became an actress at about the time I was born. It makes me wonder how old she is. I am twenty-two years old and I suspect she must be a decade past that.*

The carriage takes us at a leisurely pace through the town, down the wide streets and past beautiful homes set well back in tropical gardens. We go along Galle Face Drive, which runs along the beach just out of reach of the waves that break on the sandy banks with a deeper, more mellow roar than I have ever heard water produce.

The breakwater, which is a good half-mile in length, is a favorite promenade for the citizens of Colombo, he tells us. 'Morning and evening, gaily dressed people can be seen walking back and forth between the lighthouse and the shore. When the stormy season comes, the sea dashes a full forty feet above the promenade, which must be cleansed of a green slime after the storms are over before it can be walked upon safely.'

Sarah buys a rose from a street vendor and lays it on a plaque that says Britain's heir to the throne, Edward, Prince of Wales, placed the first stone for the breakwater fifteen years ago.

'It is considered one of the finest breakwaters in the world,' Frederick says.

I take his remark as filling a gap in the conversation because he must find her dedication to an old brass plaque a bit unusual. She acts as though it is perfectly natural to put a rose on an old brass plaque – and I do mean *acts* – and my curiosity is aroused.

A titbit about Sarah from the gossip columns back home

* Sarah is forty-five years old, but looks younger and lies about her age. As stated earlier, Nellie also lies about her age – in fact, she is twenty-five. The Editors.

stirs in my head. 'Wasn't there a rumour a while back that Sarah and the prince—'

'Quite,' Frederick snaps. 'We must hurry to make it to the magic show.'

I have inadvertently hit a sore spot relating to the British sense of total loyalty to and defence of their royals. Sarah's name, of course, has long been linked with love affairs with European royalty, but Prince Edward is not just known for his flirtation with Sarah. He is a playboy of international esteem, known for his taste for beautiful women, fine food, aged brandy, and champion racehorses.

As we walk back to the carriage, I can't help but think about Sarah's remark that her lover's family is out to kill her, but I can't see Queen Victoria setting out to commit murder. Of course, if Sarah were pregnant or had already produced a claimant to the throne, who knows what a loyal Brit might do without the Queen's permission . . .

I let out a long sigh and tell myself that I have enough mysteries to contend with without creating another.

'Did you say something, Nellie?' Frederick asks.

'No. Probably just thoughts leaking from the holes in my head.'

'I beg your pardon?'

'Sorry. It's an old American expression.'

That I made up, but it's how I feel.

# 37

'The Indian rope trick is not just considered the most amazing feat of illusion ever performed,' Frederick tells us, 'it's almost as old as the Himalayas. Claims are found in ancient Greek and Egyptian texts that this trick was observed centuries before the birth of Christ. Marco Polo saw it performed during his travels six hundred years ago.'

We are sitting on logs set out in rows opposite a mostly open-air stage, at the back of which is a tall, bushy pear tree.

A drum is beaten and a fakir comes on stage. He has the robes of a monk, wisdom's white beard and the dark eyes of a travelling snake oil salesman. A native boy about ten years old wearing a turban and loincloth joins him.

After much hand-waving and spoken incantations in which I imagine is the language of Ceylon, the old man's demand to the boy is obvious – he wants the boy to go up the tree and bring something back.

'A fruit so tasty only a god is permitted to eat it,' Frederick whispers. 'The fruit is guarded by the god's djinns in the tree.'

The fakir stands over a wide woven basket and plays a horn.

I expect an angry cobra to glide out, but instead a piece of rope emerges The rope continues up and disappears into the foliage of the tree.

'It's being pulled up by a thin line – fishing wire, maybe,' I whisper to Frederick, and get a noncommittal shrug in return.

After the rope disappears into the spread of the tree, and after a bit of coaching, the boy grabs onto the rope. He begins to climb.

The audience cheers in amazement as he climbs hand over hand until he disappears into the foliage.

The fakir stares up at the tree, then moves about the stage yelling at the boy, obviously demanding the boy come back with the fruit.

Instead of the boy descending, shouting is heard above, then cries of pain, and the tree's foliage shakes as if a struggle is taking place among the leaves and branches.

Something drops and the entire audience – including me – lets out a gasp.

It's not a piece of fruit, but an arm belonging to a small boy.

The djinns guarding the fruit are obviously bloodthirsty little demons.

Then another piece drops. A leg.

A woman screams.

I begin to laugh hysterically and Frederick grabs my arm and whispers, 'Don't.'

He's right, it's rude, and I smother my laughter.

More pieces drop, with the head coming last. By now the audience is on the edge of their seats, and staring at the basket that the pieces had been placed in.

The old man goes over to it, looks down into it and shakes his head sorrowfully. Leaning over the basket, he begins to play his horn.

Soon some hair appears . . . and then a head.

It's the boy. Stitches and a raw red gash around his neck show that his head has been sewn back on to his shoulders. As he slowly uncurls from the basket, we see that his arms and legs have been sewn on to his torso.

Finally he steps out of the basket and runs offstage, with the fakir yelling at him for having failed at his task.

The audience responds with loud clapping and coins rain onto the stage, the three of us throwing not a few.

'Amusing,' I tell the other two as we wait for the crowd to disperse.

'You're not impressed?' Frederick asks.

'Of course not. The boy disappears into the front of the tree, then climbs down the back, puts on the bloody make-up and goes through a short tunnel that ends up in the basket. There's a hole in the basket and a tunnel beneath.'

Frederick stares at the stage. 'I wouldn't be certain of that. The stage is raised off the ground enough that you can see beneath it. We would have seen the boy come up.'

'Mirrors,' I say, 'It's all done with mirrors.'

After the fakir and the boy clear the coins from the stage and leave, I make a dash for the stage to prove my point.

I grab the basket and lift it. There's no hole in the bottom of the basket, no hole in the stage beneath it, no mirrors anywhere.

'A twin,' I announce. 'There was a twin to the boy hidden in the basket. A child could easily wrap themselves around the inside of—'

Frederick grabs my arm and pulls me firmly off the stage.

'You are the most impetuous young woman I have ever met.'

'I need to examine the tree.'

'I'm getting you out of here before that fakir casts a magic spell and turns you into a mouse.'

'A mouse? I deserve at least to be a tiger.'

# 38

On the way back to the hotel, Frederick instructs the carriage driver to stop at a market. 'You'll enjoy this place,' he tells us.

The three of us split up and wander about, looking at the exotic merchandise – gems and tapestries, silk so light it seems to float and perfumes that come with a guarantee to seduce your lover.

Sarah goes for the aphrodisiacal scents, Frederick ambles to the huts of the gem merchants, and I drift over to a vendor selling cool lime and mint drinks.

I know better than to let myself get interested in beautiful things – my valise is designed to meet my needs, not my desires.

Strolling about with my drink, for the first time since leaving America I see American money. A silk vendor is wearing it – as jewellery.

He speaks a good bit of English and he tells me that American gold coins are very popular in Colombo as ornaments and command a high price!

'It goes for little as money,' he says.

I already know that. When I presented it in payment for my bills I was told it would be taken at sixty per cent discount. Gold is gold, but American gold is discounted when it is offered to pay a bill! But not if it's to be worn.

'The Colombo gem merchants are very glad to get American twenty-dollar gold pieces and pay a high premium on them,' the silk merchant says.

The only use they make of the money is to put a ring through it and hang it on their watch chains for ornaments. The wealth of a merchant can be estimated by his watch chain, they tell me; the richer the merchant, the more American gold dangles from his chain.

As I walk about, I see men with as many as twenty pieces on one chain. Women prefer daintier jewellery.

Dodging an oncoming group of children running after each other, I step off the main walkway and take a short-cut around a hut to a silk shop when a man approaches and says to me, '*Bonjour, Mademoiselle, nous devons parler.*' We need to talk.

He's a disreputable-looking sailor, a European, who has stepped out from behind the shop. His pants are stained with black smudges, his boots scuffed, and his shirt has no doubt been washed only by sweat and rum for some time. His cock-eyed sailor's cap holds down a mop of unruly dark hair. Add to all this his unkempt beard and the man looks pretty much like any seafarer who hangs around the saloons at ports all around the world – sailors who can't find a berth because their reputation for dereliction of duty and greater sins has spread.

'I don't speak French,' I lie, and turn to walk away from him.

'Hey, sorry, lady, thought you were a Frog.' He has reverted to a working-class Cockney accent.

Turning my back and walking away has only emboldened him.

'Have a drink with me and I'll show you my tattoos. I've got one that dances.'

Frederick is suddenly between me and the man.

'Get out of here. You've made a mistake. Now move on.'

The man leers at Frederick. 'And who are you to give me orders?'

'I'm the man who will beat you so you can hardly crawl away before the police drag you out of the gutter.'

The sailor's hand goes to the hilt of a knife he has strapped to his hip. He gives Frederick an appraising look.

Frederick stares back, giving the man a small smile as he taps his heavy walking stick on the ground. Walking sticks are carried for protection for good reason – they often conceal a weapon, not to mention that the head of the stick can deliver a powerful blow.

A man who has stood his ground with charging bull elephants, Frederick, tall and broad-chested, has the posture of a soldier at the ready.

'Blimey!' The sailor takes his hand off his knife and raises his eyebrows, giving both of us a look of mock surprise. 'Unfriendly blokes, aren't you?' He removes his hat and waves as he bows. 'Your lordship, ladyship.'

He moves off and Frederick offers me his arm.

'Thank you,' I tell him.

'I only intervened to keep you from harming the man.'

I warm to the great hunter. There is nothing like a man defending a woman's honour to raise her esteem of him.

'Unpleasant chap,' he says. 'Probably lost his berth for tapping into the rum cask too often and lives off the beach. You find them often enough in the warmer regions – beachcombers too lazy or dishonest to work, living off fish, fruit and what they can steal.'

As Sarah returns to join us, Frederick says, 'Here is something to remember Colombo by.'

He gives each of us a gold charm. 'This is the Monkey King, who brought peace to the island by ridding it of demons. He brings good luck to those who desire to spread peace in the world.'

We both express our appreciation, but petty woman that I am, I have still not forgotten that he was about to buy me a gift before he saw the Divine Sarah.

Oh, well, the golden monkey is quite charming.

Back at the hotel, Frederick escorts us to our rooms. First we say goodnight to Sarah, then we are at my door when he surprises me with something.

'You are a very special person, Nellie Bly. When I saw this, I knew it should belong to a special person.'

Hanging from a gold chain is a blue sapphire – the colour of his eyes.

I am speechless. Thrilled. Instantly guilt stricken because of my jealous thoughts.

'I— I don't know what to say.'

I grab his lapels and stand on tiptoe to give him a kiss on the cheek. 'Thank you.'

As I turn to leave, he takes hold of my shoulders and turns me back to face him. Before I know it, he bends down and gives me a kiss. A long kiss. 'You're welcome.' He leaves me speechless.

I float into my room and hold the necklace against my chest.

My heart is beating hard. I am breathless, and feel warm all over.

I recognize the symptoms.

I am infatuated with Frederick Selous.

★   ★   ★

The blackboard in the hotel corridor bears the information that the *Oriental* will sail for China the following morning at eight o'clock.

This is my last night in Colombo – I hope. Tomorrow I will embark on the next leg of my trip, to China – I hope. I fall asleep easily, tired from the day, but wake up sweating because I didn't leave my balcony doors open.

Getting out of bed, I take a blanket and pillow with me to set up camp on the wicker chair on the balcony and enjoy the mild night breeze and the bright moon.

My balcony looks down on the large courtyard in the centre of the hotel. It is dark, but the hotel lounge is still open and men are on the terrace, enjoying their brandy, tobacco and conversation.

A familiar figure on the left side of the terrace catches my eye. I recognize the big, broad-rimmed, rugged hat that Frederick wears.

It is too dark to make him out clearly or identify who he is talking to, but I keep watching, the thought of his special gift again warming my heart.

The discussion breaks up and he approaches the terrace doors and goes back inside. As he passes under the gas lamp, I can see that it is definitely Frederick under the hat.

The person he has been talking to is crossing the court-yard towards the exit to the street. When he walks under a gaslight, I gape.

*It's the sailor from the marketplace.*

# 39

My wake-up knock has been arranged for five o'clock and some time afterwards I leave for the ship.

Since Sarah informed me it would be much too early for her to even contemplate opening her eyes, I set out alone.

She did ask if I would go with her later this morning to buy some jewellery, but I told her I was so nervous and anxious to be on my way that I couldn't wait a moment longer than was necessary to reach the boat that was to carry me to China.

In truth, I needed to be alone to deal with all the thoughts rattling around my head.

Frederick and the sailor carried off a deception at the market. They knew each other. So why did they pretend otherwise?

What did Frederick say to the man? *You've made a mistake.* It was a message telling him he'd approached the wrong woman.

He was supposed to approach Sarah.

Frederick didn't protect me from the sailor – he protected the secret that was behind whatever they're concocting. And Sarah is part of it. Hers is a starring role, of course.

And mine? A bit player cast as the romantic interest of the leading man, but who in reality is there to draw attention away from whatever schemes the two stars are involved in. That is when I'm not being battered as the understudy of the female lead.

That special sentimental gift he gave me, the sapphire that melted my heart?

'A bone thrown to a dog.'

I speak loud enough for others on the street to turn and look.

When I think about Frederick in the light of day, my mind unaffected by my feelings, it always boils down to one thing: if it wasn't for Frederick's statement that he personally spoke to Mr Cleveland, my insistence that the man was killed in the marketplace would carry some credibility.

Then again, Frederick insisted to me that he worked on Warton and the captain to keep me from being arrested.

Why would he go out of his way to keep me around?

Is my next role the sacrificial lamb to the slaughter?

After an hour of walking the streets of Colombo for the last time, I head for the dock to find that passengers are being ferried out to the *Oriental*.

Frederick is there, talking with the Wartons and Von Reich, and Sarah arrives on my heels. I get in line to rub shoulders with my enemies as we wait for a boat to take us out. As the boys back at the newsroom would say, it's the only game in town.

Frederick turns to me and says, 'Too windy for an outrigger.'

A fresh breeze is up, creating white caps on the bay.

I agree. 'I already had a bath.'

Everyone has one hand on their hat, or they are making a mad dash for one headed for the bay. Watching the women, Sarah and Lady Warton among them, hanging on desperately to their elaborate headgear, many with veils to protect against the sun and biting insects, once again I am thankful for my simple, unfashionable cap that stays put.

A man and two women disembarking from a carriage catch my attention because of the man's unusual outfit. He wears a wide-brimmed hat not unlike Frederick's distinctive jungle tramping headgear, along with shirt, vest, pants and boots with an unmistakable Australian outback rancher look that I've seen in pictures.

While the outfit would no doubt be considered ordinary work clothing on an Australian ranch, at a Ceylon dock it looks like a very eccentric choice of male attire – or a costume.

A gust of wind comes up that nearly blows off my cap after all, and rips the hats off many a head. Lord Warton makes a dash for her ladyship's hat and Frederick uses his foot to stop his own from taking a swim in the bay.

The 'Australian' looks towards us and yells, 'Well, hello there!'

I don't know which of us he's hailed, but none of us respond and he hesitates for a moment, as if he is puzzled or unsure, then turns to the two women who even at this distance are obviously yapping at each other in a heated manner.

'That outfit he is wearing looks almost like a costume,' I voice my thoughts to Frederick as he joins Sarah and me on a steam launch.

'It is. I've been told he's an entertainer. His name is Hugh Murdock, an Australian who bills himself as the best marksman in the world.'

'Aren't you the best marksman in the world?'

'Perhaps the best hunter, if you will pardon the boast, but I have always been a terrible marksman. Quite wretched, really.

I have to let beasts get so close that I can smell their hot breath before I pull the trigger.'

He nods back at the Australian group gathering their trunks on the pier. 'I hear he also catches bullets in his teeth from a gun his wife fires. Magicians who perform on board get a discount on their fare, so perhaps he'll give us a demonstration.'

'He'd better hope the seas are calm when she shoots,' Sarah says.

I no longer have to wonder whether my reputation as a hysterical female and general troublemaker has preceded me: the purser checking off names on the passenger manifest gives me a hard stare when I give him mine. I can only attribute this to the likelihood that someone who boarded before me has befouled my reputation. My prime candidate for that someone is Lord Warton, though admittedly my list of enemies does have more than one name on it.

Too antsy to remain in my cabin, I stand at the rail and watch the steam launches deposit waves of passengers on the gangplank. As the sharpshooter comes aboard, it's not hard to see that the hostility between the two women has flared again.

'His wife and his assistant,' Von Reich tells me as he appears at my elbow. 'The one who looks young enough to be their daughter is the assistant. His wife is also a marksman, though not as good as he is.'

'Looks like the assistant has annoyed the wife.'

He grins and strokes his handlebar moustache. 'I hear the annoyance may be that the wife resents sharing the marriage bed.'

'Ah . . .'

That the Australians' personal lives are already making the rounds of the ship's passengers doesn't surprise me. A ship churns out rumours faster than a society ball.

'I've heard that the man claims to be the best shot in the world,' I tell Von Reich. 'And that he catches bullets in his teeth.'

'His claim of being the best shot is not valid. I know for a fact he has been beaten by someone much better.'

'Annie Oakley is the best I've ever seen. How can he make the claim of being the number one if he's been bested?'*

'My dear, it's showbusiness, he can claim the moon. Besides, the other sharpshooter suffered an identity crisis after rising from the dead and isn't performing. As for catching bullets in his teeth . . .' he grins, smugly.

'You know how he does it, don't you?'

'Of course.'

'Really? Tell me, please.'

He shook a finger at me. 'No, no, no, that would take all the enjoyment out of it.

I suppose he's right – I'd much rather see the trick and take a guess myself as to how it's done . . . before I'm told the secret.

As the Australians go by, I think for a moment that the wife is going to slap the assistant as the older woman hisses, '*Bitch*.'

I give Von Reich a sage nod. 'I suspect that statement sums up the relationship between the parties.'

★   ★   ★

* Nellie was taught to shoot by Annie Oakley when Nellie participated in Buffalo Bill's Wild West show. Like Nellie, Annie lied about her age to keep a 'girl' image. The Editors.

At one o'clock we sail and I stand at the bow, torn with conflicting emotions. I am on my way again! The race is still on! But I know that the mystery sparked by Cleveland's words in Port Saïd may also have followed me aboard, and I am sick to death of the shadow it has cast. With Egypt thousands of miles away, I have resolved not to play whatever game is afoot with Frederick, Sarah and whoever else is involved in the intrigue.

When I am back in the States, I will put the matter before the British ambassador in Washington, and demand that Mr Cleveland's Amelia be contacted and the odd key that is still in the heel of my shoe be given to her.

The whole sad affair has not only taken some of the joy of the journey away, but it has also put a dark cloud over me that threatens to rain on my quest to complete the trip in less than eighty days. Besides, there is one thing I know about game playing – when someone else names the game and has all the advantages, you are bound to lose.

So, I will simply concentrate on the stories I'm writing about my travels and finishing the race on time. I'll step on no one's toes and set out on no adventures.

How can I get into any trouble just minding my own business?

# 40

Hugh Murdock walks out of his cabin bathroom and into a hornet's nest. 'Will you two please shut up? You have been clawing at each other like two cats for hours.'

'Get rid of this bitch and I'll have some peace,' his wife, Irene, says.

'Go to your cabin,' Hugh tells Cenza, his assistant.

Cenza points an accusatory finger at his wife. 'She put me in a room so deep in the hole, I'll have fish for companions.'

'I hope they're sharks!' Irene hisses.

Irene and Cenza exchange one more poisonous look before the younger woman leaves.

'I'm divorcing you as soon as we get back home,' Irene tells her husband. 'You brought that little slut along to humiliate me. She approaches you just before we're ready to sail from Australia and you use some of the last of our money to buy her a ticket. She can't shoot, she can't—'

He waves away her ire. 'Be quiet, something's happened.'

'Something? *Lots* of things have happened besides your infidelities. You're not just a bad husband, you're a bad gambler and a bad businessman. What you haven't lost at cards, you threw into that crazy scheme to raise camels outback. We're stranded, we don't have the money to get back home. We don't even have the money for a hotel when this damn ship docks.'

He ignores her and stands at the porthole, chewing on his lower lip.

'What's the matter with you?'

'Someone's on board that I know.'

'Someone you've slept with? I'm not surprised, considering how many bitches you've crawled into bed with.'

He turns and meets her eye. 'You don't understand. The person I saw can solve all of our problems.'

'Our problem is that we're broke—'

'That's what I'm talking about. I smell money.'

Irene calms down. 'Tell me more.'

He grins. 'Something's afoot and I can smell money. And I'm going to get myself a piece of it.'

'You mean you're going to get *us* a piece of it.'

# PART SIX

## DAY 31

### *Against the Monsoon*

# 41

At first it is so wet – warm, so sultry and foggy, and so damp in the Straits of Malacca, that everything rusts, even the keys in one's pockets, and the mirrors are so sweaty that they cease to reflect. Then the winds they call monsoon pick up and the seas punish us as we sail for the Far Eastern ports of Penang, Singapore and Hong Kong, headwinds making the run slower than I had hoped for.

I work on the story about Colombo, both the one I will cable back and the one that will be placed in a secret journal I have begun. I am logging everything that happened since I saw Mr Cleveland leave the ship in the wee hours that first day at Port Saïd. If I am lost overboard for whatever reasons, I don't want his last wish to die with me. And I am petty enough to want to see my killer hanged by the neck if my trip to Davy Jones's locker comes from any hand but that of my maker.

The bane of ocean travelling soon strikes and almost all of the passengers disappear into their cabins to hide their misery as seasickness becomes an epidemic.

During dinner the chief officer relates the woes of people he has seen suffering from seasickness, which threatens now to overpower even the captain. I listen for quite a while, merely because I cannot help hearing, but finally his stories of miserable passengers makes me get up and run outside for the rail. After I do my duty and avoid having it slapped back at me by the wind, I straighten my shoulders and march determinedly back to my dinner plate rather than let the malady control me.

I find it amazing that Sarah is able to stay in her stuffy cabin and only occasionally seek a breath of fresh air. I am still clueless about the purpose of her goal to keep her presence a secret, but I have no doubt now that her journey is intertwined in some way with the events at Port Saïd. My nose is dying to snoop further despite my vow of abstinence from foreign intrigue, but at the moment the most I can hope for is that I keep my sea legs under me and don't have to use them to swim if the ship goes down.

While I occasionally see Frederick, he is clearly stricken with the ubiquitous nausea, and I am secretly pleased that I have fared better than the great hunter.

The terrible swell of the sea, the rise and fall of mountains of water during the monsoon is beautiful. I sit, breathless, on deck, watching the bow of the ship standing upright on a wave then dashing headlong down as if it intends to carry us to the bottom of the sea.

In a moment of insanity, I fell in love with an adorable monkey in Penang and bought it on impulse. The seller assured me it did not bite, but I soon discover that the little beast has a temper worse than Medusa, sending me fleeing for safety after I make the mistake of opening his cage after it has been banged around by the lurching ship.

During the night the sea washes over the ship in a frightful manner and my cabin fills with water, which, however, does not touch my berth. Escape to the lower deck is impossible, as I can't tell the deck from the angry, pitching sea.

As I crawl back into my bunk a feeling of awe creeps over me, and with it a definite feeling of satisfaction. I think it is very possible that I have spoken my last word to any mortal, that the ship will doubtless sink, and if the ship does go down, no one will be able to tell whether I could have gone around the world in seventy-five days or not. The thought is comforting, for I feel I might not get around it in even a hundred days.

I don't worry over my impending fate because I am a great believer in letting unchangeable events take their course. 'If the ship does go down,' I think, 'there is time enough to worry when it's going. All the anxiety in the world can't change it one way or the other, and if the ship doesn't go down, I will have wasted time fretting.'

So I go to sleep, lullabied by the sloshing water on my cabin floor, and slumber soundly until the breakfast hour. When I look out of my cabin the ship is making its way laboriously through a very frisky sea, but the deck is drained, even if it is not dry.

With the seas slowly returning to normal, I make my evening constitutional with less concern that I will be washed overboard, but more worry over whether I will get to Hong Kong in time to board the ship that will take me across the Pacific.

I'm absorbed in my own thoughts when I hear the voice of the Australian sharpshooter.

'That's my demand.'

He is standing under a stairwell. I can't see him in the darkness well enough to recognize him, but it's definitely his voice and I can make out that distinctive outback rancher hat he sports. I can't see who he is talking to, but his tone was a hard one, as if in response to an argument.

My poor nose twitches at the prospect of not finding a reason to loiter around to find out, but feeling that the eyes of his companion might be on me, I keep moving, hoping he will say something that gives me a clue as to what his demand is – and to whom it's directed.

When I mention the incident later to Von Reich, who finds little intrigue in what I observed, he suggests a way I can ask the sharpshooter myself about the conversation:

'Volunteer to have him shoot a cigarette from your lips.'

I will omit my unladylike reaction to his comment. However along with all the other passengers and crew that can squeeze into the dining room, I show up to watch the sharpshooter's performance.

Von Reich kindly signals to me to join a table that includes Lord Warton, the captain, an Italian count and his wife from Lombardy. I spot Frederick standing along the back wall with others unable to find a seat in the packed room.

I don't bother asking Lord Warton about his wife's absence. Her poor disposition to seafaring is well known.

The lights are turned down in the room and up on the stage as Hugh Murdock's wife appears and introduces her husband as the 'world's most amazing and accurate marksman!'

He emerges, stage right, to a burst of applause.

Murdock puts on an impressive demonstration of marksmanship, shooting playing cards on a spinning wheel and the flames off candles. A thick wooden barrier stage left is used to catch the bullets.

The assistant appears stage left and after she is introduced, takes up a position in front of the barrier and holds up a kitchen match.

Murdock counts twelve paces back from her, placing himself nearly in the curtained area stage right, and fires from that position, the bullet nicking the match head and igniting it.

'It's not over yet!' Von Reich whispers to me. 'I've seen these sorts of acts performed in Budapest and London.'

The assistant lights a cigarette with the burning match. Taking aim, the sharpshooter fires and knocks the tip off the cigarette.

The assistant doesn't move and he fires again, exploding the cigarette in its entirety.

A well-deserved standing ovation erupts.

Murdock holds up his hand to silence the applause.

'Now, ladies and gentlemen, we will present the most death-defying physical feat ever performed on a stage. My wife will fire a bullet at me . . . and I will catch it in my teeth.'

He holds his hand over his eyes, trying to see out into the dark audience. He is not wearing his usual hat. 'Yes, there he is, Mr Frederick Selous, the noted hunter and explorer. Please come forward.'

Frederick joins the sharpshooter on stage.

'I'm sure you all know that Mr Selous is the world's greatest hunter, a man who has trekked the wilds of the Dark Continent and bagged the most fierce creatures found anywhere. No one has greater expertise than this renowned hunter on how to load and fire a weapon. His life has depended on such skill a hundred times over when he has faced charging beasts.'

The assistant brings out a small table covered with a black velvet cloth and sets it in front of the two men. The wife places a rifle on the table and two cartridges next to it.

'Mr Selous, would you please load the rifle with one of the cartridges and fire it into the barrier. A light calibre weapon is being used to keep down the noise,' Murdock tells the audience.

Frederick fires into barrier.

'Are you satisfied that the weapon is fully functional and capable of bringing down a charging lion?' he asks Frederick.

'I wouldn't want to face a lion with this calibre, but a well-placed shot from it would certainly bring down smaller game.'

'Would it kill a man, sir?'

Frederick smiles. 'Certainly. Men are small game.'

Murdock hands Frederick a small knife with its blade open. 'Please carve your initials on the lead part of the bullet.'

Frederick marks the bullet and offers it back to the sharp-shooter, who holds up his palms to block the hand-off.

'No, please, I don't want to touch the bullet or the gun. If I did so, the audience would justly believe I had substituted another bullet by sleight of hand and have the marked one already in my possession. Please load the rifle with the bullet and place it back on the table.'

Frederick slips the cartridge into the chamber and places the rifle on the table.

Murdock invites Frederick to leave the stage amidst a round of applause and then has his wife join him and asks her if she is ready to shoot a bullet at him.

'If I must,' she says.

'Make sure you are satisfied with the weapon and that it is ready to fire,' he tells her.

She examines the weapon briefly, cocks it, and lays it back on the table.

'I am ready, but—'

'No buts, my love, these people have paid good money – well, would have paid good money had they not been a captive audience on a ship. Either way, they deserve to see the most dangerous and incredible feat ever performed on stage!'

She starts to hand him his distinctive hat and give him a peck on the cheek, saying, 'I'll try not to miss, dear,' but he steps back and holds up his hands, telling her, 'We must not touch, there must be no trick of a hand faster than the eye of the audience.'

Finally, Murdock takes up his position in front of the barrier with his wife, rifle in hand, on the other side of the stage. The assistant has gone off stage, behind the wife.

Murdock appears rather nervous and pats at the sweat on his forehead, but it's easy for me to see it's an act.

A drum-roll starts with a low tempo, which slowly builds as the wife gets into a shooting stance, cocks the rifle and slowly raises it to aim.

She starts a countdown as the drum beats louder: 'One . . . two . . .'

'Three' is lost in the bang of the drum and the sound of the shot.

The man's head snaps back, blood sprays wide and his whole body slams back against the barrier. His mouth gapes open and a bullet falls out.

No one moves or breathes in the room.

A cry of surprise and agony breaks the silence.

It comes from the wife.

The rifle slips out of her hand and onto the stage.

# 42

Before most of the ship is awake I am at Frederick Selous's door. He surprises me by being fully dressed and ready to leave his cabin.

'I was expecting you,' he explains. 'Let's go for a walk.'

'Why were you expecting me?'

He gives me a sour frown as he steps out of the cabin and shuts the door behind him. 'I've learned to expect you at the scene of a sensational news story.'

I stop short in the corridor. 'I beg your pardon, *Mr Selous* – you make it sound like I find my way to crime scenes chasing police wagons. That's hardly been the case. If anything, I've been the one chased.'

'You're right, I apologize. I was up half the night with the captain and others going over the accident.'

'Accident?' I say it with a deliberate tone of sarcasm.

He responds with a raise of the eyebrows and a shake of the head. 'Let's take a brisk walk before it gets too warm. I need to clear my head from the captain's cheap cigars and immature brandy.'

We walk briskly, indeed, with me almost running to keep pace with his long legs.

After a complete lap around the ship in stony silence, I

wait until we are out of earshot of others, then stop to get my curiosity satisfied.

'What happened last night? What went wrong?'

'Two things. The first was that Murdock chose to add what is considered magic's most dangerous conjuring trick to his simple sharpshooting act. And he got careless.'

'Was it the first time he tried to catch a bullet?'

'No, he did it a number of times over the past few months. But it only takes one error to end a life. Do you know how the trick is done?'

'No, but I think Von Reich does.'

'Yes, he volunteered to assist the captain in the investigation. However, Mrs Murdock explained the trick and we examined the weapon to confirm her statements.'

'Which were?'

'There was a malfunction. There are different ways to perform the trick, but with some common features. A member of the audience is asked to mark the bullet so it can be identified later.'

'As you did.'

'Yes. In most cases the magician uses sleight of hand to substitute the marked bullet for a fake one that will not fire because it has an insufficient load of powder, or is made of wax, or is otherwise rendered impotent. The fake bullet is fired and the magician, who has palmed the real bullet, pretends to catch it and spit it out into his hand.'

'But I watched closely. Murdock never touched the weapon. And you fired it to make sure it was real.'

'I put a cartridge with a lead bullet head into the gun and fired it. The cartridge I next placed into the weapon, the one

Carol McCleary

Murdock was supposed to catch in his mouth, was also real, but the lead head had been altered so his wife was able to slip it off.'

'How could she have slipped the head off the cartridge? It was in the gun.'

'There's a trick to cocking the gun that permits the cartridge to drop out, into her hand. The cocking action brings a blank into the chamber to be fired.'

'How does the bullet get to his mouth?'

'He had a bullet hidden in his mouth when the act started. When the blank is fired, he spits out the bullet as if it's the one I marked.'

'How does he get the one you marked to show to the audience?'

'As he steps forward with the wet bullet in his hand, his wife gives him a handkerchief to wipe it. The hand-kerchief—'

'Has the real bullet in it. And he switches bullets. Clever. It's sleight of hand, after all. Handing him the hand-kerchief would be a natural thing for her to do. So what went wrong?'

'It appears that Murdock was negligent in preparing the weapon. He placed a live bullet rather than a blank in the secret chamber. It's quite easy to do, they look alike. It's not the first time a mistake like this has happened. A moment's lack of concentration will do it, and from what his wife has said, lately he had been indulging not only in liquor, but in what the French call white angel.'

'Cocaine.'

He gives me a surprised look.

I shrug. 'You'd be surprised at what a crime reporter has

256

to deal with. What did the wife say was driving him to drink, and worse?'

'She intimated financial problems, but naturally we didn't probe any further.'

'*Naturally.*'

He doesn't miss the sarcasm in my tone and he becomes noticeably stiffer.

'All right, Nellie, why don't you tell me why we should have stretched the poor woman on a rack to get a confession out of her for killing her husband.'

'I don't know that she deliberately killed her husband. Maybe she didn't, but someone wanted him dead and she may have information that will lead us to who that is.'

'Come now, blank cartridges are made to look like real ones. It's not that difficult for a mix-up to occur.'

'A deadly mix-up.'

'With a trick that has a history of going amiss. Von Reich said that of the nine magicians who've regularly performed the act over the past half-century, five have died. Because it's so complicated, it is inevitable that something will go wrong if the trick is performed enough times. And when it does, the result is deadly.'

'Hmmm,' I reply. To keep the conversation going, I add, 'I would think that since she pulled the trigger, and everyone on board knew she was angry at her husband over whatever he had going on with his pretty young assistant, the notion of the wife shooting her cheating husband might at least have been discussed.'

'That thought was bandied about last night and in fact, the captain asked her straight out.'

'What was her reply?'

'That if she had been in a murderous mood, she would have shot the assistant and not her husband.' He grins. 'The captain found her logic rather convincing.'

So did I, but I wasn't ready to admit it.

He clears his throat. 'Nellie, my advice to you is not to go any further with your suspicions than you have with me.'

'Or once again you will police my actions?'

He stops and confronts me. 'I believe I have apologized profusely for my clumsy attempt to do what I thought was the right thing for my country in Ismaïlia. For some reason, ever since we left Colombo, you seem to have had . . . shall we say . . . a change of heart over the warm relationship we were developing.'

He is getting tight-jawed, but I don't know how to defuse the situation without lashing out with an accusation about intrigues involving Sarah and the sailor in Colombo.

'Nellie, it is inevitable that you will attempt to make something out of this event, which already antagonizes the captain. There is nothing here but an accident of the sort that has happened before. Do you understand that?'

His authoritative tone makes me fume because I know it is his way of chastising me and he has no right to do so.

'Maybe if you could see beyond the end of your nose, Mr Selous, you would learn something. I observed several unusual incidents involving Mr Murdock, the most obvious being his marital difficulties. But he also recognized someone at the dock who didn't acknowledge him in return.'

Frederick throws up his hands in exasperation. 'Perhaps the person didn't hear him, maybe he was mistaken about who he was hailing, or just maybe you are making the proverbial mountain out of a molehill.'

'I overheard him making a demand on the person.'

'A demand for what? From who?'

'I— I don't know.'

'And your interpretation of this demand you know nothing about?'

'He wanted money.'

'That's a giant leap.'

'Hardly. It fits nicely with his wife's hints that they were having financial difficulties.'

'And from this you have constructed a murder plot?'

'There are questions that need to be asked and answered. If that leads to a murder plot, then so be it.'

'You are amazing.' He shakes his head. 'Completely amazing. You really do have a lively imagination. I can understand why Lord Warton considers you a rabble rouser. The pieces you have put together, the tiny fragments that could fit in so many different ways, simply don't make a coherent picture.'

Once again he throws up his hands. 'Next you will be telling me that you believe Murdock's death is connected to the marketplace murder you witnessed.'

So that he can't see my face and read my thoughts, I turn away.

He grabs my arm and turns me back to face him. 'Don't you dare attempt to tread that path again. If you start rumours flying about that incident at Port Saïd, I will personally suggest that the captain lock you in your cabin for the duration of the voyage.'

Jerking my arm free, I take a step back. 'To protect who?'

He flinches. 'Why . . . you, of course.'

'I'm not so sure about that. I do recall that you are the sole witness to Mr Cleveland being alive after I saw him murdered. Then you handled the weapon that killed Mr Murdock. Is it possible you *accidentally* substituted a live bullet for a blank?'

His face flushes with anger and I fear I've crossed the line. I turn and leave, peddling my feet as fast as they will go. I groan aloud at my stupidity.

Why does the devil make me do these things?

# 43

It is the evening of 23 December and I am sitting by myself on deck in a dark corner, listening to men singing and telling stories. We are approaching Hong Kong and I will be leaving the ship for another after a stopover of several days.

Plagued with guilt for essentially accusing Frederick of murdering the sharpshooter, I hid out in my cabin until I could no longer tolerate the screeches of my monkey, who appeared even angrier at me than I was at myself.

In remorse over my stupidity and rudeness, I had my steward take a small parcel to Frederick containing the beautiful sapphire necklace he gave me in Colombo. The accompanying message was simple and to the point: 'I do not deserve this.'

In a funk ever since, I have come out on deck and hidden in the darkness, rather than stay in my cabin and stare at the walls while the monkey howls accusations.

I'm cursing myself silently when Frederick sits down beside me. I cringe in anticipation of the recriminations I deserve and am sure I will get.

He hands me the sapphire necklace. 'This was given to me by mistake. It belongs to you.'

'I told you, I don't deserve it.'

'You didn't earn it, it was a gift given out of respect and admiration.'

'You couldn't have respect for me after my accusation.'

'Your accusation? You mean that little matter of accusing me of murdering a fellow passenger? Don't worry about it, I simply tucked it away with the ones charging me with being Lord Warton's lackey and talking to a dead man on a beach.'

I start to get up to flee but he takes my arm. 'Please, I'm only joking. I'm guilty of throwing a few accusations your way, too. I have to keep in mind that you really do know how to punch. The moment I pushed, you lashed out.'

'I had big brothers. I had to learn how to defend myself.'

'May I escort you around the sights of Hong Kong?'

I ponder the question for a moment. I am shamelessly pleased that he seeks my company and also worried that he does so to keep an eye on me.

'Thank you, but I have already made other plans. I'm going to pay a visit to Canton to see a notorious prison. From the dock, I have to go immediately to arrange passage to San Francisco before I explore the sights.'

'Excellent. Then it's settled.'

'Settled?'

'That you will contact me once your passage is organized so I can escort you to the prison.'

He leans over, fastens the necklace around my neck and gives me a long kiss. 'Good night, Nellie.' Once again he leaves me speechless.

I go down to my cabin to tell the monkey he will soon be

in Hong Kong. 'Do you have any idea what Frederick's motives are for wanting my companionship?'

He lets out a screech as loud as the ship's emergency siren.

# PART SEVEN

## DAY 42

### *Hong Kong*
### The Bamboo Torture

# 44

Our first glimpse of Hong Kong is in the early morning: gleaming white, castle-like homes terraced on a tall mountainside. The ship fires a cannon as we enter the bay, as this is the custom of mail ships, according to the captain.

The bay is a magnificent basin, walled by high mountains. Mirror-like in the bright sun, it is dotted with strange craft from many countries: heavy ironclads, torpedo boats, mail steamers, Portuguese lorchas, Chinese junks and sampans.

A Chinese ship wends its way slowly out to sea, its strange, broad stern hoisted high out of the water, an enormous eye gracing its bow.

An exotic, graceful thing, I think, but I hear an officer say it is awkward in rough seas.

I leave the boat with Frederick and walk to the pier's end, where we select sedan chairs to carry us to the town. I expected to travel in a ricksha, but until we reach the town, the steep roads are not suitable for wheels.

The sedan carriers are as aggressive as the hackmen around railway stations in America, competing for our attention and patronage.

We follow the road along the shore, passing warehouses of many kinds and tall balconied buildings filled with Chinese families. Their washing is stretched out on poles, much as you would hang out a coat and the poles are fastened to the balconies so that it looks as though every family in the street has placed their clothes on display.

Turning off the shore road, our carriers ascend a path which winds about from tier to tier up the mountain, and then back down again. When we reach the business district, I wave goodbye to Frederick. I have to get to the office of the Oriental and Occidental Steamship Company and learn the earliest possible time I can leave for Japan to continue my race.

Only thirty-nine days have passed since I left New York and I am in China – halfway around the world. The *Oriental* not only made up the five days I lost in Colombo, but she also reached Hong Kong two days sooner than I expected, and that with the northeast monsoon against her.

I enter the steamship office feeling very much elated at my good fortune, with never a doubt but that it will continue.

'Will you tell me the date of the first sailing for Japan?' I ask a man at the desk.

'In one moment,' he says, and going into an inner office he brings out a man who looks at me enquiringly.

When I repeat my question, he asks, 'What is your name?'

'Nellie Bly,' I reply, with some surprise.

'Come in, come in,' he says nervously.

I follow him into an office. After I am seated, he says, 'You are going to be beaten.'

'What? I think not. I have made up my delay.'

Despite my optimism, I am surprised by his statement, wondering if the Pacific has dried up since my departure from New York, or if all the ships on that line have been destroyed.

'You are going to lose it,' he says with an air of conviction.

'Lose it? I don't understand. What do you mean?' I demand, beginning to think he is mad.

'Aren't you competing in a race around the world?' he asks, as if he believes I am not Nellie Bly.

'Yes, quite right. I am running a race with Time.'

'Time? I don't think that's her name.'

'Her? Her?' I repeat, thinking, poor fellow, he is quite unbalanced.

'Yes, the other woman, she is going to win. She left here three days ago.'

I stare at him stupidly. 'The other woman?'

'Did you not know? The day you left New York another woman started out to beat your time, and she's going to do it. She left here three days ago. You probably met somewhere near the Straits of Malacca. She says she is authorised to pay any amount to persuade ships to leave in advance of their time. Her editor offered a thousand dollars to the Oriental and Occidental if they would have the *Oceanic* leave San Francisco two days ahead of time.

'They wouldn't do it, but they did do their best to get her here in time to catch the English mail for Ceylon. If they had not arrived here early, she would have missed that boat and been delayed ten days. But she caught it and left three days ago, while you'll be delayed here five days.'

'That is rather hard, isn't it?' I say quietly, forcing a smile to my lips that comes from nowhere near the heart.

'I'm astonished you did not know anything about it. She led us to suppose that it was an arranged race.'

'I don't believe my editor would arrange a race without advising me,' I say stoutly. 'Have you no cables or messages for me from New York?'

'Nothing,' he replies.

'Probably they don't know about her.'

'Yes, they do. She worked for the same newspaper you do until the day she started her trip.'*

'I don't understand it,' I say quietly, too proud to show my ignorance on a subject of vital importance to my progress. 'You say I can't leave here for five days?'

'That's correct, and I don't think you can get to New York in eighty days. She intends to do it in seventy. She has letters to steamship officials at every point requesting them to do all they can to get her on. Have you any letters?'

'Only one, from the agent of the P. and O. requesting the captains of their boats be good to me because I am travelling alone. That is all,' I say with a little smile.

'Well, it's too bad because I think you have lost it. There is no chance for you. You will lose five days here and five in Yokohama, and you are sure to have a slow trip across the Pacific in this season.'

'I promised my editor that I would go around the world in seventy-five days, and if I accomplish that I shall be satisfied,' I explain stiffly. 'I am not racing with anyone. If someone else wants to do the trip in less time, that's their concern. I promised to do the trip in seventy-five days, and so I will.'

\*     \*     \*

* The woman is Elizabeth Bisland, who worked at the *World* and became an editor at *Cosmopolitan*. When the *Cosmopolitan* publisher heard about Nellie's trip, he sent Bisland with only hours' notice around the world, travelling in the opposite direction, certain that the west to east route would beat Nellie's time. Nellie relates how she learned of the 'race' in Hong Kong, but never mentions Bisland's name, in *Around the World in 72 Days*. The Editors.

I leave the steamship company office with thoughts chasing their tails around my head. My statement that I am not in a race was of course, an attempt to hide my horror that I might actually be beaten by someone who has stolen my idea.

*Put the fear away in a dark cabinet*, I tell myself. I will surely lose if I go about dreading failure rather than anticipating success.

I'm in a ricksha en route to my hotel when I see a familiar figure in another one, turning into a street ahead. Lady Warton.

I find it odd that she is alone. I'm also without a companion, but that is my way and lot in life. Her ladyship, however, is of a social milieu that would frown upon her presence on the chaotic streets of Hong Kong without an escort. She's also more reclusive and conservative in her social affairs than I imagine most women of her position to be.

More out of curiosity than anything else, I signal my driver to turn at the same corner. The first thing that comes to my reporter's mind is that the woman is on her way to a romantic rendezvous . . . with someone besides her husband, of course.

As we come around the corner I spot her stepping down from the cart in front of a restaurant.

Two men are standing by to greet her.

I'm so startled I forget to tell the ricksha driver to turn back round and end up going by them. I turn my head in the opposite direction as I'm carried past the group as they head into the restaurant.

My heart is pounding and my mind is whirling.

Frederick Selous is one of the men who greeted Lady Warton.

The other is the drunken sailor who was so offensive at the Colombo market.

# 45

I continue on to my hotel, where a room has been secured for me by the purser of the *Oriental*. The purser also had the monkey sent over to the steamship *Oceanic* with my instructions that it be cared for by my cabin steward until we set sail.

As I'm crossing the lobby to go to my room a woman approaches me.

'Miss Nellie Bly?'

'Yes.'

'I'm John Cleveland's wife'

'Amelia?'

'Yes, Amelia Cleveland.'

I suffer a rare infliction of speechlessness and simply stare at her. She's a bit older than me, about thirty perhaps. An attractive, conservatively groomed woman with heavily rimmed eyeglasses, and very blonde hair pulled back in a bun and mostly hidden under her hat, she's wearing widow's black and speaks with a British accent.

'I understand you observed the terrible incident.' She dabs at the corner of her eye with a lace handkerchief.

'Yes, yes, I did. It was . . . a tragedy.'

Getting my wits together, I direct her to a couch so we may sit facing each other.

'What a surprise,' I tell her. 'I didn't realize you were in Hong Kong. I was prepared to track you down to the ends of the earth once I returned home.' I shake my head, still bewildered by her sudden appearance.

'John planned to meet me here. His company was posting him here after he finished visiting his accounts in Egypt. It must have been dreadful for you to see him cut down before your eyes.'

I can only nod. How would I tell her about the blood gushing from his wound, the anguish on his face?

'He spoke your name to me. His last thought was of you.'

'Oh . . . oh, my.' She stares down at her lap and appears ready to collapse in grief.

'I'll get you a glass of water.'

She grabs my arm as I rise.

'Did he give you anything for me?'

'Oh Lord, I forgot! Of course he did. I'll get it.'

I hurry away towards the stairs to my room, leaving her on the couch. I can handle most things in life but I am not good with grief. I flee rather than confront it. My mother says it's because I grieved so deeply when my father was taken from us when I was six. Disappearing to my room to get the key from my shoe will give me an opportunity to regain my composure.

I'm stopped short of the stairway by a clerk who hands me an envelope bearing the insignia of the cable office. I open it and read the response from the London correspondent as I go up the stairs.

JC 34 YR OLD BACH – WORKED CUTLERY CO 8 YRS – DIED CONSUMP 2 YR LONDON – WENT GRAVESITE

I freeze in place halfway up the stairs and stare at the message. John Cleveland was indeed a cutlery salesman, for eight years. But he died of natural causes two years ago at the age of thirty-four. The correspondent visited the gravesite to make sure he really was dead and buried.

Most importantly, the man was a *bachelor*.

Spinning around, I stare at the woman, who has got up and is now standing by the couch. Whatever she sees in my face causes her to panic. She turns and runs for the door.

I start after her and become entangled with a man and woman coming up the stairs. As I brush by them, their 'How rude!' remark follows me as I race for the entrance.

Once I am outside, I look right and left, starting this way and that, but she is gone, swallowed by the crowds of people on the sidewalk and the armies of sedan chairs and rickshas flowing in both directions along the street.

Reluctant to give up the chase, but knowing it's hopeless, I slowly go back inside.

As I head for my room a suspicion strikes me and I am able to confirm it as soon as I get there and check the exact position of my personal effects: my room has been searched.

As I have so few possessions on the trip, it's easy for me to check and see that nothing is missing, not even my jewellery, which makes it a certainty that the intruder was not a sneak thief.

Standing at the window I stare down at what appears to be organized chaos on the street below. Hong Kong is a city that never sleeps and I shall get little of it myself tonight as my mind wrestles with the singular events of the day.

No matter what I do, the marketplace incident thousands of miles behind me still seems to dog my heels.

Lady Warton has apparently joined whatever scheme Frederick, Sarah, the sailor and Lord knows who else has cooked up.

My room has been searched; and now a woman has pretended to be the widow Cleveland.

However I toss the pieces, they don't fall into a revealing pattern like Chinese tea leaves, though I do have one sudden revelation: I'm glad I took Frederick up on his invitation to spend time together. While he is keeping an eye on me, I can keep an eye on him.

# 46

A chit slipped under my door the next morning from Frederick informs me that he will be delighted to see me – in an hour.

I groan aloud and stumble back to bed and under the covers to deal with the situation. I have many questions to ask the great hunter, but from experience I know that a frontal attack will not work. I shall have to be more subtle than in the past.

Mr Selous has declared war on me.

I shall respond in kind, but rather than engage in verbal fisticuffs, I must be clever and subtle, neither of which are my strong points. I must show restraint and learn something from him rather than revealing what a weak hand I have been dealt.

I have to learn how to duck.

I'm still completely perplexed about last night's incident with the woman who claimed to be Amelia Cleveland, and her desire to obtain what John Cleveland gave me.

Had she known it was a key, I'm sure she would have asked for it.

What the key is for, who the woman really is, and which of my shipmates are in league with her, are all a source of puzzlement to me.

Neither moping nor hiding my head under the blankets

will prove fruitful, so I get up to prepare my body and mind for my meeting with Frederick.

When I come down from my room and into the lobby, I give Frederick a pleasant smile. All books on etiquette decree that as a proper young lady, I am to shine in conversation – though not so brightly as to eclipse my male companion – and listen intently with eyes open a little wider than normal as he relates his triumphs of manhood.

In other words, I will know my place in the presence of a man this morning.

He gives me a gentlemanly bow. 'And how are you today, Nellie?'

'In a hurry. There are many things to see in Hong Kong and I intend to see them all. Let's get going.'

I fly by him, biting my tongue to keep from lashing out at him about his rendezvous with Lady Bitch.

Outside the entrance I let out a big sigh and pause to let him catch up. So much for Miss Manners. This will not do.

I have to change my attitude or I shall not be able to flush out the game.

'Please forgive me, Frederick. I received some peculiar news at the steamship line company yesterday and it has me quite befuddled.'

After quickly telling him that I have found myself in a competition not of my making, I ask what we will see first.

'We are going to scale the highest mountain on Hong Kong Island.'

Victoria Peak, 1,800 feet high and named in honour of the queen, is fortunately 'scaled' largely by elevated tramway, which takes one two thirds of the way up, to Victoria Gap.

Frederick explains in the tram that during the summer months Hong Kong is so hot that those who are in a position to do so seek the mountaintop, where a breeze blows all the year round.

At the Gap we secure sedan chairs, and it requires three men to a chair ascending the peak, just as it did over the rough terrain from the pier. At the Umbrella Seat, which is merely a bench with a peaked roof, everybody stops long enough to allow the carriers to rest before we continue on our way, passing sightseers and nurses with children.

After a while the carriers stop again, and we travel on foot to the signal station.

The view is superb. Indeed, they say that at night it is unsurpassed, that one seems to be suspended between two heavens because thousands of boats carry a light after dark, which along with the lights on the roads and in the houses, creates the impression of a sky more filled with stars than the one above.

'This is heaven,' I tell Frederick. I mean it, and I am pleased that I have kept my tongue on a leash.

'Quite. Now if you are game for an overnight boat ride, we will descend to Dante's Inferno – that prison in Canton you wanted to see.'

'Unlike the colony, Canton is a real hundred per cent Chinese city,' Captain Grogan tells us after we board his coastal ship, the *Powan*.

The captain, who has lived for years in China, is a very bashful man – and a most kindly, pleasant one.

Soon after the *Powan* casts off from Hong Kong, night

descends and I slip away alone and go on deck where everything is buried in darkness.

Softly and steadily the boat glides along, the only sound – and the most refreshing and restful sound in the world – is the lapping of the water. To sit on a quiet deck, with a starlit sky the only light above or about, and the sound of water kissing the prow of the ship, is, to me, paradise.

They can talk of the companionship of men, the splendour of the sun, the softness of moonlight, the beauty of music, but give me instead a willow chair on a quiet deck, the world with its worries and noise and prejudices lost in the distance, and the glare of the sun, the cold light of the moon blotted out by the dense blackness of night.

My reverie is interrupted by my own insistent sense of reality. It seems there is always a snake to spoil paradise, and the news that I am in a race not of my making has somewhat tainted my pleasant feelings about my trip. No matter how dark things have become since Port Saïd, the race has always been nothing but pure pleasure. Now I have to worry about beating not only a fictitious character, but also a fellow reporter, all the while wrestling with the intrigues and machinations that seem to be all around me since the death of 'John Cleveland'.

Frederick has not given me the slightest clue as to what schemes he may be involved in. Had I not recognized the cur of a sailor with him at the restaurant, I would have imagined the meeting between him and Lady Warton to be a romantic one.

Not wishing to work my brain or keep my tongue quiet any longer, I send a message to Frederick that I have retired and go to my cabin.

Before daybreak we anchor at Canton.

*Sedan chair*

# 47

While we are having breakfast, the Chinese guide, Ah Cum, whom the captain has secured comes aboard and quietly supervises the preparation of the luncheon we are to take with us.

The first thing he says to us is 'A Merry Christmas!' and as the date has slipped our minds, we appreciate his polite thoughtfulness.

Ah Cum tells us that he was educated in an American mission located in Canton, but he assures me, with great earnestness, that English is all he learned. He would have none of the Christian religion.

The captain says that besides being paid as a guide, Ah Cum collects a percentage from merchants for all the goods bought by tourists whom Ah Cum brings to their shops. Of course the tourists pay higher prices than they would otherwise, and Ah Cum sees they visit no shops where he is not paid his fee.

'A very clever fellow,' Frederick grumbles.

Ah Cum is dressed rather smartly, in beaded black shoes with white soles, and navy blue trousers – or tights, more properly speaking – tied around his ankles and fitted very closely over most of the leg.

Over this he wears a blue, stiffly starched shirt-shaped

garment, which reaches his heels, and atop that he has a short padded and quilted silk jacket, somewhat similar to a smoking jacket.

His long, coal-black pigtail, finished with a tassel of black silk, comes all the way down his back to touch his heels. On the spot where his hair braid begins rests a round black turban.

Ah Cum has sedan chairs ready for us as we step off the gangplank. His own chair is a neat arrangement in black – black silk hangings, tassels, fringe and black wood poles finished with brass knobs. Once inside, he closes it, and is hidden from the gaze of the public.

Our plain willow chairs have ordinary covers, which to my mind rather interfere with the view, and we have them tied back.

We have three carriers to each chair, which is not very egalitarian since Frederick's carriers are burdened with twice the weight that mine are. The carriers are barefoot, with tousled pigtails and their navy blue shirts and trousers are much the worse for wear, both in cleanliness and quality, than Ah Cum's dandyish garb.

Ah Cum's own carriers wear spotless white linen garments, gaily trimmed with broad bands of red cloth, looking very much like circus clowns costumes.

Ah Cum's chair leads the way, with ours following, as we push down the crowded streets and are carried along dark and narrow lanes through and around fish stands, until we cross a bridge which spans a dark and sluggish stream.

What a picture Canton makes. They say there are millions of people here, yet the streets, many of which are roughly paved with stone, seem little over a yard in width.

The shops, with their gaily coloured and handsomely carved

signs, all have open fronts, as though the whole side facing the street has been blown out. In the rear of every shop is an altar, gay in colour and often ornate in adornment.

I have been warned not to be surprised if the Chinese should try to stone me while I am in Canton. Their anger and bitterness over the opium wars that forced them to sell the foul substance to their own people, and other injustices inflicted by Western nations, runs deep.

Captain Grogan says that Chinese women have been known to spit in the faces of female tourists when the opportunity arises. However, I experience no trouble. Instead, as we are carried along, men in the stores rush out to look at me, not taking any interest in Frederick, but gazing at me as if I am something entirely new. They show no sign of animosity. The few women I meet stare curiously at me, and less kindly.

The people do not appear happy; they look as if life has given them nothing but hard work and little gain – expressions not unlike those of the coalminers in my own home state of Pennsylvania.

Surprisingly, the thing that seems to interest the people most about me are my gloves. They gaze upon them with wonder, and sometimes they are bold enough to touch them.

When Ah Cum tells me that we are in the streets of the city of Canton, my astonishment knows no limit. The streets are so narrow that I think I am being carried through the aisles of some great marketplace. It is impossible to see the sky, owing to the signs and other decorations, and the compactness of the buildings; and with the open shops, like stands in a market except that they are not even cut off from the passing crowd by a counter.

Sometimes our little train of sedan chairs meets another,

and as the way is too narrow for both trains to move at once in safety, we stop for a moment and there is great yelling and fussing until we have passed unscathed.

As we are approaching the prison I want to see, Ah Cum tells us that it is the place where political executions are carried out. There is much dissent against the tyrannical rule of the Dowager Empress and a great deal of that dissent ends up in spilled blood on the execution grounds.

'Why do you want to see the prison?' Ah Cum asks me during a rest stop.

'The high drama of life and death is meat and potatoes for a crime reporter,' Frederick answers.

I hope it is my reporter's instincts and not a perverse desire to see the macabre.

# 48

We go in through a gate where a stand erected for gambling is surrounded by a crowd. A few idlers leave it to saunter lazily after us. The prison is very unlike what one might suppose it to be – at first sight it looks like a crooked back alley in a country town.

As we pass rows of half-dried pottery, a woman shaping pots in a shed stops her work, apparently to gossip about us with another female who has been arranging the items in rows.

'The execution grounds,' Ah Cum says, indicating with a sweep of his hand an area about seventy-five feet long by twenty-five feet wide at the front, narrowing at the other end.

The ground in one spot is very red, and when I ask Ah Cum about it, he says indifferently, as he kicks the crimson coloured earth with his white-soled shoe. 'Eleven men were beheaded here yesterday.'

Frederick wanders off back to the pottery, telling me, 'I've seen enough blood of men and animals for several lifetimes.'

Ah Cum adds that it is usual for ten to twenty criminals to be executed at one time. The average number per annum is something like 400. Ah Cum also tells me that in one year, 1855, over 50,000 rebels were beheaded in this narrow alley.

I shudder at the thought of that many souls being violently sent off to heaven or hell because of political differences.

While he is talking I notice some roughly fashioned wooden crosses leaned up against the high stone wall. Supposing that they are used for some religious purpose before or during the executions, I ask Ah Cum about them.

A shiver snakes down my spine when he answers, 'When women are condemned to death in China, they are bound to wooden crosses and cut to pieces.'

'Good Lord!'

'Men are beheaded with one stroke unless they are the worst kind of criminals,' the guide adds. 'The worst are executed like women to make their deaths more discreditable. They tie them to the crosses and strangle them or cut them to pieces. When they are cut to bits, it is done so deftly that they are entirely dismembered and disembowelled before they are dead. Would you like to see some heads?'

Ah Cum's tales could no doubt be as tall as those of any other guide – and who can equal a guide for colourful and exaggerated tales? So I say coldly: 'Certainly; bring on your heads!'

As Ah Cum instructs me, I tip a man with a silver coin. With the clay of the pottery still on his hands, he goes over to some barrels which stand near the wooden crosses, puts in his hand and pulls out a head!

'The barrels are filled with lime,' says Ah Cum, 'and as the criminals are executed, their heads are thrown in. When they become full they are emptied out and reused. Prisoners who die in jail are always beheaded before burial.'

He tells me that if a man of wealth is condemned to death in China he can, with little effort, buy a substitute, who will be killed in his place. The Chinese are very indifferent about death; it seems to have no terror for them.

I follow Ah Cum to the prison building and am surprised to see all the doors open. But when I go inside, I see that all the prisoners have thick, heavy boards fastened about their necks, so it is no longer a surprise that the doors are unbarred: there is no need to lock them.

We go next to the law court, a large, square, stone-paved building. In a small room off to one side we are presented to some judges who are lounging about smoking opium. In still another room we meet others playing fan tan. At the entrance there is a large gambling establishment. I am not sure that justice is given its due reverence here.

'Now you must see the tools of persuasion,' Ah Cum chortles.

Two judges lead us into a room to see the instruments of punishment: split bamboo to whip with, thumbscrews, pulleys on which people are hanged by their thumbs, and other such pleasant things.

Two men are brought in who have been caught stealing. The thieves are chained with their knees meeting their chins, and in that distressing position are carried in baskets suspended on a pole between two carriers.

The judges explain to me, through Ah Cum, that as these offenders have been caught in the act of taking what did not belong to them, their hands will be spread upon flat stones and with smaller stones every bone broken.

Afterwards they will be sent to the hospital to be 'cured'.

I elect not to see the punishment.

I thought I had heard the most grotesque and painful punishment man could conceive from an American who had lived many years near Canton: a small bridge spanning a stream in the city is used to hang criminals in a fine wire hammock, with all their clothing removed. A number of sharp knives are laid at the end of the bridge, and everyone crossing while the man is there is compelled to take a knife and slash the wire-imprisoned wretch.

However, Ah Cum tells me that bamboo torture is worse – and not as uncommon in China as one would naturally suppose from its extreme brutality.

This most gruesome and horrifying punishment is exceedingly cunning in its ability to deliver not just slow, excruciating, unimaginable pain, but an unbearable anticipation of the suffering to come.

Offenders subjected to it are pinioned naked in a standing position with their legs spread directly above a bamboo sprout.

So that I understand this punishment in all its dreadfulness, Ah Cum explains that although a bamboo sprout looks not unlike the delicious asparagus, it is of a hardness and strength equal to iron. When it starts to come up, nothing can stop its progress. It is so hard that it will pierce anything on its way up; let that be asphalt or something equally dense, the bamboo goes through it as readily as though the obstruction didn't exist.

The bamboo grows with marvellous rapidity straight up into the air for thirty days, during which time it may reach a height of seventy-five feet. Then it stops. When its growth is finished it throws off a shell-like bark, its branches slowly unfolding and falling into place. The branches are covered with a soft, airy foliage finer than the leafage of a willow.

On its relentless upward course, then, it goes through the man who stands there dying, dying, conscious for a while until fever mercifully kills his awareness and at last, after days of suffering, his head drops forward and he is dead.

'But that is not any worse than tying a man to a stake in the boiling sun, covering him with quicklime and giving him nothing but water to quench his hunger and thirst,' Ah Cum assures me. 'The man holds out and holds out, for it means life, but at last he takes the water that is always within his reach. He drinks, and when he perspires it wets the lime and the lime begins to eat.'

I am dizzy and my mind is shutting down as we leave the torture area with Ah Cum continuing to describe yet more appalling punishments. Suspending a criminal by his arms and twisting them behind his back, so that as long as he keeps his muscles tense he will live, but the moment he relaxes he ruptures his blood vessels and his life floats out in a crimson stream.

The unfortunate is always suspended in a public place, says Ah Cum, where magistrates watch so that no one may release him.

Friends of the condemned flock around the man of authority, bargaining for the man's life; if they can pay the price extorted by him the man is taken down and set free; if not, he merely hangs until his muscles give out and he drops to death.

There is also the method of burying a man but leaving exposed his head. His eyelids are fastened back so that he cannot close them, and facing the sun he is left to die.

Sticking bamboo splints under the fingernails, then setting fire to them, is another merry way of punishing wrongdoers.

'Stop!' I yell at the startled guide. 'No more descriptions. You are torturing *me*.'

'Are you superstitious?' Ah Cum asks me.

'Superstitious? I suppose so, at least as much as anyone.'

'Do you wish to try your luck?'

I think about the race to the finishing line that has been imposed upon me and I answer in the affirmative.

'Come. We will go to the Temple of Five Hundred Gods and you will see your fortune laid out before you.'

With Frederick also in tow, at the temple Ah Cum places joss sticks in a copper jar before the luck god. Then he takes from the table two pieces of wood, worn smooth and dirty from frequent use, and which, placed together, are not unlike a pear in shape.

With this wood – he calls it the 'luck pigeon' – held with the flat sides together, he makes circling motions over the smouldering joss sticks, once, twice, thrice, and drops the luck pigeon to the floor.

'If one side of the luck pigeon turns up and the other turns down, it means good luck. If they both fall in the same position, it means bad luck. Since they both turned the one way, I will have bad luck.'

He does not appear pleased with the result.

I take the luck pigeon. I am so superstitious that my arm trembles and I can feel my heart beat in little jumps as I make the motions over the burning joss sticks.

Dropping the wood to the floor, one piece turns one way and one the other, and I grin with relief.

I'm going to have good luck.

It is Frederick's turn but he refuses his try.

'I make my own luck,' he says.

# 49

Ah Cum takes us to a building he says will be a pleasant place to enjoy our luncheon. Once through the high walls we come upon a pretty garden with a mournful sheet of water undisturbed by a breath of wind. In the background the branches of low, overhanging trees kiss the still water where long-legged storks stand, graceful birds made familiar to me by the pictures I have seen on Chinese fans.

The guide leads us to a room that is shut off from the courtyard by a large carved gate. Inside are hard wooden chairs and tables.

As we sit down we hear chanting to the strange, plaintive sound of a tom-tom and a shrill pipe.

'We are in the Temple of the Dead,' Ah Cum tells us.

I remember that it is Christmas Day. 'We are eating Christmas luncheon in the Temple of the Dead,' I say to Frederick.

'Let's hope the dead don't interfere with this fine food.'

While we eat, Ah Cum explains the death ritual.

'It is customary at a person's death to build a bonfire at night, and cast into the fire household articles, such as money boxes, ladies' dressing cases and the like while the priests play their pipes.

'The demon that inhabits all bodies leaves the body to save

the property of the dead, and once they trick him out, he can never re-enter, so the soul is saved.'

I climb the high stone steps to the water-clock, which, Ah Cum tells me, is over 500 years old, and has never run down or been repaired.

In little niches in the stone walls are small gods, and before them are smouldering joss sticks. The water-clock consists of four copper jars, each about the size of a wooden pail, which are placed on the steps one above the other. Each jar has a spout from which trickles a steady drip-drip. In the bottom jar is an indicator, very much like a foot rule, which rises with the water, showing the hour.

On a blackboard hanging outside the temple, the time is displayed for the benefit of the townspeople. The uppermost jar is filled once every twenty-four hours, and that is all the attention the clock requires.

I am near the gate at the bottom of the steps when a man dressed all in black suddenly grabs my purse and shoves me at the same time, sending me down while he runs through the gate.

I am on my feet again and rushing for the gate when a group of people on the outside suddenly converge upon the gate, keeping me from opening it.

Frederick is outside the gate. He yells, 'Stop!' to the fleeing man and gives chase while I push at the gate with ever-growing anger until I blow my stack and throw myself, screaming, at the obstacle.

The people pressing against the gate scatter as I hurtle through and head off in the direction I saw Frederick and the thief disappear in. I have not gone a dozen paces when Frederick comes around the corner of a building, holding up my purse in triumph.

'Got it.'

'Thieves always have time once it is in their hands; it only takes a second.' I rummage through the purse.

'He dropped it as I gave chase. Is there anything missing?'

'Nothing is missing.'

'Excellent. So the luck pigeon was right – you have good luck.'

'Luck has nothing to do with the thief grabbing my purse. And it didn't have anything to do with the people suddenly keeping me from pursuing him. Like you, some people make their own luck.'

I am steaming with anger and instruct Ah Cum to get me back to the *Powan* immediately.

It's obvious that the purpose of grabbing my purse was not to steal my money, but to search for the key.

Just as evident is how convenient it was that Frederick Selous lured me to a place where such a stunt could be easily arranged, which means that our tour guide is an accessory.

I am cold and distant to Frederick afterwards.

'Ask your friend the thief for a tip,' I tell Ah Cum when I refuse him a gratuity after he delivers us back to the ship's gangplank.

He says nothing, but glows with guilt and resentment.

I draw the line at paying to get mugged.

On our return to the *Powan* I am conscious of an inner feeling of emptiness. It's Christmas Day and I think with regret of dinner at home, although I know it is past midnight in New York.

Suffering from nausea and a headache, I go to my cabin, and shortly we are on our way to Hong Kong.

The thief got nothing from me except my last hope that

Frederick had been spending time with me because of his feelings for me.

That and my sense of security. I am in China, thousands of miles from the Mahdi and Port Saïd, and I'm still not safe.

I feel as if I have lost another battle.

# 50

On my last night in Hong Kong I am badgered by the purser of the *Oceanic* and a fellow passenger who will join me on the ship across the Pacific to see *Ali Baba and the Forty Thieves*, as given by the Amateur Dramatic Club of Hong Kong.

They tell me that the theatre in Hong Kong knows only a few professional troupes, but the amateur actors in the English colony leave little to be desired in the way of splendid entertainment. The purser says that the very best people in town take part, and they furnish their own stage costumes. The regiments stationed here also turn out very creditable actors in the form of the young officers.

We travel to the theatre in sedan chairs instead of carriages, the narrow streets posing a challenge for horse-drawn conveyances. The sight of handsomely dressed women stepping out of their chairs, with daintily coloured Chinese lanterns hanging fore and aft marking the course the carriers take in the darkness, is very affecting. It is a luxury to have a carriage, of course, but there is something even more luxurious in the thought of owning a chair and having full-time carriers in one's employ.

A fine chair with silver mounted poles and silk hangings can be bought, I should judge, for a little more than twenty dollars. Some women keep four and eight carriers; they are so cheap that one can afford to retain a number. Every member of a well-established household in Hong Kong has his or her own private chair with carriers waiting to pick up the poles.

Many men prefer a coverless willow chair with a swinging step, while many women have chairs that close entirely, so they can be carried along the streets secure against the gaze of the public. Convenient pockets, umbrella stands and places for parcels are found in all well-appointed chairs.

The *Arabian Nights* tale is a new version of the old story filled with local hits arranged for the club by a military captain; the music is by the bandmaster of the Argyll and Sutherland Highlanders. The beautiful and artistic scenery is designed and executed by two army men, as are the limelight effects.

Inside, the scene is bewitching. A rustling of soft gowns, the odour of flowers, the fluttering of fans, the sound of soft, happy whispering, a maze of lovely women in evening gowns, mingling with handsome men in the regulation evening dress – what could be prettier?

If American women would only ape the English in going bonnetless to the theatre, we would forgive their aping of us in other respects, and call it even. Upon the arrival of the Governor the band plays 'God Save the Queen', during which the audience stands.

The play is pleasantly presented, the actors filling their roles most creditably, especially the one taking the part of Alley Sloper.*

After Ali Baba discovers the cave of the Forty Thieves and

* 'Alley Sloper' was Victorian slang for a person who snuck out when the landlord came to collect the rent and sloped down an alley to sneak away. The Editors.

brings part of their treasure back to his brother's house, he meets Morgana, a clever slave girl.

I cannot take my eyes off Morgana because I recognize her. 'What do you know about her?' I whisper to the purser, who has made himself an authority on Hong Kong plays.

'Professional actress. Australian, I think. Travelling drama group went broke and stranded her here. Name's Virginia Lynn.'

I resist the impulse to tell him that not long ago she identified herself as Amelia Cleveland and fled my hotel with me on her heels.

Begging the pardon of my companions, as soon as the play is over I part company with them and station myself at the stage door.

She comes out with two men but turns off in a different direction. I catch up with her.

'Good evening, Amelia.'

She glares at me. 'Go away.'

'You can talk to me,' I reply, 'or to the police.'

That stops her. She swings around and confronts me. 'I've done nothing for the coppers to take an interest in me.'

I approach so I am almost nose to nose with her, and lock eyes. 'Nothing except attempt to steal a valuable object through impersonation.'

She takes a step back. 'No. I was just a messenger.'

'A messenger? We'll see if the Hong Kong police think that is as funny as I find it.'

'What do you want? Go, get away from here, go on that silly race you're involved in. Leave me alone, I've troubles enough.'

'You're going to have even more troubles if you don't tell me why you told me you were John Cleveland's wife.'

'It was a part I was hired to play, that's all.'

'Who hired you? Selous?'

'Who?'

'Tell me who hired you.'

'I didn't get a name. A woman offered me two quid to go to the hotel and tell you I was John Cleveland's wife and had come to get his property.'

'Which woman?'

'I don't know, she never gave her name.'

'What did she look like?'

Virginia Lynn gives that one some thought. 'I can't really say. Met me out here in the dark, just like you. I never really got a look at her. She wore one of those high fashion hats with a thick veil.'

'What was the colour of her hair?'

The actress shrugs. 'Not really sure. Maybe brown.' She shakes her head. 'Not really sure.'

'What did her voice sound like?'

'I don't know. You have an American accent. Hers was British.'

'What else did she tell you?'

'She said she was John Cleveland's wife and that Cleveland had given you something that belonged to her family.'

'Did she tell you what it was?'

'No. She said just to say I was his wife and you'd know what to give me.'

'Did she tell you why she didn't want to ask for it herself?'

'I asked her that. She said she was too emotional about it. That's all I know. I got two quid and now I've got a headache. Leave me alone.'

'Anything about the way she dressed that stood out? Brooch, necklace—'

'Her shoes. High heels, really exotic leather, light brown, had bumps on it – bumps with holes or nicks, maybe some kind of snake or something.'

We part, her almost at a run, and I secure a chair to take me back to my hotel.

Two women obviously fit the description the actress has given – Lady Warton and Sarah. The accent isn't important. I've heard Sarah imitate a British accent.

It's also obvious that half the European women in Hong Kong probably fit Virginia's vague description.

Nor does it let Frederick Selous off the hook. He has an intrigue going with both women and probably arranged the whole charade. Having a woman hire the actress was clever, because it is easy for a woman to disguise herself behind big hats and scarves and veils. A woman's size, shape and age are much easier concealed than a man's.

Murder in Egypt and international conspiracies that have already extended thousands of miles, and threaten to follow me around the other half of the world . . . it's all too much for a young woman from Cochran's Mills, Pennsylvania, population exactly 504.

Especially when I have another woman to worry about – the one causing me grief by turning my adventurous race against time into a competition.

# PART EIGHT

## DAY 45

*To the Land of the Mikado*

# 51

My first order of business upon boarding the *Oceanic* is to get quickly to my cabin and make sure both my possessions and my little simian friend were transferred from the *Oriental* in good order.

I meet the stewardess in the corridor and ask about my monkey.

'We have met,' she says dryly.

She pulls up her sleeve to reveal that her arm is bandaged from wrist to shoulder.

'What did you do?' I ask in consternation.

'I did nothing but scream – the monkey did the rest!'

I hasten away from her complaints and go into my cabin to confront the little devil. He sees me and screeches as he throws nuts at me through the bars of his cage.

'Keep that up and you will have to swim back to land.'

He replies in monkey talk that I gratefully cannot decipher.

Shortly before we are to push away from the pier for the voyage to Japan, I step outside my cabin door to find the ship's most mysterious recluse in the corridor, reading a cablegram.

Sarah gives me a grimace. 'Well, at least I am as important as a racehorse.'

I raise my eyebrows and she shakes her head. 'Nothing,

my dear, just mumbling. I came to insist that you come with me to see Madame Xi Shi.'

The monkey screeches at her from behind me.

'What is that?' she asks.

'A mistake.'

On our way to the outer deck, Sarah explains that she's heard the famous Chinese spiritualist is waiting at the gangplank for the purser to clear her boarding papers.

'I saw her perform in Paris three years ago. She has a true gift for calling forth the spirits of the dead.'

'Maybe I should ask her to give John Cleveland a call.'

We take a place at the railing along with the others who have gathered to watch Madame Xi Shi's entrance. An elegant sedan chair with tightly closed curtains is at the foot of the gangplank, with carriers standing by. A Chinese man and two women, all dressed in black – servants to the spiritualist, I assume – are also standing by the chair.

The assistant purser comes onto the deck and shouts down permission to board, and the sedan chair starts up the gangplank.

'Well, she is certainly privileged,' I say. 'I'm sure even a queen would walk up.'

'She would never make it up on foot,' says Sarah. 'You'll see why.'

At the top of the ramp, the curtains are opened to reveal a tiny woman much shorter than my own barely five feet of height. She reminds me of a ceramic doll, very beautiful, delicate and fragile. One wrong movement and she'd break into a million pieces. Her skin is pale white, emphasizing her red lips and cheeks. Her eyes are highlighted with turquoise eyeshadow and lined in a deeper green. Her raven hair is twisted in coils, making a fat bun on the top of her head. Sticking out of it are little oriental sticks with very small yellow feathers at each end. I can't see her hands; they are hidden in the folds of her flowered silk robe that conceals her figure.

Her red silk dress is exquisite, the dainty pattern embroidered with gold and silver thread, and set off with a red silk umbrella.

As she is assisted out of the sedan chair by the female servants, I realize why the gangplank would have been a mountain to her. Her feet, encased in red slippers, are abnormally short and stubby.

'Lotus feet,' Sarah whispers.

The male servant leads the way and the two female servants assist Madame Xi Shi as she walks across the deck and through a door to the interior. Even with the assistance, she sways more than a person ordinarily would . . . yet her movements are graceful, and could even be considered suggestive.

'Lotus feet?' I repeat.

'Yes. Her feet were bound when she was a child so they grew bunched up rather than straight out. They are only about three inches long. She's a Golden Lotus, because that is considered the most desirable length.'

I look down at my own feet. They are not excessively long for a woman, but compared to Madame Xi Shi's, they look like planks.

'That swaying walk is called the lotus gait. Chinese men consider it quite erotic.'

'So how do they create lotus feet?' I ask Sarah.

'It begins by bandaging the foot at about six years of age, before the little girl's arch is fully formed. Her toenails are cut way back so they can't become ingrown and all the toes and the arch are broken.'

I shiver. 'Good Lord. Why do they do that?'

'So the toes can be folded under the foot, up against the sole. That way the front half of the foot grows backwards and bunched up. Over the years, the binding is tightened each day, until the foot is fully deformed and stops growing.

I am dumbfounded by the sheer horror of it.

'Chinese sex manuals list dozens of ways for a man to play with a woman's deformed feet,' she says.

I decide to change the subject. 'Did you get to know Madame Xi Shi when she was in Paris?'

'No, I was busy with a play, but a friend was quite taken by her when she opened a channel between him and his dead mother. Her name, of course, has historical significance in China. It's the name of one of the Four Beauties of ancient China. Do you know the story?'

'Loosely,' I am lying of course, trying to appear intelligent to a woman who is proving to be as knowledgeable as she is beautiful.

'There were four women in China's history who were of such incredible beauty that many legends about them arose. Their physical features were said to be so dazzling that if they walked by a pond, the fish would drown because they forgot to swim; birds would fall out of the sky because they would stop flapping their wings—'

'Flowers would faint and fall over,' I interject as a guess.

'The legend says that flowers would close their petals in shame, but I suppose that's close enough.'

Sarah retreats to her cabin and I stay at the railing and watch two other passengers board. They are familiar to me –

Hugh Murdock's widow and his young assistant – but I find their manner towards each other strange: instead of two cats snarling at each other, they are cheerfully chatting, the widow showing the younger woman a jade bracelet on her wrist while behind them comes a line of porters carrying not just their luggage, but boxes of new purchases. Many boxes.

The widow appears to have made a nice recovery from having killed her husband in front of an audience. The gods have clearly smiled upon her financially, too, since she no longer appears to be burdened with money problems.

It is simply too much for my suspicions brain to believe that the death of the sharpshooter isn't connected to all the other strange occurances since Port Saïd. I'm still convinced that Murdock spoke to someone he spotted on the Colombo dock who he could blackmail.

I have a feeling his wife knows who it is. And if I don't ask, I won't find out.

*Mind your own business*, my good sense tells me, but I'm not listening.

# 52

Two hours later, when I'm certain she has unpacked and settled into her stateroom, I am knocking at the 'grieving' widow's door.

The door whips open. 'Put it—' She is wearing a robe, her wet hair is in a towel, and she is barefoot. She stares at me, her expression turning sour.

'I thought you were the steward. What do you want?'

'My name is Nellie—'

'I know who you are, you're that nosy newspaper person.'

I smile sweetly. This isn't going well. Her face is flushed; whisky and cheap perfume radiate from her. Rather early in the day for libations.

'I was a great admirer of your husband—'

She lets out a coarse burst of laughter. 'Well, you'd be the only one. Was he diddling you, too? He never could keep it in his pants.'

'I'd like to compose a story about what happened on the *Oriental*.'

'I know what you're up to, but you came knocking on the wrong door. I'm not telling you anything.'

'Your husband was murdered.' It is a shot in the dark to see her reaction – which is hostile. I take a step back as she moves forwards, ready to lunge at me.

'You little bitch, you'd better mind your own business or you'll be answering to me.'

She steps back into the room and I move closer. 'I'll pay you to tell me who your husband recognized at the dock.'

The door to the stateroom bathroom opens and the assistant steps out, naked, ribbing her wet hair. She sees me and stops short. 'What—' She recovers quickly and grins, not bothering to hide her nakedness.

The widow leers at me. 'What's good for the goose is good for the gander.'

I stumble back, avoiding a broken nose as the door slams in my face.

*Whew.*

At least it wasn't a wasted visit. Before I knocked on the door it had been obvious to me that someone had given the window a financial reward, but now I have added more pieces to the puzzle: she has been warned not to talk to me. And her relationship with the assistant is a far cry from what they earlier demonstrated in public.

The liaison between the two women is unlikely to have been something that happened overnight while Murdock's body still lay warm. That raises an interesting question: what was the purpose of the public clawing at each other if they were having an intimate relationship?

Had Murdock been aware of his wife's affair with his assistant? More importantly, did the affair play any role in his death?

My encounter with the woman has not resolved the biggest question of all, however: is there any relationship between Murdock's death and that of John Cleveland?

Well, this leg of my journey is turning out to be very interesting. Upside down on the bottom of the world, everything looks a bit cock-eyed.

*Steamship RMS* Oceanic
*Hong Kong to San Francisco run*

# 53

We are sailing between Hong Kong and Yokohama, Japan, as the New Year approaches. Standing at the bow, the forbidden zone, I let the wind and ocean spray blow over me as I stare at the horizon and wonder why I have been so fortunate as to find myself on this great adventure – and worry that I will not succeed, that the copycat reporter will not just steal my thunder but humiliate me into leaving my profession.

Black and white is how I've been told I see things. Win or lose. No compromises.

It is a fault, I know, but it is how I feel. It is probably why I also hold so furiously on to Mr Cleveland's memory – like a dog that's hopped into the back of a meat wagon, I have clamped my jaws onto the matter and nothing in the world will make me let go.

Casting aside these dark thoughts about my imperfections, I ruminate about the race. My fate lies with the ship because this last leg of my journey is by far the longest I've taken – over 1,600 miles to Yokohama, Japan, and then nearly 5,000 miles across the wide Pacific to San Francisco. After that, it's the iron horse across the continent to the East Coast.

The quiet of the sea and my avoidance of company on this leg have left me alone with my thoughts, a dangerous situation that too often gets me into trouble. Pondering the fact that there is a magician on board whose speciality is reading sealed messages, and he will put on a New Year's Eve performance, is exactly the sort of thing to stir up that overactive imagination Frederick Selous and Lord Warton accuse me of possessing.

Naturally, I have hatched a plot to shed some light on the mystery with a little sleight of hand myself, and before the ship's bell rings in the new year it will be time to put my plan into effect.

In just a few hours the year 1889 will be found only between the pages of history books and 1890 will be born.

The day has been so warm that we wear no wraps. In the forepart of the evening the passengers sit together in the social hall talking, telling stories and laughing. I don't feel like socializing, but I force myself to participate because the audacity of my plan has me feeling nervous and I need a distraction.

The captain owns an organette which he brings into the hall, and he and the ship's doctor take turns at grinding out the music.

Later in the evening we go to the dining hall where the purser has punch, champagne and oysters for us – a rare treat which he had prepared in America just for this occasion.

Afterwards a jolly man from Yokohama, whose wife is equally jolly and lively spirited, teaches the assembled passengers a song consisting of one line sung to a melody quite simple and catchy: 'Sweetly sings the donkey when he goes to grass, sweetly sings the donkey when he goes to grass, Echo! Ec-ho! Ec-ho!'

I sip my punch as I listen to the passengers singing and laughing. I don't dare imbibe the champagne, because I will need steady legs and my wits about me.

When the magic show is announced, we assemble in the dining room once again where a small stage has been erected.

It's time for my own magic to come into play. The plan I've concocted is to make whoever hired 'Amelia Cleveland' in Hong Kong expose themselves.

To carry out my scheme, I need Sarah, Lord and Lady Warton, and Frederick at the same table, so I sweet-talked the captain into inviting them all to his table – and threw in Von Reich for good measure because he seems to be joined at the hip with the Wartons. I will be seated with them, so I can see their faces when I spring my trick.

Getting the two recluses, Lady Warton and Sarah, to the table was a challenge, but the captain convinced her ladyship to attend, though she still wore a veil. And Sarah I coaxed from her cloister by challenging her to attend in disguise. It was a challenge she couldn't ignore and she decided to assume the character of an elderly Russian dowager, a role she once played.

No matter what my suspicions are of Sarah, I am not only fond of her as a person, but like the rest of the world, I am awestruck by her talent. Frederick confided in me that he once saw her on stage in Paris in a role in which she never left her chair – yet mesmerized the audience and overshadowed the other performers.

The magician calls himself the Great Nelson. At the beginning of the show, paper, pencils and envelopes are provided to members of the audience, who are invited to jot down a short message, no more than ten words, and place the paper in the envelope and seal it.

The envelopes are made of paper too thick for the magician to see through even if he held them up to the light.

When it is time to collect the envelopes from the passengers, the Great Nelson says, 'Now I will need a volunteer to collect the sealed messages.'

I jump up from my seat and immediately begin gathering envelopes.

'Madam, please make sure the messages are sealed and that there is no envelope among them that the human eye can see through.'

Gathering the envelopes, I slip in my own, making sure it is close to the top so it will be selected early in the performance. I hand him the stack on stage and turn around to return to my seat.

'You are not finished, young lady.' He turns to the audience. 'To prove that I am using my miraculous ability to see through the envelopes, I will have this charming lady hand them to me one at a time.'

'Oh, I can't—'

'Let's have a hand for this young woman who has so generously volunteered her services.'

I smother a groan as the audience claps. I need to be back at the table, watching my companions.

'Please hand me the first envelope,' he tells me.

I grimly pass it over. He hardly looks at it and announces, 'The message inside reads: This ship is the best ship.'

He rips open the envelope and reads the message aloud again, exactly as he did before he looked. Peering out to the audience, he holds up his hand to shield his eyes from the lights which make it much brighter onstage. 'Is that correct?' the magician asks someone, then holds up the message in triumph to the audience. 'As you witnessed, I read it correctly *before* opening the envelope.'

Another round of applause, then I hand him the second

envelope. He pronounces the message inside without looking, then tears open the envelope and reads the writing aloud, confirming its contents about the size of a hat with a woman in the audience whom I recognize as having been a fellow passenger with me since Colombo.

My envelope is the third one I hand him.

'Now this is a bit unusual,' he tells the audience before opening it. 'It reads: Virginia Lynn sends her regards.' He opens the envelope and extracts the paper I wrote on. He reads the message aloud, then shields his eyes and asks the audience, 'And would the author of this missive confirm that I am correct?'

No answer, and he repeats the question. Finally, not wanting to see the man embarrassed, or threaten his reputation because of my scheming, I timidly raise my hand. 'I wrote it.'

'And is it correct?'

'It's correct.'

Standing sadly on the stage, handing the magician another envelope, I suppress a desire to run out of the room screaming. What a fiasco! The words of Robert Burns come to mind about the best laid plans of mice and men going astray.

Defeated by lighting! I had planned to be at the table and see the faces of my suspects when Virginia Lynn's name was spoken. Instead, I am onstage and unable to see the audience because of the bright stage lights.

All I have managed to achieve is to look ridiculous to at least one person in the audience: whoever hired Virginia Lynn.

When my envelope duties for the Great Nelson are finished, rather than return to my companions I pause by the table and whisper to Sarah, 'I have a headache,' and leave for my cabin to mope.

I get only a few paces out of the dining room before Sarah is on my tail.

'You must tell me how the envelope trick is done. You're the only one Von Reich will reveal magic secrets to.'

'He made me promise not to reveal them to anyone.'

'Tell me, or I will start a rumour that you have the pox.'

'That is disgusting. All right, he never actually made me promise specifically for the envelope trick, though he did for each of the others.' A technicality, but one I will take advantage of.

'So tell me.'

'When the magician opens the first envelope, he tells the audience something entirely different to what is written on the piece of paper.'

'Something different?' she repeats. 'I don't understand.'

'Remember before he opened the first envelope, he told us that the message was about the ship being the best. Then he opened the envelope, read the note inside, and announced that he was right.'

'Yes.'

'The message he read to himself was actually the one a woman had written about the size of a hat, but he lied and told us it was about the ship, so he didn't have to reveal that he had read the hat message.'

'Someone confirmed the ship message.'

'No. If you think about it, you'll realize you never actually heard anyone confirm aloud that it was their message. The Great Nelson simply looked out at the audience and pretended someone had verified it. It was very dark in the room, so no one would be suspicious if they didn't see anyone wave or nod to confirm he was right.'

'So he makes up a message and has an imaginary person confirm it.'

'Exactly.'

'What does that accomplish?'

'It permits him to read the first *real* message. So now he knows that the message in the first envelope speaks of a hat because he has already opened and read it when he pretended to confirm his ship statement. Then he opens the second envelope—'

'I get it. He reads the second message to himself so he knows what it says, but actually tells the audience what the *first* one said. He's always one step ahead, pretending he's reading messages through the envelope when he has actually already opened up the previous envelope and memorized the contents.'

'Always such simple solutions to complicated tricks,' I tell her. 'So unlike life.'

'Exactly.' She gives me a frown and I wonder if she is going to say something about my failed attempt to expose the person who hired Virginia Lynn. If she does, I will know she is the one responsible.

'You should get off to your cabin and crawl into bed,' she says. 'You do look the worse for wear. Take your headache powders. If that doesn't work, I have a bottle of coca-wine.'

I turn down the coca-wine, a strong wine mixed with cocaine, and retreat to my room, my tail between my legs.

The monkey starts screeching and jumping up and down in his cage when I walk in, but immediately shuts up when he sees the look on my face.

I sit on my bed, unsure if I should scream with rage at myself or cry out of self-pity. What a blunder. Those damn stage lights.

'I will not give up,' I tell the monkey.

I shall simply bide my time and make my move when I am ready, while I keep moving forward one step at a time. Even if they are tiny steps I will be that much closer to accomplishing my goal.

The stewardess pounds on my door shortly before midnight. 'Your friends insist you come back and usher in the new year with them.'

Knowing that I must face the others in the morning anyway, I reluctantly return to the dining room where champagne is being passed around. Frederick hands me a glass.

'I have made a fool of myself,' I confess.

He looks puzzled and shakes his head as if he doesn't know what I'm talking about. Does he? Is he that good an actor? Or am I wrong in suspecting him of being a culprit in the Amelia Cleveland charade?

When eight bells ring, we stand and sing 'Auld Lang Syne' with glasses in hand, and on the last echo we all shake hands, each wishing the other a happy new year. 1889 has ended, and 1890 with its impending pleasures and pains has begun.

Frederick escorts me back to my cabin and we stand face to face in the hallway, knowing that we harbour secrets from one another. For a moment there is an awkward silence, then he speaks.

'Nellie, hunting big game is a dangerous business. It also requires great stamina and the ability to live under the most trying conditions. I have never taken a woman on an expedition into the unknown before and swore I never would, but after meeting you, I realize that I was wrong. You would be more capable than most men at only half the size.'

I glow with immodest pride.

'Not only are you capable,' he goes on, 'but you're also beautiful and charming.'

'And you are a great liar,' I say, still glowing. 'Go on.'

He smiles. 'I'm glad I met you, Nellie, and I hope that one day you will accompany me on one of my trips. I think we would make a good team.'

My heart melts when I look in his soft blue eyes.

'I should like that very much.' But there is a small part of me that wonders if it is just an empty declaration. I still don't trust him.

'Very well then, it's settled.'

Before he leaves, he leans slowly forward and kisses me on the lips. 'Happy new year, Nellie.'

Shortly after, I fall asleep lulled by the sound of familiar minstrel melodies sung by the men in the smoking room beneath my cabin, the taste of Frederick's warm lips on my mouth and the feel of his body against mine.

# 54

Sarah and I leave the ship at Yokohama, because we will be in Japan for five days and wish to stay in a hotel.

Full of surprises, she meets me on deck disguised as a man – clothes, hair, even a thin moustache, which, unless she can perform miracles, is false.

'What ya up to, girl,' she says, with a Brooklyn accent.

'Why?' I ask. Not why is she disguised, that I know, but why is she dressed as a man?

'I get bored just being a woman – I like variety in my roles. I've played Prince Hamlet, my dear. Believe me, playing an American will not be as challenging.'

Her voice is not terribly masculine, but it will suffice.

We are taken from the ship, which has anchored some distance out in the bay, to the pier in a small steam launch. The first-class hotels in all the ports have their own launches, but like American hotel horse-drawn omnibuses, although they're run by the hotel to assist in procuring patrons, the traveller pays for them just the same.

Frederick joins us on the launch. He is in a pleasant mood and gives me an affectionate grin, but when I see him look at Sarah with a smile in his eyes I am ready to plunge a knife into his heart.

The port at Tokyo Bay has a pleasant, cleaned-up Sunday

appearance. The Japanese ricksha men are clad in neat navy blue garments, their legs encased in unwrinkled tights, their torsos in short jackets with wide flowing sleeves. They wear comical mushroom-shaped hats, and with their wiry locks cropped just above the nape of the neck, they make a strikingly clean-cut contrast to the ricksha men of other countries we've visited. They, along with every man, woman and child I see, wear their crests embroidered on the back and sleeves of their top garment.

Rain the previous night has left the streets muddy and the air cool and crisp, but the sun creeping through the mist of the early morning falls upon us with most gratifying warmth.

Sarah and I are both staying at the Grand Hotel, a large structure with long verandas, wide halls and airy rooms, commanding an exquisite view of the lake in front.

It takes a little persuasion, but finally I convince Sarah to join me in seeing the sights of Yokohama. 'Oh, my . . .' is all I can say when Sarah meets me later in the hotel lobby. She has transformed from a saucy young man from Brooklyn to an elderly woman – white hair in a bun, a cane, a little slouch to her walk, even a big brooch in the centre of her chest, just like my grandmother always had. The lady is indeed an actress.

'Why?' I ask again, always at a loss for words around her.

'I have been informed that the Japanese are extremely respectful of their elders, so I thought, what could be more perfect than a daughter out seeing the city with her grandmother?'

'All right. I thought we'd see Yokohama and then take a trip to Tokyo, since it's nearby. Think you can handle it, Gram?'

\*　　\*　　\*

A ricksha is taking us down a neighbourhood street filled with men, women and children playing shuttlecock and fly kites, when Sarah gives me a coy smile. 'I saw you looking at that handsome devil Frederick like a lovesick adolescent. Why didn't you have him join you instead of me?'

'Nonsense, you saw nothing of the kind. Besides, I enjoy your company better than his.'

'Rubbish. I've seen the way you two look at each other with lustful eyes.'

'With *what*? You're not intimating that—'

'That you two are destined to be lovers? Of course I am. If you're going to keep your passions hidden under a blanket, my dear, do have a man there to share them with.'

'Sarah, you are scandalous. Please . . . there is nothing between me and Mr Selous.'

'My dear Nellie, you can't fool me. You're dying for him to—' She leans closer with a lewd whisper.

'Stop it! Or I'll jump from this contraption.' My cheeks are burning but I can't make up my mind whether to laugh or run from her impudence.

'Nellie, you're a grown woman, you've obviously dreamed of him whispering sweet nothings in your ear as you lie with him and he—'

'Stop! I won't listen to you.' I put my hands over my ears.

She pulls one off. 'Stop being a child. I expect better of you. I'm giving you the best advice you will ever get. Go, enjoy the magical, sensual passion he'll give you. You won't regret it.'

'And will I enjoy returning home as an unwed mother?'

'Come now, every woman knows there are ways to avoid conception. If you don't know, I'll tell you, but I don't think you're an innocent in that regard. Wait!' She leans closer and whispers, 'Do you prefer women?'

'I prefer that you stop harassing me and deliberately trying to embarrass me. But since you have raised the subject of lovers, why don't you tell me what is going on between you and the mystery man that you mentioned on the *Victoria*?'

'Look.' She points to a group of Japanese women we are about to pass on the street. 'Wouldn't you say they are some of the prettiest women in the world? One would think an artist had painted their faces . . . those perfectly shaped cherry lips and rosy cheeks. Not to mention their silky black hair. What amazes me is how gracefully they move even in those god-awful wooden sandals.'

In other words, she has changed the subject.

'My maid at the hotel says that rather than carry a purse, the women put money, combs, hairpins, anything they will need when they leave the house up their sleeves.' She gives me a sympathetic look. 'Like most women, I'm sure they carry their hearts on their sleeves, too.'

The ricksha drops us off at a covered market where everything from fish and rice to cloth and chopsticks are sold from booths. Sarah wanders off by herself to find a blind person to give her a bath and massage. 'It's a profession the Japanese reserve for the blind and they charge almost nothing.' She grabs my arm. 'Come with me; it will loosen you up for Frederick.'

I jerk my arm out of her grasp and she leaves me, laughing. I believe I'm a modern woman with a proper rein on my passions, while she is completely free and uninhibited towards men and sex. Despite her teasing, I admire her.

Wandering through the stalls, I find myself daydreaming about what it would be like between me and Frederick if I had Sarah's sense of freedom until I spot a pair of shoes on a woman's feet that cause me to stop and stare.

I can't see the woman because she is on the other side of a wall. The stalls are partitioned by bamboo with a wide space at the bottom for air to circulate, and it's in that space that the shoes are visible – and their leather has caught my attention. It matches the description that the fake Mrs Cleveland gave to describe the shoes of the woman who hired her: light brown, with bumps with little holes or nicks on them.

My heart is already racing as I make my way through the ceramic shop I'm in and into the shop next door.

I hurry around the corner and almost fly into a woman, quickly taking a step back and exclaiming, 'Sorry.'

'Perfectly all right.'

Hugh Murdock's young assistant smiles at me. I look down. She's the shoe wearer.

'What's the matter? Is there something on my shoes?'

'No, not at all,' I stammer. 'I'm sorry, I don't mean to be rude, but I saw your shoes and wondered if they are sold here.'

This is obviously a lie. Her shoes are a high, top-laced shoe similar to my own – an occidental style completely unlike the five-inch-high Japanese sandals that make the wearer look as if they are walking on stilts.

'Hardly the local style, really, are they?' she says.

I had assumed she was Australian like the Murdocks, but while her accent is British, it carries a hint of some other European country. She has dark hair, green eyes and a tanned complexion.

'It's the leather I find interesting – the bumps and all. I've never seen it before. What kind is it?'

'Ostrich, those big birds that don't fly.'

'Ostrich? Really. My name is Nellie Bly.'

'Cenza.'

She offers no last name.

'We almost met – once.'

'Oh yes, with me baring all. I'm glad you didn't appear offended. Most women have been so indoctrinated by their husbands that they would faint at the mere suggestion of love between women.'

'I have learned that there is nothing wrong with people of like desire flocking together.' I give the shoes another look. 'I've heard of ostriches. Their feathers are popular. Are they an Australian creature?'

'There are ostrich ranches outback, though I believe the birds are native to Africa.' She glances down at my feet. 'If we wore the same size, I would give mine to you – since you are so enamoured with them.'

'Actually, it was Virginia Lynn who told me about them. You were wearing them the night you hired her.'

She raises her eyebrows. 'I'm sorry, I'm afraid I don't know your friend. Wasn't that the name you mentioned during the magic act?'

So much for my frontal assault. I should have guessed she was in the audience.

She brushes against me as she leaves. 'If you want a little fun, drop by our cabin. Otherwise, get lost, bitch.'

Amazing. What a hard, nasty woman. I have a strong desire to go after her and demand she tells me what she knows, but not only am I sure I would get nowhere, I'd probably go to jail for punching her the next time she used foul language on me.

'Nellie!' Sarah comes towards me, walking much too spryly for a granny. 'What a wonderful experience. He had the hands of an angel.' Seeing the look on my face, she adds, 'And you look like the devil just spat in your eye.'

# 55

Frederick calls for me soon after I return to the hotel, and I meet him in the lobby.

'What do you know about ostriches?' I demand, before he can get a word out of his mouth.

'Ostriches? Big, fast, nasty beasts. Full-grown males weigh in at over 300 pounds and are dangerous if cornered. A man I knew climbed drunk into a corral of them one night. They kicked him to death. He probably forgot they kick forward, not back like a horse. Why do you ask?'

'When I was in Hong Kong, a woman approached me in the hotel and said she was Amelia, John Cleveland's wife.'

'*What?* Why didn't you tell me?'

'I didn't tell you because I assumed you'd hired her to get something from me.'

'What are you talking about? I didn't hire anyone. Nellie—'

'Stop.' I hold up my hands. 'You say you didn't hire her. So it could have been your friend Lord Warton.'

'I don't monitor Lord Warton's actions – nor he mine. We're not working together, we just have a common interest of Queen and country, but that is all. Did the person in Hong Kong get . . . what did you say it was?'

'Look me in the eye and tell me from the depths of your

heart that you have not worked with Lord Warton to lead me astray on this investigation.'

He locks eyes with me and says with sincerity, 'You have my word as a gentleman.'

I sigh. He's lying, of course, but there is no use pursuing it. We would simply end up in a stand-off again, each bluffing while pretending to be completely innocent, neither wanting to show their hand. 'Did you want to see me about something?'

'Quite so. A Japanese diplomat I met in South Africa has invited me to dinner tonight and there will be a special performance afterwards – dancing girls called geishas. Would you like to go?'

'I would love to,' I tell him. He has used the magic words, of course – it is not in me to miss something special.

'I'll call for you at six. Now what's this about ostriches and something you have? You must tell me—'

I step past him. 'You'll have to excuse me, I have to get ready for dinner tonight.'

Nothing is said on the way to the dinner about the Hong Kong ostrich mystery. Frederick has an uncanny ability to feign complete disinterest in this whole business while I am determined not to give him an ounce of what I know until I get a pound of his secrets.

The dinner is held in a traditional Japanese home that forms a great contrast to what I am accustomed to back in Pennsylvania. The house is small and dainty, indeed, rather like a playhouse, built of a thin shingle-like board which is fine in texture, despite the fact that our host is a man of some standing.

I find its design both unusual and clever. The first wall of the house is set back, allowing the upper floor and side walls to extend over the lower flooring, making it a portico built in, instead of on, the house. Light frames, with their openings covered with fine rice paper instead of glass, are both doors and windows in one. The frames don't swing open and shut as do our doors, nor do they move up and down like our windows, but slide like rolling doors. They form the partitions of the houses inside and can be removed at any time, bringing two or more rooms together as one.

Both the host and hostess speak English, and when I tell them that I am interested in learning more about their culture and customs, they satisfy my curiosity.

In a private moment the hostess tells me that women of her country have tested European dress, and finding it barbarously uncomfortable and unartistic, went back to their exquisite kimonos but retained European underwear, which they find more sanitary and comfortable than the utter absence of it, which was their previous custom.

'Gracefulness is taught in our schools,' she says. 'As girls, we are taught graceful movements, how to receive, entertain and part with visitors, how to serve tea and sweets gracefully, and the proper and graceful way to use chopsticks.'

It is indeed a pretty sight to see this lovely woman use chopsticks – and an ugly one to see me make use of them!

My regret as I dine with these charming people, and the only regret of my trip, is that in my haste to depart on my race round the world I forgot to take a Kodak. On every ship and at every port I meet others with Kodaks – and envy them. They can photograph everything that pleases them; the light in these lands is excellent, and they will carry many pleasant mementos of their acquaintances and themselves home on their plates.*

After dinner, in the cool of the evening, we go to a house that has been specially engaged to see the geisha girls. Several others, members of foreign diplomatic missions, are also attending.

At the door are the wooden shoes of the household, and we are asked also to remove our shoes before entering, a practice rather disliked by some of the diplomatic party, who refuse absolutely to do as requested. A compromise is effected, however, by putting cloth slippers over their shoes.

The second floor has been converted into one room, with nothing in it except the matting covering the floor and a Japanese screen here and there. We sit upon the floor, for chairs there are none in Japan, but the exquisite matting is so padded it is as soft as velvet. It is laughable to see us trying to sit down, and yet more so to see us endeavour to find a comfortable posture for our limbs. We are about as graceful as elephants dancing.

A smiling woman in a black kimono sits several Japanese stoves before us – round and square boxes containing burning charcoal. Then she brings a tray containing a number of long-stemmed pipes – I will learn shortly that Japanese women smoke constantly – along with a pot of tea and several small cups.

Impatiently I await the geisha girls. The tiny maidens glide in at last, clad in exquisite trailing, angel-sleeved kimonos. They bow gracefully, bending down until their heads touch

---

* Cameras used glass plates coated with a chemical to take pictures. The Editors.

their knees, then, kneeling before us, gently murmur a greeting, drawing in their breath with a long, hissing suction, which we have been told is a token of great honour.

The musicians sit down on the floor and begin an alarming din upon samisens, drums and gongs, and sing through their pretty noses.

The geishas stand posed, holding open fans above their heads, ready to begin the dance. They are very short with the slenderest of slender waists. Their soft and tender eyes are made blacker by painted lashes and brows; their midnight hair, stiffened with a gummy wash, is wonderfully dressed in large coils and ornamented with gold and silver flowers and gilt paper pom-poms. The younger the girl, I realize, the more gay her hair.

Their kimonos, made of the most exquisite material, are loosely held together at the waist with an obi-sash, and their long flowing sleeves fall back to show their dimpled arms and delicate hands. Upon their tiny feet they wear white linen socks, which have been cunningly divided with a place for the big toe.

The Japanese are the only women I've ever seen who can wear rouge and powder and look all the more charming. They have a way of reddening their lower lip just at the tip that gives them a most tempting appearance, so the lips look like two delicious cherries.

The musicians begin a long chanting strain, and these beautiful women dance. With a grace that is simply enchanting, they twirl their little fans and sway their dainty bodies in a hundred different poses, each one more intoxicating than the last. And all the while they look so childish and shy, an innocent smile lurking about their lips and dimpling their soft cheeks, and their black eyes twinkling with the pleasure of the dance.

Afterwards they make friends with me, examining, with surprised delight, my dress, my bracelets, my rings, my boots – to them the most wonderful and extraordinary things – my hair, my gloves, indeed they miss nothing, and they approve of all.

They say I am very sweet and urge me to come again, and, in honour of the custom of my land – the Japanese never kiss – they press their soft, pouting lips to mine in parting.

'You were a big hit with the geishas,' says Frederick as he escorts me into the hotel lobby. 'The fact that you are on a great adventure is amazing to them.'

'It's amazing to me, too,' I say, giving him a coy look. 'So many interesting things have occurred on my journey.'

'Is there something you'd like to tell me?' he asks.

He delivers the question in a stern tone, the kind used by fathers to their children and overbearing husbands to their wives.

'Yes, there is. I had a wonderful time tonight. Thank you. And I do have a question. How was John Cleveland dressed the day he told you on the beach that he was staying in Port Saïd?'

'What kind of nonsense is this? He was wearing clothes, not native garb, the clothes any British man wears in a city.'

'Ahh . . .'

He stares at me, his lips working but not knowing what revelation I have received from the gods this time. But my triumphant grin tells him he has given the wrong answer.

He stomps off, his face a map of frustration.

Why did I do that? His tone irked me, of course, not to

mention his demand that I confide in him while he keeps his cards face down.

Oh, well, it's not in me to let sleeping dogs lie, anyway. From the first time I met him, I've been bugged by his claim that he spoke to Mr Cleveland on the beach, and the business about the clothes just popped into my head. I don't know if he really did speak to a man on the beach, but even if he did, it certainly wasn't Mr Cleveland, who left the ship wearing sailor's work clothes and would have had room in his small sea bag only for his Egyptian disguise.

*USS* Omaha *warship that entertained Nellie*

# 56

Frederick doesn't send over any invitations for the rest of my stay in Japan, but I have a pleasant time and even persuade Sarah to visit Tokyo with me.

The incident with Cenza and the ostrich shoes has enhanced my wariness and I find I am continually keeping an eye out for trouble when I should be relaxing in the exotic atmosphere. I have no idea how the woman fits into everything else that has been going on, since she didn't appear until long after Port Saïd, but she spooks me. She strikes me as someone who would smile at me even as she slipped a knife between my ribs.

One of the more pleasant events of my stay is a luncheon given for me on the *USS Omaha*, an American war vessel lying in the bay. Afterwards, I return to the hotel and gather my possessions. A number of new friends escort me to the *Oceanic*, and when we hoist anchor, the steam launches blow loud blasts upon their whistles in farewell to me, and the band on the *Omaha* play 'Home, Sweet Home', 'Hail Columbia', and 'The Girl I Left Behind me' in my honour.

I wave my handkerchief so long after they are out of sight that my arms are sore for days.

Sarah simply shakes her head at the sight of the battleship hailing me. 'All my success on the stage and I have never had the entire crew of a warship adore me. All of those men . . . wasted on a woman with a virgin mentality.'

Everything augers well for a pleasant and rapid voyage home to America. Anticipating this, Chief Engineer Allen has this couplet written over the engines and throughout the engine room:

*'For Nellie Bly,*
*We'll win or die.*
*20 January, 1890.'*

The runs are marvellous until the third day out and then a storm comes upon us. The crew try to cheer me, saying it will only last that day, but the next day finds it worse and it continues, never abating a moment; headwinds, head sea, wild rolling, frightful pitching. Everyday I wait fretfully for noon when I can slip off to the dining room to see the run, hoping that it will have gained a few miles on the day before, but I am always disappointed.

When the storm doesn't pass, a rumour begins to circulate that there is a Jonah on board the ship – and, much to my dismay, I am told that the sailors say monkeys are Jonahs.

'Monkeys bring bad weather to ships, and as long as the monkey is on board we will have storms,' my steward assures me.

The chief engineer asks if I will consent to my monkey being thrown overboard. A little struggle between superstition and a feeling of justice for the monkey follows as I ponder the matter. Just then someone else declares that ministers are Jonahs; they always bring bad weather to ships. And we have two ministers on board!

I tell the chief engineer quietly, 'If the ministers are thrown overboard, I'll say nothing about the monkey going with them.'

As soon as the weather becomes manageable, I decide it is time to put into action my plan to ferret out the person or persons involved in the death of John Cleveland. People will set off in many different directions when we land at San Francisco and this is the last leg of the journey in which I can learn the truth behind his death. And discover who has tried to kill me.

Lying awake at night, I imagine the clock ticking, each moment bringing me closer to San Francisco, closer to my personal goal, but also meaning that not much time is left to expose an injustice. And I still know so little. If John Cleveland had spoken just another word, or—

I sit straight up in bed, then get out and pace up and down in my bare feet, a little silver moonlight taking the edge off the darkness.

My monkey opens his sleepy eyes and just watches me pace the floor. 'Why not have him tell us who arranged his death?' I ask him. Stepping up to his cage, I lock eyes with him. 'It's no crazier than committing myself to an insane asylum to get a job.'

He bares his white teeth, than snaps them together in a clatter, and I take it as a sign of approval that John Cleveland be brought back so he can confront the person who caused his murder. And I know exactly how it can be done.

'I'm going to raise the dead,' I tell the monkey.

He bounces up and down in the cage and screeches loud enough to wake the dead. 'Shh,' I plead, but it's too late – the man in the next compartment pounds the wall and shouts an ungentlemanly remark.

The idea stays with me as I climb back into bed. 'Too risky,' Mr Pulitzer would say if I told him what I was thinking. But he's said that about many of my ventures, and after all that's why he hired me – I take chances to make things happen. Like a rise in his circulation figures.

John Cleveland didn't live long enough to tell me everything that he wanted to. But there is a person on board who can help him say his piece.

# 57

A note to Madame Xi Shi requesting a private audience and hinting at financial reward was all I needed to arrange an interview with the famous spiritualist who acts as a medium between this world and the beyond.

'Audience' is the precise word I used in my missive, hoping it would convey the proper sense of subservience and admiration to the regal woman. Polishing an apple, the boys in the newsroom would call it.

On my way to her stateroom, I ponder over a more mundane problem: how will I account for a fee paid to raise the dead to Mr Pulitzer? Not a man in tune with the otherworldly, he'll be raisin' Cain with me if I don't find a clever way to bury the expense.

My feelings about spiritualists are similar to those of the scientist William James, who debunked many spiritualists' claims until he met Leonora Piper, a woman who experienced her first connection with the dead at eight years old when her aunt whispered to her – at the very moment that the aunt was dying elsewhere.

After studying Leonora Piper, Dr James concluded that he was not willing to dismiss her out of hand just because all the other 'psychics' he'd studied proved to be frauds. He characterized his feelings by saying that it takes only one white crow to prove that not all crows are black.

Is Madame Xi Shi a white crow?

Only the dead know for sure because a séance, is, of course, necromancy – communication with the dead. In earlier days, such attempts would be considered a black art that got the practitioner into very hot water, but it is now considered a parlour game that some take very seriously.

As for my own feelings about paths between the living and the dead, I am a practical, common-sense person, and try not to close the door on things just because I can't see them. I share the belief of many that life continues beyond the grave.

When I heard about a spiritualist in New York last year who was impressing high society with his ability to call forth the bodiless essence of dead loved ones, I decided to attempt to contact my sweet father, who passed from this life when I was six.

A friend laughed when I told her what I was going to do but it was not a joking matter to me. I hoped that love would transcend even the grave.

After listening to a shadowy figure mumbling unintelligibly while rapping was heard and the table suddenly levitated, I leaped from my chair and threw on the light to expose the fraud, showing how the medium's feet manoeuvered hidden wires to create the rapping and table movement, and the garbling came from a person in an adjoining room speaking into a tube that led to the chandelier overhead.

I had practiced a bit of fortune-telling myself for the event that night. Anticipating that my actions might provoke a violent reaction, I took along a police detective who howled with laughter as he led me safely from the angry 'spirits'.

\* \* \*

A female servant lets me inside Madame Xi Shi's stateroom and I resist the impulse to curtsey as I enter. The spiritualist is sitting in a high-back wicker chair that is low enough to the floor for her tiny lotus feet to reach, yet still manages to convey the impression of a queen on a throne.

Chee Ling, her chief assistant or henchman, whatever his function, is standing beside her with his arms crossed and his hands slipped up his sleeves. Dressed entirely in black, his features narrow, he reminds me of the bird of prey that the desert prince had back in Egypt.

Accepting an offer of tea, I take a seat and address the bird, who I'm told is her interpreter.

'Madame Xi Shi is world renowned for her ability to contact the spirits of the dearly departed,' I say.

He nods. 'Renowned in this world and *others*.'

'I have come to request that she use her great powers at a séance in which she would make contact with a man who died rather . . . violently.'

'Your loved one?' he asks.

'Actually, a stranger to me, at least until the last few seconds of his life.'

'Madame Xi Shi does conduct private sessions.' He looks pained. 'Naturally, it would be necessary to make a small gift to aid her work with the spirit world.'

'Her great work deserves to be richly rewarded so she can help others. There will be nine guests at the séance.'

Chee Ling shakes his head. 'Madame Xi Shi requires seven guests in order to achieve the proper balance of energy between this world and the spirit world. Seven is considered auspicious because during the seventh month, the Ghost Month, the gates of hell open and the dead may visit the living.'

'Uh, well, frankly, I hope the spirit I wish to contact comes from a slightly cooler climate than hell. I must have nine people. I will compensate Madame Xi Shi for the additional psychic energy.'

The spiritualist gets a translation from Chee Ling and nods her approval.

'We will need a room about the size of this one,' says Chee Ling, 'but it must be completely empty except for a round wooden table and chairs. We will need time to prepare it in a manner that will permit the entry of spirits.'

'I can arrange that; I understand that there are a couple of empty staterooms.'

'There will be no lights and no interference of any sort.'

'I will need to have a candle lit.'

He shakes his head again. 'Impossible.'

'I will need at least a small one, in the centre of the table.' I won't be able to see the effect on the guests if it is completely dark. 'I will, of course, add an extra donation for Madame's work with the spirit if a small candle is permitted.'

More discussion, then I am told the medium will make an exception and permit a small candle.

I take a sip of tea as my heart starts beating faster. 'Let me explain exactly what I need to have done.'

Lord help me if this goes wrong.

Leaving Madame Xi Shi's stateroom, I am approached by the steward assigned to the corridor.

'Mademoiselle Aisse requests that you drop by to see her.'

Sarah has booked herself under a different name on each leg of the journey. My guess is that the names are roles she has played on stage, and for reasons that I can't fathom, she may believe that her actions will confuse her enemies.

Whoever, wherever or whatever they are.

That I have been seen going into the spiritualist's stateroom does not surprise me. The steward probably saw me and told Sarah, who now wants to know if there is any juicy gossip to share. There is little privacy on a ship at sea.

Sarah lets me in. She is wearing a sailor's watch-cap, a navy shirt and bell-bottomed trousers.

'Planning to hoist the sails, matey?' I ask.

'After this long, dreary journey, I feel as if I have salt-water in my veins. Perhaps I shall play Odysseus when I return to Paris, tied to the mast with stage-hands throwing water on me as I resist the song of the sirens.'

She walks across to her closed coffin and sits with her feet extended down the lid and her back to the wall. She takes a puff from a cigarette extending from a long holder and waves me to a chair, but I am too antsy to sit.

The smoke doesn't smell like any cigarette I'm familiar with, which makes me wonder sometimes about Sarah and her bohemian lifestyle.

She points the cigarette holder at me. 'So tell me, girl reporter, what did you talk to the Dowager Empress of the Spirit World about? If she's any good, I have some questions about an ex-lover to ask her. The scoundrel passed on to the next world without telling me where he hid a diamond necklace that he promised to me.'

'You are scandalous, Sarah. I just interviewed her for my readers. Interviewed that aide-de-camp or whatever that skinny man in black is.'

'He's a eunuch.'

'*No*. You mean like a harem guard?'

'There are thousands of eunuchs employed by the imperial family, but not as harem guards. They are considered the most trustworthy servants and political counsellors in the land – and almost all of them got their status voluntarily.'

'You mean by cutting off their man things?'

She grimaces and waves smoke away from her. 'I am always amazed at how perfectly ridiculous grown women make themselves sound by using children's words to describe human anatomy.'

'They cut off their testicles?' I ask, to show I am indeed modern.

'They whack off their balls,' she says in a throaty sailor's tone. 'Not themselves, but they are sliced off by a man who travels around ball whacking with a sharp knife.'

'I can't imagine a man having that done just to get a job.'

She shrugs. 'People do worse things to themselves.'

'Why are eunuchs considered more trustworthy?'

'With no wives or children to share their loyalty, they are able to devote their entire lives to the imperial family. Like priests, except once they take up the cloth, so to speak, there is no going back. The rewards can be incredible. Some eunuchs have run China in the name of emperors.'

I shudder at the thought of what they must feel when the knife blade begins to cut. The things men will do in pursuit of power.

My next stop is the captain, to persuade him to host the séance. How else will I get my suspects there?

I approach him with the reasoning that it would be entertaining and memorable for the passengers. 'It would be a pity if we didn't enjoy the services of the most famous medium in the world while she is on board.'

'Why would anyone want to contact the dead?' is his response.

'Queen Victoria had a séance so that she might contact her beloved Albert.' I don't know if that is true, but the whole world knows how she grieved for her lost love, so it is at least a credible lie.

'Really . . .' This gets him thinking. 'Well, if the Queen can contact the dead, then I see no reason why we can't attempt it too. Besides, it's all for fun. Right?'

'Quite!'

# 58

Madame Xi Shi must have commanded all the spirits of the sea to haunt our ship tonight as the séance I arranged will unfold. A fog, heavy with gloom and swirling wisps easy to imagine as ghosts, shrouds the ship, making it impossible to see but possible to imagine anything.

Nights like this remind me of the time as a young girl when I stayed too late playing with other children and had to walk home alone through dark woods. I broke into a run, flying breathless into the house, sure *something* in the darkness was chasing me. My mother shook her head and said, 'What the eyes can't see, the mind will.'

'Oh well,' I tell the sea, pushing back from where I have been standing at the rail, gathering my courage for the drama I have schemed – my very own *dénouement*. I just hope Madame Xi Shi's Chinese spirits are up to a bit of mystery solving.

Shivering as I carry a little of the night chill back inside with me, I conclude that no one could have asked for a better setting to summon a spirit.

It is midnight, and the living I have summoned are arriving to meet the dead.

The captain has donated an empty stateroom for the

evening and Madame Xi Shi's assistants have turned it into a—

'Crypt!' Sarah declares, stepping into the room which is completely draped in black – walls, floor and ceiling. 'Even the air looks black.'

'Like the inside of a coffin,' I suggest. 'With the lid down.'

She shudders. 'That happened once.'

Amazing. Sarah is frumpy tonight, a middle-aged woman with some parts needing support. And she does it with little make-up, mostly it's just an attitude, though her drab clothes add to the dowdiness. She has a central European accent tonight.

The only furniture sits in the centre of the room: the round wooden table and bare wooden chairs have deep grooves in them from years of use. As I requested, one thin, church-like white candle is in the middle of the table, held by a plain silver candlestick.

Sarah pats the table. 'This reminds me of a set piece in one of my plays. A table in a medieval castle. When the candle goes out, the spirits of people tortured in the dungeon come to life.'

'Perfect.' Except for the candle going out, of course.

The Wartons enter, his lordship sporting a purse-lipped look of annoyance, and her ladyship an ominous frown that reminds me of the Queen of Hearts commanding, 'Off with her head!' in Alice's adventure.

Oh well. I can always throw myself overboard if everything goes to hell tonight.

The others arrive, most, like Sarah, dressed in black. I considered it myself, but I don't have a black dress. I suppose it is a show of respect, black being the colour of death. Cenza doesn't bother with respect, however: her choice of colour is red. The little tart has chosen *harlot red*, and she is clutching onto Von Reich, much to the visible annoyance of the widow Murdock.

'Isn't she the prima donna?' Sarah whispers.

No matchmaker would team Von Reich with Cenza, so unless she is attracted to the Viennese man's money, I have to wonder why this public display of affection?

Chee Ling seats the nine of us: Sarah, the Wartons, Von Reich, the harlot in red, the widow wearing a whisky flush, Frederick who doesn't recognize Sarah, the captain looking handsome in a dark navy blue uniform, and one scared rabbit.

'There must be no talking during the performance,' Chee Ling instructs us with the tone of a disciplinarian school-master. 'Complete silence is required in order for Madame Xi Shi to contact the spirits.'

The candle is lit, the door is shut and the lights go out. It's quickly evident why the spiritualist had little objection to the candle – with nothing to reflect the light, it hardly takes the edge off the complete darkness in the room. All the faces are in dark shadow and I can barely make them out.

Von Reich tells us, 'The purpose of the candle is to create a light for the spirits to find us. Isn't that so . . . uh, where are you?'

Chee Ling has vanished into the darkness.

I don't volunteer that the real purpose of the candle is to allow me to spot the guilty.

Everyone, everything is in position, except the outcome. I start to pray a little, then stop, suddenly realizing that I doubt I should bring to the attention of the Almighty that I am orchestrating black magic.

Regrets about this whole scheme are welling up in my throat as Madame Xi Shi appears, apparently floating in the air towards the table. A tiny light from the front of her clothes partly illuminates her frail features.

There are murmurs, and a gasp – I think from the widow Murdock – and a whisper to me from Sarah: 'Nicely done.' She's talking about the showmanship.

The small candle I insisted upon gives away the trick, at least to me, closest to the spiritualist. I can make out that she is sitting on a pillow placed on a small platform painted black, the tubular shape conveying an impression of bamboo. The assistants carrying her are covered completely in black, appearing as just the slightest hint of movement in the darkness.

Very clever. Without the candle, I would not have seen anything except the glow of her features from her own light. That tiny light takes another shade off the darkness, enough for me to make out that the people at the table are all focused on the spiritualist.

When I first saw her, she reminded me of a ceramic doll, one of those beautiful China dolls that Hong Kong craftsmen make so cleverly. Tonight, however, she strikes me as a goddess of the exotic and mysterious East, a deity of the shadow world.

Madame Xi Shi lowers her head, puts her hands together as if in prayer, and we hear the whisper of wind, a cold stirring that causes the candle to flicker and me to shiver.

*Wind?* The portholes are covered and the entire room is cloaked in heavy black drapes.

A sound comes from Madame Xi Shi. Not words, at least

not any that I can understand or even distinguish as words of another language, but more of a hum, a chant, and Chee Ling's voice finds us in the darkness.

'Madame Xi Shi's spirit contact is a Tibetan monk whose physical body passed beyond sorrow three hundred years ago, but whose spirit is strong. He is her guide into the world beyond.'

A childhood memory flashes into my mind – after my father died my mother stood in front of he casket, looking down at him. The minister stood beside her. She asked him, 'How long does it take for a soul to leave its body?'

His answer has never left me: 'It depends if the person died peacefully.'

Mr Cleveland died violently. Does this mean his spirit is still here, waiting for justice? Maybe Madame Xi Shi really will summon John Cleveland's ghost.

The hum slowly rises, until it fills the room with its powerful tone.

A ghostly image flashes across the room and everyone gives a start.

Cenza giggles and that releases the tension.

'Probably a light trick—' Von Reich begins to say, but is silenced by a loud hiss from somewhere in the room. Chee Ling, no doubt.

Another voice is heard, a deep rumble, and I sense someone is behind me. I want to look, but in truth, I'm afraid to. This is all getting too real for me.

A gloomy mass materializes behind Madame Xi Shi, a sort of shadowy darkness that doesn't seem to have any definite shape to it.

It *floats* closer to her and an animated conversation erupts between the dark mass and Madame Xi Shi, words that sound like the gibberish I once heard in a holy roller church; 'speaking in tongues', some call it.

A gong sounds, then there is complete silence as the dark form vanishes into the night air.

A strange guttural noise is emitted from Madame Xi Shi and she sits upright, and stares right at me.

She opens her mouth and an eerie male voice comes out: 'Amelia—'

*'You poor man!'* Lady Warton cries. *'You were murdered! God help you! You were murdered!'*

She stands up and grabs her chest, gasping for air. Then her breathing becomes laboured and she falls back into the chair. *'My heart! My heart!'*

Frederick quickly throws open the door to the corridor to let in some light and jerks the covering off the electric light next to the door.

'Someone get the doctor!' shouts the captain.

I'm in a fog. Pinned to my chair in shock, unable to move, unable to talk, as the drama around Lady Warton unfolds. A prisoner of my own sense of shame and doom, I don't even turn my head as she is lifted into a wheelchair.

The ship's doctor hovers over her as Von Reich wheels her out of the room. Lord Warton comes at me and Frederick is suddenly there, restraining him.

'You're a devil!' Lord Warton spits at me. 'If this ridiculous trick of yours kills my wife, it will be on your head and I'll make sure you are prosecuted!'

'Leave her alone!' Sarah yells at him as she puts her arm around my shoulders.

I can't say anything; all I can do is shake my head as Frederick guides the irate husband out of the room.

The captain is suddenly in front of me. 'What is Lord Warton talking about?'

Frederick approaches us and answers the question for me, as I sit paralyzed.

'Nellie, the Wartons and Herr Von Reich witnessed the murder of a man, John Cleveland, in Egypt. She also feels I had some part to play in the incident.'

I cringe when he says the words.

'The moment the name Amelia was uttered, it became obvious that she had concocted this farce to smoke out the killer. She only had the best of intentions.'

'Nonsense!' The captain glows with anger. 'That makes no difference. What in heaven's name were you thinking?'

I have no answer. I am lost.

'The poor woman has had a heart attack!' Now he's yelling. 'You may have killed the wife of a British peer with a cruel and tasteless joke. Everything I have heard about you is true. You are a troublemaker!'

The first officer has arrived and the captain turns to him.

'Officer, escort this woman to her cabin. You are not to leave your quarters without my permission,' he snaps at me. 'You will not cause any more trouble on my ship. If you do, I will have you put in chains.'

The first officer reaches for me and Frederick is suddenly there again. 'I'll escort her for you.'

Frederick offers me his arm and I slowly rise and take it, my knees so weak I must walk stiffly to keep from collapsing.

Ahead of us in the hallway, Cenza, walking with the

Murdock woman, turns and laughs. 'Everyone has a price,' she shouts.

I have no idea what she is talking about. Suppressing the urge to vomit, I keep up with Frederick, walking laboriously, like an old woman.

When we get to my cabin, the first officer excuses himself. 'Sorry, Miss Bly. You know the whole crew is rooting for you.'

I just shake my head. I have let them down, too.

Frederick puts his arms around me and embraces me. I let him pull me into him, but I don't squeeze back. I am completely drained of emotion.

He holds my head in his hands. 'I know your motives were pure.'

I bend my head down, unable to meet his gaze. 'I'm an idiot. I should be shot.'

'The captain won't go that far. I hope.' He smiles. 'Just joking.'

'Thank you for protecting me. You are truly a gentleman. And more than I deserve.'

Escaping into my cabin, I shut the door behind me and stagger to my bed.

I'm still sitting on the edge of the bed, my life passing before my eyes, when Sarah opens the door. 'Bread and water for the prisoner,' she says.

She has a bottle of champagne and a small cake.

'You'll be happy to know that Lady Warton has not slipped off to the spirit world. In fact, she never even went to the infirmary, she had them take her to their stateroom.'

'To her room? After crying heart attack? Now I know what she meant when she said everyone has a price.'

Sarah sets down my prison food and gives me a look. 'Lady Warton said that?'

'No, Cenza, the one in red. She laughed at me and said everyone has a price.'

'Meaning?'

'Chee Ling the eunuch, the spiritualist's mouthpiece, henchman, whatever. He sold my scheme to other people.'

'Ah, well that explains that.'

'Explains what?'

'Why Lady Warton's heart attack sounded so contrived. I've died from a broken heart on stage much more realistically than her pathetic moans and groans.'

I bang myself on the forehead. 'They set me up. The whole bunch of them. I *should* be shot for my stupidity.'

'Don't say that too loudly, darling. The captain might hear.'

# PART NINE

## DAY 68

*East on an Iron Horse*

*Nellie arriving in San Francisco*
New York World

# 59

I arrive at the gateway to San Francisco Bay on 21 January 1890. A grey morning with wet, chilly air and choppy seas adds to the sense of gloom and doom that grips me as I stand on the deck of the tugboat and look back at the *Oceanic* as it slowly fades into dark shadow in a bank of fog.

Frederick, Sarah and Von Reich are among the passengers lining the deck either to see me off or just to get a look at the first sight of land in nearly 5,000 miles. I'm sure the Wartons and Murdock's widow and assistant are on the crowded deck, too, if for no other reason than to make sure I have left.

Getting off the ship and onto the tug left me breathless with anxiety and anticipation, and now that the umbilical cord has been cut, I feel a sense of unease of which I know the cause: unfinished business.

So many unanswered questions are still on the ship. Sarah and Frederick – two people I am fond of, yet unable to fully trust because I know they both harbour secrets. I feel a warmth towards Frederick that surpasses friendship, despite the lies and charades we both practise, though I am not fool enough to believe that he would ever trade the green jungles of Africa for the hard concrete ones of New York.

Now, as the little tug is taking me away from the people I have travelled more than halfway around the world with, people who might have the answers to all my questions, I cannot but help feel loss and despair.

Worse than this, though, are my feelings of inadequacy. I failed to expose an injustice. I never learned why Mr Cleveland died. He entrusted to me a scarab with a key inside as he whispered a name – Amelia. Who is she? His lover? *Who?* Certainly she was not that actress in Hong Kong.

My sense of confidence has been trampled because a man died in my arms and passed to me the reason for his death, but I have been unable to interpret it.

'Nellie, stop this!' I tell the ocean air. Sulking and moping won't heal the wound and it definitely isn't making me feel any better.

I wave goodbye one more time to the *Oceanic*, Frederick, Sarah and all the rest, even though I know they won't see my gesture. I have to accept the fact that I am forever separated from the mystery and must move on.

Now I have only one thing to do: finish the race in first place.

It's no exaggeration of my feelings when I say I would rather die than suffer the humiliation of defeat at the hands of the woman from *Cosmopolitan* magazine, who showed she is without honour and common decency when she started a race against me without even telling me.

My estimation is that she has already set sail from a French port. It takes about the same time to cross the North American continent by rail as it does the Atlantic from Calais to New York by ship – if the railroad line over the Sierra Mountains is not buried in snow.

The news that it is shouldn't have surprised me – it is January, the heart of winter.

The mountains becoming impassible because of winter

storms is the reason her editor must have chosen the west to east route – she would have crossed the Sierras over two months ago.

Soon I will be at the train station, and from the telegraphic communications that the railroads use to relate the status of their routes, I'll know whether I have already lost. If by some miracle the rails are cleared, we will be neck and neck to the end and I shall have no peace until – unless – I cross the finish line first.

It is my fondest hope that my competitor will be washed overboard in an Atlantic gale and finish the race in Davy Jones's locker.

I turn my back on the *Oceanic* and move to the bow, with the silly notion that by doing this I will pass through the Golden Gate a second or two quicker than if I had been at the rear, fantasizing that these few seconds will help me win the race.

Even though there are still thousands of miles to go, I have a wonderful sense of relief knowing I'm back in my own country where I don't have to fear arrest or harm for getting mixed up in others' murky schemes. Best of all, I don't have to constantly keep watch over my shoulder for someone who wants to give me a shove overboard, or put a knife in my back.

With the key still hidden in my shoe, I still don't know what it unlocks, why it was important to Mr Cleveland, or why others so desperately want it. One conclusion I *have* reached is what to do with it: I'll turn it over to the British Embassy in Washington, after I have extracted a promise that they will assist me in contacting Mr Cleveland's Amelia. She can't have the key because it would put her in danger.

This key has already left two men dead in Egypt, another on a magician's stage in the middle of the ocean, and very nearly caused the loss of my own life, not once but twice.

If only I could rub it like a genie's lamp and have its secret revealed.

A man comes out of the pilot house and joins me at the bow.

'Welcome to San Francisco, Miss Bly. I'm Henry Stewart from the office of the Port of San Francisco. It's my job this morning to get you to the Oakland train terminal as soon as possible.'

'That's kind of you. Is there any news about the mountain passes? Are they still snowed in?'

'We won't know until we reach the terminal, but that was the case two hours ago. You know, there is another route, down the central valley and across the southern desert.'

'Isn't that much further than over the mountains?'

'Yes, it would add quite a bit of time to your record.'

As the tug steams close to the pier, I'm surprised to see a group of people waving and cheering my name.

'Welcome, Nellie Bly! Welcome, Nellie Bly!'

Smiling, I return their greeting. 'How did they know I'd arrived?'

Mr Stewart chuckles. 'You're the talk of the town – the talk of the whole country. When news came that you had left Yokohama, everybody got excited.

'If you don't mind, we'll get closer to the Frisco piers as we wrap around the peninsula to Oakland on the other side of the bay,' Mr Stewart continues. 'The people of San Francisco want to get a glimpse of you and it'll only add a few minutes to your trip.'

'That's fine,' I say, dreading the loss of these minutes. 'I regret that I don't have time to see your beautiful city and thank everyone for their support.'

'Actually, since some of the most famous parts of the city are built on hills facing the bay, you'll see a great deal right from this tug.' He points at a streetcar crawling up a hill. 'That's a cable car. Do you know why they were invented?'

I shake my head no.

'A man named Hallidie saw horses being whipped while they struggled on the wet cobblestones to pull a horse-car up a steep hill. The horses slipped and were dragged to their death as the car rolled back down the hill. He decided, enough of that, and came up with a way to pull the cars with an underground cable.'

'Thank God for Mr Hallidie.'

As Mr Stewart chats about the city's colourful history, I continue to wave at the people who stand at the piers and cheer me on. The sun has come out and some of the gloom and doom I felt leaving the ship has evaporated, but the anxiety is still with me.

People are hailing me as a conquering hero, as if my journey around the globe is for all Americans, helping to bond us with the vast swathes of the world that know so little about us. But the race is not won yet, and the cheers of success could easily turn into the sting of defeat.

No bridge has been built to link San Francisco with the east side of the bay, either, so the transcontinental railroad ends at Oakland and passengers and goods are transferred by boat to San Francisco.

As soon as we dock, Mr Stewart confers with some men

who are waiting at the pier and returns with a smile. 'The train has been waiting for your arrival and is ready to start the moment you board it. Everyone wants to make sure you win your race.'

'The pass over the mountains?'

'Still blocked, but I understand other arrangements have been made.'

'Still blocked' sticks in my head as I'm escorted to a train that has only one passenger car. I'm staggered when I'm told that it's a special train just for me.

The *Miss Nellie Bly Special* consists of the *San Lorenzo*, a handsome Pullman car; the engine called the *Queen*, one of the fastest on the Southern Pacific line; the tender car that carries coal and wood to keep the steam engine going; and a caboose.

'What time do you want to reach New York, Miss Bly?' Mr Bissell, general passenger agent of the Atlantic and Pacific system, asks me.

'No later than Saturday evening.'

'Very well, we will get you there on time,' he says quietly. 'At least the first leg – the *Queen* will carry you as far as Chicago.'

'How will you get me there on time if the pass is still closed?'

'We are taking a route that Mr Pulitzer has chosen,' he replies, 'which I must say is quite clever. Instead of going directly east to Chicago, we're sending you hundreds of miles south and then across the southwest deserts through Arizona and New Mexico before turning north to the Windy City. It's five hundred miles longer, but it has less snow and rail traffic.'

As I board, the conductor, porter, engineer and fireman introduce themselves.

'I'll keep the throttle wide open,' the engineer proudly states.

'And I will keep the boiler red hot,' says the fireman.

I'm so tickled by their enthusiasm, I feel I should also contribute. 'If you tire of shovelling coal,' I tell the fireman, 'I'll help you shovel until the *Queen* is flying.'

Changing my mode of conveyance from steamship to steam locomotive makes me reflect upon how dependent I've been for the past couple of months on the strong arms of men shovelling coal into boilers, and how fortunate I've been so far that the engines themselves have not failed me.

Crossing my fingers, I pray my luck will continue.

While we are running well on the first day, the horn blasts and there's a bump as if we have struck something. Brakes screeching, we come to a stop and go out to see what has occurred. My first thought is, now there'll be a delay.

The sky is overcast, and it's hailing when we step out and see two men coming up the track. The conductor goes off to meet them and returns to tell us, 'We hit a handcar.' He points down the track to a piece of twisted iron and a bit of splintered board – all that remains of the four-wheeled platform with a hand pump that rail crews use for transportation.

When the men arrive, one remarks, with a mingled expression of wonder and disgust upon his face: 'Well, you *are* running like h—!'

'Thank you, I am glad to hear it,' I say, and we all laugh.

'Is anyone hurt?' I enquire.

'No.' They assure me they are not.

With good humour restored all around, we say goodbye, the engineer pulls the lever, and we are off again.

At Merced, our second stop, a great crowd of people dressed in their best Sunday clothes have gathered about the station.

'Are they having a picnic?' I ask the conductor.

'Oh, no – they've come to see you.'

'*Me?* Oh, my.'

A loud cheer, which almost frightens me to death, greets my appearance and the band begins playing, 'By Nellie's Blue Eyes'.

A large tray of fruit, candy and nuts, the tribute of a dear little newsboy, are passed to me, for which I am more grateful than if it had been the gift of a king.

With waves to the crowd and cries of 'Thank you!' we are off again.

The three of us in the train car have nothing to do but admire the beautiful country, through which we are passing as swiftly as a cloud along the sky, or to read, or count telegraph poles, or pamper and pet the monkey.

Having little inclination to do anything but to sit quietly, I rest, bodily and mentally. There is nothing left for me to do now. I can't hurry anything, or change anything, and this makes me realize that the same goes for Mr Cleveland's murder. It is completely out of my control – it's done, it's over with. I can only sit and wait until the train lands me at the end of my journey, then I shall go to the British Embassy and give them the key and Amelia Cleveland's name.

With this resolution, I close my eyes and enjoy the rapid motion of the train so much that I dread to think it could stop.

At the next station, the town turns out to honour me and I am the happy recipient of exquisite fruits, wine and flowers – all the products of Fresno County, California.

The men are interested in my sunburnt nose, the delays I

have experienced and the number of miles I have travelled, while the women want to examine my one dress in which I have voyaged around the world, the cloak and cap I've worn, and are anxious to know what is in the little valise, and all about the monkey.

A man on the outskirts of the crowd shouts, 'Nellie Bly, I must get up close to you!'

The crowd evidently feels as much curiosity as I do about the man's objective, for they make way and he comes up to the platform. 'Nellie Bly, you must touch my hand,' he says excitedly.

Anything to please the man. Reaching over, I touch his hand and he shouts: 'Now you will be successful. I have in my hand the left hind foot of a rabbit!'

Well, I don't know anything about the left hind foot of a rabbit, but later my train runs safely across a bridge which was held in place only by jack-screws and fell the moment we crossed it; following that near disaster, the engine which had just switched off from us lost a wheel. At such moments I thought of the left hind foot of a rabbit and wondered if there was anything in it. I also wondered if it would counteract any of the bad luck that seemed to be associated with the key in my shoe heel.

In another place, where a large crowd greets me, a man yells, 'Did you ride on an elephant, Nellie?'

When I reply, 'No, I didn't,' he drops his head and walks away, leaving me to feel that I've let him down.

Then we stop in a town where the policemen have to fight to keep the crowd back; everybody wants to shake hands with me, but at last one officer is shoved aside and the other, seeing the fate of his comrade, turns to me and says: 'I guess I'll give up and take a shake,' and while reaching for my hand he is swept on with the crowd.

My entire trip down California's central valley and across the deserts of the southwest goes on like this – leaning over platforms and shaking with both hands at every station, and when the train pulls out the crowds run after us, grabbing for my hands as long as they can.

My arms ache, but I don't mind the pain. The journey is a haze of happy wishes, congratulatory telegrams, fruit, flowers, loud cheers, rapid hand-shaking and a beautiful car filled with fragrant flowers attached to a swift engine that is tearing like mad through flower-dotted valleys and over snow-tipped mountains – on, on, on!

During this time I find myself living in the moment and forgetting all my cares and worries. Mr Cleveland no longer troubles me. I am home, safe and very happy.

'Come out here and we'll elect you governor,' a Kansas man says, and I believe they would, if the splendid welcomes they give me are any indication.

It's impossible to say that any one place was kinder than another. Over 10,000 people greet me at Topeka. To say I feel honoured is an understatement. Everyone has been so kind and so anxious that I should finish the trip in time, it's as if their personal reputations are at stake.

It's only when I'm alone in my bunk at night, listening to the rails sing as we roll along, that little doubts and fears sneak back into my head. Sometimes I feel as if there's a devil in my ear, whispering the question that has become a mantra to me when things are going badly.

*When will the other shoe drop?*

# 60

I'm sleeping late when George the porter knocks and tells me we will shortly be arriving in the outskirts of Chicago.

I dress myself leisurely and drink the last drop of coffee there is left on our train, for we have been entertaining anybody who cared to travel any distance with us, before inviting my two train mates to join me in the stateroom.

There is little for us – Henry, George and myself – to do in the Pullman car except watch the fields and hills slip by as we roar down the tracks with the throttle wide open.

I listen with interest as they talk about the history of the Pullman car, how not too long ago it revolutionized train travel, creating a hotel on wheels for the ordinary traveller and palatial luxury for the rich.

The inventor of the sleeping car, George Pullman, designed his car after spending too many miserable overnight trips sitting up in a train seat. The only other option was to sleep on the dirty floor, using one's bag as a pillow.

Mr Pullman's concept of berths that fold up by day, a wash-room for men and one for women, clean sheets, towels and pillows, proved very popular.

The car on my special train has thick carpeting, draperies, carved mahogany panelling, French upholstered chairs, a well-stocked bookcase, a card table, a chandelier and oil lamps rather than candles, plenty of headroom, and water provided from an overhead system of tanks. And, of course, 'George' the porter. I hadn't realized until he told me, but all Pullman porters are called George – in tribute to George Pullman.

George tells me my special car pales in comparison to the private cars for wealthy people that are built exactly to their specifications, with as much attention to detail as the construction of their yachts. But Abraham Lincoln apparently so disliked the ornate railroad car supplied for his service as president that he only rode in it once – when it carried his coffin.

'The Lincoln funeral train is still running on the tracks, filled with ghosts,' George says. 'Every April it comes through at midnight, following the route it took when it carried his body home. It passes by with long black streamers waving, a band playing and skeletons sitting in the carriages.'

I stare out of the window, watching telegraph poles fly by as I listen idly to their conversation about railroading, when I hear a name that gives me a start.

'What did you say, George?'

'Ma'am?'

'What was that name you just said?'

'You mean Amelia?'

'Yes, what about Amelia?'

'Why, *Amelia*'s the finest private rail car in the country. I spent a month serving on it last year when a porter friend took ill.'

'Who does it belong to?'

'To Stirling Westcot, the wealthy railroad magnate.'

Westcot. His name is recognizable not just to me, but to people in all forty-two states as one of the richest men in the nation. He owns railroads and coalmines. His name is also synonymous with ruthless business practices.

'Is Amelia his wife's name?'

'No, ma'am, it's the name of his horse that won the Kentucky Derby last year.'

What did Sarah say to me just before we sailed from Hong Kong? Something about her being as important as a *racehorse*.

A coincidence?

The hair standing up on the back of my neck says it's not. So do the knots in my stomach. Getting up, I pace back and forth, thoughts flying through my head, none of them forming a coherent pattern.

How do I make the connection between a murder in an Egyptian marketplace, a holy war to drive the British from Egypt and the Suez Canal, a train car named *Amelia*, the world's greatest actress, and an American racehorse enthusiast as rich as Midas?

No matter how the pieces are twisted, they don't fit together. Connecting them requires a romantic link between Sarah and Stirling Westcot. While he is immensely wealthy, he is also very short, with an oversized head, and is famous for being as mean as a snake and cheap as a Memphis minister.

A man with enough money can attract beautiful lovers, even if he looks like a toad and acts like a cad. But when Sarah spoke of her mysterious lover, there was real passion in her voice. A fire lit up in her eyes and she acquired that glow only real love can produce.

Stirling Westcot doesn't fit with her passion. And neither do fanatical terrorists halfway around the world and the struggle to control the Suez Canal. Westcot makes money, not nations.

'There's no connection between them, despite the name,' I tell the conductor and George.

They both agree without knowing to what they have assented.

Sitting down, satisfied that I have reached the correct conclusion, it occurs to me there is one more item concerning Mr Cleveland that I have not resolved.

As the men go back to talking, I slip off my shoe and twist the heel to let the key drop into my hand. 'What do you turn, little fellow?'

George stares at my key and then checks the ring he carries on his belt.

'What is it, George?'

'Sorry, ma'am, for a moment I thought you had my key.'

'You have a key like this?'

'Of course I do. All porters have them. It opens the storage area beneath the car.'

*Oh my God.*

# PART TEN

## DAY 70

### *Chicago*
The key to *Amelia*

# 61

Just before the train is about to pull into a station outside Chicago, I slip back into my compartment with the excuse of wanting to bathe my face and hands, but I want the time alone to get my wits about me.

No longer is there any doubt as to what John Cleveland's key opens – for over 12,000 miles, I have carried a key to the storage bin in the underbelly of a private Pullman car.

Now I am completely stumped by its importance.

Why it was hidden in a scarab seems obvious – so it could be passed on secretly to someone without attracting attention. Whoever passed it or received it must have believed that they would be watched, and didn't want the key to be seen exchanging hands.

But Mr Cleveland did see it and intercepted it, grabbed it and ran, so it wasn't meant for him. And it got him killed.

A scarab was a good choice for a hiding place. Of all the things a European tourist might purchase in an Egyptian marketplace, a souvenir scarab ranks very high on the list – probably at the top – beating cartouches and papyri painted with hieroglyphic art. It would be unlikely to attract attention.

The scheme to pass on the key starts to take shape in my mind. The person who was supposed to receive it was a European, probably someone from our ship. While many passengers on board may have visited the marketplace, only a few of them stand out in my mind – Lord and Lady Warton, and Von Reich – and only because I accompanied them. It was Lord Warton who insisted we go to that area of the market because he wanted to purchase something for his sister.

That doesn't mean there weren't a dozen other passengers in the area, or that the handover wasn't to take place later. The snake charmer had me engrossed and I wasn't paying attention to what was happening around me.

Whoever picked up the scarab-key intended to carry it to America and use it to open the storage area underneath Westcot's private train car. But why?

From the news stories I have read about Stirling Westcot, he is an unlikely candidate to be involved in any kind of international scheming. He prides himself on making money, period, and the only business he has with politicians are the stuffed envelopes he slips them when he wants something. Other than gouging as much money as he can from coalmines and railroads, his only passion is horseracing.

I still have no idea about the contents of the storage box, but no matter how I stir the pot, it all boils down to one thing: when the key is used on the *Amelia*, it will open Pandora's box. And it will trigger something with international consequences. There is no other explanation for a Mahdi connection.

Somehow Sarah is mixed up in the intrigue, but I'm certain it's an innocent involvement. I find her too blunt and open about her thoughts and feelings to picture her as a schemer. Nor does she strike me as politically zealous. I'm sure she couldn't care less whether the Suez Canal belonged to the Egyptians, the British or the man in the moon, and she is definitely too melodramatic for spying.

Whatever earthshaking events are unfolding, they don't seem to relate to Sarah but to the important man she is clandestinely seeing. And try as I might, I still can't see her romantically connected to Stirling Westcot. A man has to have more than money to capture her heart. Perhaps Westcot has a son Sarah has become involved with? One in the diplomatic corps?

Now I'm worried for Sarah. I need to contact her, find out where she is going and where this train car *Amelia* is. But how?

I must finish my race. Too many people are counting on me. I've gone this far, there's no turning back. *Damn!* What I desperately need is time, which I don't have.

George knocks on my door. 'Miss Bly, there's a reception committee here for you.'

I find the social area of the car quite filled with good-looking men.

'Hello, Miss Bly, I'm Mr Cornelius Gardener, the vice-president of the Chicago Press Club.' He steps forward, his hat in his hand. 'We've come to Joliet to escort you to Chicago.'

'Thank you.'

Before the train departs the station, I give Henry a telegram to run in to the station office: a query to Mr Bissell, the kind railroad executive I met in Oakland. I request a most urgent reply; I'm hoping that I will find a response at Chicago, our next stop.

Before we are into the station I have answered all the newsmen's questions, and even joked about my sunburnt nose and discussed the merits of travelling around the world with only one dress and a devilishly clever – and bad-tempered – monkey.

I bid a teary-eyed farewell to the wonderful men of the rails who have brought me safely and speedily two thirds of the way across the continent at record speed. The crew on my train and many dozens of other trainmen on the Santa Fe route made my winning the race a part of their own lives, and I shall be forever grateful to them.

The *Miss Nellie Bly Special* was given the right of way along the entire route and all speed limits were ignored. As news of the train's impending arrival flashed over the telegraph lines to the next station, switchmen, engine changers, coal and water tenders were standing by and went into action like a race crew, breaking many records, including switching an engine in forty-five seconds.

Because of their efforts, we set a new record for a run from the San Francisco Bay to Chicago – nearly 2,600 miles at an average speed of thirty-seven miles per hour and occasional bursts of sixty miles per hour.

The rails between Chicago and the Eastern Seaboard are too crowded with traffic to permit my special train to dominate the tracks, so now I must leave the *Miss Nellie Bly Special* to board a regular passenger train for the rest of the race.

My train in Chicago is not ready to depart when we arrive, so carriages are waiting to take me and the group of newsmen to the meeting room of the Press Club.

As I step aboard a coupe I shall share with Vice President Gardener, George the porter comes huffing and puffing from a good run to catch up with me, and thrusts the reply to my telegram into my hands.

'Here you are, Miss Bly. God's speed to the finish line!'

My query to the Oakland manager requested information about the onward journey of certain passengers from the *Oceanic* who docked after I left the tugboat. It is easy for a railroad man to determine the progress of trains in a very short time because most of the telegraph lines across the country follow the train tracks.

My specific question was about Sarah, Frederick, the Wartons and Von Reich. The answer: they left together on the train that crossed the mountains, and are due to arrive in Chicago several hours after I am scheduled to leave.

Mr Gardener interrupts my contemplation.

'Sorry, I was lost in thought,' I apologize. 'What did you say?'

'My dear Miss Bly, I am strongly tempted to steal you. You are quite a lady.'

'Well, Mr Gardener,' I say, giving him my innocent young woman smile that worked many times with Mr Pulitzer, 'that is an opportune suggestion. I do indeed need you and the Press Club members to steal me for a few hours. I'm changing my departure time so I can join up with friends coming in from the west.'

'Isn't that risky?'

'I hope not.' But I know it is.

I can see the headlines: 'NELLIE BLY FAILS AMERICA AND WOMEN!' Instead of hurrays, I'll be receiving boos.

But there is no other choice. Delaying my departure to join my former shipmates is the only honourable thing for me to do. I'm certain Sarah is in danger, more than she realizes.

War, death, illicit love – deadly sins are all in some way wrapped up in Sarah's journey, events not far from my description of armies marching on darkling plains.

'You appear sad, Miss Bly.' Mr Gardener gives me a kind smile. 'I hope it's simply because you know that you will only spend a few hours in our beautiful city.'

'I was just thinking about how peaceful life was when I was very small and had not one care in the world.'

# 62

In the beautiful rooms of the Press Club I meet the president, Stanley Waterloo, and a number of clever newspapermen. They weren't expecting me in Chicago until noon. The club had arranged an informal reception for me, but when they were notified of my speedy trip and consequent earlier arrival, it was too late to notify the members.

After a most delightful reception they escort me to Kinsley's, where the club has a breakfast prepared. Owing to some misunderstanding, none of the men have had anything to eat since the night before. After breakfast the members of the Press Club, acting as my escort, take me to visit the Chicago Board of Trade, the commodities exchange, where I encounter two surprises.

First – their billboard lists my name as today's guest speaker to the commodities traders.

Second – *Mr Stirling Westcot* is listed below my name. He is going to address the traders tomorrow night.

I must have been staring at his name, for my escort notices. 'Are you acquainted with Mr Westcot?'

'Only by reputation, but I would like to meet him.'

'Unfortunately, you'll miss him on this trip. He addresses us tomorrow and leaves for the West Coast the following morning.'

Going west in his private train car, of course. And I'm going east. So are my shipmates. Sarah wouldn't come all the way to Chicago just to turn around and head west again. Maybe there is more than one Amelia in this world and I have been focusing on the wrong one.

When we enter the commodities trading room, the pandemonium which seems to reign during business hours is at its height.

My escorts take me to the gallery and just as we get there, a man raises his arm to yell something to the roaring crowd, but he spots me and yells instead: '*There's Nellie Bly!*'

In one instant the crowd that has been shouting like mad becomes so quiet a pin could be heard falling to the floor. Every face, bright and eager, turns up towards me, instantly every hat comes off, then a burst of applause resounds through the immense hall.

I am in shock. People can say what they please about Chicago, but I do not believe that anywhere else in the United States could a woman receive a greeting which would equal that given by the Chicago Board of Trade.

The applause is followed by cheer after cheer and cries of '*Speech!*'

I take off my little cap and shake my head at them, for I can't speak. I just pray I can hold back my tears; I can't have these men seeing me cry . . . it's just so incredible.

My gesture only serves to increase their cheers.

It is late afternoon when the Press Club members escort me to Pennsylvania Station, where I reluctantly bid them goodbye, unable to thank them heartily enough for the royal manner in which they have treated a little sunburnt stranger.

From Mr Bissell's telegram I already know the Wartons and Von Reich have compartments in one car. Frederick Selous and Sarah are in other cars. My compartment is in the same car as Sarah's; she and I will be next-door neighbours, and the rest closer together than when we were at sea. It will be interesting to see what happens with all of us sandwiched together like sardines.

Right now I'm very curious as to how they will react when they see me. And to know what Sarah will tell me when I demand answers from her.

A group of people boarding the train pause and look in my direction as a man takes off his hat and yells, 'You're on the last lap, Nellie! Get going and get across that finish line!'

Smiling, I wave and mouth a 'thank you' to him. God, I hope I will cross that line.

Well, now the cat's out of the bag.

Lord Warton, who is entering a Pullman two cars down from the one I will be riding in, turns and gives me the sort of frown and grimace I would expect a hanging judge to cast on a prisoner in the dock. As for her ladyship, she merely glances in my direction, lifts her chin, and shows me her back. An ice-cold wind would have been a warmer welcome.

Inside, I drop my bag and ulster in my own compartment and knock on Sarah's door.

'This is the police,' I whisper at the door. 'We are investigating a mystery woman.'

A scream of joy comes from the other side of the door, and it flies open. 'Nellie!' She gives me a genuinely warm, enthusiastic hug. 'Come in!'

Pretending to peek around the tiny compartment, I ask, 'What, no coffin to sleep in?'

Dramatically she puts the back of her hand against her forehead. 'Alas, it ended up in the baggage car. I'm so delighted you are here! I thought for sure we had seen the last of each other.'

'Me too.' I close the door behind us. 'Sarah, I have to talk to you.'

She takes a seat, while I remain standing.

'What is it, dear? You look positively alarmed.'

'We need to talk about your rendezvous. You have to tell me—'

She almost shakes her head off her shoulders. 'No—no—no, you must not ask, you must stay completely out of the matter.'

'I have to know. Especially about Amelia—'

'Out!' She jumps up and slides open the door.

'Sarah—'

'Out.' She gives me a little push. As I start to step out she gives me a kiss on the cheek. 'Some day I will make it up to you, but right now you are *persona non grata* to me.'

'Sarah, I think you're in danger.'

'That's so sweet, you are such an innocent little thing. Sometimes I feel like the whole world is in danger.'

'Armies marching on darkling plains . . .'

'Exactly.' She gives me another peck on the cheek. 'Now run along, dear, and –' she leans close and whispers, 'Don't come back unless I call for you.'

She slips back into her compartment and closes the door.

For a moment I stare at the door, tempted to slide it back open, then I hear the lock engage. Well, for now that takes care of that, and I start to enter my compartment but change my mind.

I find the porter. 'George, what car is Mr Selous in?'

'The next car up. But I saw Mr Selous in the smoking car a moment ago. That's three cars up.'

'Thank you.'

Smoking cars are my least favourite part of a train. I'd rather ride in the coal tender with the fireman and the smoke from the furnace blowing back at us than be forced to breathe thick clouds of evil-smelling cigar smoke – a fact that I have shared more than once with men on a train. To no avail.

Lord and Lady Warton are there when I enter, with her ladyship's charming personality fortunately hidden behind her veil, along with whatever her thoughts are about the fact that we have been reunited as travelling companions. They're in a group that includes Frederick, who is engrossed in conversation with another man and doesn't realize I have entered.

The Bluenoses both completely ignore me despite the fact that I hear my name buzzed around the room and several people give me a friendly smile of recognition. I feel like asking her ladyship if she's faked any more heart attacks, but decide to leave well enough alone.

'What do you gentlemen think of the Westley 303?' a man asks Frederick.

'A what?' asks Lord Warton.

'It's a tiger gun, isn't that so, Frederick?' says his wife.

'Yes, it can bring down a tiger,' he says, giving me a big smile as he spots me, 'but you'd better hit it at a kill point or you'll end up facing six hundred pounds of charging beast with the force of a locomotive.'

I move along, waiting for Frederick to disengage himself from the men who want to ask questions of the renowned hunter, when I spot more familiar faces.

The widow Murdock and Cenza, her assistant, or lover, and the gregarious Von Reich are sitting together at the back of the car. The latter is leaning back in a chair, glass in hand, and appears to have enjoyed quite a few drops of the nectar of the grape. The widow is smoking a cigarillo and holding a glass of brandy, and from the flush on her cheeks it isn't her first.

Cenza gives me a smirk that implies she knows something I don't, and it's about to drop on my head.

Smirking, it seems, is a permanent deformity of her lips.

It's still difficult to imagine Cenza with Murdock's widow. They are just not a match, whatever their sexual preferences. There has to be something else binding them together and the only thing I can think of is the pot of gold the widow appeared to have acquired after her husband's untimely demise.

I reverse my direction to stay away from them and find Frederick breaking away from his interlocutors, calling out, 'Nellie! I'm so delighted you're here.'

Lord Warton turns his back again, takes his charming wife by the arm and exits. I catch something like 'the bad penny is back' as they leave.

'I apologize for Warton,' Frederick says, taking me out of the others' hearing range. 'He's a discourteous wretch. Under different circumstances, I would take him to task for his boorish behavior towards you.'

'What exactly are the circumstances that make the mere sight of me so offensive to him, and prevent a gentleman from coming to my rescue?'

He chuckles. 'Nellie, you have a wonderful sense of inquisitiveness. But you must learn to control it.'

'Does Amelia control it?' It's a shot in the dark.

His eyebrows go up. 'Amelia? Isn't that the name you thought you heard—'

'Yes, *thought* I heard, but I realize now that I was wrong. The truth is I never heard anything. I was never in Port Saïd. I don't even know who you are. Or who I am.'

'Nellie, I think—'

'Please do. In the meantime, I'll take some headache powders, or something stronger, for my weak feminine disposition, or maybe I'll just have some of Sarah's damn coca-wine.'

If I wasn't a lady, I'd ... instead, I spin on my heel and am out of there without looking back, retracing my steps to my compartment. I enter and slam the door shut behind me. And lock it.

Why did I do that? I went to talk to Frederick in a civilized manner. I was happy to see him and could tell he wanted to see me. And what did I do? Blow up at him.

My only excuse is that I'm angry, frustrated and bewildered because what I'm certain is a murderous conspiracy seems to be unimportant to others.

'What is going on?' I demand from the wall separating me and Sarah.

Maybe I am just a fool. I must be. I have risked losing my race to save Sarah and she doesn't want to be saved. She doesn't even want me around.

I'm beginning to wonder if they are all right, that *I'm* the one with the problem.

Why else would I jeopardize the race of my career and my reputation to come back and travel with people who appear surprised – and some definitely annoyed – that I am still on the planet?

Sarah seems to adore me, but slams her door in my face

and tells me to stay out of anything involving her. Frederick is laughing at me, or at the very least has developed a patronizing amused tolerance of my antics. Lord and Lady Bluenose treat me like a leper. Von Reich ignores me. And Cenza, who radiates malice with her smug grins, gives me the creeps.

*What do these people know that I don't?*

*Railroad Parlor Car*

# 63

Instead of having an entire deluxe Pullman car at my disposal, I have but a stateroom, and my space is so limited that all my floral and fruit offerings had to be left behind, which I very much regret. I also miss the speed of my first train. This one creeps along like a snail, and I fear I will not make this last leg of my journey on time.

Before I reached my compartment, George gave me a telegram that was meant to be delivered in San Francisco, but has only just caught up with me.

The message gives me great pleasure and changes my mood: 'Mr Verne wishes the following message to be handed to Nellie Bly the moment she touches American soil: M. Jules Verne addresses his sincere *félicitations* to the intrepid Miss Nellie Bly.'

Oh, how I could use Jules's help right now.

The train is rather poorly equipped and it's necessary for everyone to disembark for meals. Our first stop is Logansport for dinner.

When I reach the platform, a young man whom I've never seen before or since, springs up on another platform and waves his hat, shouting, 'Hurrah for Nellie Bly! Hurrah for Nellie Bly!'

A delegation of railroad men wait upon me and present me with beautiful flowers and candy, as do a number of other people. The crowd claps and cheers, and after making way for me to pass to the dining room, they press forward and their cheers go up again. They even crowd the windows to watch me eat.

After I sit down, several dishes are put before me bearing the inscription: 'Success, Nellie Bly.'

Despite all the attention I've received since I left the *Oceanic*, I'm not comfortable with these public displays of admiration. It makes me sad and angry with myself – here are people who think highly of me and are counting on me to finish, and I may have betrayed them because I could be hours ahead. How stupid I've been.

I spoon my soup very carefully, so at least these wonderful people won't have the memory of my dinner running down my chin or dropping on my blouse.

An ancient old dowager at another table has a note delivered to me. I open it, reading between sips of soup: 'I don't even get this type of treatment when I'm in a hit play. Next time I need attention I shall travel around the world at great speed.'

Glancing over at the old woman, I get a subtle nod and give back a wry grin.

What an actress she is.

On my way back to the train, I'm informed there will be a delay, because a switching locomotive is adding another car to the one behind mine. It provides a golden opportunity for me to walk along the tracks in the cool night air and enjoy a moment to myself after all the fuss of the last few days.

Even though there are other people about, every now and then I can't help taking a look behind me. It's dark, and I still have the key someone has killed for.

A short distance down the tracks they are connecting the new Pullman car. It's beautiful, polished forest green with a substantial gold trim that shows it obviously belongs to someone with an abundance of wealth.

I stop and stare at the plate on the side of the car, the name engraved in gold on a silver plaque.

*Amelia.*

My heart beats a little faster, and I get a flash of a man speaking her name as his life blood pours out onto the ground.

A porter steps down from the *Amelia* and lights a cigarette. I saunter over to him.

'Good evening.'

'Evenin', ma'am.'

'Isn't this Mr Westcot's car?'

'Yes, ma'am, it is.'

'I met him once. Would you mind taking my card to him?'

'Can't do that, he's not aboard.'

'Really? Who's using the car?'

A grunt comes from above us. A man is standing at the top of the Pullman's steps, looking down at us.

The porter mutters, ''Scuse me,' and goes up the steps, the man moving aside for him without ever turning his eyes from me.

Another man, of the same school as the one that's staring down, appears from behind me.

Obviously they are plain-clothes policemen – they have the thick necks, beefy frames and Irish whisky noses of New York City's Finest, with their roomy cheap suits cut from the same cloth. Or I suppose they could be private detectives.

Whichever they are, why are they guarding the *Amelia*? Or, more likely, whoever is in it. It certainly isn't its owner, Westcot, if he's on his way to count his money out west.

Turning around, I smile politely and give them a 'Good evening'.

They return my greeting in a not particularly friendly manner, and tip their hats.

Very interesting . . . they are coppers, for sure. But one thing surprises me – their accents are British.

Why are two British dicks protecting the train car of Sarah's lover?

*Who* is important enough for one of the richest men in America to give up his luxurious Pullman for his guest to have a romantic tryst with an actress?

It's a very short list, for sure . . . but who?

An answer springs to mind as to the lover's possible identity, but it's so incredible, so far-fetched, that not even my vivid imagination will accept it. It's simply not within the realms of reason that one of the most important men on the planet is in that train car. Not even what Frederick thinks is my overworked imagination can make me believe that he is in there. If that were the case, it would be on the front pages of every newspaper in the country.

No, it just can't be . . . which only leaves me aching to find out who *is* in that Pullman.

I can't sleep.

Lying awake, I listen for the tell-tale sound of Sarah leaving her compartment for a romantic rendezvous with the mysterious occupant of the *Amelia*, but I don't hear it. She might have sneaked out too quietly for me to hear over the noise of rolling wheels on the rails and the creak of the train cars.

I finally doze off, but in the middle of the night I'm jolted awake as the brakes screech, bringing us to a stop to take on coal and water.

The moment I wake up I know what my next step must be. I quickly dress, remove the key from my shoe heel and slip it into my pocket. As I put my hand on the compartment's doorknob, I pause for a moment and ask myself . . . should I really go through with this?

The train has stopped, it's the dead of night and the rest of the world is asleep. I have the key to the *Amelia*. This is an opportunity that might not be repeated.

If there are easier ways to find out what's in the storage locker than sneaking around in the dark, they all elude me at the moment.

Fighting the jitters, I lean my forehead on the door and close my eyes. Do I really want to do this? *Now or never*, that's the answer. If I am ever going to do it, it has to be now.

I squeeze the key in my hand. I made a promise to a dead man to get the key to 'Amelia'. Well, this is the only way that promise can be kept.

It's time to open Pandora's box and see what is inside.

# 64

Slipping by the snoring porter's curtained bunk, I quickly open and close the exit door behind me to keep a breeze from sneaking in and awakening him.

The night is dark and cold as my feet touch the rocky rail bed and I immediately regret that I didn't wear my ulster.

Down towards the front of the train, I can make out the chute that is feeding coal to the tender car and a line from a water tank to the boiler. It's a fuel stop in the middle of nowhere, with no houses, no station. I am at the far end of my train car from the *Amelia* and I have to walk slowly and cautiously to keep my footing on the rocky bed. After everything I have been through, it would be a fitting conclusion to my race around the entire world if I were to fall and hit my head and be left on the side of the tracks while the train continued to a triumphant entry into New Jersey – minus me.

No light shows in any of the *Amelia*'s windows. The storage locker is about halfway down the length of the car.

Despite the crunch-crunch-crunch noise I'm making, I pick up my step because I don't want to run into someone who has decided to stretch their legs and get a breath of fresh air.

Crouching down in front of the locker, I wish I had had the foresight to slip a kitchen match into my pocket because it's too dark to see the lock. Exploring with my fingers, I find it.

A serious case of the jitters has set my nerves on fire, as if my body knows something I don't – but should.

Fumbling, I drop the key onto the rocky train bed, which is black from soot and coal dust. Patting the ground I find it again and using two hands to guide it, I slip the key into the lock and turn it. The brackets make an awful metallic grating noise that makes me cringe as I lift the lid. *Damn.* I'm so jittery, I'm sure the scraping is loud enough to wake the dead. And I can't see anything in the locker, it's just a black void. Either it's completely empty or whatever is inside is further back, hidden in the darkness.

I reach back as far as I can, but feel nothing. Pandora's box is empty? I edge back and stare at the locker, refusing to believe the obvious – the key to *Amelia* has opened an empty box.

Footsteps crunch to my right and I turn to find a gun in my face.

'You called that one right, Mr Selous. The woman's a troublemaker – that's a certainty.'

The speaker is one of the British coppers, a redheaded one. The train has finished fuelling and we are in the common area of the car containing Frederick's compartment. While the redheaded copper pointed his gun at my nose outside, his mate ran up behind me, putting aside his own pistol only long enough to handcuff me.

Treating me as if I'm a dangerous criminal when I'm investigating a case does so remind me of my interactions with New York's Finest.

Lord Warton has joined the others trampling my good person, figuratively at least, but the night is young – they may still kick me like a dog.

His lordship has a whisky glow and he's unsteady on his feet. Obviously he has been sucking on a bottle in the middle of the night. Whatever demons drive him to find relief with John Barleycorn seem to have intensified since I last saw him aboard the *Oceanic*.

Frederick came to my rescue and had the coppers put away their guns and remove the cuffs, telling them, 'She's not dangerous – just nosy.'

Now, listening with a sense of cold fury to the men boasting and patting themselves and each other on the back, I keep my mouth shut because I have no defence.

Frederick refuses to meet my eye, which is fine with me because I'm more angry at myself than I am at him. He guessed my intent and told the coppers, and they set a trap. Walking into it was inexcusable.

Other passengers, who poked their heads out of their compartments to see what all the commotion was about when I became incensed at being manhandled, were ordered back to bed. Sarah never showed her face.

A vigilante committee: that is how I have come to think of these Brits who have seized me as if I am a criminal. Like the groups of men who clean up San Francisco and many another Western town by stringing up the bad guys from the nearest trees, these coppers act with authority when they have none. That they have guns and muscles makes them the natural administrators of justice at the moment.

When I reach my fill of abuse as they debate how to 'restrain' my 'wild impulses', I start throwing verbal punches. 'At the next stop, I'll have the sheriff remove all of you from the train,' I tell the redhead, 'and place you, your cohort and the rest of this posse of vigilantes under arrest for manhandling a woman.'

'I'll have you know *we* are police officers,' the redheaded copper snaps back.

'Then you're thousands of miles outside your jurisdiction. You're a bunch of foreigners who have attacked an American citizen.'

Frederick reaches to pat my hand and I jerk it away. 'Nellie—'

'What is *your* authority, Mr Selous? And the rest of you, tell me – who granted you a licence to kidnap a woman and hold her prisoner?'

I look from one to the next, giving each of them a good stare. 'It's pretty obvious that you have plotted with my competitor to keep me from winning. In case you haven't noticed, the local police have been at every stop to cheer me on.'

This is not completely true, but I throw it in for good measure.

'When I get out at the next stop and inform the crowd that you have physically assaulted me, do you have any idea what the men in that crowd will do?'

The redheaded copper looks at Selous. 'I thought you said she wasn't dangerous?'

'She needs to be locked up,' Warton manages to say.

His drunken slur reminds me of my alcoholic stepfather, who abused our entire family with his bad words and beatings. I hated that man. I step up to Warton to make sure I am right in his face.

'I am filing charges of slander and abuse against you at the next stop. You can look for your next bottle of whisky in a jail cell, if the crowd doesn't string you up from the nearest tree first.'

Lord Warton takes a step backwards, almost falling as he stumbles. The man is so horrified, he appears ready to collapse.

'I'll have you horsewhipped.' He points a shaky finger at me.

'Another threat for the police!' I snap.

Frederick steps in between us. 'Show his lordship back to his compartment,' he orders the redheaded officer. 'Return to your duties,' he tells the other.

He grabs my arm but I jerk it loose. 'You're also going to jail.'

He starts laughing and that spikes my rage.

'Stop, please,' he begs, 'I'm not laughing at you, I'm laughing at the way the others got out of here so fast.'

There seems to be an eternal silence as we stand staring at each other.

Naturally, I break it. 'I meant it when I said I'd have the whole gang of you arrested.'

'I'm sure you could do it, you're America's sweetheart. But after what I've been through since I met you, a long prison term sounds like paradise.'

'What *you've* been through? I have blood on me from a murder and I was nearly killed myself – not once, but twice. I hope a big, strong man like you wasn't too terrified as I fought my would-be killers.'

Satisfied that I have gotten the last word in, I start for my room. He follows, whispering the magic words, 'I have answers to your questions.'

Weak person that I am when it comes to a story, I stop.

He touches my arm again, gingerly, as if he's afraid I'll bite. 'Please join me for a moment in my compartment where we can talk in private.'

In his room, we sit across from each other. Pushing the wrinkles out of my dress, I sit back and clasp my hands together.

'First,' he says, 'let me tell you what I meant when I said I'd had nothing but trouble since I met you. You aren't the cause of the trouble, it just happens that it began about the time we met.'

'Tell me everything,' I command. 'Everything. Start at the beginning. And try not to lie too much.'

'Before I begin, I must have your word of honour that what I'm about to tell you will never find its way to the public during the lifetimes of anyone involved.'

'I can't promise that, I'm a reporter. Besides, I already know a great deal.'

'Your promise is required for me to go on.'

'How can I make a promise when I don't know all the facts? What if you tell me something that in good conscience should be revealed to the public or the proper authorities?' I hold up my hand to stop his objection. 'I will commit to this: if you give me a good reason why I shouldn't do the story, I won't do it. *But* only if I find the reason compelling. I've already put together much more than you realize and I don't care which country ends up controlling the Suez Canal. And I'm positive that I know the identity of the mysterious personage that Sarah is visiting.'

Much of what I 'know' qualifies as wild guesses, but I doubt he's going to be completely honest with me anyway. I don't know how many chords I've hit, he appears rather amused, so I lock eyes with him so he gets the full impact of my knock-out punch.

'How is good old Bertie?' I ask, attempting a Cockney accent.

That wipes the humour from his face. His eyes narrow and his forehead folds into wrinkles. 'You *are* dangerous.'

'Start talking,' I command again. It feels good to have the upper hand after scraping bottom for so long. 'Start with the murder at Port Saïd.'

'Fine. The events that led up to that began some weeks earlier, at least for me. I was visiting an old hunting chum in Cairo – a Turkish collector of exotic animals who has deal-ings with a wide variety of individuals in Egypt, including some ardent followers of the Mahdi movement. Let's call him Bey. He heard a story that I didn't find credible, but when I passed it on to the head of our mission in Cairo, I was shocked to discover that there was credence to it.

'Bey told me that a plot had been hatched by the Mahdi to galvanize the support of the entire Egyptian population by striking a blow against Britain that would shock the world. The plot was to assassinate a very important personage—'

'Bertie,' I interject.

'The plot was to kill the individual while he was on a, uh—'

'Romantic tryst?'

He clears his throat. 'While he was on an unreported horseracing venture in America. As you must know from reading the newspapers, the gentleman is an ardent racing fan and race horse owner who regularly enters his horses in important British meets and on the Continent. For a number of years he has had a friendly competition with Mr Westcott about who has the fastest three-year-old filly in the world. The track time of the two horses is the same, and the only way they can settle the matter is to race them against each other. So, the . . . uh, the personage decided to bring his horse to America and hold a private and, of course, secret meet at the track where the Kentucky Derby is run.'

I raise my eyebrows. 'Obviously such a race could have been arranged much more easily by simply shipping horses rather than people, so my guess about a romantic rendezvous is most likely correct.'

Selous gives me a diplomatic smile. 'Let's just say that there is more than one motive for the trip. The person we are speaking of is noted for occasionally travelling incognito.'

'Fine. So how did word of this trip get all the way to Egypt and to the ears of terrorists?'

'In a manner that is not as unusual as you might think. The individual who is second in command of Britain's mission in Egypt is part of the personage's inner circle back home. The friend learned of the trip while in London. When he returned to his duties in Cairo, one night over dinner he told his wife about it—'

'With servants present,' I interpose.

'Yes.'

'You're right, it's not unusual. There's more than one servant in New York who got rich leaving his ears open while serving an employer who talked business over cigars and brandy. It's pure arrogance on the part of men who don't consider servants to be people.'

'Quite so. The servant was a Mahdi loyalist who passed the information on to some higher-ups, who hatched the plot. They knew that their target would be travelling by Pullman car. It so happens that they once killed an important member of the British government, along with several high-ranking Egyptian officials, with a bomb on the Alexandria to Cairo run.'

'You're going to tell me they placed the bomb in the locker under the train. And stole a Pullman key to do it.'

'Exactly. The keys are easy enough to get hold of; there are Pullman cars in Egypt.'

'And Mr Cleveland intercepted the key. I take it he was a British agent?'

'A naval officer—'

'Mr Cleveland's been dead for two years.'

Frederick clears his throat. 'We used Cleveland's identity not only because he no longer needed it, but because his profession as a cutlery salesman serving Egypt fitted the need for a cover. The naval officer was given the assignment because he spoke Arabic. The British government doesn't have many full-time spies, and none fluent in Arabic. My own initial involvement was simply to fulfil a request that I meet Cleveland in Port Saïd and fill him in on what I had learned from Bey, who had told me that the key was to be passed by a scarab merchant in the marketplace to the hired assassin.'

'The Mahdi hired an assassin rather than use one of their own? Because their own people would have stood out?'

'Yes. Cleveland was to go to the marketplace to observe the hand-off, as you know, and ended up with the scarab in his own hand. We don't know why he suddenly grabbed the scarab, perhaps from inexperience in dealing with such a situation, or maybe the man mistook him for the assassin and at first offered him—'

'The scarab and then called for his death when he realized the mistake.'

He nods. 'Poor devil. He appears to have acted on impulse, as a soldier would have, not realizing the subtleties of spying.'

'Your Cleveland disguised himself as an Egyptian when he could have blended in with other Europeans in the marketplace. Isn't that true?'

'Yes, I agree, Nellie. What does that tell you?'

'He planned from the first to get the key. And he had had a conversation with the man selling the scarabs, at least enough to be told that the target car was *Amelia*.'

'You're quite right, I see what you mean. He didn't go there just to observe, as he'd been ordered, but to pull off a coup.'

'How close were you when he was killed?' I ask.

'Not as close as you. Back quite a way, as a matter of fact. I didn't see the killing. I made contact with Lord Warton after you and her ladyship left.'

'Uh-huh. And began trying to make me the fool.'

He shrugs and spreads his hands on his lap. 'Not out of malice, let me assure you.'

'And you took Cleveland's place?'

'Right. His superior drafted me to continue the mission because there was no one else available. As it so happened I had already obtained a ticket for India to attend a safari, so I knew my appearance on the boat wouldn't arouse suspicion.'

'And you concocted the story that Cleveland was alive.'

'It seemed the appropriate way to proceed at the time.'

'Why didn't you just ask me for the key?'

'Nellie, you never told me you had it.'

'True . . . actually, I didn't know I had anything of significance until I began to see conspiracies swirling around me.'

'There was also the question of your potential involvement. Bey was told that the assassination team was composed of two people. It could have been a man and woman.'

'You thought I was an assassin? And planned a race around the world to disguise my true plan?'

'I didn't know who you were at the time. I soon decided you were a genuine reporter—'

'Well, that was kind of you. And clever.'

He clears his throat. 'But then another problem arose. The scarab wasn't on Cleveland when I searched his body. And I found fragments of a scarab when I searched your room.'

'So you knew I had the key. And we began a game of cat and mouse.'

He smiles. 'And you were the cat. With sharp claws.'

'So after you realized I had it, why didn't you just ask me for it?'

'There were complicated reasons.'

'Complicated reasons . . . ah, I think I understand. The hired assassins would also want the key. And if you watched me, you would see who they were . . .'

'Quite.'

'As they murdered me.'

He clears his throat again and grins. 'I was hoping to prevent that eventuality.'

'And you are just an innocent bystander, roped in to serve Queen and country.'

He tries unsuccessfully to smother a smirk. 'I thought I adapted well to the role of spy.'

'You're not bad,' I shrug, 'though you must watch your back more. I was able to follow you to your meeting with Lady Warton and that rather offensive sailor friend of yours in Hong Kong.' I don't volunteer that I stumbled upon them by accident.

'So, the spy was spied upon! Very good. Gary plays the

role of offensive seaman quite well, don't you think? He's actually with Naval Intelligence.'

'He didn't play it that well. He spoke French to the wrong woman, so I knew you had hatched something with Sarah. I take it there was an effort to get Sarah to go home and forget the rendezvous?'

'Yes, but like you, Sarah follows her own drummer.'

'What were you hatching with Lady Bluenose in Hong Kong?'

'Lady Warton wanted to confide her feelings about Von Reich. Her husband is quite taken with the man, but her ladyship doesn't like him and was offended by some anti-British statements he had made.'

'Her husband's tolerance, I take it, is a result of him being paid to introduce the man to government officials.'

'Quite.'

'So . . .' I think for a moment. 'The plan was to put a bomb into the Pullman locker. As they did in Egypt.'

'Yes.'

'But you prevented that?'

'The attempt was blocked, yes, hours before your use of the key. We knew the attempt would be made and we were ready. When the culprit was spotted, he dropped the bomb on the ground and fled. But we know who he is and your police will catch him. If nothing else, his heavy accent will trip him up.'

'An accent? Von Reich? Von Reich's the assassin?' My astonishment is evident.

'Yes, he fits the bill rather nicely, don't you think? An explosives expert, a foreigner, he was at the marketplace—'

'He's not the type.'

Frederick raises his eyebrows. 'Nellie, dear, assassins aren't produced from a cookie cutter.'

'But—'

'No buts. You simply must accept it.'

'You and those coppers actually saw Von Reich?'

'It was too dark to see the man's features, but his hat fell off as he ran away.'

'What's his motive?'

'Money, of course. The Mahdi can pay vast sums in gold. They may have done business before. Perhaps he also prepared the explosives for the Egyptian train car assassinations.'

'You have no confession. You don't know where—'

He holds up his hand to cut me off. 'The man is on the run. And I'm sure you're aware from your reporting that fleeing the scene of a crime is tantamount to a signed confession.'

He gets up, leans over and kisses me on the cheek. 'Get some rest, sweet lady. We'll talk about this some more in the morning. You must conserve your energy to finish your race.'

Back in my compartment, I undress and climb back into bed again, tired to my very marrow. Frederick's right, of course – the mystery of the key to the *Amelia* is finished and I still have a race to win.

I didn't fail to note that Frederick forgot to obtain my promise not to use the story. The revelations will be sensational. Mr Pulitzer will be thrilled, not to mention there will be extra benefits for me – a pay raise, choices of stories to cover. Not only will I finish my trip on time, but I will come back with another sensational story.

This settled, I close my eyes and will myself to sleep when a thought electrifies my tired brain . . . *poor Von Reich.*

Now why did I have such a thought? The man's an assassin, a murderer— I sit straight up in bed. But he's not a runner. The portly gentleman would hardly have gotten far before the coppers caught him. And dropping his hat. 'How convenient,' I tell the ceiling. He leaves his hat behind so there will be no mistake in identification?

The shoe doesn't fit Von Reich no matter how I try to slip it on.

*Stop it, Nellie!*

It's over with, done, finished. Time to move on.

Von Reich is the obvious villain. He's a professional bomb-maker; the crime fits him like a glove, so why can't I accept it? I pull the blanket over my head. I hate it when my mind won't shut off and let me sleep.

There's a light tap on my door and the porter asks, 'Miss Bly? Are you still awake? I have a note for you.'

Giving me the note, he apologizes, 'Sorry, ma'am, I was given this hours ago and forgot to give it to you.'

'Who's it from?' I ask as I unfold it.

'Don't know, ma'am. Another porter handed it to me. Good night.'

George leaves and I step back into my compartment to read the message.

I MUST SEE YOU *7201C – VR*

The author's initials blaze with fire in my mind's eye.

*What does he want with me?*

# 65

*Not a creature was stirring, not even a mouse*, plays in my head as I step lightly down the corridor to the porter's bunk. The only evidence of life in the train car are the rasps of snoring. Once again, everyone is asleep except lucky me.

Standing next to the bunk curtain, I whisper George's name and he sticks out his head.

'Sorry, George, but which car is 7201?'

'Two cars up, ma'am.'

'Who occupies compartment C in that car?'

'I can't say, ma'am. The porter in 7201 has that information. Did you want me to—'

'No.' I slip him a silver dollar. 'Thank you. Go back to sleep.'

Two cars up is the one that I saw the Wartons entering. Frederick's car is next. The corridor is as deserted as my own, as is that of 7201 when I reach it. Hushing the porter with a 'shh' and a silver dollar, I ask who occupies compartment C.

He unhooks a clipboard from the will and consults it. 'A Mr Lazarus, ma'am.'

'What does he look like?'

'I don't know. He's sick, never comes out of his compartment.'

'How do you know he's sick?'

'The young lady told me, the one with the other Australian woman. She said not to disturb him 'cause he's under the weather.'

Questions rattle around my head as I make my way to compartment C. Who's Mr Lazarus and why is he harbouring Von Reich? Why is the caustic Cenza making excuses for Lazarus? And what does Von Reich want with me?

Gathering my courage, I stare at the compartment door, knowing that I might be throwing myself into the hands of a dangerous killer, that I should get Frederick. But then I'd never get to the truth of what's happening. He'd burst in, arrest Von Reich and I'd still have no final answer.

Looking up and down the corridor to ensure that I am not being watched, I tap lightly with just the tip of my fingernail. No response and I tap again, a little louder. Silence. Taking a deep breath, I slowly slide open the door an inch, just enough to see that it is dark inside.

I pull the door open wider and give a startled cry.

Von Reich is on the bench seat, hunched over, his right shoulder against the window frame. A streak of blood has run down the side of his head. On the seat beside him is a derringer.

A woman pokes her head out of the next compartment.

'What's going on?'

'*Murder*! There's been a murder.'

She screams. I stare at her, dumbfounded.

She screams again.

Compartment doors start opening, heads poke out.

I feel like screaming myself, so I take a deep breath and let out a wail of pure frustration.

# 66

I am back in the hands of the coppers and the other vigilantes. Under ordinary circumstances I would welcome the professional attention being given to the matter, but since the high-handed flat foots are treating me as a suspicious person, if not an actual suspect, I find no fault on my part in challenging their conclusions and their authority.

Shocked, sick at seeing a man dead that I knew and rather liked, a companion on a long trip who had shown me courtesies, I permit myself to be ushered to the common area in Frederick's car. I don't know what to think. I'm out of answers, at the moment. I'm even out of questions. Everything is too unreal for it to really sink in. For a moment after I opened the door my first thought was that the death had been staged, that it was a joke by Von Reich, but that thought was erased when I saw the funeral pallor of his skin.

Half the train was woken by the hysterical cries of '*Murder!*' that resounded down the aisles. Order was finally restored, people assured of their safety, and the vigilance committee met to receive the 'official' pronouncement from the coppers who were examining Von Reich's body – which they have now wrapped in blankets and are transferring to the baggage car.

Frederick is with me, as is Lord Warton, looking the worse for wear and carefully not looking in my direction.

No one is happy I found the body. No one considers me completely innocent.

They look at me as if I have been caught rustling their cattle and will soon be kicking at the end of a rope.

Frederick reads my mind and rubs his forehead as if it will remove a headache.

'I find you completely amazing. A friend of mine in the Raj is quite taken by the Indians' belief that our lives are predestined, that the paths we take are determined at birth by our fate, our karma. Nellie, I have to wonder what it is about your karma that draws murder to you like bears to honey.'

The two coppers return, saving me from trying to justify my existence.

They nod at Frederick and glance at Warton, who appears to have slipped into a drunken slumber. His lordship's chin has dropped down to his chest and a dribble of saliva threatens to drop off it at any moment.

'Suicide,' the redheaded copper announces.

'Nonsense.' That retort comes from me, of course.

The copper sucks in a sharp breath through bared teeth and Frederick throws his hands into the air. 'Why does that proclamation not surprise me? Officer, let's hear the facts of your thorough investigation before Miss Bly entertains us with her guesswork.'

My temper spikes but I clamp my mouth shut.

'It's all quite clear, sir. There are no powder burns around the wound; however, there are burns on the small pillow he used to muffle the shot.'

'Why would he use a pillow to muffle the shot?' I ask.

The copper chews on this for a moment before deciding

to answer me, using a tone he obviously reserves for children – and women. 'Clearly, one muffles a shot so it can't be heard.'

'It doesn't make sense that someone on the run from the police and so panicked and depressed that they are driven to take their own life, would bother muffling a shot.'

'Crazy people don't have to make sense,' the copper replies, miffed.

'Well, I spent weeks travelling on the same ships with Von Reich. Being crazy was not one of his faults.'

'I warned everyone about her.' Lord Warton has come to life.

His drunken, slurred statement, made without opening his eyes, grabs all our attention for a moment, but he quickly falls back into his slumber.

The redheaded copper gives me a stern look that I'm sure has frightened a confession out of more than one criminal.

'This is a police matter and I am informing you in no uncertain terms that you will find yourself in serious trouble if you interfere in an official investigation. Do we understand each other . . . *madam*?'

'As I have pointed out, you have no *official* authority in this country. And if you interfere with my *official* investigation as a journalist, I shall have the sheriff of the next town take you into custody. Do you understand me . . . *sir*?'

He mouth flaps open in an attempt to deliver a reply, but the words don't come. He looks to Frederick for help.

'Nellie, please, the officer is just trying to assist with a delicate situation. Let him finish his report. Officer?'

The copper clears his throat. 'Yes, sir. The most important and telling piece of evidence is the weapon used by the deceased. It is a Rhine brand single-shot derringer. And on the bottom of the butt,' the officer gives me a look of triumph, 'appears a plate containing the name Von Reich.'

The other chimes in, 'Naturally we considered the matter of motive. The deceased was on the run from the law, facing financial ruin, and the rest of his life in a prison cell. There's motivation for suicide if ever I heard it.'

Frederick nods. 'Quite so; good work, officers. Isn't that so, your lordship?'

Lord Warton snaps awake with a splutter and looks around him as if he's unaware of his whereabouts.

The redheaded officer gives the peer a frown and says to Frederick, 'We'll be moving on.' He nods in the direction of the *Amelia*. 'We have to make a full report of the matter.'

I wait until they have stepped past me before I direct a comment to Frederick, who has started up from his seat: 'There is that unanswered question . . .'

He flops back down and looks to the two officers who have paused in the corridor. Poor devils – they would very much like to ignore me, but they don't dare, out of fear that a mere woman will show them up.

'All right, Nellie,' Frederick sighs, 'we're all tired, as I'm sure you are. Please, do tell us what you're referring to.'

*That's it.* I get up and head for my compartment.

'Nellie!' Frederick yells. 'You'll not be able to sleep unless you get it off your chest.'

He is right, of course, but I would like to make them sweat a little, so I pause at the compartment door before I turn and give them a wan smile.

'What about Mr Lazarus?'

'Lazarus?' Frederick asks.

'This investigation is not over with until the matter of Mr Lazarus has been resolved.'

'Why should we care about this Lazarus person?' the mouthy redheaded copper demands.

'Well, I would be curious as to the man's whereabouts since Von Reich was found dead in his compartment. If you are actually right about Von Reich being a bomber, and if he knew Mr Lazarus well enough to kill himself in his compartment, well . . . I guess I would be wondering about whether this invisible man makes bombs, too.'

Passing halfway into my compartment, I toss another volley over my shoulder. 'It's kind of strange, don't you think, that no one has ever seen the man? I think I'd ask Murdock's assistant, Cenza, why she made excuses for him.'

'She left the train,' Lord Warton says. 'I saw her get off at the last stop.'

I throw my hands in the air. 'Well, there it is. You spent so much time harassing me that all the bad people were able to duck for cover. Good luck finding a man no one has ever seen after you let the only witness to his existence escape.'

As soon as I have closed the door behind me, I lean back against it. My heart is ricocheting in my chest, my mouth is dry, and my stomach feels ready to erupt. Despite my attempt at a firm tone, I am shaking. However, I'm glad I threw that last punch.

The devil oils my tongue and makes me do these things, but it feels good, at least for the moment.

# 67

*Lazarus rose from the dead.* That's what it says in the Bible, if my memory of that particular Sunday school lesson remains true.

I was lying awake, listening to the rumble of the train wheels in the early morning, when I remembered about the name, and now I can't shake it. Lazarus rising from the dead is connected to something Von Reich said on the dock at Colombo when Murdock shouted to someone as if he recognized the person.

Von Reich also said someone else was a better shot than the Australian, and something about an identity crisis and rising from the dead.

Another thought grips me. If no one saw Lazarus besides Cenza, a doubtful source, was he ever actually in the compartment?

I try to move on but my thoughts are fuzzy. Being in a room so small and confining doesn't help, and I decide to try again to persuade Sarah to work with me.

A knock on her door reveals that she has not returned from her previous engagement. Sliding it open to see if she has simply slept through my knocking – my excuse for being nosy – I find her personal effects have been removed. The Divine Sarah has either moved into the baggage compartment to sleep in her coffin, or she is ensconced in her lover's bed. I'd guess the latter.

Knowing that she is enjoying the tender caresses of forbidden love while I wrestle with the world's problems doesn't endear her to me at this moment.

The parlour area at the head of the car is empty and I go there to pace. Most of the passengers on the train boarded after attending a wedding and got off at the last stop, leaving me as the only occupant now that Sarah has taken up residence in more luxurious quarters.

George comes up behind me carrying a long, narrow box. He gives me a smile as I eye the odd-shaped package.

'Golf clubs for that British lord. I stored them for his porter because there was no room in his car. I can't imagine why he'd want them while still on the train.'

'Maybe he plans to hit his balls down the aisle.'

George finds the idea amusing and is still chuckling as he goes through the connecting doors to the next car.

I also find myself wondering at the odd item of baggage. Unless Lord Warton has had a miracle cure, he will be fortunate to get out of bed today, never mind play golf aboard a train.

I kneel on the bench seat, leaning my arms on the windowsill and stare out, miserable. I hate it when I can't shake off that unsettled feeling I get when things just aren't right and there's no easy solution to putting them back on track.

The train is travelling through hilly terrain, snaking around turns that permit me a good view of the other cars on the inside bends, and give me the opportunity to stare shamelessly at the *Amelia*, hoping to get a look at the 'personage' within her. Like all passenger cars, Westcot's Pullman has large windows, but my car is too closely attached for me to get a good broadside look when the opportunity arises. Cars further up the train would have a clear view.

What I do get is a glimpse of the storage locker beneath the car and that gets my thoughts churning again.

I have been so busy defending myself as a woman, a reporter and a human being to the vigilantes that I have not shared with them a thought I've had about the storage locker, and haven't given it enough reflection myself. Now it tugs at me: *when the key was taken by Mr Cleveland, the locker became useless as a hiding place for a bomb*.

The full impact of this realization threatens to overwhelm me. Resisting the impulse to run and tell Frederick, I keep my feet firmly planted where they are, because my thinking isn't completely organized.

While the blood was still wet in the marketplace, the conspirators had to have known that Mr Cleveland had passed on the key and the name of what it fitted. And they could pretty much have guessed that I had been the recipient. Cleveland died in my arms and I made no secret that he spoke the name to me. Not long afterwards Frederick worked out I had the key and told Lord Warton, who would have passed the information on to Von Reich and Lord knows who else.

When that happened, the plot to place a bomb in the *Amelia*'s storage locker became unfeasible – not because they couldn't get another key but because it was obvious that the locker would now be carefully watched. But the storage locker could serve another purpose for the plot – a red herring to direct the authorities' attention elsewhere while the killing is carried out another way.

The thwarted attempt to place the bomb in the *Amelia* was at best inane – walking up to the train car, bomb in hand, knowing that the authorities had been forewarned and knowing that two armed guards were standing by was hardly a workable scheme. Managing to leave behind a hat conveniently allowed the perpetrator to be identified.

It made sense only if it was done to disarm the suspicions of the guards. They were told there would be a bomb attempt; there was one; the would-be assassin was identified, and is now conveniently dead.

With a wave of a magician's wand and a shout of abracadabra! everyone can relax and the lovers can enjoy their forbidden tryst.

So what is the real plan? Guns, knives, another bomb plot . . . ?

We go around another inside bend and I get view of Sarah and her lover through the window, briefly but enough to see the broad build and the dark beard of the man. Too far away to see him well enough to be sure of his identity, in my heart I believe I know who it is, but I dare not utter his name even to myself until I am positively certain. Still, it does strike me that he would be an easy target for a sharpshooter on the ground or even on the train. In fact, because a marksman in another carriage would be travelling at the same speed, it would make it a much easier shot.

Why, going around the curves as we are, if I had a rifle, I could—

A thought petrifies me.

A man named Lazarus is somewhere on the train, a person who is a world-class sharpshooter.

But Frederick and the British coppers must have searched

the train and it would be extremely difficult for Lazarus to hide – unless someone is helping him, someone who is above suspicion and whose quarters won't be searched.

Lady Warton demonstrated her knowledge of a high-powered but little-known rifle last night. One even her English huntsman husband wasn't familiar with. She didn't name the rifle out of necessity, more to show off – hardly the sort of thing a proper woman, a well-bred lady, would, especially one that prides herself on her womanly social skills as she does.

If she and her husband are working with Lazarus, it is information that she could have gotten from the mysterious marksman. It sounds far-fetched only because Warton is a British peer. But he's also a drunkard, a gambler and apparently so broke he has to sell his integrity to act as a doorman for businessmen who want access to government officials. Is he desperate enough to aid an assassin because he might lose his estates? Men have done worse for less.

Thinking about it, Warton has always been Johnny-on-the-spot. He took charge in the marketplace, set out to discredit my suspicions from the very beginning, and kept possession of Mr Cleveland's effects even though he could have sent them ashore to British officials in Port Saïd. Von Reich knew something about Lazarus and was involved in some way with the man. Lord Warton was Von Reich's sponsor and even volunteered the information that Cenza had left the train, thus ensuring no one would look for her.

Now he has ordered his golf clubs to be brought to him. A golf bag would be a perfect place to hide a rifle.

My mind is whirling and I press my temples. Is this all nonsense? A house of cards? But it fits so nicely.

'Head hurtin' from all the excitement?'

*Cenza.* With a gun; a small, wicked-looking one.

'There are people looking for you. And they have bigger guns.' It's brave talk, but I'm petrified.

'This? It's only a back-up. When the two guards come out of *Amelia* and run down this corridor, I'm going to step out of a compartment and shoot them – hopefully in the back. If I don't get them, my brother will.'

'Lazarus?'

'That's his stage name, from an act he did when he was a kid and rose from a coffin that had been burned to cinders. Bela kept it when he became a sharpshooter.'

'He's the one who Murdock recognized in Colombo and tried to blackmail. He shot Murdock backstage with you. He fired at the same time Murdock's wife did. She knew, of course. Bought off?'

'Bought off in more ways than one. Bela's very smart. He knew the Murdocks were booked on the ship and sent me down to join them. It wasn't hard. I just climbed into bed with both of them.'

A strange calm engulfs me as I talk to the woman who has come to murder me. Electrified shock, not courage, keeps my lips moving.

'Why didn't you just buy him off instead of killing him.'

'I tried. But Hugh had a big appetite.'

'What about Von Reich? When you didn't need his explosives—'

She scoffs. 'He knew nothing about explosives. He was a road manager for Bela's magic and sharpshooting act and made some money selling gunpowder to the Mahdi. He talked too much. You are clever, I give you that. You have the curiosity of a cat.' Her malicious grin widens. 'But with eight fewer lives. Have you figured it out?'

'I think so. It'll happen around one of these bends, when your brother can get a clear shot at the man in the *Amelia*. The rifle's in the golf bag. You paid off Lord Warton to help.'

'Very smart. You would make a good detective – if you weren't going to be dead very soon. But you're not all right.'

*Keep her talking, someone will come along.*

'How much did you pay Warton?' I ask. 'Even if he needed the money—'

'That souse's so desperate, he'd sell his soul to keep off the foreclosure of his estates. But there's more than that. Bela could destroy his reputation, too. A sex scandal that no one could crawl out from under.'

'Did you—'

'Turn around.' She checks her watch. 'Now. We're through talking.'

'They'll hear you if you shoot me.'

'Don't worry, I'm not going to shoot you.'

There is wicked glee in her voice.

I turn, my knees suddenly weak. I can barely keep them from folding. I hear a movement and out of the corner of my eye I can see she's taken off her belt and folded it. My head explodes in a burst of sparks. The leather strap loops over my head and around my neck, her knee goes into the small of my back and my wind is shut off as she jerks back. My neck feels crushed and I can't break her hold, even with the strength of my panic.

Suddenly, the pressure snaps and she falls against me, sliding to the floor, as I push myself away and get up, nearly falling back down.

'You okay?'

Holding my burning throat and gasping for breath, I stare into the wonderful face of my porter. He's holding a silver platter, and there are breakfast rolls scattered all over the floor.

He gestures at Cenza. 'She was choking you. Is she crazy?'

'Mean crazy.'

Cenza starts to push herself up and I grab the heavy platter from George. Lifting it high in the air, I bring it down on the back of her head, collapsing her back onto the floor. Just for good measure I give her another whack.

'You could kill her!' cries George.

'I doubt it, but I hope so.' She's still clutching her small pistol and I take it. 'Watch her, she's dangerous.'

'Who is she?'

'A killer.'

Giving him the platter, I make a dash for the connecting door to the adjoining car where Frederick's compartment is, yelling back at George, 'Tell those British coppers to make sure their man is away from the windows and then come to Mr Selous's compartment.'

Dashing into the next car, I slide open Frederick's door. His compartment is empty.

'Where is he?' I shout at his porter, who stares at me like I'm a maniac.

He shakes his head as he backs away, holding up his hands. 'I don't know.'

I realize I'm pointing the gun at him and aim it instead at the floor. 'Find Mr Selous. Tell him it's the Wartons.'

'What about the Wartons?'
'Tell him they're the ones.'
I rush by him.
'Where are you going?'
'To stop a murder!'

# 68

A few feet from the Wartons' compartment I stop and stare at the small calibre revolver in my hand.

*What am I doing?* I'm about to face a sharpshooter who's armed with a rifle and I've got a peashooter. Cenza's small revolver holds five bullets in the cylinder – less than the six-shooter I learned to fire, but it feels like a cannon right now.

'Don't think,' Annie Oakley said when she gave me my lesson. 'Just look where you want the bullet to go, then point and shoot.'

*Point and shoot.* Pulling back the hammer to cock it, I fumble and nearly drop the gun.

Forcing myself forwards, one step at a time, I'm shaking so badly I have trouble opening the connecting door out of the car and the one into the next.

The corridor is deserted and I move slowly down it, holding the gun out in front of me with both hands. A shadow created by someone in the parlour area at the other end of the car moves, and I freeze in place.

Lord Warton steps into my line of fire, swaying, and almost loses his balance.

'Go back to your hole,' he slurs.

He's so drunk, I'm not sure he even recognizes me.

'Put your hands up!'

'Stupid woman.' He goes back around the corner, out of my sight and aim.

Half from panic, I run towards the parlour area holding the gun bouncing out in front of me. As I go by a half-open compartment door, Lady Warton flies out, swinging a rifle stock that knocks the revolver from my hand.

She jerks the rifle back and slams the butt into my stomach, crippling me with pain and shock. My knees fold and I grab at her for support as I start to fall, getting a hold of her hair – which comes right off, revealing a bald head.

She – he? – grabs me by my own hair and jerks me up, sticking the gun under my chin as I rise onto wobbly knees. My eyes are glazed, my wheezing breath feels like it's on fire.

'Give me any trouble and I'll blow your head off.'

Her voice is no longer feminine, though softer than most men's. The identity problem Von Reich spoke of is obvious – Lady Warton is not a woman. Now I understand Cenza's remark about Lord Warton facing a sexual scandal.

'Bela,' I spit out.

He hits me across the side of the face with the back of his hand. 'Shut up.'

His features are so similar to his sister's, I might have made the connection if I had seen them side by side – without a netted veil.

He forces me down the aisle, one hand on my hair, the other holding the rifle he has stuck against my side. Tears roll down my cheeks from the excruciating pain.

In the parlour area he shoves me down on the couch next to Lord Warton, who's clutching a bottle of Scotch as a life-preserver.

Bela lifts my chin with the tip of the rifle barrel. 'Where's my sister?'

Unable to speak, I shake my head as the tears flow and I'm still trying to breathe.

He slaps me and my neck stretches as my head feels like it's ready to fly off.

'If they have her, I have you and we'll trade when I'm ready. And if she's been harmed . . . I'll kill you.'

He raises his hand to slap me again and I slide down the couch, turning my head away and sobbing.

Bela looks beyond me, leaning down to squint as the train rounds an inside bend, giving him a clear view of the *Amelia*.

'Can't do this,' Lord Warton slurs. 'Not what we agreed. Can't do it.'

'Shut up, you old sot. I'm saving your estate from the creditors.'

Warton shakes his head. 'Can't do it, not this.'

'Shut up and drink your milk.'

The window suddenly explodes behind my head and I fall forward as glass shatters before me. Bela drops to his knees and I grab onto the rifle with both hands. He jerks it, rising up from his knees, but I hang on for dear life and move with him until we are standing face to face with the rifle between us. He lurches forwards to shove me back and I push up on the rifle, displacing his force, as Carolina Magnet did. He lurches again and I push up, shrieking with glee as his face turns purple from rage.

Jerking me to him, he twists the rifle, but I hang on as he pulls me around in a circle when he can't break my hold. He tries again, this time pushing me back towards the wall; I push up again and we stop in the middle of the parlour. His rage has now turned into a wild animal howl.

He takes one hand off the rifle and hits me across the side of the head, sending me sprawling. Rifle now to his shoulder, he aims down at me, but Lord Warton comes to my rescue as he flies off the couch with his bottle of Scotch and swings, hitting Bela on the side of his head.

Bela falls back against the opposite wall and screams, 'You stupid fool!' He fires, slamming Lord Warton back onto the couch.

Gunfire erupts and I lay flat on the floor as bullets smack the walls around me. Bela is knocked backwards but stays on his feet and fires his rifle from the hip once before his body jerks as a rain of bullets hits him.

My ears are ringing and the air is full of gunsmoke. Both Bela and Lord Warton are down and neither is moving. Or apparently breathing.

The redheaded copper is coming down the corridor with a gun in his hand.

'Don't shoot!' I yell at the top of my lungs as I lie my head back down. If he says anything, it is lost in the ringing of my ears.

A few minutes later I am seated in Frederick's compartment as he makes me an apology my numb brain can't process.

'Cenza—' I interrupt.

'Jumped from the train. Probably dead.' He kneels before me. 'Sweet Nellie, I almost got you with that shot through the window, but I had to try it.'

'Had to try it? Had to risk killing me to get a shot at that man, woman, whatever he is?'

'You have to understand—'

'That you were willing to risk killing me for Queen and country?'

'I fired from the *Amelia* at Lazarus, Lady Warton, whatever that monster is called.'

'And almost got me? You – the world's greatest hunter?'

'I told you I was a poor shot. I have to—'

'See the whites of their eyes, I remember.' I get up slowly, resisting Frederick's offer to help me.

'Nellie, I need to talk to you about what you've seen and heard. A revelation about the personage in the *Amelia* having an affair with an actress could have a dire effect on an elderly woman whose health and welfare is of prime importance not just to my country, but to the world at large.'

I brush by him and slide open the compartment door.

'Where are you going?' he asks.

'To get washed and remove the glass from my hair. And keep myself from finding a gun and showing you what it's like to nearly get your head blown off.'

'Please. Another Nellie nearly killed her with grief. Don't be the one that actually puts her in the grave.'

'I still have an issue to resolve with you.'

His eyebrows go up. 'Just one?'

'One at a time. Did you fight off that assasin the night I was attacked on the bow of the *Victoria*?'

'Nellie, sweet Nellie, I wish I had, so you would remember me for something besides a near miss.'

'Then it must have been Von Reich.'

'Lord Warton saved you.'

'What?'

'Sarah confided in me that she saw him running away when she found you lying on the deck. Warton was not a good man, nor even a very pleasant one, but as you found out today, he will stop short of murder.'

'I will have to thank him in my prayers. After I forgive him for almost getting me murdered in the first place.'

'You are not a forgiving woman, Nellie Bly.'

'Mr Selous.' I tap his chest with my forefinger. 'I have been battered, slandered, beaten and kicked – and I have endured and fought for truth, justice and the American way. Or something like that. And right now—'

He pulls me to him, embracing me and smothering me with his warmth and masculinity. Our lips touch and a warm flush flows all the way down to my toes.

I finally push him back with weak knees. 'Don't go away.'

Before I slip out of the compartment door, I tell him, 'I'm taking you up on your offer to join you on a safari. You need someone to teach you how to shoot properly. Point and shoot, just point and shoot. Don't aim. I'll show you how.'

'Don't make promises you can't keep,' he looks back at me with those blazing blue eyes, 'because I'm going to hold you to that one.'

For a moment we just look at each other, then I race down to my compartment and start picking the shards of glass from my hair.

He almost killed me. And yet I want nothing more than to rush back and have him take me into his arms and never let me go.

The race is still on. I will crawl to the finishing line if I have to, but for just a few precious moments I want to be held in his strong arms, feel his warm breath against my neck, and have him kiss me.

Maybe I'll cry, but that's a woman's prerogative, isn't it?

'Take a deep breath,' I tell myself. I have people counting on me to finish the race and that is exactly what I am going to do.

*Nellie arriving at the finishing line in Jersey City*

# L'envoi

Almost before I knew it I was at Philadelphia, and all too soon to please me, for my trip was so pleasant I dreaded the finish of it.

A number of newspaper men and a few friends joined me at Philadelphia to escort me to New York. Speech-making was the order from Philadelphia on to Jersey City.

I was told when we were almost home to jump to the platform the moment the train stopped at Jersey City, for that made my time around the world. The station was packed with thousands of people, and the moment I landed on the platform, one yell went up from them, and the cannons at the Battery and Fort Greene boomed out the news of my arrival. I took off my cap and wanted to yell with the crowd, not because I had gone around the world in seventy-two days, but because I was home again.

To so many people this wide world over am I indebted for their kindnesses that I cannot, in a little book like this, thank them all individually. They form a chain around the earth.

To each and all of you, men, women and children, in my land and in the lands I visited, I am most truly grateful. Every kind act and thought, if but an unuttered wish, a cheer, a tiny flower, is imbedded in my memory as one of the pleasant things of my novel tour.

From you and from all those who read the chronicle of my trip I beg indulgence. These pages have been written in the spare moments snatched from the exactions of a busy life.

## For the Record

I covered 21,740 miles in 72 days, six hours, and 11 minutes.

I spent 56 days, 2 hours and 4 minutes in actual travel, and lost by delay 15 days, 17 hours and 30 minutes.

My average rate of speed was 28.71 miles per hour.

First class tickets around the world (ships and trains) cost $805 (not counting the special train).

Nellie Bly, *Around the World in 72 Days*

*Cover of Nellie's book,* Around the World in 72 Days

# Historical Note

Who was the man in the *Amelia*?

For reasons that are not clear, but perhaps arose from a sense of respect that Nellie had for Queen Victoria – the grande dame that an entire age of history is named after – Nellie never, even in her secret journal, revealed the name of Sarah's lover, 'the personage' in the *Amelia*.

However, looking at the evidence, the man did indeed have British 'coppers' as bodyguards when he travelled, his very presence in the United States was a well-protected secret, and he was an aficionado of horseracing.

These facts all fit Edward, Prince of Wales, Queen Victoria's oldest son. Well known to be a playboy, Edward angered his mother when her beloved consort, Prince Albert, died two weeks after travelling while ill, in the dead of winter, to an army camp, to chastise their son for having an actress smuggled into his tent.

This was the probable source of Frederick Selous's comment that another Nellie had almost killed the Queen with grief: the actress was Nellie Clifton.

Queen Victoria never forgave her son. She wore mourning black for the rest of her life and wrote to her daughter about Edward, saying, 'I never can, or shall, look at him without a shudder.'

Prince Edward, who enjoyed the nightlife of Paris, was rumoured to be a lover of Sarah Bernhardt, but the 'smoking gun' of the evidence was Nellie's facetious remark, 'How is good old Bertie?'

Edward, Prince of Wales

'Bertie' was the pet name given to Edward by his family.

Prince Edward ascended to the throne after the passage of his mother and is remembered by history as Edward VII, an able monarch who also has a period of history that carries his name: the Edwardian era.

THE EDITORS

# Acknowledgements

*The Illusion of Murder* was a labour of love that I could never have accomplished without my dear friend Junius, thank you, kind sir. And without the wise and insightful guidance of my fabulous and incredible editor, Sue Fletcher. She kept asking, pushing, probing, questioning me into making the book work. And Swati Gamble who is always there, checking, rechecking and making sure everything is in its right place, what would I do without you?

And then there is Harvey Klinger, my Maxwell Perkins.

And David Grossman, as always, 'Thank You.'

As Nellie Bly so adequately put at the end of *Around the World in 72 Days*:

'To so many people this wide world over am I indebted for their kindnesses that I cannot thank them all individually. They form a chain around the earth. To each and all of you, men, women and children, in my land and in the lands I visited, I am most truly grateful. Every kind act and thought, if but an unuttered wish, a cheer, a tiny flower, is imbedded in my memory as one of the pleasant things of my novel tour.'

*Carol McCleary*

As I wrote the book, there were people around the world who made Nellie very special and I want to thank a few of them for their kindness, love of Nellie and support, and that 'un-uttered wish and cheers. They are:

David Headley & Daniel Gedeon
Hilde Heyvaert
Ian Kern & Sally Owen
Barbara Peters
Raffaella Vitangeli
Miyo Kai
Daniela Micura
Richard at Flowers by Richard, in Manhattan, N.Y.
Heather Rees

# List of Pictures

Sources of Illustrations

*Around the World in 72 Days*, 1980, Nellie Bly: 432.

*History of Egypt*, c. 1881, G. Maspero: 114.

*Illustrated London News*, 1882: 70.

*In the Heart of Africa*, 1890, F. Selous: 56.

Library of Congress, Washington DC: x, 67, 428.

*New York World* 1889 & 1890: 66, 356.

Private Collections: 158, 280, 434.

*Scribner's Magazine*, 1888: 386.

*Sears Catalogue*, 1890: 68.

*Steamships and Their Story*, 1910, E. Keble Chatterton: 184, 310.

US Navy Archives: 334.